LOW

By Mike Duke

Edited by Donelle Pardee Whiting
And Lance Fling

WWW.STITCHEDSMILEPUBLICATIONS.COM

ISBN-13:978-1-945263-21-7
ISBN-10:1-945263-21-0

Table of Contents

PROLOGUE 1

SECTION I 5

NOVEMBER 1, 10:00 A.M. 7

NOVEMBER 3, EARLY MORNING 33

NOVEMBER 4, LATE AFTERNOON 39

NOVEMBER 5, 1:02 A.M. 47

WEDNESDAY, NOVEMBER 23 51

NOVEMBER 24, THANKSGIVING DAY 61

BLACK FRIDAY, NOVEMBER 25 77

MONDAY, NOVEMBER 28 83

DECEMBER 1 109

DECEMBER 6 115

DECEMBER 11 117

DECEMBER 15 119

DECEMBER 16, 8:05 a.m. 129

TUESDAY, DECEMBER 22 133

DECEMBER 24, 6:30 a.m. 139

CHRISTMAS DAY 143

SECTION II 149

CHRISTMAS DAY 151

FRIDAY, DECEMBER 26 163

DECEMBER 27 177

DECEMBER 28 185

DECEMBER 31, NEW YEAR'S EVE 193

JANUARY 1, NEW YEAR'S DAY 201

JANUARY 3 205

JANUARY 4 209

THURSDAY, JANUARY 5 217

JANUARY 6 239

JANUARY 7 255

THURSDAY, JANUARY 11 277

FRIDAY, JANUARY 12 281

SATURDAY, JANUARY 13 297

SUNDAY, JANUARY 14 305

SECTION III 311

SUNDAY, JANUARY 14 313

MONDAY, JANUARY 15 319

TUESDAY, JANUARY 16 367

WEDNESDAY, JANUARY 17th 12:05 a.m. 403

EPILOGUE I 425

EPILOGUE II 429

ABOUT THE AUTHOR 431

PROLOGUE

October 31 Full Moon

The old man and his dog walked into Pleasant Grove at a leisurely pace, picking their way across a recently harvested corn field. Stepping over tractor tire trenches, mounds of dirt, and corn stalks left behind, they looked toward the hotel parking lot just ahead. The man stopped, gazed up at the full moon, then bent down to tighten the laces of his boots. He spoke, calm anticipation warming his voice.

"It's our time again Phobos. The Hunter's Moon, and quite appropriately, the Traveler's Moon, as we now find ourselves selecting another territory to call home for a time. Even more auspicious, this year, it falls on the sacred moon Sabbat of Samhain."

With an ease that belied the weathered appearance of his elderly frame, he stood, sturdy and confident, before he pulled a pipe from his jacket pocket and thoughtlessly pressed the dark matter inside the hollowed wood. A brief incantation escaped his lips, followed by a puff of air; light glowed, smoke swirled. He drew the grey tendrils deep inside and held them captive for a long time before slowly breathing out and releasing them to the darkness.

"I remember nights like this, special nights when sacrifices were necessary to divert the dark flood bearing down. Villagers stacked their neighbors, men and women both, like cordwood and burned them as such, marching between the blazing pyres of charred bone and sizzling flesh, seeking purification, the blood of the dead smeared on every forehead, a ward against the roaming demon hordes crossing over for the Hunt. We were a scourge upon mankind, at times eradicating whole settlements. So they killed the weak and the old and begged for their lives, pleaded for good fortune and ample provision throughout the winter. Each sacrificial throat slit was an attempt to placate the gods of the harvest, to earn protection; and on rare nights like this, people needed protection from duplicitous spirits glutting themselves on the pain of others to relieve their own misery. Better living through sacrifice, I suppose … at least for the survivors. Probably why they remembered their dead and bound them before burial or placed rocks in their mouths … just in case they came back."

The old man kicked a particularly large dirt clod on the field's edge, watched it spray into the air, and fall back to earth. Phobos sneezed. They stepped off and headed toward the downtown area, the silence comfortable between them.

After a while, they entered the city park and turned north, walking towards the far corner, a glowing light visible from a distance.

"I tell you, Phobos, there are few things in this world like the hunting of men, people scattering before you, fleeing with screams, the smell of fear so rich you could taste it in the air long before you sank your teeth into their skulls, crunching down like a dog eating a raw egg in the shell.

"Of course, I had standards, mind you. I enjoyed running down the ones who had killed family and neighbors to save their own skins. Their rites held no sway over our kind, Phobos." The old man motioned with his hand back and forth, indicating himself and the dog as the special 'our kind.' "And I tell you, the irony was absolutely juicy. Yum!"

He paused as they approached a small group of men huddled around a small fire, far from the main walkways.

"Hmm … Yes, Phobos, those were the days. Good times."

They walked right up to the circle of homeless men, who remained apparently oblivious to their arrival until the old man spoke, his voice assuming a kind British accent typical of the peasantry many years ago.

"Hullo, gents. Got room for me and me dawg by chance?"

They startled at his voice, but once they looked him over and saw all the wrinkles and age worn eyes, they decided he wasn't a threat. A middle-aged fellow with a full beard spoke up for the rest.

"Yeah, old timer, grab a bucket and take a seat. What's yer name?"

"Phailees. Mister Phailees. And thank ye for the warm welcome."

Three others greeted them. Mister Phailees smiled. Phobos licked his chops and whined ever so quietly, focusing on the large framed man sitting mute.

"So," Phailees piped up, "got anything good to eat? We sure are hungry."

"Ralph here is good at trapping squirrel. It's not much, but you can have a bite or two."

"Yes, that would be tasty, indeed, till something more … substantial can be found."

They ate in near silence, occasional comments on politics, weather, or sports. One guy carried on about government conspiracies and UFOs. Everyone sat warming themselves by the fire. One by one the men wandered off in time, each back to his chosen slumber spot, to bundle up in blankets, trash, and cardboard shelters. Only the large man who would not speak stayed behind, seated across the fire from them.

Phailees stared at the man. He knew his kind. The man served 10 years for rape long ago, but had never been caught for all the other times he'd violated women since then.

Phailees wet his mouth and stood, his posture becoming uncommonly erect. He set his jaw and took the first step. Tonight, this man would pay for his sins.

Turned out the brute wasn't mute, just rude. No one heard his screams, but it made Phailees think of long ago, of the dog and the egg, teeth piercing the hard shell, the golden treasure exploding across taste buds.

Later, wiping his lips clean, he mumbled to himself in fond recollection. "Oh yes. It was just like that."

SECTION I

"We are each our own devil and we make this world our hell."
OSCAR WILDE

"Lust is the craving for salt of a man who is dying of thirst."
FREDERICK BUECHNER, BEYOND WORDS

"The only demon you need to save yourself from is you."
ANONYMOUS

NOVEMBER 1, 10:00 A.M.

"Officer Adams, my client, Johnny Greene, swears that you planted that crack pipe in his pocket, but I know better than to think that is true with the reputation for integrity you have. If by some chance it wasn't his, it was probably one of his friends that slid it in there. He's an idiot for even suggesting you would do such a thing, and I'm not going to pursue that line of questioning. However, he insists on testifying, despite my objections. In fact, the bastard threatened me earlier if I didn't let him testify. As far as I'm concerned, the stupid fucker can hang himself."

Chad Bigleby hated the days when he had to take his turn at being a public defender. Adams nodded in acknowledgement and chuckled a little, his face showing he felt Chad's pain.

"So basically, my only point of contention will be with the validity of the pat-down. Since his aunt lives in the same project where you stopped and interviewed him, this could give him a valid reason for being in the neighborhood, and he wouldn't have been trespassing. Did you ask for consent to search my client?"

Adams was completely candid.

"No, sir, I sure didn't. Based on the time of day and the location being known for its high drug traffic and numerous shots-fired calls, I felt it was necessary to ensure the safety of my partner and myself."

"Humph. The judge might agree with you on that. I guess we'll see. Thank you for your honesty, Officer Adams."

"Of course."

Adams stared at his watch every five minutes for the next hour until the case was finally called. He did not want to be late for his and Amy's counseling session.

The longer Chad sat and waited, the more he stewed over Johnny having the audacity to threaten him. He decided to show Johnny who was in control of whom here.

"Commonwealth vs. Greene."

Adams approached the stand and gave his testimony, recounting who, what, when, where, how, and why. When finished, the judge spoke.

"Your witness, Mr. Bigleby."

"Thank you, Your Honor. Good day, Officer Adams."

"Good day to you, sir."

"I just have a couple of questions, Officer Adams. Let me see if I have this right. You're saying that you stopped my client in a known drug area and that, upon patting him down you felt something that, based on your training and experience, you believed to be a crack pipe?"

"That's correct, sir."

"And you found this in the right pocket of Mr. Greene's jacket?"

"Yes sir. The right pocket."

"And the lab results showed that it tested positive for cocaine?"

"Yes, sir."

"Your Honor, I have no further questions of the officer at this time, though I would like to reserve the right to redirect after my client's testimony."

The judge looked slightly puzzled, but agreed. Adams recognized Chad's game plan.

"I call Mr. Greene to the stand, Your Honor," Chad smiled as he did so.

"Mr. Greene, before Officer Adams stopped you, was there a crack pipe in your jacket pocket?"

"No, sir."

"Well, how do you think it got there?"

"Officer Adams put it there while he was patting me down."

"Why do you think he did that?"

"Because he's crooked, and he don't like me. We've had words before."

"Those words, that would be the last time you got arrested for cocaine possession, wouldn't it?"

"Uh, yeah."

Johnny's face looked confused, not tracking where Chad was going.

"And you were convicted of that charge, weren't you?"

He paused, and looked at the judge, then glanced around briefly.

"Um, yes. I was."

"But you're positive that Officer Adams put that crack pipe in your pocket?"

"Absolutely."

"Can you think of any other way it could have gotten in your jacket pocket?"

"Nope."

"Very well. Your Honor, I'm done with this witness."

"Mr. Grant. The witness is yours," the judge declared.

The Commonwealth Attorney was trying not to smirk as he spoke.

"Your Honor, I have no questions of the witness."

Chad spoke up. "Your Honor, I'd like to call Officer Adams back to the stand."

Officer Adams strolled back up and sat down, trying not to laugh.

"Officer Adams, is there any truth to my client's claim that you planted that crack pipe on his person?"

Adams looked right at Johnny.

"Not one bit, sir."

"Of course not. I expected as much. Officer Adams, I have no further questions, and I thank you for your service and dedication to our city. Good day. Your Honor, the Defense rests."

Adams winked at Johnny then left the stand.

"Your Honor, the Prosecution rests as well," Mr. Grant declared.

The guilty verdict came quickly and the guards led Johnny out of the courtroom before it could even dawn on him what just happened. Chad nodded to Officer Adams and the Commonwealth Attorney, looking innocent as could be.

Mark Adams left court and quickly made his way across town to his old church. He walked into the Pastor's office ten minutes late for the marital counseling session, tired from working the midnight shift and then staying awake for court. His wife's irritation was obvious.

"Sorry, Pastor Dave, court ran longer than I'd hoped."

Pastor Dave was gentle and sincere. "It's ok, Mark. It's good to see you again."

"Typical," Adams' wife, Amy, spat under her breath.

"Amy, for God's sakes don't start! You know I don't have any control over how long court lasts."

"No, you don't, but I'm tired of you being late all the time, getting called in all the time, and working all the overtime."

"You don't seem to mind the money, but do I hear any appreciation for that? No!"

Amy redirected without a hitch.

"And if it's not work, it's you working out. You spend more time at that damn dojo than you do at home."

"Hold on! First, you know I have to maintain a certain level of training and fitness. You do want me to come home at the end of each shift, right?"

Mark might as well have slapped Amy in the face, the offense spreading red across her cheeks.

"Of course I do! What the hell kind of question is that? You shouldn't even have to ask!"

Mark ignored her protests and continued on.

"And second, why should I want to come home and spend time with someone who doesn't show any affection? Do you even know when the last time we had sex was? No? Five weeks. It's been five freakin' weeks. That's not normal. Hell, it's not even healthy."

"Why should I want to have sex with someone who's rarely home, and when he is, he's in his own little world: reading books, watching training videos, playing Xbox. I might as well not even exist. You certainly don't treat me like I matter, at least not until you want me to spread my legs! Apparently, that's the only way for me to get your full attention! I'm sick of it! It makes me feel like a piece of meat, like I don't matter to you for who I am. You only value me for sex. The rest of the time, you're a sarcastic smartass. Hell, you're kinder to the criminals on the street than you are to me!"

Amy shut down, arms and legs crossed, chin tucked to her chest, glaring eyes barely visible from beneath auburn bangs, anger vividly displayed on her face. Bitter tears welled up.

Mark took a deep breath and spoke through almost gritted teeth.

"You know, I get more respect from the criminals on the street than I do from you. I know it doesn't excuse my behavior, but it sure as hell doesn't help. Combine that with all your criticizing and complaining about me and my job, and you make it real hard to be kind. Oh, and by the way, I'm not the only one with attitude. You can be a real ... you know what, all on your own. You know that. You're not even the same person I married. You're harder, meaner, more uncaring, and distant than ever. It's like you've redefined who you are and who you're supposed to be. You have no problem spewing venom in my face, and you can hold a nasty grudge for weeks and not miss a step. You've got ice in your veins, and you don't give a shit about how you make me feel."

Mark paused, several seconds ticking by, breathed deep, sighed, then lowered his voice to almost a whisper.

"God, it's a vicious cycle. The worse I get, the worse you get ... but I know I'm responsible. I have to break this cycle."

"Ooooo, Mark Adams, ever the martyr ... everyone feel sorry for him and all his sacrifice: 'he's such a hardworking, loyal officer and such a patient man' ... don't make me gag! You disgust me! Everyone thinks you're so god damned perfect, and all your coworkers feel sorry for you because you have to put up with your 'unstable' wife. Well, they'd be unstable too if they lost a baby and had no husband around to help them through it."

Mark inhaled sharply, but held his tongue and only glared at Amy, his hands overlapped, thumbs covering his lips, an unconscious indicator of restraint. Amy met his gaze, cold eyes stabbing into his from across the couch.

Mark looked away first. He sat quietly, breathing shallow and fast, trying to relax by staring off in a corner of the room, focusing on the titles on the pastor's bookcase.

Pastor Dave remained silent during the exchange. He felt it was often informative and beneficial to let couples say what they're really thinking. Much can be learned about a person by what kind of tactics they use when arguing, and often what's really inside of them will slip out in the heat of the moment, and a counselor can find out things he would have never seen otherwise.

"All right, folks. Take a deep breath and exhale. It's obvious that there is some very entrenched animosity running in both directions. I know we're only seeing the tip of the iceberg."

Amy exploded. "You're damn right it's only the tip of the iceberg! I've had enough. I can't take it anymore. I don't want to take it anymore! I don't want to live with someone who doesn't want to be around me anymore. I'm done! I need space, and he needs to fix his shit and decide what's important."

Pastor Dave interjected calmly, "Amy, let's not be rash. Let's discuss the ramifications. Let's look at options …"

"No! I'm done! I want out … Today!" The last word communicated the finality her expression displayed. Talk time was over. Mark knew that face well.

He took a deep breath and blew out the shock of the moment, accepting the situation for what it was, focusing forward, not behind.

"Ok, Amy. I'll give you what you want. I'll get a motel tonight and find an apartment tomorrow. I'll need to grab some stuff when we leave here, though."

Amy sat silent, but her shoulders relaxed as if a weight had been lifted.

Mark hesitated for a second, then asked one more question. He did not want to be ignorant or float in limbo, not knowing her intentions.

"You don't want a divorce, do you? This is just a separation, right?"

"I don't know yet!" she spat. "For now, it's a separation. So don't think you can go see other women, because I surely won't be seeing other men! You've ruined that for a while!"

Mark sighed, wishing he hadn't even asked.

"Ok. Well, thanks for your time, Pastor Dave. I appreciate your seeing us, despite the fact we haven't attended in almost three years. I'm going to go ahead and leave. We're done here for now."

Mark stood and exited the room without another word. Once outside, he stared up at the grey sky and misty rain. "Dreary day," he said aloud. "What a dreary fucking day."

The rain was coming down hard now and dread seemed to burst from every drop smacking on the windshield of his cruiser as he drove away.

"Dreary fucking day," he mumbled again, sighing deeply.

Chad Bigleby was a man with a plan, and it was about to come to fruition. He closed his office door and sat down to review the file Annie O'Reilley placed in his desk. He was about to break it off in Brad Buxton's ass and take his position as partner, all thanks to Annie. She had provided all the details—the hidden fees, billing statements, deleted files, missing funds, automatic transfers to offshore accounts that were hidden within other records in remote locations. Being Brad's paralegal assistant—and quite the hacker, he had learned—Annie was able to access Brad's files and retrieve enough proof to confirm what Chad suspected for some time. Tomorrow, they would drop the hammer on Brad Buxton together.

Harry Fitzwell was seated at the Blue Pelican Lounge slamming drinks. His workday would start early in the morning, but he didn't care. He had hit it big today; promoted to VP of Sales at last.

He had climbed the mountain of success, firmly gripping the knife in the back of everyone in his way. Sly and coy, innocent and sometimes bumbling until the moment of truth, everyone knew Harry came through in the pinch, but no one ever suspected him to be the shrewd, cold-hearted backstabber in the bunch, least of all Jack Walters. When Harry made sure that merger didn't go off, Jack was done. Getting fired was the least of his worries. His reputation in the field was ruined. Harry consoled him, helped him pack his things. Two weeks later, they made the decision and here Harry sat, friends and coworkers toasting him and cheering one last time before they left for home.

Around midnight, Harry set off for his vehicle sitting a few blocks away. It was a full moon, high in the sky, clouds bunched like huge cotton masses stuffed together, light escaping through every crack, a huge luminous ring encircling its glowing ivory mass.

Harry located his vehicle and dug for his keys, his back to an alley.

"Do ya have some change, good sir?"

The slightly English-accented voice was polite, low, and had a pitch that was a bit rough, like sifting gravel. Startled, heart suddenly pounding, Harry spun around, hands rising instinctively. A man stepped into the light and, for a moment, almost seemed to separate from the shadows themselves.

He was tall and wiry, his complexion olive, face and hands sun-weathered and wrinkled. He held a worn and crumpled bucket hat in his left hand with a tight-fitting stocking cap pulled over his head, scraggly salt and pepper hair protruding along the bottom. A slightly scruffy grey goatee and dead eyes that only feigned feeling rounded out his facial features. He wore a dirty, old, black sports jacket over a dark hoodie, along with a pair of jeans made filthy by some kind of grease spread over the tops of the thighs. There appeared to be multiple layers of long johns and t-shirts beneath the outer clothing. The man was definitely a vagrant.

But the shoes were impressive, Harry noticed: Allen Edmonds black Penny Loafers. Ultimately, they were the one inexplicable detail that distracted Harry from the obvious ... this homeless man was moving closer the whole time.

Harry snapped back to attention as the man's upturned palm stretched out further to beg. It was etched with dirt in every line, black grime lining the underside of each fingernail tip.

"I said, good sir, do ya have some change?"

Harry stepped back, his butt touching the car door.

"No. I do not."

"Please sir ... just some change for a hungry old man. Is that so much?"

The homeless man stepped forward again, reaching, almost touching. Harry pushed the man away.

"Get back!"

Immediately, a black German Shepherd shot from behind his master and moved up almost in between Harry's feet, mouth at a very vulnerable level ... for Harry.

Harry froze, frightened to move even the slightest bit. The dog growled low and rumbling, teeth bared, yellow eyes almost glowing in the moon's light.

"I don't think he particularly likes yer attitude, sir. Nothing a few dollars wouldn't fix, though."

"Fine! Here, take it! It's ten dollars—smallest thing I have." Harry eased his hand forward slowly.

The old man smiled, and suddenly clenched Harry's hand in a firm shake, grasping his wrist with the other. Staring intently into Harry's eyes, he whispered something briefly in a foreign tongue. A chill penetrated Harry's hand and ran throughout his whole body, a tremendous shiver rattling every bone for the briefest of moments that left him feeling violated. The homeless man's fingers closed on the bill, crumpling it out of sight, then released Harry's arm and faded into the shadows, the dog growling one last time before following his master.

Harry stood there, dumbfounded and off kilter for a minute, wondering what the man meant by his parting words: "Sweet dreams."

Sgt. Roger Rose sat behind his desk, roll call paper in hand, eyes apparently half crossed, as usual, looking down his nose through thick lenses set in a pair of outdated frames scarcely hanging onto his face.

"Woo Eeee boys ..." he said in a slow, deliberate Southern drawl that pervaded every word he spoke, while shaking the paper in his hand as he shifted his large frame within his seat. "I'll tell ya what, we've had a hell of a day ... helluva day. All the crazies were up in a tizzy. Lil Buddy, Hanafi Khadafi, Eleanor Ricks, the Newton kid, and even old lady McLean. Lil Buddy was ten times as paranoid as usual, walkin' all over town, refused to stay in one place. Damn if 'e hadn't lined his trench coat and winter hat with aluminum foil. Said 'e needed to be invisible from the gub-ment aliens roaming the city. Hanafi was preachin' again, this time about some avenger of Allah come to punish all the infidels. Eleanor was creepin' round her house with a big ol' butcha knife. Kept freakin' out old man Alberts next door. Her yard though, so she can tote a sword around if she likes. Swore she was guardin' against evil spirits. Couldn't convince her otherwise, so she's probably still out there now. The Newton kid was just scared shitless. Wouldn't come out of his closet and had a lantern with a shitload of batteries inside and Christmas lights strung through all the clothes hangers. Couldn't talk him out of there, but he wasn't a threat to himself or others, so nuthin' we could do about that neither. And Old Mrs. McLean just kept whisperin' 'the devil is a'comin', the devil is a'comin',' shakin' 'er head and rockin' to and fro in that creaky ol chair of 'ers."

"Then, in the middle of all that," he said, a chuckle escaping as he shook his head in mild disbelief, "damn if I didn't roll up on a couple in the brickyard. Boy had some girl bent over the trunk of his car railing 'er good, I tell ya. I flipped the spotlight on 'em, and that boy's head spun around like in The Exorcist and froze mid-stroke."

A hearty laugh, belly shaking and all, forced a pause in the story, perhaps even a calculated effort for dramatic effect.

"Right then he eased back all slow like, and I thought it would never stop. I tell ya, that boy pulled enough meat out of her to season a pot of collards!"

Sgt. Rose slapped the desk for emphasis and broke out into another deep belly laugh, his glasses almost slipping off his nose. He caught them with his index finger and slid them back up into their former precarious position. Everyone else laughed, accustomed to the off-color humor.

Sgt. Hicks spoke up, "Anything else of note, Roger?"

"Oh yeah, day shift had a hell of a find this morning," he said, shaking his head back and forth slightly, "a hell of a find. You know that old pervert Rory Blunt, always hanging out in the back corner of the city park?"

"Yeah. Got convicted of rape years ago, right?"

"Yes, sir-ee. He's the one. His sorry ass was found dead right where all those crazy homeless fuckers sit around together by their little bonfire. Spooked that rookie Leander a good fashion. Boy still looked half pale at roll call."

"What about it?"

"Well, from the pictures it looked like some kinda animal gnawed a hole in his skull and licked his brains right out like it was candy or somethin'."

"Holy shits" escaped a couple of mouths, including Adams'.

"What the fuck?" Hicks mumbled. "Any idea what exactly it was?"

"Big. That's all they know for sure right now. Bear maybe. A really freakin' big Rottweiler perhaps. Hard ta say right now whether someone cracked his skull with a hammer and then the animal came in or whether it was just a critter did all the handywork. If it's an animal, I'd like to give him a whole damn bag of treats. Good work, if you ask me."

"Do they think it happened last night?" Hicks was concerned about an ass-chewing from command if it happened on their shift.

"Yeah. From time of death it had to be sometime around midnight. Don't worry about it though. Nobody hardly ever rides back there. I don't think the Chief will say anything."

Hicks rocked forward in his chair. "All right, I suppose that's all then, eh?"

"You know it. Me and mah boys are out of here … Oh! Almost forgot … there's a good size crowd hanging out at the Gas N Go. We cleared them a couple of times, but they were back again on my way into the office just now. Y'all be safe now, ya hear?"

Everyone said their goodbyes, and Sgt. Rose's shift shuffled out.

"All right, guys." Hicks got their attention. "Make sure we check out that area a couple of times tonight, but make sure you have someone with you; no one goes alone back there. Copy?"

After "yes sirs" all around, they all left for patrol prepared for more craziness, but as it turned out, it was rather quiet after all.

NOVEMBER 2, 3:00 A.M.

Harry Fitzwell's sleep was fitful and full of vivid dreams. Covers bunched and twisted, the corners of the fitted sheet pulling away as he continually shifted, gripping the linens wherever he laid his hands.

The fear was palpable, the anxiety pushing his blood pressure up with every minute he wandered the office building in his dream, uncertain who lurked in the shadows and waited for him behind each cubicle and closed door. They were all after him; everyone he had ever betrayed knew his secret. Now they were all out to get him and were hidden, waiting to pounce and drive the blade of vengeance through his cowardly spine.

There was nothing he could do. They would all turn on him. They would all go to his boss. They would all go public. He would lose his job, his reputation, and his friends. Everyone would hate him. He couldn't live like that.

His dream shifted, and Harry found himself on the fifth floor, looking out the wall of glass there. He decided right then there was no fate worse than being exposed for all to see and having to face the consequences. I don't have to, and I won't, he thought determinedly, then took a deep breath and sprinted towards the glass. He hurled himself forward, elbows first, through the splintering shards and out into the void, gravity quickly dragging him to hell.

A gasp escaped his mouth as he suddenly woke up, whole body soaked in sweat, his torso trembling from chills as his heart raced with the fear that still lingered. Glancing at the clock revealed only an hour passed since sleep had so readily come. His wife slept on, undisturbed. He grabbed a towel to dry off and another to cover the sweat-soaked sheets on his side then went out to the living room to watch TV.

Harry had no desire to go back to sleep right away.

Chad rose early, getting out of the house long before Samantha woke; leaving a note for her on the kitchen counter, which read:

"Sorry I missed you, but I have to finish some work for a trial later today. I'll see you tonight. Have a good day, Chad."

His first stop was for coffee before he hit the road, arriving at Emily's by 6:30 a.m. She met him at the door, freshly showered and in her bathrobe. A quick flash of flesh and she backed across the floor to her bedroom door, index finger curling, beckoning. There she dropped the robe and dragged him to her bed, undressing him every step of the way, kissing him vigorously, deeply, suckling his lips as she pushed him down and kneaded his lap with a firm, rhythmic grip. Chad was unbuckling his pants and pushing them down as he kicked off his shoes. Emily pulled away long enough to strip his pants and underwear, then paused.

"Oh my," she said with a serious tone.

Chad was caught off guard as she stared at his naked frame.

"What?"

Deadpan as possible, Emily answered.

"A naked man in socks. Totally unacceptable."

They both laughed as she pulled them off and crawled on top of him. Sliding into place, Emily rode him aggressively, the very act a cathartic release of all the stress she was carrying inside her. She continued long after Chad reached climax, until finally she was overcome by powerful waves rolling up from within. They swept over and through her, delivering her into a deep sea of bliss as the world disappeared for an indefinite time. When she finally came ashore once more, her head lay on Chad's chest, wet hair splayed across his torso. She closed her eyes and slept the sleep of the dead, it seemed.

Chad dozed as well until Robbie knocked on the door at 8:00 a.m.

Chad roused himself, dressed quickly, and went out to be with Robbie. They made pancakes and eggs together, chit-chatting about cartoons, toys, comic books, games, and of course, Christmas. Robbie brought in his drawing pad, showing Chad his robots and dragons he worked on recently. Chad "ooohed" and "aahhed" at all the right places, not out of duty, but because they were really that good. Robbie was gifted; he could have a real future in art one day, Chad thought.

I'm doing everything I can to make that possible, buddy, he thought.

When the food was ready, they went to wake Emily. Robbie waited outside while Chad entered to make sure momma was covered. Once inside, he stood for a minute, plate in hand, just looking at Emily's lithe frame as it stretched along her belly, curves wrestling with the sheets, her face a painting of cherubic peace. It was times like this the whole playboy thing faded, when he was a real dad with a real son, and Emily clung to him like he was the man of her dreams. If a wife loved her husband for all the days of his life like she did him, why go elsewhere?

He pulled the sheets up to cover her body then let Robbie in to crawl up on the bed and ease her out of sleep with some feather kisses.

Emily came around, a smile spreading over her face.

"Somethin' smells reeaaallll good."

Robbie piped up.

"Daddy and me made pancakes and eggs, mama. You gotta get up and eat some before Daddy and me eat them all!"

"Oh no! Don't do that! My! I better hurry, then. All right, munchkin, scoot out for a minute so I can dress."

"Okey dokey."

Robbie climbed down and ran out of the room, arms pumping in exaggerated form, giggling all the way.

"Love you!" Emily called as he shut the door.

A muffled "love you too" sounded through the walls.

Emily grabbed the plate from Chad and stuffed a forkful of pancake in her mouth, wiping a little butter from the corner of her mouth and licking her fingers. She swallowed, then looked at Chad.

"Oh my God, you were absolutely fantastic! You felt so good I don't even want to leave the bedroom now. I could eat you up all day and forget about work. Maybe dip you in maple syrup this time and have at ya!"

Emily smiled before filling her mouth again. Chad grinned a little and admired her genuine beauty of character and physical form.

"Thanks for breakfast. This was real sweet of you."

"I try to be … sometimes. C'mon, get dressed, and we'll go finish eating with Robbie. I've got some possible good news for you."

Chad leaned over, kissed her gently on the forehead, then stood.

"I'll be waiting out there with Robbie."

Chad moved to the door. Just as he turned the door knob, he heard Emily's voice, quiet and timid.

"I love you."

He paused, hand on the door knob, looked back at her warmly.

"Emily Rideout, I think I love you too."

He smiled then slipped out.

Chad was stirred inside for Emily as he had never been before. There was something different inside him, some attachment taking hold; an anchor in his heart that never held firm before for any woman, not even his wife, Samantha. He didn't know how to explain it. It felt dangerous, but good.

Minutes later, they all sat around the kitchen table, eating pancakes and eggs, talking and laughing. Robbie was in great spirits with Chad around, and old Transformers reruns playing in the background. Eventually, Robbie left the table and went into the living room to watch more Transformers. Chad seized the moment.

"All right, so here it is. I've got a fish on the hook, so to say. Don't know just how big it is yet, but hopefully, sometime soon, I will. It could be a major payday. Nothing guaranteed yet, but there's a big possibility it could help out a lot with financing Robbie's treatment."

"O-my-God! Get out of here!" She slapped his forearm for emphasis. "Seriously!?"

Chad just smiled big as he kept talking. "Aaaannnnd … I may be in line for a promotion to full partner status in the next month if things at the firm unfold the way I think they will. That would be a HUGE pay raise. Can you believe it?"

"Holy crap, Chad! I mean, that's incredible. This is freakin' awesome!"

She jumped up, gave Chad a big hug, and slid right into his lap, leaning back as she held onto him and kicked her feet in the air.

"Thank you, God! I swear I can't believe it!"

"All right," Chad cut in, "don't get too worked up. Nothing is in stone yet. It's all just possibilities right now. No counting chickens before they hatch, and all that, 'k?"

"Yes, sir," she pouted, her bottom lip pushed outward. Her facial expressions indicated she was dejected, but grudgingly agreeable.

"But we can still be excited at the hope of an immediate answer. So, no pouty face, soldier! Got it?"

"Sir, yes, sir!" Emily said as she gave a little salute.

"So," Emily continued, smiling with devilish charm, "what time do you have to be to work?"

"Since I did all my prep work already, I don't have to be in till noon. It's 8:30 now. What's on your mind?"

"Well, I can get Robbie's babysitter to come grab him for a while. She could be here in a half hour. That would leave about an hour or so free before you have to leave. What do you think?"

"My, that sounds riddled with delightful possibilities. Make it so, private!"

Emily saluted and kissed him deeply, long and slow; her lips pressed firmly to his, while her tongue found its way inside his mouth. She pulled away, pecked him on the nose, and then stood. A phone call and 30 minutes later, Robbie was walking out of the house with a big hug from Chad and a kiss from mom. Emily dropped her robe and sauntered into the bedroom, hips tilting dramatically from side to side, inviting Chad into her lair. She climbed up onto her bed on all fours, and looked over her shoulder.

"Come and get it, if you think you're man enough!"

"Oh! I know you didn't! Someone needs a lesson."

"Well come give it to me then!"

Mark Adams' alarm went off far earlier than he normally would care for, but he needed to find an apartment … today. He hit snooze and rolled over, his mind slowly drifting onto the shores of consciousness. Waves of overwhelming bitterness towards Amy lifted him up before slamming him headlong into the concrete truths he could no longer avoid: how incredibly unloved he felt, how discontent he was with their life, with his life, how angry he was at Amy, angry at himself for his part, and angry at God for another tragic moment in his life when, once again, He wasn't there.

Why had they struggled so much when others were at ease? Why did they live paycheck to paycheck when drug dealers sold dope and had money by the handfuls? Why had they lost a child, when unwed crack-whore mothers abandoned their children to grandparents to raise? Why did he worry about being faithful when society barely perceived it as a virtue? Why him? Why did he have to suffer, and why couldn't he just be happy for one fucking moment?

Adams' mind wandered to Megan.

It wasn't uncommon for officers to come in and chitchat with a dispatcher to pass the time during the slow hours, or to call them up on a cell phone while on patrol and talk to help keep them awake on night shift. Megan, however, wanted more than friendship; she made that evident. Adams clearly communicated to her he was faithful and wasn't going to cheat on Amy, and to knock it off, but Megan continued to flirt in both subtle and, at times, aggressive ways. He would give her the 'cut it out' look, and she would give him the 'whaattt!?!' look and act innocent. She was beautiful, but more importantly, he knew she wanted him. That made him feel special, important, valued, and sexy. And that kind of influence made her nigh irresistible. He knew all it would take would be a word, and she'd be there … anytime, anywhere. She had said as much.

"Ya know, if you could just set those silly morals aside, we could both be really happy." She stared at him when she said it, her eyes hungry.

Adams replayed it in his head. Really happy, even if just for a little while, was really fucking tempting right now, and those hungry eyes made him hunger, too … a deep, gnawing hunger that wouldn't stop. It made him feel like a real man … and happy. But being 'happy' was not the chief aim in life; of this he was sure. He had convictions concerning right and wrong he believed were true, even if his convictions concerning God had waned.

His integrity was the one thing he knew no one could take away from him, but as of late, he certainly had been tempted to trade it for a chance at being happy, content—even if just for a while. Yet, he doubted it would really deliver. In fact, it would probably just make matters even more unbearable, particularly on his conscience. Still, the bitter temptation seemed sweet.

"Damned if I do, damned if I don't," he muttered out loud.

Crawling out of bed, he missed Toby, his honey colored lab. By now, the dog would have moseyed over to nuzzle his hands and steal some loving. As soon as Adams secured the apartment, he'd swing by and get him. Toby was his. Amy wouldn't dare deny him that.

An hour later, after a shower and shave, Adams checked out of the hotel and was on his way to the Merriweather Heights apartment complex to sign the paperwork he already discussed with the manager, Terry, over the phone.

He dialed Amy, kept it dry, monotone, matter of fact: information exchange only. Told her what he'd be by to get and when; she had no problems with it.

"Good," he told her, "have a nice day."

"You too," she said flippantly. A cold "bye" from both and the lines clicked dead.

Chad arrived at work shortly before noon and invited Brad and Annie to lunch. Brad tried to decline, but they both insisted until he finally agreed, though with a distinct look of trepidation on his face.

They made their way two blocks down to a local panini restaurant. Annie grabbed a secluded corner table while Chad and Brad placed orders. Annie occupied a seat facing the corner so Brad would sit facing out, and likely would be more conscious of keeping his facial expressions and demeanor in check.

Chad and Annie started sipping soup and eating their sandwiches when Brad finally decided to acknowledge the elephant in the room.

"All right. Let's get this over with. I know you didn't invite me here for the company. Something's up, and I doubt it's good. Out with it. I don't like the suspense."

Brad glanced at Annie then locked eyes with Chad, his stare challenging.

Chad sprung the trap mercilessly.

"All right, Brad. You are absolutely right. We didn't invite you here for the company. Hell, I don't even like your company, never have. So, here's the deal straight up. We know you have been essentially embezzling from the company by overcharging all your clients. We know exactly what line item it is; we have found it in all your accounts, buried there, out of casual observation. We know that you have been having that money deposited into other accounts of your own. We know about all your offshore accounts, your whole little nest egg. We know you have been illegally screwing over all your clients and that, if this saw light of day, you'd be locked up at worst and disbarred at the least. To sum it all up, we know you are totally fucked right now, and the pucker factor on your ass is trying to suck up that seat cushion at warp speed as I speak. Anything else you need to hear right now?"

Brad sat there, jaw slack, mouth wide open, like some dead Venus Flytrap, impotent to catch the buzzing flies descending on his paralytic tongue. He stared, heart pounding, mind scrambling for a rabbit hole to escape down, some possible way out of this predicament. The moment stretched out, nearly strangling his cognitive function with his own inaction. Then his mind, finally feeling the inability to flee from this life altering threat, shifted to a fight mode, fueled by pious, egotistical hubris.

Brad fired back. His tone was aggressive, but he kept his volume in check—a calculated rage.

"You think you're going to blackmail me? You think I'm going to just roll over and admit to everything you said just because you make a bunch of unfounded claims and huff and puff and think you're going to blow my brick house down? Are you fucking stupid, or do you both just want to get fired? I'll have both your jobs before you get back to the office. In fact, I can take care of you right now, Annie, you fucking white trash whore. You're fired, effective immediately! I'm done here."

As Brad began to stand, Chad grabbed his wrist with vice-like force and looked Brad in the eye again. Chad's gaze was cold, uncaring ... a shark bearing down on its prey.

"That wouldn't be prudent, Brad. We have it all. Hard-copy, hard drive, you name it. Show him, Annie."

Annie was already opening her laptop. A couple of key strokes and she turned it around so Brad could see the power point presentation unfold. Copies of billing statements, electronic deposits, bank statements and screenshots from his off-shore accounts, passwords, hacked files, investments, interest—it all flashed past his eyes in two second intervals, a train wreck in staccato sequence.

Brad slumped back into his seat as Annie spoke.

"We have everything we need to get you fired, disbarred, and jailed if you don't do what we tell you to do. So, yes, we are blackmailing you, and there's not a damn thing you can do about it, you condescending, bald headed, ugly yuppie bastard. Try us. I dare you."

Brad resigned himself to the outcome. He knew resistance was futile at this point.

"So," he croaked, mouth dry, his stomach a knotted balloon attempting to float away, "what do you want?"

Chad spelled it out.

"You will go back to work and submit your resignation with some made-up personal reasons, today! You will include a recommendation that I fill the void. That's all. You leave—I move up. Tomorrow afternoon, you will meet me at the Pelican Lounge to confirm. You will give me a copy of your resignation and a letter addressed to me admitting to all this with your John Hancock on it. I will keep said letter. Any questions?"

"No," Brad managed to squeeze out of his constricted chest.

"Good. Now, you don't look hungry anymore, so leave us alone and head back at the end of the lunch break. Bye."

Chad raised his hand and silently waved his fingers bye.
Brad stood without a word and left. Annie gripped Chad's
arm and leaned her head on his shoulder.

"We did it!" she whispered. "We totally did it!"

"Damn straight we did. Everything gets better from here,
girl, everything."

They finished their meal, fantasizing over all they could
do together. But ticking along in the background of Chad's
thoughts were other plans, plans Annie had no knowledge of.

"113 to Dispatch."

"Dispatch, go ahead."

"60 and I will be out on foot at the Gas N Go."

"10-4, 113."

It was the beginning of their shift and things were already
hopping. Adams and Hicks exited their vehicles near a crowd
of about twenty people milling about on the convenience
store lot. Several began to shuffle away from the gas pumps,
distancing themselves from the "No Trespassing" signs and
muttering beneath their breath. Adams spotted a familiar face
and approached him. Hicks wandered inside the store for a
minute.

"Rodney Hall! How're you doin' man?"

The light-skinned black male seemed happy to see Adams.

"Yo, Adams! What's up?"

Adams extended his hand, and Rodney grasped it firmly.
They pressed shoulders and patted each other on the back.

"It's good to see you, Rodney. You back in town for
long?"

"I'm visiting the family for a few days. Came down here
to grab a beer and saw some of my old homeys. You know
how it is. I'm chillin'. You still puttin' the fear of God in
these people?"

"Fear or respect, baby, you know how I roll."

They both laughed. One young guy standing in a small group of thugs spoke up.

"Man, whatchu talkin' to him for? He's fuckin' 5-0!"

"What? You don't like Adams?" asked Rodney, with a look that showed he really couldn't care less. "Well too fuckin' bad! I don't give a damn what you think, son. I respect this man. As a matter of fact, I am honored to shake this man's hand and call him friend."

Rodney shook Adams hand again as he spoke.

"And if you don't like it, you can kiss my black ass. This man saved my life, talked me out of committing suicide. He treats people fair and does the right thing no matter whether you're white, black, or whatever. He's earned my respect, so fuck off."

At that, the boys shut their mouths and walked away without a word. Adams was sincerely touched and impressed.

"You are still the man, Rodney." Adams made his voice crack, as if he were crying, and joked, "I love you, man."

"Hey, I'm standing here right now because of you and the grace of God. Ain't nobody talkin' shit about you while I'm around."

Radio traffic interrupted their reunion. "Dispatch, 113."

"Sorry, Rodney, hold on. 113, go ahead."

"Respond to 425 Lacy St., reference to a domestic between father and son."

"Copy Dispatch. 113 and 60 are en route." Adams released the shoulder mic and turned back to Rodney.

"Gotta go, man. I'll catch you around. Tell your folks I said hi."

"Will do. You stay safe, Adams. Get 'em before they get you."

"You know it brother. Later."

NOVEMBER 3, EARLY MORNING

Harry Fitzwell felt eerily disturbed and on edge all day. Questioning every glance and gesture, every phrase, thinking someone at work knew more than they should; anxiety gripped him at every turn over the possibility. At the end of his work day, the Blue Pelican Lounge was a welcome diversion.

Now, at 1:00 a.m., after one last drink, Harry stepped outside, swaying beneath the alcohol's influence. He noticed the creepy homeless man and his dog from the other night standing across the street. Ignoring them, he turned to head north on 1st Ave., performing the drunken man's shuffle as he meandered along. His car was two blocks over. His peripheral vision caught sight of the man and dog paralleling him. His throat suddenly dry, his Adam's apple stuck in his throat as he reflexively swallowed and picked up the pace. They matched his speed then began to close. Terror gripped Harry. Instinctively rejecting the option of fight, his body prepped for flight.

The dog took off running across the street. Harry sprinted for his life, taking a short cut down a dark alleyway.

Only seconds later, Harry's screams echoed in the night air. Raw pain electrified his nerves relentlessly until the blackness consumed him.

Adams finished processing the son for assault and battery from their earlier domestic disturbance call. Afterwards, the night ticked by, uneventful after about 3:00 a.m. Adams had his fill of driving around and decided to go back to the office, knock out the arrest paperwork, and pop in on Megan to talk.

His ID card opened the door to Dispatch, and he strutted in 'gangsta'-like, throwing hand signs.

"Yo-yo-yo! What's happnin', home-girl?"

"Not a damn thing. I'm bored, and the night is draaagginng. God, I want it to end, along with this thumper of a headache."

"I'm sorry you're hurting, Meg. Anything I can get for you? I've got some Excedrin in my desk," he offered.

"Oh my God, that would be a lifesaver!"

"Sure, no problem."

Adams slipped out and returned a minute later with two pills. Megan swallowed them and thanked him.

"Anything else I can do for ya?"

"Yeah. Rub my neck, big boy."

She smiled, a twinkle in one eye while she winked with the other. She was half-joking, but serious at the same time. Adams thought about it. Bells and whistles were going off inside his head.

Suddenly, the image of the robot from Lost in Space popped into his head, exclaiming, "Danger, Will Robinson! Danger!"

He told himself there wasn't anything wrong with rubbing her neck in this setting, but something inside warned otherwise. Once his hands touched her, the temptation for something more would certainly increase, and probably embolden her to more aggressive flirtations.

Screw it! he thought, as the justifications flowed freely through his mind. She's a friend and coworker, and it's only a neck rub. Besides, I'm only doing it because she has a real bad headache, he reasoned with himself.

Adams laid his hands on her shoulders. Just touching her felt electric, exciting. He massaged her shoulders first then worked up the neck with deep, methodical strokes, gripping, pinching, and pressing. Megan relaxed, sinking into her chair.

"Can you rub my head too? That usually helps a lot." She looked up at him with puppy dog eyes and pouty lips, begging.

"Pleeaasse …"

"Ok, girl, no need to turn on the charms." He began rubbing his fingertips over hair and scalp.

"I thought my charms were the only way I'd ever get you to do something like this."

"Nah,. I can tell you're really hurting tonight."

"God, you're a sweetie … Can you pull my hair too? Just get a handful and move the scalp around."

Adams paused for a second, realizing all the sexual connotations that were running through his mind as he started to run his fingers deep beneath the surface of her hair and clinch as many locks as he could get a firm grip on. He used both hands, swirling her hair around, moving the scalp in circles, releasing, moving and gripping again, over and over, pulling tightly until eventually she moaned. Right then he stopped and let go abruptly, catching himself. It was too much.

"I think that's enough, Megan. I hope it helped." He felt unbalanced, as if suddenly realizing he had almost walked off a cliff and was now back peddling away from the edge, seeking safer footing.

"Oh, it helped all right, so well I might need a cigarette or something, and I don't even smoke. My goodness, Mark, I had no idea you had such seriously passionate energy in those hands. You should moonlight as a massage therapist; I'll pay you a nightly rate. How 'bout that?"

"I don't think you could afford me." Adams said, carelessly slipping into a slight flirt. It left a door open.

"Oh, I'm sure I could work out some form of compensation to take care of you, don't you think?"

"I'm sure you could more than compensate me for my efforts … if I let you."

Adams took a deep breath and exhaled slowly. Leaning down to speak, he caught a whiff of her perfume. It was earthy, sensual, invigorating. He noticed things in that moment that usually didn't even register with him, such as her earrings, painted fingernails and toenails, makeup, well-styled hair, and a business casual outfit that said she was classy, yet approachable at the same time. She was utterly intoxicating. All this and an alluring fragrance drawing him like a bug to an electric blue zapper, just waiting to execute his integrity if he gave in. Amy rarely utilized any one of these tools from the feminine arsenal, let alone using them all together. He stood up to distance himself from the temptation that was poised like some serpent ready to strike.

"But I can't."

"Dammit, Mark, why won't you let me?" she said, turning in her chair to face him. "You don't think I can't tell how miserable you've been for a long time now? You don't think I can't tell that your coldhearted bitch of a wife is sucking the life out of you? That you aren't full of passion just waiting to get out? That you aren't dying to be wanted desperately? I know frustration when I see it, Mark. You want it, almost as much as me. Give it a little longer, and you'll be ready for some relief. And I'll be waiting, babe. I'll be waiting."

Megan leaned back in the chair and smiled knowingly, like some drug dealer ready to feed an addiction, her gaze daring him to turn away first.

Mark stood silent, taken aback by her penetrating analysis. It was a gut punch on the money to hear her say what he had known all along. He was trying to formulate an answer when the door beeped and in walked Kaitlin, her dinner break finished.

Megan's eyes held his gaze with a sultry confidence for a moment longer. Part of him wanted her so badly, wanted to see her demonstrate her want for him, but he still had his convictions, and despite his feelings, frustrations, and angst over his dysfunctional marriage and now separation, he couldn't bring himself to sacrifice fidelity for fleeting pleasures. He was weary but not beaten, at least not yet. He broke eye contact, turned away, and acknowledged the newcomer.

"Hey, Kaitlin." Backing toward the door he remarked, "Well, I gotta go. See y'all later."

"Yup. See ya later, Mark," said Megan, applying one last twist of the screw. "Oh, and by the way, I'm sorry to hear about your separation. Let me know if I can help you out in any way."

"Uh … yeah, thanks. Later."

At that, Adams quickly walked out the door and didn't poke his head back in the rest of the night.

Harry Fitzwell was cursing everything he could think of as he dragged himself to his feet.

The dog had lunged at him, and as Harry's arm reflexively rose up to protect his face, the dog's teeth sank into his forearm. With a violent jerk from the dog, Harry was brought to his knees. He screamed as he hit the ground and flailed at the dog's head with his free arm. It released him, and with blinding speed, slipped to his side, then clamped its jaws down on his left calf, its teeth penetrating deeply and causing his leg to burn. The dog held his leg for several seconds before giving it a violent shake, then released it. Harry stayed very still, listening, until he heard a low growl followed by padding feet moving away. The dog's shadow slid across the concrete walls as it exited the alley.

Pain throbbed to the beat of his heart, every pulse a stabbing pain in both arm and leg. Harry staggered out of the alley to his car. At home, his wife helped cleanse and dress both wounds; he'd go to the doctor tomorrow.

A few beers later, Harry fell into a fitful sleep, unprepared for what lay ahead.

NOVEMBER 4, LATE AFTERNOON

Brad walked into the Pelican Lounge at 5:30 p.m., looked around until he saw Chad in a booth, then slowly made his way over, a dead man walking death row for the last time, trying to delay the hangman's noose as long as possible. He stared helplessly down at Chad.

"Sit down, Brad."

Brad sat.

"Let's see the paperwork."

Brad produced the resignation letter and his confession, laid it on the table with a long, unconscious sigh, and awaited Chad's inspection. Happy with its contents, Chad slipped it into his briefcase, then withdrew a sticky note pad and slid it over to Brad. There were numbers written on it and a name.

"What's this?" Brad broke the silence.

"That's the bank account number and bank that you're going to deposit $500,000 into right now. I'll only say that once. You know what I can do to you."

Chad hit send on his phone and handed it to Brad.

"Your bank. It's 4:30 p.m., their time. Tell 'em what to do or you're done. This is non-negotiable."

Brad had been waiting for the other shoe to drop, but $500,000 was like a tidal wave slamming into him face first. He wanted to fire back, say something, anything, but it was hopeless. Of course, that's all part of being a lawyer, Brad thought, knowing when you're hopelessly screwed. You'll take whatever plea they give you because you know it's better than the alternative.

Brad took the phone, pressed the buttons, and when the teller spoke, he told her exactly what to do and read the numbers off, each one like a kick in the teeth. He kept telling himself it was the only way out. It didn't help.

He finished and handed the phone back. Chad pulled out his laptop, accessed his account, and confirmed the deposit was pending. It could take some time to actually hit, but it was on its way. Then he would need to set about maneuvering the funds into other accounts so when he gave it to Emily, Samantha would never be able to get her hands on it in a divorce.

"Nice doing business with you, Brad. Remember, if you try to cancel this deposit, there will be no warning. I'll just go to the police, and with all our evidence plus your signed confession, you know it will be a slam dunk."

Chad paused long enough to see recognition dawn in Brad's face, then dismissed him.

"You can leave now."

Brad stood, but couldn't move, his body rigid, his mind in a tailspin. He wanted to say or do something, anything except go out with simply a whimper, even if it did feel like swatting at a storm.

"I hope you burn in hell, Chad Bigleby."

"Don't worry, Brad. If I'm in, you're doubly so, and I'll watch you suffer all the more." Chad grinned as he said, "I can live with that."

"Now leave," he coldly told Brad, the grin disappearing as suddenly as it appeared as he took a sip from his frothy mug.

Brad's face twitched, once, twice, then he turned and walked away without another word. "Like a boss" Chad told himself, riding the high of victory.

Adams had a long morning in court after working all night, yet still sleep had not come easily when he got home.

He had been far too frustrated after the Darrel Weathers case. "I just knew we had that prick this time," he kept telling himself as he drove to the station for roll call. But, as it turned out, they did not. Detective Milton's confidential informant had skeletons in his closet they did not know about, but somehow the defense did and Commonwealth Attorneys do not like open court embarrassment, not one bit.

It didn't matter they had video, and Adams positively identified Weathers in the video giving the drugs to their informant. The Commonwealth Attorney would not stake his reputation on a witness who had perjured himself in another state. It was scandalous and humiliating, and he would not bear the responsibility or the burden of pushing on with what they did have. The case was dismissed, and the blame thrown back on the Narcotics Division for a poor background check on the confidential informant.

May as well call the Commonwealth Attorney 'Pilot', Adams thought in disgust. 'I've washed my hand's' must be his professional motto.

Apparently, the word was out, because the streets were full, the criminal element emboldened, more boisterous, yelling as his police cruiser rolled by, laughing at him and all he represented. There would be no respect tonight on the street unless they took it back somehow.

"Fuck this!" Adams said to himself. "This place is in need of a little intervention."

Adams made his way to the station and sat down.

"What do you know, good Roger Rose?" Sgt. Hicks asked, knowing almost certainly what the answer would be.

"I know a bag of flour makes a mighty big biscuit," Rose replied dryly. "But, I di-gress," he said, adjusting his glasses.

"First off, have fun tonight. The natives are restless and full of piss and vinegar because of the ruling today, but you probably already knew that. On a more interesting note though, Detective Andrews passed on earlier the autopsy re-

sults showing Rory Blunt's death was not a criminal homicide, but purely an animal attack. Animal Control swears it
couldn't have been a bear; they don't come that far into the
city, but that the size of a dog and the necessary jaw strength
would have to be pretty god damn impressive to do the deed.
Also, there were defensive wounds consistent with fighting
an animal, and they found hair under his nails. Weird thing
though ... lab couldn't identify the hair. Genetic markers
didn't come out conclusive or something like that. Anyway,
Animal Control is going to set up some kind of wildlife camera in the area to see if we can get a picture of it."

"Pret-ty freak-ee," whistled Dexter to break the silence.

"No shit, Sherlock," quipped Rose as he stood to leave.

Roll call completed, Adams immediately piped up, his
desire for justice burning hot in his chest.

"Sarge, I want to put these bastards in check tonight,
right out of the gate. I say we get out at every place we have
an agreement on file to enforce trespassing and write as many
people as possible. Any lip, we bring them in and hope they
resist. Especially, Darrel Weathers, if he shows his face."

Hicks took a deep breath, "Mark, I know you're pissed
about earlier today, and I don't care if you decide to step up
enforcement tonight ... just don't cross a line we can't step
back over. You know what you can and can't do legally. Stay
within it and don't run your mouth off making threats you
can't back up legally. Good enough?"

"Works for me boss. All right, Dexter, Greer, let's get
busy."

"Right behind ya," Dexter said.

Greer downed his coffee, burped, then stood and saluted.
"Aye, aye, sir!"

Adams, Greer, and Dexter got out at several locations often used for loitering and drug transactions—projects, convenience stores, abandoned houses, and empty private lots on

the main drag. Some people had sense enough to start vacating when the cars pulled up, some didn't. One suspected drug dealer was written for trespassing and searched incident to arrest. Dexter found some crack cocaine, enough for distribution charges. It put him out of service for a while, so Hicks stepped in to fill his spot.

Just after midnight, Adams spotted Darrel Weathers in the Gas N Go lot, two thugs with him for protection. Darrel leaned against the "No Trespassing" sign by the gas pumps sipping on a 40-ounce beer (not even brown bagged, Adams noted wryly), just daring the police to mess with him.

Adams exited his vehicle, notifying Dispatch via radio. Greer and Hicks were nearby and pulled up a few seconds later.

Adams walked straight up to Darrel. "Well, I can understand you might feel a bit invincible after today, but seriously?"

Darrel just ducked his head and laughed; his boys, keying off him, snickered at his side.

Adams continued, heat rising at the back of his neck. "You know, I really shouldn't be nice, but I'm gonna give you one chance to trash that open container of alcoholic beverage and stop trespassing by leaving this lot … now."

Darrel flashed his smile of almost all gold teeth and shook his head again. "Yo dawg, ain't no one scared of you and yours. You can't touch me. Anything you do right now will be considered 'retaliatory'." Darrel used his free hand to make bunny ears for quotation marks. "My lawyer said so." Darrel tilted back the 40 ounce and took several gulps, then lowered the bottle and tipped it in Adams direction. "So fuck off, yo!" Darrel laughed harder. The "Thug" twins followed suit.

Adams stood there for a second, staring Darrel in the eyes as he took a deep breath and, nice and steady, reached his hand out and grabbed the bottle, slowly pulled on it, waiting for Darrel to release his hold. Darrel held his gaze, sniggered a little, and let it go. Adams slowly tipped it on its side, the remainder of the contents pouring out onto the concrete lot. Adams let his eyes scan behind Darrel and his boys, beyond the lot, across the street. People were gathering nearby now, expecting fireworks. He could hear someone saying "Dayuuum!" in that high pitched "oh shit I can't believe he just did that" tone.

Darrel's smile fled his face, anger taking its place. Adams just crossed the line of public shame. There was no turning back now for either one. But in this case, Adams had the law on his side.

Adams spoke first, loud enough for everyone to hear.

"Darrel, I don't give a damn what your lawyer said. The law is the law, and I'm going to enforce it. I don't care who you are. You're trespassing, you're in violation of the open container code, and you just cursed and abused me." Adams tossed the bottle into the garbage can next to him and Darrel.

"Fuck you 5-0! You and all your bullshit codes!" Darrel blew up, dropped his arms in a bowed-out manner, stepped up to Adams with his head cocked, his chest puffed out, daring Adams to engage in the "alpha male dance for territorial pissing rites".

No one heard Hicks mutter "Oh shit …" then quietly ask Dispatch to call for backup from District Two, just in case.

Adams wanted to punch him dead in the mouth, choke him unconscious, and drag his body through the streets, but he pushed the rage down, checked the anger, and remained calm. Stay between the lines, he told himself as his gaze became predatory.

"And now disorderly conduct." Adams grabbed Darrel's right wrist with his left hand as he said, "You're under arrest." He held his other hand palm forward in between Darrel's face and his own, a barrier in case Darrel decided to lash out suddenly.

Thug number two stepped forward, and Adams immediately finger jabbed him in the eye. The sound of an injured animal escaped from behind the thug's gritted teeth as he flinched away.

The scene exploded. Darrel tried to jerk away, but Adams clinched the back of his neck with his right hand, pulling him square. Darrel scrambled to back away at a sprint, but Adams stuck to him, not letting go.

Hicks pounced on the guy reeling from the finger jab, kneeing his lower thigh. The leg gave out and Hicks shoved him face down to the ground, leveraging his arm behind his back. The other thug turned to help his boss, exposing his back to Greer who, in two quick steps, grabbed the clothing at both shoulders and snatched backwards, kicking his legs out from under him. A moment of horizontal hang time, then the thug's back landed square, air leaving his lungs in a rush.

Adams stuck to Darrel as he travelled three, four, five steps and slowed. Letting go of the wrist, Adams reached around behind the upper thigh. Darrel's feet suddenly pointed straight up in the sky, and his face planted into something unyielding. The world went black momentarily, the color of pavement, his body stunned as it came to a rest face down. Adams cupped Darrel's chin and rotated his head, turning his eyes away from him before Adams pinned Darrel's skull like a bug to a board with his right hand. He underhooked Darrel's right arm, cranking it high on his back, before putting his knee in the nearest kidney. Adams looked up, scanning right.

Hicks had his guy under control, one cuff on, the other getting ready to slide in place. Adams head turned a little further right, over his shoulder. Greer had a knee in his guy's solar plexus, the guy's head pinned with Greer' left hand. He looked up at Adams and smiled. Adams smiled back for an instant then saw Greer's face change, his right hand jerking back to his hip. Adams tried to turn his head quickly to the left to see what Greer saw, but everything seemed to be in slow motion. As his eyes began to scan the scene, not three feet away he saw a man's body go rigid, fold sideways and hit the ground, the large chunk of brick falling from his hand.

Adams snapped his head back around to the right, saw Greer's Taser in his hand, the metal wires catching the street lamp light as they stretched between the two men. Adams quickly pivoted on Darrel's head, swinging around to the other side so he could see the unknown clearly. More people had been coming across the street, but appeared to have stopped at the sight of the guy being tased. Adams wrenched both of Darrel's arms behind his back and cuffed him with no resistance. The throw did the job, Adams thought. A complete will breaker.

Hicks looked at Adams. "Watch this guy too. I'll help Greer." He then quickly pulled out a spare pair of cuffs, rolled Greer's thug over, and cuffed him.

"All right, Greer," Hicks directed, "cuff Taser boy there." Greer moved swiftly to the downed, would-be attacker, telling him, "Squirm and I'll tase yer ass again, you chicken shit bastard." He received a submissive nod, and the cuffs smoothly clicked into place.

Greer lifted the man to his feet in one motion, the taser electrodes still in him. "Walk to that car on the right, and remember, any shit and you get tased again. Comprende?" A quiet "yes, sir" came out of the man. All the patrolmen stuffed their guys in a backseat and secured them for the ride to the station.

NOVEMBER 5, 1:02 A.M.

Glenda Harris was leaving the Gas N Go, a large colorful coat covering her heavy dark-skinned frame, when she saw a creepy old man and his dog lingering beside the building, almost invisible, the shadows wrapping them like a shroud, eating the streetlight's glow. If her skin hadn't prickled when she passed them, she might never have even glanced over, much less paused, to stop and stare. The man's lips parted in a smile and white teeth were suddenly all she could make out clearly, the brightness casting a cloak over what she had seen before. Like some Cheshire cat, his smile hung in the darkness, tilting slowly to the right and then to the left before righting itself at last and revealing his face.

She stood frozen, struggling to find words to break the spell of fear gripping her.

"Umm … sir … this ain't no place for an old white man to be all by himself at this time of night. Are you lost?" Her heart was beating out of her chest. She gripped the aluminum foil packet in her pocket that held the blessed roots and herbs and prayed they would do their job of warding off evil.

A voice, smooth like sand sliding over glass, a southern gentleman's accent, projected from the shadows as the teeth disappeared.

"Why, mah lady, how absolutely kind and considerate of you. I appreciate your effort, but I assure you, I am quite dandy and in need of no assistance. You may be on your way without the slightest worry for my well-being."

The man tipped his head down and in her direction in parting recognition, then raised his right hand up and waved his fingers up and down to say goodbye, each finger falling and rising in succession.

Glenda's feet came alive, paralysis gone and flight kicking in. She ducked her head to look only at her boots and began walking away from the strange man, an unexplainably abhorrent aversion gripping her bowels. She clenched her buttocks as she placed one foot in front of the other, struggling to not mess herself before she made it home.

Mr. Phailees stood silent after the lady passed, waiting for his mark. It was mere minutes before the older man exited the convenience store with a 40-ounce beer stuffed in a brown bag and started his off-balance strut. He reeked of alcoholic beverage and days-old body odor. Poo-Dick turned behind the store and headed for the cut through that would take him home, passing right next to Phailees and his dog. The path led through a small wooded lot which was bisected by a large ditch. Phailees knew about Poo-Dick, knew about all the times he chased young girls down and threw them in that ditch when it was dry, held them face down to muffle their cries, and raped them from behind. That was how he got his nickname. Phailees glided behind him, unseen and unheard, until the ditch came into sight.

"Get him, Phobos."

In an instant, the dog was off and running without a sound. Poo-Dick was stepping onto the makeshift two by four bridge that stretched across the ditch when teeth sunk into his left calf and jerked hard. His legs shot out. His upper body slammed down on the bridge, knocking the wind from his lungs. Before he could grab any purchase, Phobos dragged him into the ditch. Phailees' hand shot out in a 'C', wrapping around the base of Poo-Dick's skull and pinning his face into the dirt and leaves. Phailees leaned close and whispered in his ear.

"Not used to being on this side of the action are ya, laddy?"

A muffled cry was barely audible. The next sound was the crunching of bone.

At the office, Adams peeked into Darrel's cell through the thick glass pane. "How's the head, yo?"

Darrel looked up, a large hematoma bulging on his forehead, his speech slow and quiet. "Yo, don't fuck wit' me, man. I just want my call."

"Don't worry; you'll get your call. I just wanted to make sure you understand."

"Understand what?"

Adams pressed his head to the door.

"That in the future, you shouldn't test me like that. You obviously don't know me."

"Huh. Yeah. Obviously. But now I do. You're a crazy white muthafucka."

"I can live with that," Adams said. "And I know you're a drug dealing piece of shit, whether a judge ruled in your favor or not. You'll get caught again. One of us will catch you. One way or another …"

"Well happy huntin,' muthafucka. That's all I got ta say."

Adams focused his eyes intently on Darrel's.

"The hunt always makes me happy, Darrel. Always."

Adams walked away wishing he was judge, jury, and executioner. Wishing justice was swift and he was the sword for a change instead of just a man catcher, a simple tool that can only hope to deter and restrain the wickedness of men, rather than eradicate it and make a real difference.

WEDNESDAY, NOVEMBER 23

It was Adams' day off, and he was grabbing some items at the grocery store when he spotted Amy. She was wearing scrubs, on her way home from work at the hospital. She spotted him and moved in his direction, her face uncomfortable but softer than he had seen it in months. Adams met her halfway.

"Hello, Mark. How're you doing?"

"Pretty good. How was your day?" He tried to be kind and civil.

"Not too busy, but strange."

"How so?" His curiosity was piqued.

"We had some guy come in the ER this morning for a panic attack. His wife said he had been having nightmares and could hardly sleep for about two weeks now. He was on edge, and his vitals were way up, especially his blood pressure. I overheard him talking to the doctor about his dreams. Man, you want to talk about some freaky stuff. I only caught bits and pieces. He didn't want to talk above a whisper, as if he didn't want 'them' to hear him, whoever 'they' are."

"So, what was the freaky stuff?"

"Oh, yeah. Well, he was complaining about some homeless guy with a dog that keeps following him in his dreams, except the dog wasn't always just a dog, just like the man wasn't really homeless and wasn't really just a man. I heard him say something about 'changing' and 'huge fangs.' Then he swore up and down that all his coworkers just knew how he had screwed them over, and they were going to kill him. The homeless guy said he would make sure of it, he'd make sure the man paid for all his sins."

"Sounds like a potential committal."

"Yeah, and it sounded like he honestly thought it all was real, and then it was like he caught himself, realizing how it sounded, and he told the doctor he knew it was all a dream but he just couldn't take it anymore. He wanted Valium, Prozac, something that would make it all go away, or at least make him not care. The doc gave him both medicines and lined him up for a sleep study."

"Do you remember who he was?"

"Yeah. Some middle aged white guy named Harry, Harry Fitzwell I think."

Annie O'Reilley's luck with men was, unfortunately, the tragic sort. She usually felt like the world favored her with a kiss until one day it turned Judas, and the kiss was no longer that kind of a kiss.

But Annie wasn't the type of girl to lose heart. She was a glass half full kind of gal and would often remind herself, "Momma always said, 'You have to crack a few eggs to make an omelet.'" Well, at this rate, she figured it was going to be one damn big omelet, and it better be gourmet, at that.

She sat at her desk daydreaming for a few moments that morning. She had finally left her husband, Marcus O'Reilley, and Sachs, a partner at the firm, was processing her divorce paperwork. It would be served on Marcus today. She wanted it expedited as quickly as possible, so when Chad left Samantha, there would be nothing in their way.

Speaking of Chad, she thought he was cooking up quite nicely, as far as omelets go. He would be the one. Annie just knew it. Brad quit, and Chad was promoted to full partner. The plan was working.

She focused back on finishing up her pet project. Brad swindled too many people out of too much money. It just wasn't right. Once she tracked them all down, she was going to talk to Chad about forcing Brad to pay back the money to each one. Send out anonymous money orders for the amount he charged them plus the interest he had accrued. He wouldn't like it, but he wouldn't really have a choice, now would he?

She spent the last couple of days searching through files for dates, people's names and amounts, establishing an exhaustive list of people Brad screwed over, when, how much, and a rough estimate on interest gained. It was extraordinarily thorough. She just needed to compare her totals with Brad's account balance to make sure there was enough money in there to cover it all.

She hacked Brad's offshore account one more time to check her figures. The screen popped up, the total balance present.

"What the fuck!?" escaped under her breath. "This is bullshit," she thought. "The sorry bastard has withdrawn all the money!"

Annie sat back in her chair.

"Motherfucker!" she said aloud, but quietly. "I'll fix his ass." She grabbed her cell phone and went downstairs. A short walk in the park would give her sufficient privacy for the call.

Annie dialed Brad's number, took a deep breath, and steeled herself for the animosity she knew would spit right through the phone.

Brad picked up on the other end, eyes on the caller ID.

"Yes, Annie. What can I do for you now?"

"Well, for starters, how bout tell me what you did with all that money in your account."

"What the hell do you think I did? I pulled it out before you got the bright idea to fuck me over even more, which I suppose occurred to you if you went looking, bitch! Leave me the fuck alone you little white trash whore! I've given y'all all the money you're going to get. I swear! It wasn't enough to take my job, you had to rape me financially, and now you still want more, huh? Greedy, greedy bitch! You and your backstabbing, ladder climbing boyfriend can go fuck yourselves!"

'I don't know what you're talking about now, Brad. What the hell do you mean, financially raped you?" Annie was indignant.

"Oh, sure you don't. And you probably don't have any plans right now to acquire outrageous jewelry, a sports car, an account in the Caymans that's all yours, and y'all are probably looking for a little vacation home to top it all off. Fuck! I bet you're shopping right now as you speak. The money cleared my account this morning. God, Annie, you're such a lying bitch! I can't believe I ever thought highly of you. Fine. You want to lie, lie, but I already gave y'all two-thirds of my nest egg. Y'all aren't getting another dime from me. So, piss off and die!"

With that, Brad slammed the phone down in its cradle, leaving Annie holding the dead line, bewildered at the rabbit hole opening up beneath her feet, a sinkhole threatening to destroy everything she was dreaming of. There was only one explanation for Brad's accusations.

"God damn you, Chad Bigleby! I'm not a fucking thief!"

It looked like she had another broken egg, but no omelet.

When she was done cussing, she cried, then wiped her face and went back inside. As she entered the office, she ducked into the women's restroom to check her makeup. Still holding onto hope, she went to find Chad.

He wasn't in his office. She looked at her watch then walked over to the main office window and scanned the lot for his car.

Chad Bigleby was, at that very time, walking out the door for an out of town conference. He had an hour and a half drive ahead of him. He hopped in his car, suitcase and coffee in hand, turned on the satellite radio, and pulled away, heading for Route 95N.

Annie cussed her timing under breath as she watched from the fourth-floor window, then quickly made up her mind and walked out to Judy's desk.

"Judy, would you be willing to run downstairs and grab me a sandwich. I've got something I'm working on."

"Sure honey. No problem. What do you want?"

"Parmesan eggplant sounds good. Thanks. Here's the money."

Judy locked the computer, grabbed her purse, and headed into the elevator. As soon as she left, Annie slipped into Chad's office and closed the door. Five minutes later, with Chad's agenda memorized, she asked Mr. Krumbacher if she could cut out early for the holiday to take care of some personal business. She grabbed her sandwich from Judy on the way out the door.

She knew where Chad was headed. At home, she changed clothes and made coffee for the road, but dropped it on the way out the door, spraying it all over the siding of her apartment building. She cursed, but thanked God it hadn't gotten on her clothes. She didn't notice the door neglected to click shut all the way. Frazzled even more now, she hopped in her Nissan Altima and sped off to confront Chad when he finished with his meeting. The whole way there she fought for focus, for calm amidst the growing storm, thoughts twisting in her head and heart, sharp and nauseating, the dream beginning to burst ... again.

When Chad exited the law firm, the parking lot was dark and almost empty as he walked briskly to his car, just outside the edge of light. He was nearly to it when he noticed the shapely form leaning on the front quarter panel and clicked the unlock button to illuminate things. In the flash, he could tell it was Annie, but she didn't look her usual chipper, sexy self.

"Crap, Annie. You could have scared the hell out of me sitting there. What's up? Couldn't wait for tomorrow night?"

"No, Chad. We need to talk." She was dead serious.

"About what?" Chad's tone dropped and his countenance turned to stone. His brain started trying to compute the variables and figure it out. Had she followed him to Emily's? Did she want to push the issue of him leaving Sam sooner than he planned? Was she pregnant? He couldn't read it.

"I think you know, Chad. I spoke with Brad today."

Chad's brain cringed at the unexpected turn of events.

"What are you talking about?" he asked. Deny. Deny. Deny.

"Don't screw with me, Chad!" Annie barked. "I'm not stupid. Blind and trusting, apparently, but not dumb. You didn't just blackmail Brad to get his job; you got most of the money he had embezzled!"

Annie was working herself up into a frenzy, and her voice carried.

"Dammit, Annie! Not out here. Get in the car."

Chad hopped in the driver's seat, and Annie pursued him inside, slamming the door on her way in.

"I was good with getting rid of Brad. Stealing money from all those people was wrong and I was happy to help make him pay, but I did not agree to blackmail him for money. In fact, I was planning on talking to you about forcing him to pay back what he took. This makes you as much of a dirtbag as Brad. And legally, if the police ever get wind and investigate, it makes me an accessory! Me! Little Annie O'Reilley. That much money stolen from that many people is serious shit, Chad! It wouldn't be a little slap on the wrist. It would be serious time! Federal time! And those bastards don't play."

Chad tried to turn on the charms, his voice calm, full of sincerity, honesty, integrity.

"Annie, c'mon, who are you going to believe, me or that lying bastard, Brad Buxton? Huh?"

"I'm going to believe my own damn eyes Chad, and the offshore bank account balance statement … your account statement!" Annie brandished the printout that had been folded in her hand. "I found it in your deleted email folder. That's what I'm going to believe."

Chad's heart sunk. Denial was useless at this point. She knew too much and had hard evidence. It was all damage control from here.

"All right. So, I got money, a lot of money. You haven't complained so far. And tell me, just how else do you think I'm going to be able to afford to maintain this lifestyle for us once I divorce Sam, and she rapes me for alimony? She's already on antidepressants and sleep meds. The judge will bleed my accounts dry to satisfy her. I won't stand a chance."

"I don't care about alimony, Chad! You can't buy a clean conscience. My momma raised me better than this. I'm no thief, and I'm not going to be looking over my shoulder wondering if I'm going to get caught for something I didn't even want to do. I couldn't live with myself if I enjoyed all those poor people's money, anyway. It's not who I am. No, Chad. You have one choice and only one. Do the right thing. Give the money back to Brad so it's all on his head, and we'll be fine between your salary and mine, or so help me God, I'm going to go to Mr. Krumbacher and tell him everything."

Annie's face was pure defiance. Chad had no idea she could be so strong. He hadn't seen that in her. Chad's mind scrambled for options like a cornered animal looking for a hole in the fence. There wasn't one. He was caught. All his plans were beginning to burn. Either he was going to lose all the money and everything he planned for, or lose everything when she told Mr. Krumbacher and the authorities. He wasn't prepared to lose it all, wasn't prepared to go to jail, but most importantly, he wasn't willing to let Robbie down. It was his fault Robbie wasn't medically insured to begin with. His responsibility. His oversight. And Chad refused to let Robbie's innocent life slip away when the money would pay for his treatment. Saving Robbie was a higher moral ground than all this other bullshit, he was sure of it. Damage control was all that could be done now. Tough decisions had to be made to ensure Robbie was taken care of.

Chad didn't hesitate.

His tone relented to one of dreadful resignation as he spoke, the unwanted acceptance of an unavoidable path.

"Dammit, Annie. Why'd you have to go and jack the train? I was on course. I was on top. Everything was going according to plan."

Chad gripped the wheel tightly, his forearms bulging.

"I don't care about your plans, Chad. I'm not going to be a part of this. You know what you have to do."

Annie shifted to grab the door handle and exit strong.

Chad calmly spoke as his left hand slipped down and hit the door lock.

"Yes. I do."

The bolts plunged and Annie turned back. She managed to get, "What the ..." out before the bottom of Chad's fist slammed into her forehead. It caught her flush and stunned her. He followed up with a barrage of blows, driving his triceps into the side of her face until consciousness left, and her limp frame collapsed against the passenger door.

Chad's brain turned a key, unsealed a locked cellar, and loosed some deep, coldly calculating evil, hidden and restrained until now. It worked with methodical efficiency. Quick assessment, then rapid formulation of a simple plan, executed with disturbing composure.

A white gym towel in the backseat made an easy tool to strangle the life from Annie's unconscious body, limbs twitching only slightly before all was still.

Chad left the body there long enough to locate her car nearby in the parking lot and bring it over by his, lights out, slipping through the shadows, making sure no one else was about. Moving swiftly, he put on leather driving gloves and stuck her body in the trunk of her own vehicle after stripping jewelry, purse and wallet. As he shut the trunk, green eyes stared up at him, dumb disbelief seemingly causing the pupils to swell.

"Damn shame," he muttered underneath his breath as he casually got in her car and drove off to dispose of matters properly.

He found an abandoned warehouse and tossed her body in a dumpster that probably hadn't been serviced in months, then drove half an hour south to an alley a few blocks from a bus stop, abandoning the car there behind a small strip mall. A stack of empty wooden pallets made an easy place to dispose of Annie's purse and wallet, less the cash she had been carrying. Some homeless guy was nearly passed out in a cardboard box full of popcorn packing material. Chad gave the wretched man the hundred dollars from Annie's wallet, as well as her jewelry in exchange for his coat and hat, then put it on and walked to the bus stop.

The bus dropped him off three blocks from where his car was. As the bus pulled away, Chad took the coat and hat off, cursing the stench, stuffed it in the trash can, and walked back to his car, pulling out his gym bag for a different shirt and stuffing the old one in the trunk.

He drove the speed limit all the way back to the gym where he entered, showered, and then disposed of his clothes in the dumpster after putting the gym towel in the bin for laundering. He slipped back out, catching the form of a man out of the corner of his eye, walking into the shower, his back erect, posture abnormally perfect, whistling some tune Chad couldn't place.

Chad arrived home to find Sam awake. Endorphins were still flooding his body, and he felt aroused enough to try and entice her into having sex. Her defensive mode gave way to his flattery and seemingly genuine interest. They had rough, passionate sex, the best in a very long time for them. Sam couldn't believe how good it was, how good she felt afterwards. She felt like a woman who was valued and desired, like a woman alive from the grave. She refused to let it go quickly, worked Chad into arousal, and they went again. Afterwards, she collapsed in pleasure and slept sweetly.

Chad fell asleep as well, without a hitch, resting like a baby.

NOVEMBER 24, THANKSGIVING DAY

Chad woke, refreshed and vitalized. Lying there, he considered his next move. This being a holiday weekend, no one would even know Annie was missing until she failed to show up for work. He would hit a car wash somewhere this morning and do a once over himself, then drop it off on his way to work on Monday for a thorough cleaning that would leave no evidence behind. Annie hadn't bled any so he didn't have to worry about trying to erase that CSI nightmare. It could be weeks or months before someone found the body. Act normal at each stage of the game and who would know? He was golden, he thought.

He sat up on the bed and stretched. Sam's arms encircled his waist, her hands cupping his groin, and kneading. He grew erect quickly and didn't fight it when her hand wrapped around his girth and gently pulled him back into bed, guiding him inside for another healthy romp.

Samantha had been slaving in the kitchen just about all day, cooking turkey, yams, cranberry sauce, stuffing, ham, pumpkin and pecan pies. It was a nice spread, and she hoped to impress her friends, as well as Chad. She wanted Chad to value her, think highly of her, adore her, want her, but it had all seemed beyond her grasp … until last night.

She considered Chad while she worked. Last night had been amazing, had come out of nowhere. He had been distant for a long time now, their sex life nearly nonexistent. She feared something was wrong but didn't have the strength to face it square on. No, she had Prozac and Valium to help her face things, or rather to never have to fully think about facing things. A few pills, and who really cared. She told herself she didn't, but the anxiety and insecurity said otherwise. She longed to impress Chad in some way, to solidify her value in his eyes, to assure longevity. Was last night just some freak anomaly or a new direction? Lately, a happy marriage seemed more and more of a pipe dream, their house built with brittle bricks, and the Big Bad Wolf was lurking somewhere outside in the shadows, waiting to huff and puff and claw his way in if necessary. Hell, he could already have found his way inside and be hiding in the closet or under the bed, eating her marriage up a bite at the time.

Her gut said the passionate sex was a fluke, perhaps even a dying gasp. She felt inadequate, mentally and emotionally hamstrung and in denial, incapable of mustering the chutzpah to really commit to the cause and go all out. Slowly, she had been cocooned within a thickening web of inaction, detachment, and lack of zeal. Too late to struggle. Smothered and spent, it was just easier to take the pills and fake ignorance, oblivious and wrapped in bliss for a while.

The doorbell rang. She moved to open it, a smile already framing her face. Happy pills make happy people, she thought. It was her sister Kristen and her boyfriend Jay.

"HEY, sis!" Big hug for sis, little hug for Jay. "Hey, J! Man, it is so good to see you both. Come in," she said, enthusiastically ushering them into the living area. "I swear, I am so glad y'all came. I've missed you so much, sis!"

Samantha held her big sister tight, then collected jackets and hung them in the foyer closet.

"Have a seat guys. You want something to drink? We've got wine, egg nog, beer, soda, juice, water ..."

Jay piped up. "I'll take a beer, please."

"Egg nog for me," quipped Kristen. "Hey, do you need any help in the kitchen?"

"Nope. Finished a few minutes before you got here. Thanks though."

Samantha distributed drinks and held onto a glass of wine for herself. Chad exited the bedroom and greeted Kristen and Jay warmly. He liked Kristen. She had spunk and initiative, if a bit feminist; but better the energetic, active sort than a lame fish like Samantha, he thought.

"Hey honey, grab me a beer too?" Chad half asked, more a commanding interrogative.

"Sure, dear."

The doorbell rang. Chad answered it.

It was his law school buddy Gerry and his wife Ginny.

"Hi, guys! Glad you could make it. Come in. Let me take your coats." Chad hung the coats then man hugged Gerry. Ginny gave a warm, friendly hug, her full breasts pressed tightly to his chest momentarily, impossible not to notice.

Samantha rushed in to greet them and play proper host.

"Hi guys! Good to see you. Gerry and Ginny, this is my sister Kristen and her boyfriend Jay. Kristen and Jay, meet Gerry and Ginny. Gerry and Chad were law school buddies, Gerry and Ginny were together back then, too. Ginny made more pots of coffee than she could remember for the two on all their late-night study sessions." Gerry laughed. Ginny giggled. Kristen smiled and nodded in between sips of egg nog.

"Well, guys, what would you like to drink. We've got wine, egg nog, beer, soda, juice, water …"

"What? No hard liquor?" Ginny gave a sad puppy face.

"Well, actually, we have that too."

"Vodka and orange juice, girl! It's been a long day around his mother. I need something good."

"Easy …" Gerry said in a bad dog, low voice.

"Oh, no." Ginny said, immediately adopting a correcting, check yourself tone. "I'm a virtual saint just for staying in the same room with that lady for three plus hours, much less for actually talking and doubly so for taking her pious, condescending criticisms without ripping her fat head off and using it for an ashtray. Sooooo … I don't want to hear a word about my vodka and juice tonight. I've got a halo round my head and a spare in my pocket."

Ginny crossed her arms and smiled with all the angelic charm she could muster, excessive cleavage spilling over the top of the deep V-neck shirt she wore.

"So, Ginny," Chad inquired sarcastically, "what will Gerry have to drink tonight?"

"Oh, he can have a beer or two, sure, but I'm the one getting sloshed tonight."

Samantha smiled broadly then spun on the ball of her foot and headed to the kitchen to prepare drinks.

For the next hour it was all food, drinks, and football. Ginny was definitely getting tipsy. When the game ended, everyone's conversation slowed to a trickle. Chad was irritated. A good host should be able to help start and carry conversation, but Sam was socially handicapped.

He hadn't cared when they first met. She was hot, liked sex back then, came from a wealthy household, and looked like a good trophy wife. But now he found her lack of passion for anything and her contingent inability to get a conversational erection that lasted longer than a minute of stimulating talk, quite unacceptable.

Chad steered the conversation toward Gerry's most recent legal endeavors and Ginny's accounting business in its second year. He even drew Kristen in with some talk of recent developments in legal precedent with regard to environmental activism. Sam pretty much kept everybody's drinks full and said "wow" a lot and "that's interesting." Chad was all smiles outside but progressively more irritated inside.

Jay was flipping channels after the game ended and landed on a movie channel. 28 Days Later. It was at the part where the soldiers were going to make the two girls dress up and have sex with them after they got around to executing their male friend who wouldn't go along.

"Now this is an awesome movie," Jay said.

Samantha piped up. "Yeah, it really shows you who the real monsters are in life. Zombies represent people who are full of desire and drive, compulsive and lacking clear intellect. But the soldiers are in full possession of their faculties and still decide it's ok to rape two young girls. Just goes to show, people are the real monsters. What one person is willing to do to another to get what they want is bad, but when it is carefully calculated, thought out, and then carried out, it's even worse. It takes a very inhuman heart that has disconnected from humanity. To them, people are just resources to fulfill their needs."

Chad stared at Sam, a look of defiant pride briefly rising on his face. Sam's audacity was surprising, but it was her contempt for the man he knew dwelt deep inside him that provoked an indignant bitterness he had to hide.

Samantha sipped her wine and looked around. Everyone was quiet. Kristen broke the silence.

"Wow, sis. That's pretty deep …"

Jay turned on the caveman voice, deep, gravelly, and slow.

"Big words … me no know … what you say … killing good … sex goooood."

Kristen punched him hard in the arm, and he went proper quick.

"Umm … Yeah, sure, you're right, Sam. People are the real monsters. I just don't think about movies like that. It's just an escape to me."

"It's ok, Jay. I understand. A lot of people are like that, and that's fine. I just like looking at the things a movie represents or what views the writer and director have of the world and how they think things are or should be. I find it interesting."

Ginny's brain was on an alcoholic delay but finally kicked in. "Guys are just Neanderthals, Sam." Her speech was a little broken in rhythm and slightly slurred in places. "They don't actually use their brains for anything that doesn't involve securing food, money, or sex ... oh, or organizing sports."

Chad didn't care for Sam's contribution. He felt it had placed a spotlight on a part of his life he desperately needed to keep hidden.

Gerry weighed in. "Sam's right. It's an age-old question. When somebody really wants something, how low will they go to get it? We see it every day as defense attorneys, and I've seen a few monsters in the last several years that kept me up more than one night."

Gerry made a quiet, minimalist clapping motion, fingertips to palm, like high society people commending someone at one of their soirees. "Bravo, Sam, bravo."

Kristen praised her again. "Smart girl. Good to see you speak up for a change."

Sam blushed a bit but quickly diverted the conversation, finding a reason to walk away. "Anyone need a refill?"

Everyone said they were fine. Sam downed hers and said, "Well, I want some more wine," then got up and walked into the kitchen.

Chad looked at Gerry and decided to test the waters for his conscious sake. "I suppose the whole issue of how low you are willing to go can be justified depending on what it is you need, don't you think, Gerry? I mean, if the cause is righteous and good?"

"Dangerous line to play on though, Chad my boy. Like walking down the center of a busy traffic road, one step off to either side and you're road kill, metaphorically and ethically speaking."

Kristen was the new ager, and threw her hat in the ring.

"Well, morality is so subjective. Who says what's right and what's wrong? It's all relative, no absolutes. Each person has to find their own path and embrace the good within them instead of the desire to screw over their fellow human beings for their own benefit."

Gerry bit back hard, playing devil's advocate.

"But if that's the case, then who's to say whether or not screwing over other people for personal benefit is wrong? I mean, I think it's wrong, but on what basis do we say it's wrong if everything is relative and subjective. Take 28 Days Later, for instance. I could say that I think rape, in a world where the population has been incredibly depleted, is ok. Evolution baby, preservation and procreation of the species; someone's got to take the lead and show some initiative, even if others aren't quite agreeing with the program yet.

"If it's all subjective and relative, then it's just your opinion versus my opinion, and if I can beat your ass or if I have more friends than you or more friends with bigger guns than yours, I can say my way is right. Will to power and all that Nietzsche stuff. The Romans sure as hell did it for years. But if right and wrong is objective … well, that's an entirely different beast …"

"All right," replied Chad, instinctively going on the offense to defend his case, "I can buy that to a degree, but what about weighing value? For example, is it more important to not screw someone out of money or is it more important to, let's say, ensure someone can get proper medical care to save their life by securing said money through deceptive or physically violent means, even murder? Isn't life more important than just someone's money? Or, if someone threatens another's life in indirect ways, doesn't it warrant defense of that life? Or, how about the whole good of the many exceeds the good of the few argument? If I can save 100 lives by ending one isn't that morally superior?"

"Maybe to the 100 it seems that way, but to the one, he has just been screwed out of life, liberty, and the pursuit of happiness. And what about self-sacrifice or self-interest? If he gave up his life for the 100 to save them that's one thing, but if one of the 100 kills him, maybe they're just a selfish coward too afraid to die. But, if a totally disconnected party chooses the same act, he could be acting from a higher moral ground, because he is not swayed by his own interest. So, what's the right moral choice?"

Samantha walked back in, sipping her wine. "Complicated."

Gerry chimed in again. "Succinct and to the point, even if a generalization. Above all, quite true, Sam, quite true. Bravo again. Well guys, I thank you immensely for this last minute mental challenge, but alas, I must bid you all adieu. Ginny just grabbed my crotch, her subtle way of saying she's peaked on alcohol and ready to ravage me on the way home."

Ginny flipped her hair and smiled big and sexy. "Yup, my love meter is running hot. I can't wait no more. Sorry, guys. We gotz ta go."

Everyone said their farewells as Kristin and Jay gathered their things as well. The girls hugged goodbye. The guys shook hands. The door shut behind them, leaving Chad and Sam on their own. Chad felt compelled to pick a fight and lash out at Samantha, but unable to say anything about her actual opinions that deemed him a monster, he found another avenue to harass her.

"Well, Sam, you did well with food and drinks, but until the end there your conversation sucked. You need to work on that, especially if you want to host in the future."

"Seriously, Chad? You're going to critique me on every little thing, right now, already?" The wine had finally loosened Sam's tongue. "At least I wasn't staring at Gerry's cock all night, like you were staring at Ginny's tits. I thought there for a little while you were going to ask her to join you in the bedroom for a quickie. I mean, for the love of God, Chad, you could at least be discreet."

"Well, Sam. Ginny is not only attractive but a socially vivacious girl who knows how to talk, and I'm a guy with a wife who's taking so many meds to avoid life she doesn't have a lick of passion left in her for anything, including sex. So pardon me if I find my eyes wandering. I'm just a man,

Sam. If you don't like it, step up to the plate and do something about it." Chad stood across the living room, arms folded and cocksure.

Samantha downed her glass of wine, sat it on the coffee table and walked straight up to Chad, pushing him into the recliner. Without a word, she dropped to her knees, freed him from his pants, and began sucking at a frenetic pace. Chad watched her intently, enjoying the sheer energy of effort, but her eyes were still distant, disconnected, an academic exercise in attempting to disprove her accuser more so than a sincere longing for him. He enjoyed it more like someone would a prostitute than a lover, both parties detached from one another emotionally.

Samantha finished him, swallowed once, then wiped her mouth and slipped him back inside his underwear. She stood and looked at him, "See, I've still got it." Chad didn't feel like a fight after that, so he went along with it. "You certainly do."

Samantha was temporarily emboldened by the wine and her performance. "And don't you forget it! Oh, and tomorrow, we can talk politics or something."

She walked into the kitchen to clean up and get ready for bed.

Later, Samantha stared in the bathroom mirror, disgusted with herself. She had just thrown away her dignity, a level of her own self value and esteem, sacrificed on an altar of twisted need for acceptance and affection. She was driven by the moment to prove to Chad and herself she could be passionate, that she had not turned off the switch inside, that medication and repeated retreats from the world had not numbed her permanently to the possibility of deep, vigorous, emotional experiences. She had to prove she could still not only taste the sweetness of life, but still had the appetite for it.

But what was sweet soon turned bitter in her bowels, her heart palpitating in angst, her stomach turning on itself. She sold a piece of her soul to a devil who did not care, and she had done it out of a twisted, desperate, and spiteful desire for vindication.

The image in the mirror was dark, scandalous, degraded, and overwhelmed with a burden of shame she could not fully articulate. She felt worse than a common whore; at least they got something in return for their services. Her efforts had been a mere gamble, a poorly calculated immolation of her own moral standards in pursuit of some demented stab at relational significance, a pathetic attempt at validation of her humanity. Ironically, both of these goals were impossible to attain by virtue of the very lowly means she chose to employ, her goals frustrated from the start. Samantha could not feel alive, much less passionate. She felt degraded, humiliated, her identity obliterated, as if she had just strangled what goodness remained within and was already rotting, a putrid odor of sex and death infusing her breath.

The sickening noise came first, followed by the vomit suddenly hurled into the sink, the seed of the serpent mocking her as it slid down the drain hole. She buried her head in both hands and cried quietly, unable to look at herself any longer.

"I'll be God damned if it ain't gettin' crazier than a couple of shithouse rats smokin' crack out there today. All our regular nutcases are fit to be tied, sure, but we had normally sane folks losing it."

Sgt. Roger Rose sat back in his chair, pulled out his handkerchief, and dabbed his forehead dry.

"I'm tellin' ya, I've known Bill McCormick since he was knee high. Always had a good head on his shoulders, but today he was rantin' about nightmares and people out to get him. I mean full on hallucinations, paranoid schizophrenic-like. So was Wanda Bennet. Same exact shit and they don't even know each other. Both of 'em had to be committed 'cause they were talking about killing themselves. I mean, we all know we have a bunch of crazies in this city, always have, but neither one of these folks has any history of mental illness. They just seem to have gone off the deep end. Like a bunch of fuckin' lemmings 'round here, all headed for some goddamn cliff. Hell, even the mental health lady was at a loss. She said her initial suspicion was acute paranoia but didn't have a clue what set it off."

He wiped his forehead again then wiped his glasses.

"Anyway, better luck for y'all tonight, but we're out of here. Had our fill for more than a day.

"Oh, and somebody found Poo-Dick's missing body. Looks like the same animal got to him days ago and hid him under some brush in a ditch in the cut through behind Gas N Go. Apparently, Poo-Dick hadn't been seen in a couple of weeks or so, but nobody noticed enough to give a damn. Like anybody cared about that sum' bitch anyway."

Adam's thought about how creepy these animal murders were as he gathered his gear and got in the patrol car.

A half hour later, Megan's voice cracked the radio silence as he patrolled the city.

"Dispatch to all Zone 1 units, respond to Edward and Brock's Import Exports building at 5th and Vine. Report of a man standing on ledge of third-story window. Possible jumper."

"113 direct. En route."

Adams hit the lights and sirens and sped away as other units acknowledged and marked en route.

Dexter and Greer were first on scene, advising Dispatch they were parking on the north side of the building, out of sight of the potential jumper. They peeked around the corner, confirmed his location, then checked the side entrance. It was secure.

"119 to Dispatch. See if you can get a hold of the business owner and get them to come down here and unlock this door before we have to force entry. Also, call out our crisis negotiator."

Dexter looked at Greer. "Good call. What do ya think? Stay here out of sight so he doesn't even know we might be entering?"

"Yup."

"Dispatch 119."

"119 go ahead."

"No answer from business owner."

"Copy that. 119 out."

"Dexter, you got your Hooligan tool in the trunk?"

"Yeah."

"Get it"

Dexter nodded and scurried off to the back of his car to retrieve the Hooligan tool, which fire and police often use to make entry to buildings, amongst other uses. Resembling a long, overly beefy crowbar frame, it's topped by a trio of implements—a flat hammer head, a thick prybar, and a large spike—which certainly makes it a versatile device.

Hicks and Adams arrived out front. Adams shined the spotlight up at the guy before exiting his vehicle. The man was middle aged, average build, nondescript, a little paunch above the waistline, balding but hanging on with a comb over. On the surface, a normal looking guy, except for his face, a contorted portrait of terror and conflicted angst. There was obviously something dogging this man's mind, something he could not escape, and facing it wasn't an option. Desperate eyes stared out over the edge at Adams. The man's butt low and pressed against the building along with his hands on each side, he looked scared of heights, afraid to jump, shaking his head back and forth in short jittery movements as he moaned.

Circumstances were volatile and exigent, for sure, and it would take time for the crisis negotiator to get on scene. Adams would have to try talking the guy down.

"Hey. Sir," he called out. "Whatcha doin' up there on a nice Thanksgiving night like this? Shouldn't ya be eatin' turkey and yams somewhere, laid up in bed knocked out cold with a full belly?"

The man looked at him and tried to speak, closed his mouth, swallowed hard, and tried again.

"I ... I'm going to jump!"

"What in the world would you want to do that for? Let's talk about this. Tell me what's wrong. Maybe we can find a better solution."

"There is no other solution! I've thought it all through. I know they know. It's too late! Too late!"

"Who knows what? Who are you worried about, sir?"

The man groaned, slowly building in volume, his face widening equally in dread.

"Aaaaaahhhh! O God! I don't want to die, but there's no other way! All my coworkers know how I betrayed them to get the promotion. I can't face them. I can't face my wife! I have to jump!"

The man eased his weight off the building to stand erect, though still trembling head to toe.

"All right now, buddy. Let's just think this one through. It takes a real man to admit when he's done wrong and accept the consequences for his actions. That's something your coworkers and your wife can respect. You can save face. Refuse the promotion, come clean, and start fresh. We can all respect that. What do you think?"

"N ... N ... No way, man! I cannot face them. It's too much. I'm not strong enough to face them, but I can do this."

Adams knew it was spiraling out of control.

Dexter popped the side door lock, prying it open with the Hooligan tool.

"119 to 113. Be advised we are making entry from the side door and proceeding to the third floor. Keep him talking."

Perhaps a different approach, Adams thought.

"All right, guy, let's say you're right. You're not strong enough. You can't face them, and taking yourself out of this world is the only way out. I still think you have a pretty big problem you haven't thought about."

"What the hell would that be?" The man was incredulous.

"Well, looks to me like your whole jumping plan here isn't going to work out too well."

"What the fuck do you mean? I'm three stories up. That's plenty high enough, 'specially if I go head first."

"Well, yeah, yer three stories up, but there's a bunch of bushes down here. They're just enough to cushion your fall so that you don't die, but break all kinds of stuff. You wanna be a cripple facing all those people? Unable to take care of yourself and having to rely on everyone who knows what you did, and knows that you couldn't even kill yourself right? Well, do ya?"

"You … you're full of shit!"

"I'm thinking not. Seriously. Look at all the bushes down here. Does that really look like it will do the trick?"

The man stared down over the edge, quietly assessing his odds.

"119 to 113. We're almost there. Keep him talking."

"Come on, sir. Go back inside, and meet me down here. You can talk to someone and figure out a better way—whatever is best for you. I'll even grab you some turkey and mashed potatoes or something for while we talk. How 'bout it?"

The man appeared to slump back against the wall, his eyes squeezing so tightly it twisted his face into pure despair. He appeared defeated, shaking his head slowly, some unholy nightmare playing out on the insides of his eyelids.

Suddenly, he looked sharply at the window on his right, as if he heard something. Recognition dawned.

"I don't think so, officer. I can't live another moment like this. They won't let me."

A surge of confidence rushed across his face as he made peace with his final decision, and his body swelled with adrenaline courage. His legs coiled from despair to determination, arms bending like springs, before he launched himself out into the night, diving head first into hell. Adams sucked wind and held his breath involuntarily until the man's body impacted with the concrete sidewalk, just barely clearing the bush line. There was a loud crack, like a steel ball bearing being thrown against a cement wall as the skull met the pavement, his body toppling over as joints and tissue gave way to gravity's unyielding follow through.

Adams stared at the body, mere feet in front of him, the pool of dark, viscous blood expanding in a slow pool around the man's head and shoulders, bits of skull and gray matter floating along, the moon and street lights reflecting in the crimson flow. Adams looked up and saw Dexter and Greer looking down, shaking their heads.

"Fuck," was all Adams said at first. Hicks called for EMS and told them to call the detective, and cancel the crisis negotiator.

"Fuck me," Adams mumbled and squatted down, running his hands through his hair.

Hicks came over to him, placed his hands on his shoulders, a sergeant reassuring his man.

"It's ok, Mark. You tried man. You tried real hard. Better than I could have done. I know that for sure. It was his decision. You didn't do anything wrong. I got your back."

Adams stood and turned back to the car.

"I appreciate that, Sarge. It means a lot."

Adams pulled the crime scene tape from his trunk and started cordoning off the area.

Hicks knelt by the guy's body, fishing in his back pocket for a wallet.

"So, who is he?" Adams asked.

Hicks flipped open the wallet and located the driver's license.

"Harry. Harry Fitzwell. Age forty-six."

"Ho-ly fuck! Hicks, that's the guy Amy said came in the ER the other day acting all weirded out and talking suicidal. Shit!"

"Man … that's some coincidental shit there. Look, just take a seat in your cruiser, and start writing your report. I got this stuff, and I'll coordinate with Detective Andrews when he gets here. The sooner we're done the sooner I can let you off early."

Adams glanced around, dejected, "epic fail" the only descriptor for his life right now. Vehicles were starting to slow to a crawl as they passed by, staring, trying to ascertain what might have happened, steal a glance of darkness normal people rarely see. On the perimeter, standing calmly munching on a cheeseburger was a scraggly looking homeless guy, dressed in a worn sports jacket and jeans. He smiled at Adams, stared at the body again, then took another bite. Adams thought he might have seen the guy before but couldn't really make out his features. His mind released the puzzle quickly and moved on, not even trying to hold onto the memory under the circumstances.

Adams headed to his car, the blood seeming to slowly follow him, until the little red soldiers no longer marched forth from the wound.

BLACK FRIDAY, NOVEMBER 25

Adams woke around 1:00 p.m., visions of pavement covered in gray chunks and red spray still vivid in his mind's eye. He tried to shake the images, but they held on firmly. He knocked out a quick kettlebell workout in his living room, showered, shaved, and got ready for work. He had switched with Rider from evening shift for the day so he could take off and head to a Filipino martial arts seminar Saturday and Sunday.

Everyone asked him how he was doing, and he responded, "just dandy" to each inquiry. Truth be told, right now he was quite dandy, hell, even a bit jolly, ready for the hiatus to arrive.

The day was nearing an end. The digital clock in his cruiser read 10:45 p.m.

"Hmmm. 15 more minutes, and it is clear sailing. Yes!"

Dispatch called on the radio.

"Dispatch to 113."

"Dammit." Adams cursed quietly as he shook the steering wheel once before picking up the radio mic.

"113 go ahead."

"Respond to Harris Teeter. Manager advises there is a vagrant with a dog outside the business begging from customers entering and exiting the store. He wants the subject to leave, but he will not comply."

"113 direct. En route."

A deep breath, then a forceful exhale.

"Fuck! Fuck! Fuuuuuuck!!!" Each word emphasized with a palm strike to the steering wheel.

"Grrrrrrrrrrrr! Why me? For the love of God, why me? Can't I get off without incident on a Friday evening when my vacation is starting? Jeez!"

Adams continued to cuss intermittently until he saw the tall vagrant and his dog as he pulled into the lot. The man was speaking to some lady who seemed to be holding her nose and keeping her distance. He was rolling a quarter through his fingers, back and forth on top of his knuckles, then caught it momentarily between thumb and forefinger before snapping his fingers. The quarter disappeared, and the woman gasped lightly. Adams stopped the cruiser, and when he opened the door, the conversation was audible from his position.

"Dollar for the entertainment, my lady? Perhaps one for my companion here as well?"

The lady dug in her purse and withdrew two one-dollar bills and extended them.

"Phobos." Phailees simply said his name and nodded toward the woman. Phobos stood and walked slowly forward. Head down, tail wagging.

"Don't worry, my lady. He won't bite."

She lowered the bills, and Phobos gently took them from her hand. She giggled at this display. Phobos turned and gently laid the bills in Phailees' hand.

"Good boy." Phailees patted Phobos' head twice then looked up at the lady.

"Thank ye much, lady, and God bless yer comin' and yer goin'."

"Phobos. Tell her thank you." Phobos barked once and then extended his right paw in the air a couple of times, waiting for a similar response. The lady squealed then put out her left hand, palm up. Phobos laid his paw in her palm, shaking hands in thanks. The lady beamed.

"Good day to ya, ma'am." Phailees removed his crumpled bucket hat and bowed at the waist.

"Good day and good luck to you and your friend." She smiled once more then walked into the parking lot, headed to her vehicle.

Adams sauntered up to where Phailees stood, adopting a relaxed expression and natural body posture, genuine and non-threatening, though erect, professional, and prepared.

"That's a neat trick you got there, mister. How are you doin' today?"

"Why sonny, that's awfully polite of ya, especially since yer here to run me off."

Phailees' semi-British accent shifted seamlessly into a slight southern drawl.

"Well, that's true. Management doesn't want you out here. He thinks you're bothering the customers, especially with it being after dark."

"Horse wash! Nothing further from the truth. Only smiles from everyone who's stopped long enough to talk."

"I'm sure you're right. Problem is it doesn't matter whether he's right or wrong. It's his place, and he can choose to not have you on his property if he feels like it."

"I know, Officer Adams. I know you hear this all the time, but I actually do know the law. I was a law graduate … a very, very long time ago. I will comply with the manager's lawful, though potentially asinine, request."

"I appreciate that, sir. By the way, do you have some ID on you? I didn't get your name."

"Certainly. I have no desire to give a lawman such as yerself a hard time."

Phailees flicked his right wrist, flourished his hands, and an ID card appeared. He stepped forward, extending it to Adams, his stench rolling forward as well, disturbed by the sudden movement.

Adams took it, suddenly feeling the need to hold his breath.

"First Name Mister. Last Name Phailees. And this is my partner, Phobos. At your service." The southern accent fell away.

Adams looked at the card and called in a wanted check. Phailees was much neater in the photo and significantly younger. Looking back up, he noticed Phailees had extended his hand.

"It's a pleasure to meet someone in your profession with such a reputation for excellence."

Adams shook his hand. Phailees' grip was firm, and he grasped Adams' elbow as well, establishing the dominant position. Adams grabbed Phailees' elbow back, instinctively not allowing the dominance move to go unchallenged. Phailees stared Adams in the eye and mumbled several words, possibly in German, Adams thought, then suddenly Phailees let go and stepped back, his hands reflexively rising in a palms out submissive posture.

"Yes. You certainly seem to have ... a gift for justice. Exactly what people on the street say."

Adams chalked the mumbling up to one of numerous possible behavioral oddities many homeless people with a bit of crazy can display, then made a mental note to use the hand sanitizer in his workbag when done. Often, it does more harm to not shake a man's hand, unless you've just seen him piss or do something else unclean. Then you can point it out, and they understand. Otherwise, you just screwed any kind of positive connection you might have made and most likely offended them beyond recovery.

"Hmm, you're askin' round about me, are ya?" Adams said as he handed the ID back.

"Not at all. You just hear people talking as the police cars ride by. Most of yer kind they just cuss. Yer one of the few they either seem to respect or fear. Either way, you seem to have made a lasting impression."

"Well, didn't think I was quite so popular. Anyway ... so, legal name Mister, huh? Your parents name you that?"

"You might say that. Yes."

"I've seen you around once already haven't I?"

Phailees smiled. "Why yes you have," he said gleefully, returning to the southern accent. "Go fish." He flashed a devilish grin momentarily.

Adams searched his memories, but there was nothing there. "Where at? I can't recall."

Phailees jerked his left hand to his heart, and the back of his right hand to his forehead, feigning surprised distress.

"Officer Adams! How quickly you forget me! I am crushed! Why it was that pathetic suicide last night, of course! I saw you from the fringe. I smiled, but you did appear rather distracted. I suppose you didn't notice Phobos and me after all."

Adams face twisted just slightly, unable to hide his surprise at the matter of fact callousness displayed in that two-word judgment, "pathetic suicide."

"Why would you describe that event as a pathetic suicide, Mister Phailees?"

Phailees' accent turned scholarly.

"He was a coward, unable to deal with the consequences of his actions, unable to face his victims, and do what was right. He could not linger long enough for this world to exact its due justice. A pathetic shame. The backstabbing bastard got off far too easy if you ask me. But, really, what are you going to do? Every man can tread the coward's path if he chooses. You cannot stop them if they are committed to it. They will find a way. I heard you speak to him. You certainly gave it a valiant effort. I hope you won't let it trouble your soul. Such men are not worthy of losing sleep over. Do not be distraught."

Adams was a little taken aback. This guy was more cynical than most cops.

"How can you make such a harsh judgment? You didn't even know him and his colleagues."

"Actually, we met once, briefly." A sly smile tugged at the corner of his mouth.

"Still, seems a bit ignorant of the details."

Phailees turned his head away, a thousand-yard stare waxing over cold eyes, his accent bland but his tone deadly serious.

"I assure you, Officer Adams, I see the truth, I see the lies; I see the wicked in a man before he dies."

Phailees blinked and turned to face Adams again. It was all a bit disturbing and disorienting to Adams.

"Dispatch to 113."

"Go ahead," Adams mumbled thoughtlessly.

"No wants on record."

"Copy."

Phailees cut in.

"Well, I shall excuse my companion and myself to comply with your request. I'm sure we'll see you again soon. The wicked are populous amongst the sons and daughters of men, no matter where you go. Good day."

Without waiting for acknowledgment, Phailees walked away; Phobos trotted behind.

Adams stared after Phailees, trying to fit him into the proper box. Yup. He's got a crazy streak, Adams thought to himself. But somehow that didn't seem sufficient.

MONDAY, NOVEMBER 28

After a weekend of hard training, Adams slept in until noon so he could get well rested before work. He was doing a twelve-hour split shift, 3:00 p.m. to 3:00 a.m. He felt good, despite his sleep having been restless, full of fitful dreams, strange, and unusually vivid. Recollection was fading fast, a blur of images and vague impressions swirling into a fog of forgetfulness.

The homeless man and his dog were prominent, speaking to him again, gripping his arm, whispering foreign incantations, declarations of a "gift" and a blessing ... and an invitation. There was a hunt, an evildoer fleeing. Adams ran with two others, pursuing. His lungs sang with the wind, howling one moment and hissing through clenched teeth the next.

He saw a man, or the mask of a man, saw desperation turn to hopeless surrender as he ceased fleeing through the park, turning to face them, back to the brick wall of the Civil War Memorial. The mask dissolved, humanity falling away to reveal greedy eyes, drooling tongue, a panting gluttony of rabid selfishness, his voracious appetite for wealth at the expense of others consuming anyone he touched, their addictions feeding his own. Exaggerated features sculpted his form into the very image of cunning, narcissistic avarice that had defined his entire life. There was nothing human about him any longer. He was just a predator who saw others as a resource to feed his needs. There was no remorse for all the pain and harm his actions inflicted, no internal pause of conscience. Every ounce of empathy fled long ago, a ravenous indifference his defining quality.

Adams sensed all of this in moments in his dream.

They descended in mass, devouring him with their own teeth, glistening white, bright like the righteousness of God's own wrath, avengers gladly delivering the justice due, executing the reprobate in an emotional ecstasy that left Adams elated and invigorated, while simultaneously disturbed and guilty for the joy he felt.

The two conflicting feelings coexisted until he got to work and walked into roll call and heard Sgt. Mitchum recounting the day.

"Damn boys, I tell ya what, score another one for the dogs or whatever the hell it is doing all this damage. First Rory Blunt, then Poo-Dick, and now, last night, the one and only drug dealin' son of a bitch Rashid Whitman."

"You gotta be kidding, right?" Adams spat out.

"Would I look this happy if I were kidding, Adams? In fact, it was in rather grisly fashion."

"Fuck yeah! Tell us the details," Williams said, unable to contain his rookie excitement. Rashid was one of the biggest drug dealers in their city and had nine lives. This was good news to all.

"Well, this time, whatever it was it must have been real hungry. Not only did they crack the skull open again, but they gnawed off his mouth, tongue, and his genitals to boot. Medical Examiner thinks there were multiple animals involved this time. We might have a pack of the bastards running around. Chief's all over Animal Control to figure this out."

Adams' mouth was dry, his brow hot.

"Where did it happen this time?" he asked.

"City Park, right in front of the Brick Wall at the Civil War Monument; blood all over the concrete sidewalk too. Quite a mess."

Adams almost puked. Turning away, his stomach lurched repeatedly, and he began to cough.

"Something got your goat there, son?" Sgt. Mitchum asked.

Adams held up one finger as he continued to cough. Finally, when he could speak again, he lied.

"Just breathed in some spit or something. I'm fine, thanks."

Adams' mind ran rampant. His dream. The hunt. The kill. The exact same location. It was all too much, too much to be coincidence. He was freaked out and trying to hide it. This was more than weird, too weird to even possibly be true, totally out of the box. He mentally clamped down on the growing whirlwind of thoughts. He couldn't dare consider it right now. It was so much more than his worldview could hope to process.

One-time coincidence, he reassured himself, slamming the door in his gut's face. If it happens again, then I'll shit myself and swear I've gone crazy.

That was that. Adams tried not to think about it the rest of his shift. Particularly the fact that he recognized the man in his dream. It was Rashid Whitman.

On his way to work, Chad dropped off his vehicle at a local shop to be thoroughly detailed. Just five blocks away from his office, it was a quick morning walk.

At work, everyone wondered where Annie could be. She left early on Wednesday to take care of personal business before the holiday, but no one heard from her since. After lunch, even more concerns were raised. Judy was particularly distressed, having tried multiple times to get Annie on the phone. Chad was pretty sure Judy knew about his and Annie's affair. On his way out, he insisted Judy call the police and ask for a welfare check at Annie's residence. She hadn't called him all weekend, and he was worried, he told her.

"I've got this meeting at 3:00 p.m. sharp. Can you please keeping trying to reach her?"

Judy nodded, wrung her hands, and tried calling Annie's cell phone and home phone once more. She even looked up Annie's mother's number and called that. Her mother hadn't seen or heard from her either. Judy finally worked up the nerve enough to call the police.

Dispatch answered the phone. "911, what is your emergency?"

Judy felt like crying suddenly, the act of having to explain the situation to someone who could possibly help, was breaking the dam holding her emotions back.

"Ma'am, my friend and coworker is missing. She hasn't been seen since she left work early last Wednesday, before the holiday weekend. I can't get her on her cell phone or her home phone, and her mother hasn't heard from her either. It's highly unusual for her to miss work and not call, very unusual indeed."

Judy nervously fiddled with her dress as she paused.

"Well, what was your name again ma'am?"

"Judy."

"Yes, Judy. I can have an officer go by your friend's residence and do a welfare check. Also, if you give me her vehicle description and some personal information I can put out a Be-On-The-Lookout to all my officers and surrounding jurisdictions. Does that sound good?"

"Yes. Yes, it does, ma'am. Thank you. I'm just very worried about her."

"I understand. So, what's her name?"

"Annie O'Reilley."

The dispatcher shifted Judy over to a non-emergency line and proceeded to get all the pertinent information. Judy thanked the dispatcher, and they hung up.

"Dispatch to 113."

"113 go ahead."

"Respond to Oak Grove Commons Apt. 150C for a welfare check. Call me for the details."

"10-4 Dispatch. Stand by."

Adams picked up his cell phone and dialed Dispatch. Gloria gave him the info she gathered from Judy. A short time later, Adams pulled into the apartment complex. It was 3:15 p.m. Parking space 150C was empty. He parked a few doors down, then approached her residence scanning for anything unusual.

Adams noticed a brown stain on the white vinyl siding next to the door along with a coffee cup sitting on the concrete, the lid lying up against the wall near the door. Left in a hurry? he thought, then knocked firmly on the door.

It swung open smoothly.

He drew his gun and held it down at his side, slightly behind his leg, pressed tightly to his pants to reduce its visibility. He didn't want to alarm any neighbors just yet. He took partial cover behind the doorframe and called out.

"Annie O'Reilley! Are you home? Police department." Adams spoke firmly and loudly into the apartment. There was no response.

"Police Department!"

He pulled back behind the wall and keyed his radio shoulder mic.

"113 to Dispatch."

"Go ahead 113."

"I have an open door at Apt. 150C. I'll be doing a sweep of the residence. Put a backup unit en route to me just in case."

"10-4. 111, were you direct?"

"111 was direct. I'll be en route from downtown. ETA five minutes."

"113, 111 is en route to your location. ETA five minutes."

"Thank you, Dispatch. I'm entering the residence now."

"10-4, 113."

Adams reached in his pocket and slipped his tac-light attachment onto his Glock pistol. If there were any dark corners it would come in handy. Another added benefit of being on the Emergency Response Team, he thought, cool equipment.

From the front door, he had a clear view of the living room and kitchen. He eased his weapon up to a low-ready position and slowly crept out on an angle across the threshold, clearing as much as possible, one sliver at a time, before entering. As he moved into the room, he rolled out to his left to see behind the couch and recliner before moving to the kitchen, where he swept around the island, putting eyes in every dead space. He continued through the rest of the house, clearing each room methodically, but with swift and concise movements, checking closets, behind doors, inside the shower, under beds. Within two to three minutes he had swept the whole residence.

"113 to Dispatch."

"113 go ahead."

"Residence is clear."

"10-4, 113. 111 were you direct?"

"111 direct."

Adams glanced around the apartment trying to tell if anything was significantly out of place, and for any personal affects that might provide context and background. He noticed numerous pictures in the living room. The same red headed girl was in many of them. Based on the physical description he was sure that was Annie O'Reilley. On the mantle, above a set of gas logs, was a 5x7 of Annie and a man. He was well dressed, sharp, handsome, and fit. Adams recognized him but couldn't place the face. The man wore a wedding band. Annie looked very happy, a knock out green cocktail dress complimented her ivory skin and emerald eyes. She was not, however, wearing a wedding band.

Adams pulled out his cell phone and took a picture of the 5x7, playing a hunch. Could be useful later on, he thought.

He walked out, pulling the door shut tightly, and walked around back. There was nothing of note, and the rear door and windows were all secure.

Adams knocked on a few doors, without any luck, until one lady in 148C answered. She had one child on her hip and two playing in the background.

"Yes. Can I help you?" She seemed surprised and concerned they had a police officer in their apartment complex.

"Hi, ma'am, I'm Officer Adams. I was doing a welfare check on one of your neighbors, but she's not home. Are you familiar with Annie O'Reilley in 150C?"

"Yes, a little."

"What can you tell me about her?"

"She just moved in about six months ago. Keeps to herself, but very nice and talkative if you catch her when she's not busy. Spends a lot of time at work and the gym. Her husband's a butthole though, been over here a few times since they separated, yelling and pounding on the door. Nothing physical that I've seen, and the police have never been called that I'm aware of. Um, is there something wrong? Is Annie ok?"

"That's what I'm trying to figure out. She hasn't been seen since around lunch last Wednesday when she left work early. When was the last time you saw her?"

"Oh no! I mean, I just figured she was off seeing family or friends for the holiday. Actually, the last time I saw her was last Wednesday, a little after lunch. I remember she pulled up, hurried inside, and within ten minutes she came back out dressed a little more casually, more than a little irritated, and definitely in a hurry when she left."

"Do you know of any friends that she might go and visit? Any boyfriends?"

"No. I don't know her that well, and I've never seen any men over at her apartment besides her husband."

"Ok, ma'am. I appreciate your time. If you see her, how 'bout giving us a call? Here's my card. You have a nice day."

The lady smiled and turned away, a little one peeking around the closing door. As Officer Adams walked to his car, he winked at the kid. The kid winked back.

Adams reached the fourth floor of the H.P. Arkham office building, occupied by Krumbacher, Sachs, and Bigleby, around 4:00 p.m. The elevator door opened, and he walked straight to the front desk.

"I'm betting you're Judy," he said, extending his hand in greeting. "Hi, I'm Officer Adams." Judy took it, a little smitten.

"Why yes, I'm Judy. Did you find Annie?"

"I'm afraid not, ma'am. Her car was gone, and she was not at her residence. There didn't appear to be any foul play at the residence. A neighbor saw her leave Wednesday afternoon in a hurry after stopping in to change clothes. Any idea where she might have been going in such a rush?"

"No. She told Mr. Krumbacher she needed to leave early to take care of some personal business and left in a hurry. God! I wish I had asked her something. I feel so useless."

"It's ok, Judy. No one's psychic. Lots of people take care of personal business every day and don't disappear. There was nothing shouting, 'ask questions' in this situation. Don't beat yourself up. Ok?"

She whispered a tentative "Ok," not entirely convinced, but it did make her feel better coming from an officer.

"All right, so here's the plan. I've got Annie's cell phone number. I'll keep trying it. I'm also going to go talk to her mother and see if she wants to file a missing person report. In the meantime, Dispatch has entered Annie's vehicle description in the system for a Be-On-The-Lookout to all states. I'll keep checking by her residence periodically as well. Ok?"

"Sounds good."

"Also, tell me her physical description again."

"Oh, she's a looker, a regular bombshell. About five-foot-eight, long red hair, spiral perm, bright green eyes, oval face, minimal makeup—she doesn't need much—fair skinned, extremely busty, and very much in shape, not petite, just a solid frame that any woman would kill for."

"Yeah, I thought I saw some pictures of her at her house. Is this one recent?"

Adams pulled out his cell phone and showed her the green cocktail dress picture with the unknown male.

"Oh yes. Very. Just a few weeks ago, or so, I think."

"Is that her boyfriend?"

Judy ducked her head a little and looked around, lowered her voice before answering.

"Well, I can't say for sure, but I have a hunch that it might be. That's Chad Bigleby."

"As in Krumbacher, Sachs, and Bigleby?"

"Yes. That's his office over there, but he's not in right now; he's at a meeting and won't be back till later."

"Were they real close?"

"I think they were having an affair, but trying to keep it under wraps. Annie is in the middle of a divorce, and Chad's marriage has been rocky for a long time. Course, I think he's a bit of a player anyway, if you ask me, but he's nice enough to work with."

"All right. I'll want to talk to him later. He might have a better idea right now of other friends' names, possible locations she might have gone, etc. Tell him to give me a call later. Here's my card. Thanks, Judy."

"Thank you, Officer Adams. You'll call if you find out anything, right?"

"Yup. You'll do the same?"

"You bet."

"Deal then. Try to have a better day, Judy."

"You too, Officer Adams."

Mister Phailees sat on the wooden park bench, continuing his vigil. Patiently, he watched the jostling crowd doing their afternoon waltz from work to home. Phobos lay at his feet, head erect, eyes scanning, whining, salivating. He gulped deeply at the sight of a chubby teenage boy, slapped his chops a few times in a staccato rhythm, and sat at attention, straining, motionless. Ink black pupils swelled in the canine skull, staring at the disheveled Metallica t-shirt, iPod headphone wires dangling down to the hips, baggy jeans with visible butt crack, and the lazy zombie shuffle of fat ankles and leather boots, the left shoestring trailing behind, inviting the dog to play.

"Plotz!" came the command to lie down, a deep, guttural voice edged with disapproval. Phobos flattened back down against the grass, and Mr. Phailees patted his companion's still erect head reassuringly, his gaze returning to the crowd, but his mind wandering in fond recollection. He did so love the German tongue: medieval incantations, Goethe's Faust, Nazi sorcerers, and gas chamber attendees begging for their lives. The sound of it warmed him.

"Who knows, Phobos? Some day perhaps, but today we are fixed on a middle-aged Caucasian male, fit, slightly tanned, dark, short cropped hair, sports jacket, manicured nails, and perfect white teeth. Yes, his is a tragic tale of lust, greed, and a desperate need pushed to the extreme. He is the fraudulent, the betrayer, a predator, and the prey on which we shall soon feast." Mr. Phailees' face brightened, exuberant and gay, in a most disturbing way. A little girl walking by clung to her mother's leg and cried out, hiding her face.

"Chad Bigleby, Phobos, he's our man: smooth operator, forked tongue and shrewd as a serpent, Don Juan suave with the ladies, father to a deathly ill boy, and desperately in too deep to make it up for air.

"He is like the fattened calf, obese with sins, a juicy bug fallen into our web, waiting to be slipped the pointed poison, then drained at our leisure, a fine wine aged to perfection, an aroma of dread, and the anesthetic for our souls."

People walking by gave wide berth to what appeared to be a very old, thin and dirty, possibly schizophrenic, homeless man talking to his lanky black dog.

Phobos sat at his side, ears erect, watching the ever-moving crowd, waiting for their man.

"It's 4:55 p.m., Phobos. It won't be too long now."

Chad exited the meeting at 3:30 p.m. and headed straight for the Blue Pelican Lounge, a mere block from their building and a quick walk across the park to the detailer's shop.

He ordered a drink, downed it, then gave Judy a call to see what the police had to say about Annie. Judy gave him the run down and told him Officer Adams wanted to talk to him soon. He thanked her and told her he'd take care of it in a little while. Despite the officer wanting to talk to him, Chad felt safe. He would play the distraught lover. Nothing could be connected to him. But he would not make any call until after he picked up his car and knew it was clean.

Chad shifted gears.

"Judy, I thought of one other thing that had slipped my mind till just a few minutes ago. It might be important."

"What's that?"

"Didn't Annie's divorce papers get served on Marcus last week?"

"Oh my god! You're right. I should let the police know."

You do that, thought Chad.

At that, Chad sighed heavily and paused for a long time, beginning to scrunch up his face a little with fear, letting his voice crack in a concerned, helpful way. He cupped his hand above his eyes, shielding his face from common view.

"What can we do, Judy? It's like she vanished, and there's no clue where she might have gone. I can't even go somewhere and look for her. Where would I start?"

"Chad, I'm sorry but there's nothing we can do but tell the police everything we can think of and let them look for her. Go home, and have a few stiff drinks and rest. Maybe tomorrow we'll know something. Maybe she'll just pop back in here like nothing ever happened."

"You're right, Judy." He sniffled. "I could worry myself to death. I think your prescription is spot on. Thanks. Call me if you find out anything."

At that, Chad hung up the phone and ordered another vodka and juice, pushing his glass forward.

"One more time, Joe."

Joe was right on it.

"Here you go, Mr. Bigleby. Just the way you like 'em."

"Thank you. You know, Joe, I think you're a swell guy, no matter what your boss says about you."

They both laughed. Joe turned away, and Chad pulled out his cell phone and keyed in a number from memory, his thumb pausing over the Send button. He had finalized the money. He had the account set up and ready for Emily to use for Robbie, and it wouldn't come back to him. The money was safe. He pushed Send. It rang a few times before the female voice answered. He tried to focus on what he had accomplished instead of how he got there.

"Hi, babe. How are ya?"

"Just dandy, Emily. How about you?"

"It's been tough. Robbie hasn't been feeling well at all today."

Chad's heart sunk.

"Geez, I wish I was there."

"So do I."

There was a long pause. Chad hated to hear his little trooper was suffering again. There were good days and bad days, but the longer the Leukemia drew out the harder it got on both Robbie and Chad.

He hated he couldn't be there for his son more often, but he could only get away so much without being noticed. Samantha wasn't that observant, but one couldn't be too careful. He hid Robbie from her for a long time now. The odds were against him at every turn. From the beginning of this tragic ride, it had been an incredible shot to the gut, realizing, despite his fairly wealthy income, he was hopelessly impotent in the face of the staggering cost of treatment for Robbie without insurance, not to mention the horrible sense of guilt at his oversight. But Chad hadn't given up. He challenged the house and made his own rules. And now he had more than enough money to cover Robbie's treatment. It felt good to just say it.

"Em. I've got the money."

He just threw it out there.

"What did you say?" Emily's voice dropped to almost a whisper, breathless, unbelieving, unwilling to embrace for fear her ears heard wrong.

Chad repeated himself, slower and with appropriate emphasis.

"Em. I've got the money."

A cackling scream cut through the phone. "Oh my god!"

The screaming continued. Chad held the phone away from his ear. Joe's shoulders reflexively shrugged, his knees dipping in surprise.

Chad laughed and waited for Emily to calm down. Finally, she spoke intelligently again.

"How the hell did you do it?"

Chad lied.

"That insider tip really paid off. I invested everything I've managed to stick aside the last few years for Robbie. It was a gamble, but the share value shot through the roof, and I made a killing. Robbie can get the surgery, Em."

"Oh my god. I can't believe it." Her voice had quieted again, a sense of euphoric shock setting in.

"Believe it, Em. He's going to be ok, no more worries about what ifs and life expectancies past eight years old. He's gonna grow up healthy, like a normal kid, and meet a girl, and you'll be a grandmother. A normal life, I promise."

Chad was choking back tears, while Emily began shedding enough for both of them.

"I don't know what to say. It's … it's incredible … a miracle … it's crazy. Oh god, Chad, I am so glad I finally called you months ago …" Her voice trailed off in a light and happy sob.

"I'll get you all the account info. It's in your name. A card should be in the mail."

"Sure. That's awesome." She paused for a couple of seconds then resumed, her voice dripping like honey in his ear now. "When can we see you again, Chad?"

"Maybe I can swing it tonight. I'll call you if I can."

"I'll make sure I wear the outfit you like so much, for after Robbie goes to sleep. Sound nice?"

"Sounds real nice, Em. I'll do my best. Bye, babe.

"Bye."

At that, Chad hung up the phone, looked at the time, and slipped it in his jacket pocket as he picked up the vodka and juice and slammed what was left. He placed a hefty tip on the bar as he got up to leave for the detail shop.

It was 5:00 p.m. sharp.

Phobos yipped, jerking Mr. Phailees out of his thoughts.

"Ah, and here he comes, Phobos! I told you it wouldn't be long. Time management is oh so crucial in this line of work. So many fallen people to prey upon it's easy to miss a meal if you can't juggle well. No rest for the wicked, or for us. You need an astute eye to recognize the ones with sharp teeth and where they lie on the food chain. We must respect the caste system, of course. We all have to feed on someone, but we have been granted a position of affluence. The fraudulent betrayers of their own kind, descendants of Judas; anyone who deceives and does harm in order to feed their own greed at the expense of trust violated, they belong to us."

Phobos whined and smacked his chops.

Mr. Phailees stared at Chad as he walked past them. A shiver ran up Chad's muscular frame, until it made his head twitch hard to the left. Chad looked around, noticing only a homeless man on a bench with a mid-sized dog staring intently at him. Chad watched the man watch him and thought he looked rather familiar, until some busty girl jogging by caught his eye and dragged his attention ahead.

"Oh, my child, he will be vintage," Mr. Phailees said, smiling and shaking his head slightly side to side in tickled delight.

"Sic him, Phobos."

The dog rocketed after Chad, muscles rippling, legs pumping like powerful pistons, devouring the distance in an instant. Phobos' head suddenly convulsed then grew wide and thick, flattening, his dark fur thinning to reveal rough, blackened skin beneath, almost leathery. His lower jaw unhinged and dropped open. Needle sharp fangs of frightful proportions unfolded from the upper palette, flaring out into place then slammed into Chad's left calf, driving deep into the flesh and ripping Chad from his feet.

A yelp escaped as Chad flew in the air. He landed on the right side of his back, his arm flailing out to the side. The wind went out of him with a loud thud and hiss. He tried to breathe, but couldn't. His left leg was on fire. Gasping for air, he tried to look down, but couldn't sit up; the dog was still latched on to his calf, jerking him around.

Phobos' jaws worked quickly—distending, squeezing, and pumping the viral venom into the flesh. He cut his eyes to look at Chad, shook the leg once for good measure, then released it and ran off.

Those passing by only noticed a young, healthy man fall down and paid no mind, consumed with the bustle of their lives. No one even saw the strange dog bite Chad, except for a young kid sitting on a park bench who would have been pale white if he weren't black.

Chad managed to roll on his left side and look after the animal. He saw a black dog trot up to a homeless man who seemed to be waiting for the dog and praising his behavior.

The man looked right at Chad, winked and turned to walk away across the lawn. Chad staggered to his feet, favoring the left leg while trying to keep his eye on the homeless man and dog through the crowd. There were too many people obstructing his view. He hobbled toward the grass, but by the time he had a clear line of sight, the homeless guy was gone. A well-groomed black German Shepherd of similar build and appearance was now walking next to an olive complected gentleman in a white sports jacket and matching pants wearing dark oval sunglasses whose posture was absolutely perfect. They were too far off now, and Chad's leg was too jacked up to follow.

He cursed, brushed off the dust, and limped over to a bench where he sat down to have a look at his leg. Two large puncture wounds were already looking swollen and angry but had bled very little. Oddly, it didn't really look like much of a dog bite. He decided to continue to the detail shop, pick up his car, then drive to the ER to get it checked.

When Adams arrived at Annie's mother's place and knocked, it took a minute for Mrs. Fontaine to answer. She invited him in, looking his athletic frame up and down like a piece of meat. It disturbed Adams. He felt the unnaturalness of it, a cougar grown far too old, still dreaming of what she could have done in her younger days.

He glanced around the dilapidated apartment, wishing he was done already. The Virginia Slim cigarette drooped absentmindedly from her gnarled fingers, the length of ash somehow defying gravity's might.

For God's sake, flick that thing won't ya? Adams thought, distracted, ready to leave.

"Any idea where your daughter might be, ma'am?"

"She's a big girl. I'm sure she can take care of herself. Rarely calls me anyway. Couldn't tell you what her habits are beyond work."

She took another drag on the Slim then finally flicked it … in her hand.

"Well, ma'am, I thought you would be concerned and might want to go ahead and file a missing person's report."

She blew the smoke out the side of her mouth. "Does that cost anything?"

"No, ma'am."

"Do I have to go to your building or anything?"

"Nope. You can just sign a form right here, and I'll enter it into the system."

She grunted slightly. "All right. Where do I sign?"

"Right here, ma'am." Adams pulled out the form, got her signature, and left.

He called Gloria and had her enter Annie O'Reilley as missing; a BOLO was put out to all agencies for her vehicle as well as her physical description.

"Oh, Adams, by the way, that lady Judy called back. Wants you to call her on her cell phone for some further info … I think she has the hots for you."

Adams sucked wind, surprised, then sputtered, "Say what?"

"I could be wrong, but, hey, I'm just sayin'."

"She is sooo not my type. Nice but too old and not exactly what I call attractive."

"Aww. C'mon Mark. Big old girls need lovin' too."

"Ok. I'm hanging up now. Later."

Adams picked up his cruiser radio mic.

"113 to Dispatch."

"113 go ahead." Gloria's voice was syrupy, singsong, and subtly sarcastic. She was a mess, but fun to work with.

"Clear from last location, I'll be busy on that follow up call."

"Copy that, 113."

Adams made his way across town, keeping an eye out for the homeless man. He wanted to ask him what he meant when he mentioned a "gift" the other night. At the same time, he didn't want to think about what connection it might have to his dream and Rashid Whitman's death.

He closed the door on that mystery and considered what info he had on Annie O'Reilley: separated, seeing a married man, a man who is technically a boss, a daughter of white trash, but working for a nice legal firm, sexy and playing the field, perhaps. Too soon to judge—just guessing, hunches, following the gut- Adams' gut told him he needed to talk to Chad Bigleby.

He dialed Judy's number and waited for her to pick up.

"Hello?"

"Hi, Judy. Dispatch told me you had some more info for me?"

"Oh, Officer Adams, yes, I do. I completely forgot earlier that Annie had divorce papers served on her husband, Marcus O'Reilley, last week. It was that Wednesday she left early as a matter of fact. To say the man has a temper would be kind. Annie showed up at work a couple of times with bruises on her upper arms. And once, she called in sick for four days because she 'fell' down the stairs.

"Now, all of this is speculation mind you, but Marcus did show up here one day, madder than hell. I thought for sure he was going to beat her right in front of us. I think if Chad hadn't stepped out of his office when he did, Marcus would have dragged her to the elevator.

"As it was, I thought Marcus was going to attack Chad when he told him this was a business, and that if he was going to act like this he would have to leave. Chad told me to call 911. I picked up the phone and Chad stared him down until he left. That was the day Annie left Marcus. She went to a shelter for a couple of days until a girlfriend of hers helped her line up her current apartment. She got a restraining order. Anyway, I thought you might need to know all that."

Adams nodded unconsciously in agreement. "Absolutely, Judy. Thank you so much. I will definitely need to talk with Marcus. Do you know where he lives or works?"

"His address is 120 Lakeland Drive. I know he's a mechanic, but I'm not sure exactly which business he works for. Probably someone shady though, I bet."

"Judy, what about Chad Bigleby? Does he have a temper too? Do you think he would ever get violent with Annie?"

"Oh, gracious no, Officer Adams! Chad is always calm and respectful. Shows a lot of self-control and discipline. Anyway, he was out of town on a meeting all day. Didn't end until somewhere around 8:00 p.m. or later. Up in Westport, a good two-hour drive north of here."

"All right, then. I guess that's a pretty good alibi. Do you know if Annie called him over the weekend?"

"No. He said he hadn't heard from her either."

"Ok. Well, I'll probably still need to talk to him to see what he may know about Marcus, but that helps guide my investigation a lot. Thanks so much, Judy. If you think of anything else that's important, just call me direct, you've got my card."

"Ok, Officer Adams. Thank you."

"Talk to you later, Judy. Bye."

"Bye."

Adams hit End on the phone, then drove back to the station. Gloria ran a criminal history and, sure enough, it popped up two misdemeanor assault convictions as well as one felonious assault conviction, all from other jurisdictions. Records also showed the divorce papers and court subpoena were served yesterday at an attorney's office. The address matched the one Judy provided, and a report entry a couple of years old showed Vic's Garage as a place of employment.

Adams called up Vic.

"Hey, Vic. Officer Adams here. How ya doin'?"

"Just dandy, young fella. What can I do for ya?"

"I was just checking to see if Marcus O'Reilley still worked for you by chance."

"That twisted snake in the grass? Nah. I fired his ass months ago."

"Any idea where he's at now?"

"Don't know off the top of my head, but I can check around and see. Has he done something wrong again?"

"Not sure yet. Need to talk to him and get some answers. It may be nothing, but I appreciate your checking on that for me. You know where to find me, Vic. Thanks again. Have a good one."

"You too, son. Take care out there. And be careful with Marcus if you find him. He's a live wire when lit."

"Will do. Thanks!"

Adams grabbed Officer Spencer to back him up and rode by 120 Lakeland Drive to check Marcus' residence. It looked lived in, but the mail was addressed to an Emily Hunter. No joy.

Chad arrived at the ER around 5:30 p.m., his calf throbbing and his mood bitter. Nurse Jenkins sat in the triage room, her face scrunched up in confusion as she faced him.

"You sure a dog bit you?"

"No. It might have been a rabid wombat." Chad's voice dripped sarcasm.

"You don't have to be a smartass."

"And you don't have to ask stupid questions. Of course I'm sure it was a dog. I looked right at it. Just get me a doctor, for God's sake."

The woman's mouth twitched as if she were going to fire back, but she bit her lip and simply left the room. A different nurse came in and took him back. A half hour later the doctor finally came in and looked at his leg. After a minute, he simply stood shaking his head and staring at the wound.

"What's wrong doc?"

"Not sure. I know you say it's a dog bite but it doesn't look like just a dog bite, and it's definitely not acting like a typical dog bite. For starters, the spread on those puncture marks is close to five inches wide. That would have to be a very, very large dog. Far larger than what you described. I'm not saying you're lying or anything. Just, based on known factors, past experience, it isn't consistent with a normal dog bite." The doctor paused and scribbled something on the clipboard.

"I want you to wait here for a couple of hours for observation, just as a precautionary measure. In the meantime, we already called Animal Control. They should be here anytime to take a report."

"Hey, doc, what the hell does it look like, if not a dog bite?"

"Well, strange as it may sound, kind of like a snake bite, but I'm fairly certain that won't be the case. It would have to be an extremely large snake. Just relax; I'm sure it'll be fine."

A little while later, Animal Control Officer Winslow tapped on the curtain and announced himself before sliding in to speak with Chad. Notepad and pen in hand, he ground his way through the standard questions: who, what, when, where, how, etc.

"So, let me make sure I've got it. A homeless guy's black dog, maybe a German Shepherd, ran up and bit you then took off? Right?"

"Yeah, in a nutshell."

"O … K. Well, I'm sorry, but I really can't make any promises. That's like telling the cops it was a black male with a white t-shirt and blue jeans. The chances of me finding this animal are slim to say the least. If I am lucky enough to find it, I'll give you a call—I've got your number. If you see the man and his dog again, give us a call. Try to have a better day, sir."

Around 9:00 p.m., the doctor cleared Chad for release after treating his wound as a dog bite.

"Unfortunately, if Animal Control can't find the dog, you will need to come back here within three to five days to begin a course of rabies shots. Not pleasant, but there won't be any other options. Here's some sample painkillers and a scrip you can fill tomorrow."

"Thanks, doc."

Chad gathered himself and left, still walking with a pronounced limp. Once in his car, he fired off a text to Emily.

Sorry. Ur not gonna believe this shit. I got attacked by a dog today. Bit my leg good. Just left ER. Can't make it tonight. Love you and Robbie. C ya as soon as I can.

Chad arrived home to find Samantha crashed on the couch, prescription sleeping pills on the coffee table with a note, "So sorry—REALLY bad day. : ("

The TV played faintly in the background.

"Yeah, you and me both," he mumbled.

I do believe I'll join you, Sam, he thought and popped one of her sleeping pills. He limped into the kitchen, got an ice pack, mixed a vodka and juice to chase the pain meds, then limped back into the living room and kicked back in the recliner, elevating his leg and turning on the sports channel. It wasn't long before he fell asleep to some Rally Racing highlights.

Chad walked into the office building before dawn feeling just peachy except for the pain in his calf. The elevator opened quietly at their suite. It should have been peaceful, serene, and pretty much soundless. But he could hear the copier working overtime, spitting out page after page.

As he approached the copy room, a piece of paper came skidding out the doorway. He bent to pick it up and noticed a heaping mound of papers in front of the copier, another one landing and sliding towards his feet. He lifted the paper in his hand and read it.

"I, Annie O'Reilley, do solemnly swear that I have died a very untimely and unnatural death and that my killer is none other than Chad Bigleby. God damn his soul! Someone, please, give me justice!"

Beneath the message was a clear thumbprint.

Chad dropped the paper and stared into the room in disbelief. How in the hell did this thing not run out of paper? popped into his mind first, followed by Who the fuck did this? Who knows?

He quickly started picking up the papers, and eventually the copier stopped. He collected all the papers, stuffing them into a trash bag.

For a minute he was relaxed, but then an anxious but valid thought burst his bubble. Did the copier just run out of paper or is the job done? If the job isn't done Judy will find it.

"Fuck!" he shouted and took off for the copy room again. "Fuck! Fuck! Fuck, fuck, fuck, fuck, fuck!" escaped his lips in cadence with his rushing feet.

He stared down at the screen. It said "567 of 1000" in one corner and "Load Paper Tray" in the center.

"FUUUCK!" he yelled and hit the machine.

For what seemed like an eternity Chad tried everything he possibly could to cancel the job, but nothing worked. When all else failed, he decided to find more paper and help it finish. No luck. All the paper was gone. Judy would be here soon. She would run to the FedEx down the street when it opened, replenish supplies, and he would be found out.

Chad paced back and forth, cussing and trying to think of a solution. Instead, his mind thought only of every possible consequence that could occur if he were found out. His anxiety and frustration built to a level of desperation. At last he snapped, grabbing hold of the copy machine and lifting it off the table with uncanny ease for something so large and heavy. He pressed it overhead and then screamed as he slammed it to the floor. Pieces shattered and crunched, but it was not enough. He picked it up and repeated. Again and again, he pressed it overhead and hurled it to the floor as forcefully as possible. Each time, there was less and less of it left to lift. Eventually he exposed the hard drive, ripped it loose, and grabbing it with two hands, started slamming it on the edge of the table, as if he could snap it in half.

After it was sufficiently bent, he found a pair of scissors and stabbed it until he was sure nothing could be read on it. He dropped both and turned to exit the room, sweat pouring down his face and arms.

Pain blossomed in his leg, and his eyes were filled with bright white sparkling lights. He had whacked the bite mark on a large chunk of the copier. His leg buckled and as he fell to the floor, hands reflexively clamped over the injury. He screamed in pain until speech returned and then spat "motherfucker!" from between clinched teeth.

His body began to shake, and he realized the sparkling lights were fading. He heard a TV, felt flesh on his flesh. He heard a distant voice, followed the sound and the touch, and looked up into Samantha's eyes.

"You ok, Hon?" she asked, true concern filling her face. "You were shouting and holding your leg in your sleep when I woke up."

Chad tried to make sense out of the chaos swirling in his head. The dream was so lucid; he was having a hard time deciding what was real. Eventually though, Samantha bringing him pain pills and coffee convinced him he was safe, for now. There was no malicious copy machine threatening to expose him. All was well, his secret safe. But doubt tickled the back of his brain where paranoia had taken root like some black mold in hidden recesses, out of sight.

Chad woke feeling like a Greyhound bus had run him over then dragged him from one stop to the next. He was feverish, chilled to the bone, and ached all over. It didn't even feel like he had slept. It would seem the dreams kept his body too active and tense. He called Judy and told her all about the dog bite and how bad he felt. She gasped and told him to stay home and rest.

"Oh, and by the way, Chad, Officer Adams is probably going to want to talk to you today. I told him you were out of town last Wednesday on business, but I think he wants to ask you some questions about Marcus."

"No problem. Just ask him to please call me and not come by the house."

"Ok Chad. Go back to sleep."

DECEMBER 1

Adams decided to call Chad Bigleby at work when he woke up around 3:00 p.m. Judy told him he was sick and home today but gave him a phone number. Adams dialed it and waited. A groggy voice answered on the other end.

"Hello?"

"Mr. Bigleby, Officer Adams. You up to talking with me for just a few minutes?"

"Sure. Judy told me you would probably be calling today. I feel like shit. Got bit by a dog last night?"

"That was you huh? I heard the call go out."

"Yeah, I'm the poor unlucky bastard. I hope y'all spot that homeless fucker and his dog. Thing needs to be put down."

"Homeless guy? Yeah. I've seen him around. We'll see what we can do. Anyway, I needed to ask you a few questions and hopefully get some information that might help me in the missing person investigation of Annie O'Reilley."

"Sure, anything I can do to help. We both want her found. Shoot."

Nice opening, thought Adams. A little bit of forced teaming. Wants us to feel in this together. Calculated, or so damned used to doing it he doesn't even think about it? Can't say.

"Well, why don't you just start off by telling me your relationship with Annie? I know that you two were engaged in an extra-marital relationship. Correct?"

Chad's mouth dropped open slightly, and he quickly shut it. "Well, yes. We've tried to keep it hidden for the past couple of months, but, yes, we have been involved in a relationship together."

"Thank you, Mr. Bigleby for your candidness. Now, first, I need to know, when was your last contact with Annie?"

"I saw her last Wednesday morning at work before I left for an out of town business meeting, about two hours north of here in Westport. I was in that meeting until after 8:00 p.m., grabbed some dinner at a sushi place before driving back. I drove straight to Pleasant Grove, no stops except a gas station for coffee. When I got back into town I went to the gym and worked out for a little while before going home. Annie and I didn't talk all weekend because of Thanksgiving and me having to spend it with my wife, Samantha. Monday morning Annie didn't show up for work. My secretary said she had left work right around lunch, probably a half hour after I left for the meeting."

Chad paused for a couple of seconds. "God … you mean you don't have any leads? I can't believe this …" Chad sighed. "Is there anything I can do to help? I promise, if there's anything I can do, I will."

Geez, Adams thought as Chad continued to talk, that's way more detail than the average person would supply. Course, he's a lawyer. Cops and lawyers both are used to providing details. Our job is in the details and anticipating what details will be required. But the unsolicited promise there at the end. He seems to really be trying to convince me he's innocent and a good guy who's on my team. My gut says he could be guilty, but there's nothing concrete pointing at him right now.

"Well, Mr. Bigleby, let me cover my bases, and then we'll see what you might be able to do to help. K?"

"Sure."

"First, can you provide me contact info to verify your whereabouts on last Wednesday?"

"Sure. That's not a problem, except for the sushi restaurant I had dinner at. I paid in cash, and the place was packed. Doubt anyone there would remember me."

Adams interrupted. "You didn't keep a receipt for business expenses?"

"No. Was in a hurry and forgot it on the table. But my secretary can tell you what time I left the office, I can give you a number for the business meeting location, and they can verify my arrival time and what time the meeting let out. I scanned my membership card at the gym, so that should be on their computer system. Good enough?"

"Certainly should be," Adams said, though his gut wouldn't be quiet. He wished he was sitting in front of the man to read his body language. "Next, what do you know about Annie's ex, Marcus?"

"I know he got served with the divorce papers that week. Man's got a hell of a temper. We almost got into it once before Annie and I even started seeing each other. Marcus showed up at the office having a fucking fit: cussing, yelling, slamming his hands on her table, even threw her cell phone across the room. He looked ready to beat her ass right there. I told him to carry that shit elsewhere, and get out. He wanted Annie to go with him, but she said no. I told Judy to call 911. Marcus and I stared at each other for a bit then he cussed me out and left."

Silence filled the void for a few moments, as Chad thought back.

"Oh, and there were a couple of times Annie showed up with some bruises on her arm. Once we started seeing each other she told me Marcus would grab and shake her all the time, and he hit her pretty good on a couple of occasions too. He's a piece of shit. I don't particularly like my wife, but I've never laid a hand on her. I swear, if he hurt Annie, I'll fucking kill him myself." Chad let his temper flair, breathing deep over the phone.

"All right, that could be very helpful, but just let us do our job. How 'bout your wife, Mr. Bigleby? Does she know about you and Annie's relationship? Could she have possibly found out and been angry enough to hurt Annie?"

"My wife?" Chad almost laughed. "Oh no, detective. My wife is not the violent type. She'll take a bunch of pills and crawl in bed to escape the world before she'd try to face it head on. And no, I'm sure she doesn't know."

"What do you know about any friends she might choose to hang out with? Some place she might have gone?"

"Not much. Annie and I work together, and we've slept together on several occasions, but we never went out and socialized locally, so I haven't met any of her friends. How about her mother? Did you check with her?"

"Yeah, I spoke with her. That lady is a useless piece of work. Didn't seem to give a shit about Annie."

"Yeah, I've never met her," Chad said, "but based on everything Annie told me, the lady's a useless bitch who only cares about herself."

"Well, Mr. Bigleby, I think that pretty much covers everything." Adams was almost ready to end the conversation, but his gut just wouldn't quit nagging him. He paused for a long moment.

"Just one last question. Mr. Bigleby, why did you kill Annie O'Reilley?"

Chad sputtered to get out words.

"What? ... Umm ... Ex ... Excuse me! Are you serious?"

"Dead." Adams kept his tone flat and cold, matter of fact and let the silence bring its weight to bear.

Chad cleared his throat multiple times and then took a deep breath. Finally, he released the wind in his chest in a rush of words.

"This is ridiculous! Have you not listened to a goddamn thing I've said? I loved that woman more than my wife. We were discussing me leaving Samantha. I most certainly did not kill Annie, and if you are going to pursue that line of questioning any further I'm not dumb enough to entertain it without representation. Are we done?" Chad's tone was irate, but Adams felt he still detected a level of detached calculation present.

"Yes. We're done Mr. Bigleby," Adams assured him. "I'm sorry, but you know how things go. Sometimes we have to ask the question, no matter how unpleasant or unlikely it may be, and the more of a surprise it is the more of an accurate response people tend to give. Sorry to offend. Thanks for your time and cooperation. Hope you feel better soon. If there's anything else you think of please contact me."

Chad's response was annoyed but polite. "Ummm. Yeah. Will do. Bye."

Adams hung up the phone and sat processing the conversation. He certainly felt like Bigleby was feigning emotional concern and attachment. His whole demeanor and tone wasn't naturally distraught enough. Of course, lots of guys have very little emotional connection with their side pieces. Still, Adams would not let Bigleby off the hook. For now though, he needed to talk to Marcus, who obviously had more motive.

DECEMBER 6

It took a few days for the fever to break and the aches to diminish. The bite wound wasn't healing very well and still hurt like hell, worse than the rabies shots. He hadn't worked in days, and his sleep sucked too. Dreams were frequent and freakish, Annie always haunting him. A guilty conscious, he assumed.

He had called Emily to let her know about the dog bite and sickness. She was sweet and understood he wouldn't be able to visit right now, but Robbie's disappointment was heartbreaking.

When Chad finally went back to work, he found it hard to focus. He could swear everyone was looking at him funny. He was sure he detected a distinct sense of distrust in their gazes and in how they talked with him. It made him uneasy … a little paranoid even. Did they know? was the constant question burning through his brain.

Day after day the feeling compounded, but he knew there was no way they could know. He was just projecting his fears of the police finding out onto his coworkers.

Everything was going to be all right. At least that's what he kept telling himself, no matter how he felt.

DECEMBER 11

Adams' efforts at locating Marcus for questioning were completely unsuccessful thus far. Maybe he left town completely after he did the deed, Adams thought. Also, there had been no luck with the BOLO dispatch put out to other jurisdictions for Annie and her vehicle.

Eventually, Annie had to take a backburner role. The calls still poured in and people were still breaking the law daily. It never stopped. The truly wicked can never be deterred, only motivated to work harder not to get caught. Police cannot make them obey the laws or care about the harm they inflict on others. They are a sword of justice and a sword for punishment, never deterrence. But who will punish them when Lady Justice has been hobbled and disarmed? he thought. Who indeed?

Deep inside, Adams could hear the scratching whisper digging its way to the surface.

"I will," it said clearly. "I will."

DECEMBER 15

Chad opened his eyes, the throbbing pain in his leg slowly dragging him out of a dream he could not recall. Eyes circled the room. Boxing was on, and Sam was asleep on the couch; the mantle clock said 3:00 a.m. Chad limped into the kitchen, popped a pain pill, and washed it down. He stood at the sink looking out the window over his backyard.

Movement caught his eye.

He saw a female figure emerge from the shadows, creeping around the edge of his pool. His eyes followed her until they fell on the pool itself. The water was a horrible dirty brown. It appeared oddly viscous, almost gelatinous, and it was undulating, the rhythm broken and unnatural. Gently, it began lapping at the edges, as if hungry, climbing higher with each interval, precisely where the young lady now paused momentarily by the shallow end, looking around warily.

Chad noticed something move beneath the surface, a thick tentacle squirming, curling, and slithering forth, burrowing through the coagulated mass filling the pool. The length of it suddenly shuddered, beginning at the deep end, as if snapped by some force. It shot through the surface, wrapping around the girl's left leg. Panic struck her face for a split second before it snatched her feet from beneath her and dragged her body into the water, all in one fluid move. She reflexively grabbed the pool ladder, right hand a vise, forearm muscles a knot of steel wires bulging. She looked toward the house and screamed for help, the moonlight clearly illuminating her face.

It was Annie.

More tentacles crested the murky film, brown slime sliding down their milky skin. They seized hold about her torso and neck, jerked explosively and she was gone, a small bow wave rippling outward from where she disappeared the only evidence she had even been there to begin with.

Chad took another sip of water.

"Good riddance … bitch."

The whole affair was quite surreal and, strangely, did not seem to violate his expectations of the universe. Across the pool, Chad noticed the black dog that bit him, sitting erect, smiling. The pool began churning, a roiling mass of filth, critically agitated.

The surface exploded, a thousand bits of phlegm-like matter spraying the backyard and house. A large piece smacked sickly against the kitchen window, making Chad flinch. It stuck like pitch for just a moment before a writhing mass of tentacles burst through the glass, slamming into Chad and knocking him to the hardwood floor. The weight smothered his efforts to stand, wet flesh coiling about his lower body. He wrapped his arms around the kitchen table leg and screamed for Sam, looking to the living room. She was oblivious.

The tentacles twitched a coordinated, spasmodic popping motion that wrenched his arms loose. Helpless, it dragged him up and over the sink and through the window, a vestigial piece of glass cutting a path along his hip and severing his left oblique muscle in half. The tentacles flopped to the ground, smashing him into the cobblestone patio. They constricted further in preparation, then began yanking him towards the pool, spastic jerking motions tracing a dogleg trail of slime and blood.

Chad heard a dog bark and looked up. An olive-complected man with perfect posture stood beside the dog, looking on as if an avid spectator, his white sports jacket crisp, his sunglasses reflecting the moon, like two huge, white orbs for eyes. Chad recognized in that instant it was, in fact, the homeless man and the dog who bit him. He was sure.

As he slid into the pool, Chad flailed desperately one last time and grabbed the pool ladder, hanging on to not only the

ladder but to hope and sanity as well with a determined resolution, his mind denying the reality confronting him now, defying what could only be his pending death. He looked over
at the man again.

Mr. Phailees smiled broadly, immaculate white teeth
brilliant against the dark. He chuckled briefly, then repressed
his mirth.

"Please, Chad, don't look at me," he said, patting his
chest and shaking his hand. "You'll miss the best part." A
bony finger pointed to the deep end of the pool, and Chad's
eyes followed it with dread.

The mucous-like waters began churning sharply, a seeth-
ing current diving to the bottom then cycling upward in a series of agitated convulsions to lift some unseen mass to the
surface. Chad watched as the gelatinous surface tension quivered violently with the waves of force pushing out from some
buried epicenter. Slowly it began to swell and bulge, fissures
breaking forth to ooze some noxious emulsion. Finally,
something heaved beneath and a huge bulk of malformed
convexity broke the surface. Rising above the gruesome caul-
dron, puss sloughing off at unnatural angles to reveal the
pulpy, bulbous head of some squid-like beast, the flesh pale
with purple blotches, firm yet soft and almost pithy. Worst of
all, it was sickly slick like an eel, except for the small barbed
teeth gripping his flesh. There was no hope of escape without
severe injury.

Inner and outer eyelids worked in opposition to blink off
the oozing flow, revealing large, white, veiny orbs rolled
back in lustful anticipation. Intertwining tentacles, bunched
tightly together, stretched out from a mouth with frightfully
human-like proportions for its size, the lips full and curled
back, jaws yawning, the flesh gesticulating in a gross panto-
mime of rhythmic ingurgitation as the tentacles broke Chad's
tenuous grip and jerked him closer with each esophageal con-
traction despite his panicked scrambling for freedom.

The moment elongated to allow Chad's fear to reach its pinnacle. Mr. Phailees called after him, a chiding, judgmental tone.

"Your sin has found you out, Chad. There's no escaping the punishment you deserve."

Exhausted, Chad gave up his struggles and turned to see death approach. Both the creature's eyelids pulled back, revealing blue iris eyes with pulsating pupils, greedily staring at him. Chad filled his lungs one last time in preparation to scream, but was cut short as a plump, pulpy tentacle forced itself down his throat, choking off his cry of disbelief before dragging him into the belly of hell.

Chad knew those bright blue eyes … they were his own.

Samantha startled awake, jumped off the couch, and landed upright; her head swinging around in search of information faster than her eyes could follow. Her ears triangulated the awful commotion, drawing her attention to Chad on the kitchen floor, arms wrapped around the table leg as if the devil himself was attempting to drag him away.

He was screaming—staccato, hyperventilating screams mixed with uncontrolled weeping. Unresponsive to all Samantha's attempts at communication, his shrieking continued unabated, escaping in between increasingly raspy inhalations.

Samantha called 911 and simply held him as she waited, helpless and frantic.

By the time EMS arrived, Chad was hacking blood and phlegm; his throat hoarse, his vocal cords hemorrhaging and raw, his howls now gross guttural croaking. Both of the medics stood frozen for a time, their minds overcome by the shock of what they saw.

Chad's whole core heaved, knotted and flexed, drawing his knees up and pulling on the table leg, as if dragging himself back from some yawning precipice. His cries turned to racking sobs mixed with retching noises. His mouth and chin were bloody, thick white mucus hung from his nostrils, stuck to his cheeks, and pooled on the hardwood floors.

One of the medics turned pale and puked. The other called for assistance.

Chad was combative from the start, kicking wildly at anyone who touched him besides Sam, refusing to let go of the table leg. One medic got kicked in the knee, hyperextending it. Three more medics struggled to subdue Chad after the first went down.

Adams advised dispatch by radio he and Dexter had arrived on the scene as they pulled up out front of the residence together, parking next to the ambulance before heading inside. The ruckus was audible as they approached the front door. They rushed in to see the melee with a crazed man wheezing between gross barking sobs. The problem was immediately apparent to Adams—the heavy oak table and Chad's death grip on one of its legs. He flipped the table over on its side, removing any purchase Chad's arms had, but then the flailing began. Another medic got his nose broken. They finally dog piled Chad's upper body, Adams pinned Chad's head to the floor while he instructed Dexter to put one shin across Chad's calves, in order to limit him from getting his legs into play to resist them. Next, he told the medic to wrap his belt around Chad's legs and cinch it up, enabling them to immobilize the lower body long enough to get Chad on the stretcher and strap him down.

Everyone breathed rapid and deep, as Chad was finally secured to the gurney. The medics who were not self-assessing injuries, looked around to ask Samantha for Chad's information before they rolled out.

Sam, relieved of responsibility at last, fainted.

Adams followed behind the medics in case they needed a hand, Chad's unnatural croaking wails carrying through the parking lot and building. Heads turned in anger then disgust as they realized their source. A wide berth was given by the patrons on the way in; and even some nurses veered away.

Amy heard the gurgling shrieks before she saw the ungodly face producing them. Despite her revulsion, she jumped right in, instincts blocking out the horrific chaos filling the ER. Medics provided personal info and event details on Chad to one of the nurses. Adams caught the name "Chad Bigleby" over the relentless din of shrieks and sobs.

I'll be damned, he thought. "This can't be coincidence. Can't be," he mumbled to himself, staring at Chad's writhing frame as his brain tried to see how the pieces fit.

Nurse Jenkins was working a double and immediately recognized Chad from his ER visit. Never forget a smartass, she thought. Everyone scurried about, grabbing what was needed, trying to block out the cacophony of screams, grunts, gurgles, and hoarse rasping noises. Adams helped restrain Chad's arm long enough for Amy to put an IV in, then used a spare pair of handcuffs along with a couple of zip ties to make sure Chad wouldn't jerk the IV out. The doctor ordered a strong antipsychotic and a sedative, then left. Adams stepped outside the room when he saw Nurse Jenkins walk out, pulling the door almost shut to muffle some of the noise.

"Hey, Nurse Jenkins, you got a second?"

"What can I do for you, Mark?" She was a bit cold; stoic, but professional.

"I heard you say that Mr. Bigleby was seen here recently. I was curious; would that be relevant to his current condition?"

"Well, patient confidentiality and all that HIPPA stuff limits what I can tell you, but I don't think it's a big deal. He came in complaining of a dog bite. That's all. No cure for his other problem though." Nurse Jenkins let her voice trail off.

"What was that?" asked Adams.

"He's a smartass," she said flatly.

Adams laughed. "Good to know. Anything out of the norm, by chance?"

"Well," and suddenly her voice lowered to a whisper, "actually, it didn't look like a dog bite at all. Weird. Looked more like a snake bite. You didn't hear it from me, but look for yourself. Probably healed up a lot by now, but something that nasty is going to leave a serious scar." She pointed in the room. "Left calf," she mouthed, then, louder, "I'll be right back, ok?" and walked away quickly.

Adams slipped inside the room, closing the door behind him then moved around to Chad's left side, lifting the sheets. Adams peeled the bandage back, exposing the wound.

He dropped Chad's leg, backing away reflexively and sucking in air. "Holy shit," escaped his lips. The wound did look like it was made by two large snake fangs. But it was not healed at all. In fact, it was inflamed and aggravated looking, like it was infected or maybe the effects of venom. It would have to be a really freakin' big dog for the spread on the puncture marks. Course that would mean it would have to be a huge freaking snake too. Adams pulled out his cell phone and snapped a quick close-up, then pressed the bandage back into place and pulled the sheet over Chad's legs. He quickly slipped back around to the door and went outside.

Nurse Jenkins walked right by him a minute later, avoiding eye contact.

Adams stood outside, his brain wondering what the fuck was going on in his city. As always, he questioned coincidence and tried to connect the dots. Weird suicide, increase in crazy people activities, homeless man with bad vibes and a dog, a drug dealer killed in my dreams by a pack of unknown animals, turns up dead, missing girl and a boyfriend gone loony, and now bite marks from a dog that look like a snake bite the size of a huge Rottweiler's mouth. Do they connect? he thought, And if so, how?

He visualized the puzzle pieces, attempting different combinations but was unable to perceive a big picture.

Adams stepped outside to call Dispatch and update her on his status. As he came back into the ER, orderlies were wheeling Chad up to the psych ward. Desperately wanting a Diet Mountain Dew, Adams walked down to the employee lounge. Amy was seated, sipping coffee and staring at the wall, appearing a bit shell-shocked. He got his drink and sat down next to her.

"You ok, kiddo."

Amy glanced over and realized it was him. She set her coffee down and quickly wrapped her arms around him, holding on for a long time, her sobs quiet but steady. Adams held her firmly, lightly rubbing her back and telling her it was ok. After a while, she relaxed her grip and eased away, wiping her eyes and grabbing a paper towel off the table to wipe her nose.

"Thank you," she whispered then blew her nose. "I'm sorry I got all emotional on you … and snotted on your shoulder. Oh geez, let me clean that off." She hurried to wet a paper towel and wipe the shoulder of his uniform.

"Don't worry about it, Amy. It's nothing, comparatively," he said, thinking back to the house earlier tonight.

Amy sipped her coffee again. "Man, I've seen a lot of bad stuff in my days, but that was so horrible sounding, and so grotesquely bizarre. That man was absolutely terrified. I mean the fear was palpable in his bugged-out eyes. And the screaming, God, the longer he went the more awful it sounded. I just know his throat is hamburger. Man, I've just never seen anything like that. I handled myself in it, but, I gotta say, it freaked me out."

She sipped her coffee then tucked her hair behind her ear on Adams' side. "But I feel a lot better now. I'm glad you were here, Mark. Thanks." Her hair fell out from behind her ear. Mark reached up and tucked it back again.

"No prob. Glad to be here."

They both smiled.

"Well, I for one, am almost glad I'm going up to the psych ward in a few days to cover for some girl on maternity leave. At least I might avoid some of all this craziness that's in the air. It's usually just the regulars up there to deal with."

Adams' face became a question mark. "What do you mean all this craziness in the air?"

"Are you kidding me? People are acting flat-out funny. More crazies in general, and even some apparently sane people are feeling something strange. We've had several panic attacks come in. Say they can't put their finger on it, they just feel scared, terrified, think they're going to die or their life is about to go to shit or something. Just plain weird."

"Yeah, sounds like it. Funny, we've had a few more crazy folks here lately, but the big difference I've seen is that the regulars have been absolute doozies."

Amy nodded, then smiled at Adams. "Well, I better get back to work."

"Yeah, me too."

They stood, both staring at each other with aching hearts they tried not to show. Adams missed her bad.

"Thanks again, stranger. Stay safe out there, you hear?" Amy's eyes betrayed a restrained sense of longing.

"Yes, ma'am. I sure will."

Amy walked out. Adams was distracted by all the weirdness. When he wanted to give his brain a break he liked to people watch. He eased his way through the ER, sipping on his soda as he took in everything. It was always good to practice reading body language, part of the job really. However, tonight Adams felt he could read people like a book, effortlessly pinpointing intent.

Eventually, his mind a bit more at ease, he left and headed home.

DECEMBER 16, 8:05 a.m.

Samantha was sleeping in the waiting room when Dr. Danner came out to give an update on Chad's condition. He was fit and quite attractive, relatively young, probably mid-thirties, with bright blue eyes that gave you their full attention.

"Mrs. Bigleby?" Dr. Danner called out in a soothing tone, just loud enough to stir her into consciousness.

"Yes." Samantha, half startled, sat up stretching as she spoke, shaking off the tiredness. It was light outside.

"Your husband is displaying some very peculiar symptoms, as I understand you are quite aware."

Samantha nodded.

"We have him heavily sedated right now. My preliminary diagnosis is an extraordinarily acute case of night terrors."

"Night terrors?" Samantha was incredulous. "Night terrors can do that to a human being? I thought he was dying."

"Well, they aren't usually quite that dramatic, but it is possible. I'm going to commit him for further observation and treatment. It took an unusually high dose of Haldol to knock him out and give his body the break it needed. I suggest you go home, get some real sleep, and come back this evening or call for an update. If he wakes and is lucid, we'll call you immediately."

"Thank you so much, doc. God, I can't thank you enough."

Dr. Danner walked away and Samantha gathered herself and went outside in the bright morning, squinting and pulling her sweater tight in the crisp, cool air.

After sleeping all day, Samantha arrived at the psych ward around 6:00 p.m. She thanked God when she found Chad asleep, his features peaceful by comparison to the previous night, yet still uneasy, a tenuous stillness hiding behind an almost haunted expression.

The silence broke sharply. A clip of club music blared from a bag beside the bed. It was Chad's phone ringing. Samantha scrambled to pick it up before it disturbed him, desperate to avoid witnessing another night terror. She dug through the bag as frantically as possible without making more noise, seized it, pressed the phone image and answered.

"Hello?"

A female voice immediately responded. "Oh ... I'm sorry. Wrong number." The line clicked dead.

Samantha stared at the phone for a second then pulled up the call history. "Private number," she read with a mumble. She slid Chad's phone in her purse and put it out of her mind, watching Chad sleep soundly.

Later, back at the house, three glasses of wine gone and a fourth one filled nearly to the rim, seated by the couch, she spoke with Dr. Danner by phone.

"Mrs. Bigleby, first I want to tell you that my colleagues and I are doing everything we can to figure out how to manage your husband's night terror delirium, but I must also tell you that this is an extraordinary case. None of us have seen anything like this, though I have read of a few documented cases over the years. We are pushing the limits of narcotic treatment with nearly hourly doses of Haldol, and your husband is still waking at times with screaming fits, though of much lower intensity and duration than at the initial onset. We are reaching out to our medical community and personal connections. In all honesty, Mrs. Bigleby, we're at a loss here, but we hope for a break in your husband's condition. Once again, let me assure you, we are doing everything we can. It's not pleasant, but as of right now, his vitals are stable, and there's no degradation in his physical health, other than the damage his vocal cords have possibly suffered, which, given a little time, should heal up."

Samantha sat still and quiet, afraid to say a word and have the world unravel.

"Mrs. Bigleby, do you have any questions? Do you understand all that I've said?"

She forced herself to speak.

"Ummm, no, no questions, and yes, I understand. Just keep me posted, and I'll keep visiting. Thank you, doctor. Bye."

She hung up, her mind numb. It wasn't long before glass number four was gone and five stood in its place.

TUESDAY, DECEMBER 22

Adams was happy for the day off and had to finish Christmas shopping anyway. By 11:00 a.m., he managed to arrive at West Gate Mall. People were abundant, and personal space reduced, everyone slipping past each other.

His shift was planning a White Elephant gift exchange Christmas Eve since they weren't working Christmas Day. Everyone kicks in a gift, each one draws a number to establish the order of opening, and then, once the first gift is opened, you can either choose to "steal" a gift from someone else or open a new one.

Adams knew exactly what he wanted to get—a Shake Weight.

"It'll be a hit for sure," he thought. "They'll be desperate to get rid of it, or they'll start using it and the jokes will flow. Either way, we'll all get a great laugh."

He hit the novelty store and wasn't disappointed, plenty in stock. He bought two, one men's model and one women's model. The clerk looked at him a little funny.

"Grabbing these for a couple of friends," Adams said, momentarily feeling uneasy beneath the clerk's disdainful look.

"Sure. 'Friends,'" the clerk said, making the bunny ear quotation marks as he said it. "Right …"

Adams decided to roll with it.

"What? You've never used one of these? It's an awesome arm and shoulder workout. Don't knock it till you've tried it. I've got one at home of my own."

The smartass clerk didn't know how to take it.

"Well … um … I hope they enjoy them then," was all he could think to say.

Adams smiled and walked out, feeling good about the small one-ups in life. Hunger got him heading for the Food Court next, but as he passed a Bath & Body Works he happened to see Amy standing near the entrance, smelling various fragrant lotions and candles. She was dressed up more than usual, hair and makeup nicely done. She looked great, he thought.

His stomach knotted up as he stopped and watched her for a few seconds. He missed her, wanted to talk to her, but he was scared of things going wrong, getting even worse. What if he said something that pissed her off even more, pushing her further away from considering reconciliation? Last time, she was vulnerable and needing comfort after the horrifying episode in the ER. She was glad to see him. But that was then, he thought. A moment of weakness perhaps. She doesn't even know I'm here. I can just walk away."

He stood there for what felt like an eternity, torn, dissonant, the man inside who always avoided conflict in his personal life struggling with a man of desire and courage, who wanted to fight for his marriage. Seconds later he acted, walking right over to Amy, her back still turned, candle to nose. He got close before speaking.

"Personally, I think the lemon smells the best. What about you?"

Amy didn't flinch.

"I was wondering how long it would take you to come over here and say hi."

Adams' face twisted reflexively as "dammit!" shot through his mind. Amy continued talking.

"Yeah, the lemon's real good, but there are times you're just in the mood for something different. What do you think of this one? It's called Snowbound Cherries."

She held it up, and he smelled it. It was crisp, fresh, the cherries strong, a slight nuttiness running underneath it all.

"Nice. I like it. And you?"

"Yeah. Nice fragrance and clean. I think I'll get it."

Amy started walking for the cash register and motioned Adams to follow her. They chitchatted over some other items while waiting in line.

"So," she asked, "whatcha up to now? You finished shopping or what?"

"Well, actually, I was getting hungry and heading for the Food Court when I saw you."

"Oh my!" she exclaimed, hand to mouth. "You mean I stopped your stomach in its tracks? Wow! Didn't know I was that good."

Adams gave her a playful "you're a smartass" look then rolled his eyes.

"Well … I was going to invite you to have some lunch with me, my treat."

"Oh, and now that I've been a smartass, what now?"

"Annh, I'm thinking Dutch, maybe."

They laughed together, finished checking out and walked to one of the Chinese food places to share some Bourbon Chicken. Getting the food was easy. Locating a seat was the difficult part, but eventually they found a small table tucked in a corner beside one of the landscaped brick islands.

They sat down and began eating, one dish two forks.

"So, what's in the bag?"

"Shake Weights." Adams threw it out matter of fact and kept chewing.

Amy sputtered, almost spit out her food then swallowed wrong and started coughing.

"Geez, girl, don't choke; I might have to give you mouth to mouth or something. Eww!"

Amy cough-laughed some more then sipped some water and made sure she could breathe ok before saying anything else.

"So, you bought two huh? One for each arm?" Amy smiled, in that mischievous way he had always loved.

"Nah, one's for you. Thought it might help you get ready to play the field again."

"Oww! Shots fired!" Amy played offended, but she was still laughing. "And who's the other one for then?"

"Oh, that one's mine," he said. "When I switch teams, I'll need to build up my endurance, you know?"

Amy made the mistake of sipping water and sprayed a little on Adams as she busted out laughing hard.

"Wow," she said, wiping tears from her eyes. "I've driven a flaming heterosexual man to forsake women. Damn, I'm impressive!"

They both laughed for a long time, Adams wiping his jacket with a napkin then Amy giggled and asked, "Ok, so who's it really for?"

"We're doing one of those gift exchanges at work where you can open a gift or steal someone else's. I thought it would be a good laugh. I figured I buy both the men and women's models and just return whichever one we don't need."

"Oh yeah, I'm sure it will be a hit." Amy chuckled while continuing to wipe tears from her eyes. "So, do you have any plans for Christmas Day, other than work?"

"Nah. Not really. I'm off Christmas Day but work Christmas Eve, night shift. I'll get off at 7:00 a.m., probably sleep till three or four in the afternoon. You know the deal. My family is too far off to think about driving up on the same day after work. It'll just be me and Toby Bear, chillin'. Maybe I'll go catch a movie or something, don't know. How about you? You off?"

"Yeah, I get off that morning too, but I don't want to have to drive two hours up to my mom's on no sleep. I don't know. I might sleep and then drive up, or I might just stay home … not sure."

A lengthy pause, a bite chewed, and Amy continued. "You wouldn't want to go to mom's place with me when you wake up, would you?" Amy's expression was hopeful, but her body steeled, anticipating rejection, hands folded in her lap suddenly.

"Ummm … Amy …" Adams put the fork down and looked her in the eye. "Don't get me wrong. I get along with your family ok, but right now, circumstances what they are; I think it would feel really freakin' awkward. I don't want to be the splinter in the mix, making everyone feel uneasy, you know?"

Her body stiffened a little as her face fell with a sigh.

"Yeah, I get it. I understand. It's just …" she looked away, unable to hold his gaze, feeling tears welling up. She took a deep breath, wiped her eyes with a napkin quickly.

"It's just that I'm really lonely this season, and what, I miss is you. I want us to work things out Mark. I do." She touched his arm lightly, craving the connection touch established. Adams rested his hand on hers and squeezed easy.

"I miss you too. I've been working extra just to try and keep my mind occupied so I don't get depressed. I do want to work things out, but let's be honest. It's definitely going to take some real effort for us to get through the issues. We'll need counseling."

"I know, Mark. I know. Can we line something up for after Christmas or New Years?"

"Definitely. Do you mind seeing Dr. Wilkins, the lady psychologist on retainer at the PD? I think I can get her services for free, and she's good."

"Yeah, I'm fine with that. Sounds good." Amy sniffled a little, blew her nose, picked up another napkin and wiped her eyes some more. She flipped her hair, tilted her head down a little to one side and looked at Mark.

"So, Mr. Adams, how 'bout a Plan B? Would you like to come over to the house when you wake up? I'll make dinner. Maybe we can watch a movie and talk?"

"It's A Wonderful Life, maybe?"

"I thought your favorite was Jingle All the Way."

"Well … it is a holiday classic, you know?"

They both laughed, not too loud, feeding off the hope they each felt.

"A double feature then?" suggested Adams.

"Sounds great! And bring Toby Bear. I miss him too." Amy beamed.

"Deal. Well, I guess that means I'm not done shopping yet."

"Why's that?"

"Well I can't show up at your place empty handed, now can I? That's just bad manners. I'll have to go get you something."

"Well, don't go crazy right now. We can't afford it. It's ok."

"Oh, it's all right. I'll just go grab another Shake Weight." Adams cracked as soon as he said it. Amy smacked his arm, mouth an O.

"Well, I know you're out of practice and everything, and if we're going to work things out you'll want to get back in fightin' shape."

Amy sat back in the chair, "Oh, you are so wrong. But," and she raised her index finger, "I bet you don't need any extra practice right now, do ya?" Amy's smile gloated over the swiftly landed jab.

Adams spread his hands in non-protest. "True ... true. You got me."

He gave an impish smile. "Anyway, it's been real nice, but I need to finish my shopping. I hear a Shake Weight calling my name."

"Ooo, you rat. You better not."

"Don't worry; I'll bring you something nice." Adams slipped out of his chair, walked around behind her, and bent to kiss her head. "It was nice talking with you. I'll see you Christmas Day, around four, ok?"

Adams couldn't see it, but Amy melted at the brief kiss. "Yup. four o'clock is fine. Stay safe out there."

"But of course," he called over his shoulder. "Later."

DECEMBER 24, 6:30 a.m.

It was almost the end of his shift when Mark's phone rang.

"Hi, Megan. What's up?"

"Just got a call from Vic at Vic's Auto. He finally found an address on that guy Marcus you've been looking for. He works over at Sutter's Body Shop and Repair. They open at 7:00 a.m."

"Sweet. Thanks, Meg. I'll head over there now and wait."

"No problem."

It was 6:50 a.m. by the time he took up a position across the street from Sutter's Body Shop and Repair, waiting for them to open. If he couldn't find reason to pursue Marcus further, he could at least cross the man off the suspect list. Either option could help get this investigation moving again.

He suspected Marcus might already be there. He ticked off the next ten minutes reviewing the file and calling Dispatch on his cell to inform her where he would be and what he was doing.

Adams walked through the door at 7:00 a.m. on the dot, a bell jangling as he did. An older man stood at the counter, who he recognized as Sutter Sr. It had been awhile since he had to come by here, but the man remembered him.

"Officer Adams. Rather early for you to be calling. What can I do for you?"

He looked a bit wary, but not overly concerned. Probably hoping he wasn't about to lose a worker for the day.

"Actually, it's rather late for me. Getting ready to sign off. I just needed to talk to one of your guys for a couple of minutes so I can cross him off my list. It's about a missing person. I need to talk to Marcus O'Reilley. I'm hoping he might be able to shed some light on where his ex Annie O'Reilley might have run off to."

"Ah. Marcus. He in any trouble?"

"I'm not expecting him to be. If it's foul play involved, I have my money elsewhere. Can you have Marcus step out here for a minute?"

"Yeah. Just make it quick as you can. Got a lotta work lined up for him today."

"No problem, Mr. Sutter. Appreciate it."

Adams twiddled his thumbs and looked around, eyed the parking lot outside through the window a couple of times to make sure Marcus didn't run off. A minute later, Marcus came through the door leading to the garage, a scowl across his face. Not a happy man. Not now and probably not ever.

"Hi, Marcus. Sorry to bother you this morning, but I need to cover my bases and clear your name off the list of persons of interest on this case I'm working. I just need to ask you a few standard questions; then you can go back to work, and I can sign off and go to bed. Sound good?"

Adams maintained a positive tone and disinterested posture, totally nonthreatening and lacking suspicion. Marcus eyed him for a few long seconds, sighed big, his broad shoulders settling, some of the tension bleeding out of them.

"Yeah. This is about Annie goin' missing, right?"

"Yup. How'd you know?"

"'Her mom called me the week after Thanksgivin'."

"All right. Well, first off, she was last seen leaving work after lunch the Wednesday before Thanksgiving. I know you were served the divorce papers that morning. Did you have any contact with her that day, physical or by phone, email, whatever?"

"Nope. I knew the papers were coming. She had someone give me a head's up so I didn't get totally surprised. She knows I hate surprises. I didn't need to talk to her one lick."

"Ok. Good. Do you have an alibi for your whereabouts on Wednesday afternoon into Thursday morning?"

"Sure do. I worked late here until around 8:00 p.m. that night, then left, grabbed a beer at O'Connell's Pub, stayed there until about 9:30 p.m. then came back to my house and met my buddy Phil Barrows. We worked on his motorcycle in my garage until after midnight, drinking beers the whole time. He crashed on my couch, and I slept like a baby in my bed until I had to get up and come back in here. Good enough for you?"

"Yeah. I just need a number to call Phil and verify your story. I'll verify the rest with Sutter Sr."

Marcus reeled off a phone number, and Adams scribbled it down on his pad.

"All right, Marcus, almost done. No one's seen or heard from Annie. Not work, not her mom, and I haven't been able to figure out any friends she was close to yet. Her mom's a piece of work, as I'm sure you know, and not a lick of help. So, can you tell me, any girlfriends she might have chosen to stay with if something went wrong?"

"Jenny Pages is about the only one she ever really spent much time with. Works over at The Body Shop, you know, the Go-Go bar. Annie was a quiet one. Stayed at home a lot, though can't see her going long without having a man. She got a new boyfriend yet?"

"As a matter of fact, yes. I've already spoken to him. He appears to have an alibi."

"Who is it?"

"Don't think you need to know that right now, Marcus, but I appreciate your concern."

"Humph. Concern my ass. Just make sure you find that car she was driving. My name's still on the loan. I could fucking care less for all the rest. She made her bed, whatever it is, I lay money on it."

"I'll see what I can manage and let you know if I find that car. Thanks for your time, Marcus."

Marcus frowned and turned back through the shop door. Adams spoke with Sutter Sr. briefly, confirming Marcus' alibi, then left. Adams needed to speak to Jenny Pages and then revisit Bigleby, try to press him. Chad was still unconscious in the hospital, and The Body Shop would be closed Christmas Eve and Christmas Day, so both would have to wait until after the holiday.

CHRISTMAS DAY

By 3:00 a.m., it was snowing and calls were non-existent, so the whole squad met back in the office next to Dispatch. Megan and Kaitlin propped the door open and wore their headsets, just in case. Another squad was out on the street covering both zones temporarily. They'd switch in an hour or so.

They wrote down numbers one through six, mixed them up and drew from a hat. Dexter drew one, Kaitlin was two, Adams three, Greer four, Hicks five, and Megan was left with six, and she was absolutely, diabolically happy about it.

"Yes!" she said, rubbing her palms together, "Hah, hah, hah. I get my pick of the litter, my little pretties."

"All right, Megan, Halloween was two months ago. Don't scare the kids." Hicks looked at her and laughed. Megan blew him a raspberry.

"All right you two," Adams intervened, "no sibling rivalries." Hicks was married to Megan's sister. They might as well have been real siblings though, the way they picked at each other.

Everyone looked over the six gifts and all eyes, except Dexter's, seemed to linger on what appeared to be about a foot and a half long by three-inch diameter tubular present. Megan hefted it while everyone was still sitting down.

"Holy crap this thing is solid and heavy. Scary ..." Megan put it down as Greer snickered.

Dexter chose first, picking a small gift. Greer smirked, trying not to laugh out loud. It was a yellow container, a monkey with a bright red butt pictured on the front. Dexter mumbled, "What the hell?" then read the label out loud. "Monkey Butt Powder? Seriously?"

Greer clapped his hands and laughed. "I was hoping you'd pick that one, Dex!"

"Gee, thanks, Greer, buddy of mine. Want a picture?"

Dexter held it up with his left hand, smiled, and flipped Greer off with his right hand.

"Merry Christmas, motherfucker," Dex said. Everyone roared.

Kaitlin was next. She picked a six-by-twelve box. It was unmarked on the outside once the paper came off. She opened it up and pulled out the newspaper packing. Kaitlin suddenly shut the box, her cheeks blushing bright red.

Megan egged her on, "C'mon, Kaitlin, what's wrong? Show it to us."

Kaitlin covered her mouth, stifling a laugh and shaking her head, embarrassed. Greer spoke up.

"C'mon, Kaitlin, you know the rules. Gotta show the gift to everybody in case they want to take it from you on their turn."

"Oh, they can have it. I don't need it. I don't want it."

She pushed it over to Greer, who quickly opened it back up. He laughed big and hearty, then reached in and pulled it out—an economy size bottle of personal lubricant with the pump dispenser. Everyone cracked up. Greer dropped it back in the box and shoved it back over to Kaitlin, who didn't even touch it.

Adams piped up. "Well, it's my turn, and seeing how I'm the one separated here, I think I can use that more than Kaitlin." Everybody burst out laughing hard, Adams turning almost as red as Kaitlin. "I'll take it off your hands, girl. Give it up." Kaitlin gladly slid it over to him.

"All right, Kaitlin, I took yours. You get to pick again."

Kaitlin went with the safe looking envelope attached to a small, skinny bottle shaped item that felt really light. First, she opened the bottle shaped item. It was a small metal flask. The envelope had a $20 gift card to the ABC Liquor Store.

"Yes! Now, that's more like it," she said. "Working with you guys makes a lady need a stiff drink fairly regularly."

"What's the other card say, Kaitlin?" Hicks was probing, making sure they saw everything he bought.

"Oh, I almost didn't notice it stuck to the back of the gift card. Um … Hah!" she laughed loud once then held it up for everybody to see. "'Licensed Alcoholic Card, state certified to be functional and safe at as much as a .16. Present to Law Enforcement if stopped for D.U.I.' I guess the bottle ensures I keep my dosing up to date to maintain proper tolerance levels, huh?"

"Now you got it," said Hicks. Everybody got a good chuckle.

Dexter was impressed. "I'll be damned. Wish I could think of something that funny, boss."

"All right, Dex," cautioned Greer, "don't get your nose too far up his ass." Dexter flipped Greer off again.

Greer was up next. "Well, as tempting as the lube and the alcohol package is, that big red box has been calling my name since we walked in. I gotta go with that." Kaitlin smiled big as Greer dragged it over between his legs and began opening it. Once inside, he lifted out a large crocheted afghan, folded up. It was mostly white with scattered specks of red. He unfolded it and held it up.

"Holy shit!" Greer was impressed. Everyone else but Kaitlin said "ewww" in unison. "It's a fuckin' crocheted blood spatter pattern, isn't it? Holy shit! Kaitlin, you're awesome, girl!"

"Yeah, it is." Kaitlin was smiling but a little self-conscious. "I know it's on the morbidly funny side, but … you really like it?"

"Hell yeah!" said Greer. "Can I take you home? You are definitely my kinda gal. Damn, this is cool!"

"Well, Greer, I don't think you have to worry about any of us stealing it from you, no offense, Kaitlin. It's beautiful … if you're into that kind of thing."

"All right, boss," said Greer. "You're up."

Hicks looked at the big tube and quietly said, "I'll be damned if I'm picking that one. Guess I'm stuck with this box here."

Adams couldn't hold back the shit-eating grin spreading across his face. Hicks looked at him and paused. "You bought this one didn't you, Adams?"

"Yes, sir. I did. And may I say, I think you picking it is an absolutely fortuitous sign from God above that He exists and loves me very much." Hicks cautiously pulled the rest of the paper off. He didn't need to open the box. There was a big picture across the front with a woman demonstrating its use.

"A Shake Weight! You rat bastard, Adams. I can't believe you got a friggin' Shake Weight."

"Break it out, Sarge," hooted Adams. "Show us how it's done!"

Megan opened up next. "Yeah, Sarge. Shake it, baby. Shake it!"

Hicks was red, but laughing hysterically. "Ahhh, what the hell? You only live once, right?"

He pulled it out and started shaking, posing in various positions as he did so.

Adams looked at Megan. "Could you imagine if we had been off and gone to a restaurant somewhere and got wasted before doing this?"

"Oh yeah. It could have gotten crazy." Megan smiled at him, just briefly, but it was that sexy, flirtatious smile.

Hicks brought all the merriment to an end. "Holy shit, my arms are burning! I'm done. This thing works! Whew!" Hicks nodded at Megan. "All right, Megan, last man."

Megan stood with her arms crossed, one hand beneath her chin, index finger playing with her pursed bottom lip. She scanned over all the gifts, assessing each one out loud individually.

"Well, Monkey Butt powder is definitely not on my wish list, Alcohol is tempting, and so is the economy size lube, but yeah, Adams needs that more than any of us. She smiled directly at him again, more smartass than sexy. "And Greer, no, you don't have to worry about me stealing your afghan, which leaves me with stealing the Shake Weight or going with the possible incredibly huge dildo Dexter might have bought."

Dex perked up, a confused, "what the hell" look plastering his face. Megan never broke stride.

"I'm sorry, Hicks, I'm fairly adventurous as far as women go, but Dex's gift scares me. I'm gonna have to steal your Shake Weight. Besides, this is the bitch weight women's model. You need the beefier men's model for developing those macho, manly biceps." Megan sauntered over and took the Shake Weight from Hicks.

"Damn you ... you ... you bitch," Hicks said flatly. "Just when I thought I could get sexy arms, you steal my dreams away."

"Don't worry, boss," said Greer, "for 19.95 you too can own one of these heavenly machines."

"Hold on, Greer," said Adams. "How'd you know its 19.95? Hmmm?"

"Uhhhh, ummm ... I saw it in the store ... just like you ..."

Dexter blew his whistle. "Bullshit! Flag on the play! Ten-yard penalty. Repeat down."

"No. No. He's not lying, Dex. He saw it in the store. Actually, I saw him when he saw it in the store," Adams said.

Greer's face went pale, his jaw a little slack, tongue useless.

Adams laid it on thick. "What's wrong, Greer? Cat got your tongue? Come on, now. Nothin' to be ashamed about, except maybe your total lack of situational awareness. You never even saw me. I figured I'd wait and see if you showed up here with one, but … alas, ye have not. So, did you buy it for yourself?"

Greer initiated player self-defense mode. Deny, deny, deny. "Nooo. I did not."

"Well who'd you buy it for then?" pressed Adams.

"Umm …" Greer paused a little too long, and his right eye twitched twice before finishing, "my girlfriend."

"Bullshit! One, you took too long to answer. Two, your right eye always twitches when you lie. It's why you suck at poker. And three, why'd you buy the male version then, huh? Case closed. Guilty as charged." Adams sat back in his chair and beamed. Greer hung his head.

Megan walked behind Greer, put her hands on his shoulders and leaned down next to his ear. "It's ok, Greer. Don't let Adams bully you. You can be my Shake Weight workout buddy!" She scrunched his trap muscles once then patted them. "And if the bad man picks on you anymore about it, just let me know, and I'll give him a good spanking for it. Ok?" Megan eyed Adams flirtatiously for a moment while Greer played the upset but consoled child part, knuckling his eyes as he spoke.

"O-K, Sissy."

Adams sat across from him playing the imaginary little fiddle in his fingers, ignoring Megan's charms.

"Now," said Megan, "brother-in-law of mine, let's see what that big thing is."

Hicks grabbed the package and hefted it. "Holy crap this thing is heavy, but … I think your brain lives in the gutter, Megan. I know what this is." Hicks ripped the paper off quickly, revealing the gift just as he declared it. "Beef summer sausage, and a big one at that. You're right though, Megan. You couldn't handle this, you and your vegan ways."

They all had a good laugh and the city stayed quiet for another hour before it was time to get back to work. Adams couldn't stop thinking about meeting Amy later in the day, though.

SECTION II

"A beast does not know that he is a beast, and the nearer a man gets to being a beast, the less he knows it."
GEORGE MACDONALD

"A man without ethics is a wild beast loosed upon this world."
ALBERT CAMUS

"'How can you act so glibly? Look what you've done to me. How could you do this? Doesn't this effect you at all?!?'

'No ... Your friend Feuerbach wrote that all men counting stars are equivalent in every way to God. My indifference is not the concern here. It's your astonishment that needs study.'"
THE ADDICTION (FILM)

CHRISTMAS DAY

Chad woke abruptly as Robbie climbed up on the bed and excitedly announced the new day like some little rooster.

"Wake up, Dad! It's Christmas Day! It's Christmas Day! C'mon!" Robbie straddled his chest, squeezing Chad's face between two tiny palms, his mouth transformed into fish lips.

"Waaake up, Dad!" Robbie lowered his forehead to Chad's forehead and took on a quiet, solemn voice, emphasizing each word.

"Daddy, we've got to open presents." Robbie broke out into uncontrollable giggles and cackled loudly as Chad tickled him relentlessly.

Robbie squirmed his way off the bed and ran for the living room, shutting the door on his way out. "C'mon, Daddy!" he hollered. "Wake Momma up, and c'mon out here."

Chad laughed to himself and called out "Yes, sir, Captain, sir. Aye, aye!"

Emily was already awake and smiling when he rolled over to kiss her.

"We've got our orders ma'am, and we cannot delay."

"You got it, Big Daddy Bigleby."

Emily sat up, holding the covers over her chest in case Robbie rushed back in, pulled her knees up and stared at Chad.

"You know, this right here is all the Christmas I need— Robbie, you and I, all together."

A heavy knock at the bedroom door.

"We'll be right out, Robbie. Just have to get dressed."

A muffled "K" drifted through the door. Then a deep, scratchy noise rumbling in a throat, a throat far too large to be Robbie's.

"Robbie?" Chad called. "Are you ok out there?"

"Of course, Daddy." The voice made Chad's bowels loosen for a moment. It was pregnant with doom and darkness, the very tone a carrier wave for fear, terribly different in sound but still definitely Robbie's words. "I'm fine. The nice man is just showing me how to be a little boy transformer."

Chad froze, a fevered sweat instantly breaking out all over as his heart skipped at least two beats before launching into a frenetic pace.

"I can change all my parts around, Daddy." Robbie's voice was deep, and gurgling. "Let me show you, Daddy."

The door knob turned, but wouldn't open. He was standing, his fingers on the lock. How did I get here? shot through his mind.

"Let me in, Daddy." The gurgling phonics sputtered obscenely, now accompanied by a sickly wet strike against the door.

"Let me in, Daddy." THUD!

Another impact sounded on the door, and another, and another until they were coming faster than two hands could possibly deliver in so many different places all over the door. Like a twisting mass of tentacles spinning and flagellating in angry rhythm, the door a war drum that could not withstand the driving beat.

It splintered all at once, the center mass an explosion of shrapnel impaling Chad's body with a thousand tiny, wooden shards. His world went instantly dark, but his ears detected a multitude of wet slithering and thrashing noises bearing down on him. Somehow, he was sitting up. He tried to butt scoot away from the unseen threat, but something soft and warm enveloped his back and held him tight. He froze, fear making it impossible for him to move while his mind tried to gather more information. He needed to see. He reached up and gently touched his eyes. Splinters pinned his eyelids shut. Several things wriggled just above his shins, barely brushing his legs in a sporadic squirmy fashion, waiting for him to open his eyes.

Chad gently pulled out the splinters and forced his eyes to flutter open just enough for him to see. He was thankful the world was somewhat blurry and out of focus. Clarity of vision would have been a greater death, but it was death nonetheless. A death he desperately tried to flee from; his whole core exploded into rapid fire, flailing movements that sent each limb into a frenzy and his head spastically trying to escape the limitations of his spine and fly away all on its own.

Robbie's arms and legs were split twenty times over, a bundle of tentacles propelling him along as they covered both floor and ceiling, his body suspended above Chad. The torso was inverted somehow, and the head was where the groin should have been; a bulging head with black holes for eyes and hundreds of bony splinters for teeth, each polished shiny white and needle sharp. The jaws distended and stretched beyond what the laws of physics would seem to allow. It lingered above him, a cavernous pit slick with saliva that stuck like pitch when it dripped on his face.

His body seemed to be sinking backwards the more he struggled, and it obeyed him less and less, numbness spreading everywhere. Something long, thin, and wormlike wiggled into his ear even as many others constricted his neck and held him firm. He reflexively turned to look, but only his head obeyed. A bloated face floated next to him at the end of a long and twisted eel-like neck, its tongue was forked and dripped venom, a paralytic. The face was Emily's. She smiled and, as his jaw dropped, her tongue forced its way down his throat and writhed in pleasure, feeding it to him, in and out, over and over. When the violent kiss was complete, the tongue tore itself free and slithered down his esophagus, his mind wanting to vomit, but his gag reflex was numbed beyond function. Emily lifted Chad's body, tubular fingers propping his head up, extending him to Robbie like some mama bird preparing to feed its young.

The gaping maw descended upon him, a razor forest encircling his head. Chad tried to scream, but his vocal cords were incapable of movement. Insanity consumed him as smooth muscle propelled him into a tar pit that would preserve him and bind him to its belly. He was unable to escape the unending and unbearable violation that filled him and would not cease to squirm.

Sleep had been somewhat restless, anxiety over talking with Amy infiltrating his subconscious. Still, he was looking forward to the opportunity. He arrived on time, the front inside door already open, welcoming him as he walked up and rang the doorbell anyway. Amy appeared around the corner, an oven-mitt in one hand, hair nicely styled, makeup on but not too heavy. Adams was smitten already.

"Silly goose," she chided. "I left the door open for you. Come in."

Toby barged in, happy to see Amy, running circles at her feet, whining then lying down on his back so she would rub his belly. After a minute of catch-up bonding, Amy spoke up.

"So, what did you bring?"

"Well, let's see. I have gifts."

"Giftsss?" She emphasized the 's'. "Plural, huh? Rotten."

"I also have my world famous triple chocolate caramel brownies and vanilla ice cream."

"Oh, yum! Thank you!" Amy grabbed them right out of his hands.

"And a little wine. Nothing crazy.

"Want to get me drunk on wine and chocolate and have your way with me huh, mister?"

"Now you're rotten. That is a no-win question for a man in my position right now. Say 'yes', and I'm just the average sex addict man who has no other priority than getting himself laid. Say 'no, that's not what I intended' and it becomes an issue of offense, the woman asking 'what, I'm not attractive enough to make you want to have your way with me?' See, either way I'm screwed. You've won already."

Amy disregarded Adams' jibe, smacked his arm, and took the wine. Ice cream went in the freezer, brownies on the kitchen counter, and the wine on ice. She bent over to open a drawer, flipped her hair and smiled, glancing at Adams as she pulled out the wine bottle opener and set it on the counter.

"Well, mister, as to the latter, I doubt you would be here today if you didn't still find me attractive." She stood, turned sideways, dipped one hip and batted her eyelashes in jest, then grabbed a brownie and leaned on the counter. "And as to the former ... well, we've both known for a very long time that you're a sex addict. So, no surprises here. Eyes wide open and all that."

"Gee, Amy, that last bit hurt me ..." Adams put on his puppy dog eyes and patted his chest above his heart, "right here."

"Puh-lease! You're a mess. I'm not questioning your chivalrous motives, mind you, I'm just saying it wouldn't be unnatural, that's all. Ok, enough of that. I have turkey, gravy, some honey ham, stuffing, and collards. Oh yeah, and brownies." She finally popped the brownie she had been holding in her mouth.

"God! You make the best brownies. I love these things!"

"All right, it's feeding time," Adams declared.

"Ok. Let's dish up, and I'll get It's a Wonderful Life started."

"Sounds good."

They ate mostly in silence, just happy to be in each other's company, and not alone on Christmas Day. Once done, they sat close, Amy leaning on Mark, in a boyfriend-girlfriend date kind of way. How two kids who haven't ventured into making out yet would sit. They watched the movie, both wishing someone would swoop in and make everything right in an instant. But healing is never easy. They knew this, but set it aside and focused on finding what they had always loved in each other. After It's a Wonderful Life ended, they decided to exchange gifts.

"All right," said Mark, "you open first, and you have to model the gifts, Ok?"

"Ok …" a slight sense of hesitancy in her voice. "Which one first?"

"The bigger one."

"Cool!"

Amy tore into it, pulling the paper and bow off in a hurry. Halfway through, she cried foul.

"Mark! You didn't! You are sooo rotten! O my God, you are rotten!"

She pulled the box into clear view, revealing the Shake Weight packaging, the woman on the front in mid-shake. Mark laid back on the floor laughing heartily.

"O God! You should have seen your face! That was worth every penny and any payback coming, especially since you agreed to model it. Break that bad boy out, and show me how it's done!"

"You're kidding, right?" Amy was laughing, but she wasn't going to make it easy. "You actually think I'm going to shake this thing for you?"

"Well, I can think of better things to shake, but this will do for now." Mark smiled with devilish charm. "But … I suppose if you're not a lady of your word, you might be able to convince yourself that you didn't really agree to model this gift, when in fact you did. Either way, it's entirely up to you. No pressure." Mark laughed some more, smiling like the cat that ate the canary the whole time. Amy's forced glare said he was going to choke on that canary.

"All right. Fair is fair. You got me, and I'm a woman of my word." Amy reached in, pulled it out, made sure it was functional and proceeded to work the weight, first with two hands, then one hand, alternating above her head and behind her back, and finally on her back with only one hand and one foot on the ground. It was like watching someone use a Shake

Weight while trying to play a game of Twister. She finished up, blew on it like it was her six- shooter or something, then set it down beneath the tree."

Mark had run out of laughs a while back. "Wow," he said, wiping his eyes. "I am beyond impressed. Holy cow, if I'd known bringing one bottle of wine would get this much mileage, I'd have brought two. All right. The small one now. The 'nice' gift."

"You sure? You got me gun-shy now." Amy picked up the small box and eyed Adams suspiciously.

"Geez, girl! You don't have to be paranoid. I got you with the Shake Weight; now this is the real gift. Open it up."

"All right. I just needed a little reassurance, that's all."

Amy pulled the wrapping paper away to reveal a small jewelry box. She opened it up to find a beautiful set of circular stone earrings. They were polished smooth and with a clean sheen, a deep, bright red with streaks of black.

"Oh my God, Mark. They're beautiful. Really, really beautiful! What kind of stones are they?"

"They called it Red Jasper."

"You spent way too much, Mark. You shouldn't have."

"Nah. Not really. It wasn't as bad as it looks."

"Seriously? Man, it looks expensive. It's beautiful!"

"Well, put 'em on. Let's see how they look on you."

Amy slipped each one into place, primped her hair a little and gave an exaggerated model pose for Mark.

"Yes! I knew they would look awesome on you with your auburn hair. Go look in the mirror."

Amy smiled, then got up and scampered over to the nearest mirror to get a look. She turned right, left, flipped her hair back then forward to let it hang, assessing from every angle.

"I love 'em!" she called from the other room.

She came back in and hurried over to give Adams a hug, then kissed his cheek. "They're perfect! Thank you so much. Ok, now it's your turn."

Amy went to the Christmas tree, reached down and picked up a fairly large box, long and wide, but not very tall. Mark carefully unwrapped it then pulled the top off. Inside was a white Jiu-Jitsu Gi, pants and top.

"Oh my, Amy. This is nice. Really heavy-duty, reinforced stitching. Great weave for gripping. Man, this should last for a long time. Thank you!"

"I remembered that yours was about shot. Thought you'd like it."

"Well, yeah! You didn't have to spend this much though."

"Don't worry. I got a deal." Amy winked.

Mark smiled. "Touché, Rotten."

"Well, sir, what say you? Should we get some brownies and ice cream and start our second feature film? I hear Jingle All The Way is a real holiday classic; can't miss it!"

"Absolutely," said Mark.

They dished up dessert and watched the movie, laughing off and on. When it was done, they sat and chitchatted about work.

"Oh, by the way, that guy Bigleby is still knocked out in the psych ward. Hasn't been able to stay conscious yet."

"Yeah, I know. I'm still waiting to talk to him again."

"I hear there's still plenty of crazies coming into the ER, too," Amy said casually.

Mark's brain gave a sideways jog, and he remembered the jumper.

"Oh my God, Amy! That reminds me. I hadn't told you about the jumper last month."

"What jumper?"

"You remember that day we ran into each other in Harris Teeter, and you told me about some weird guy who came into the ER swearing his coworkers were out to get him and a bunch of other crazy stuff? Name was Harry."

"Yeah." Amy suddenly looked borderline ill.

"Thanksgiving Day, evening shift. He jumped off a building downtown. Swan dive, head first, pavement cracker, right in front of me. I'm talkin' dead right there."

Amy's body twitched, her hands coming up over her mouth with a gasp.

"O God, Mark! I just knew something was wrong with that guy. That's freaking me out, Mark, and I wasn't even there. How are you with it? I mean, you saw the whole thing. Did he say why? Did someone talk to him before he jumped?"

"Yeah, me, I talked to him. He kept swearing up and down that all his coworkers knew how he was screwing people over to get some promotion. Said he couldn't face them or his wife, couldn't live another moment like that. They wouldn't let him, whoever 'they' were. Guess he couldn't take the shame of people finding out."

"Oh, Mark, it was more than that. Don't you remember what I told you about his dreams?"

"Not really. Just remembered you said he was paranoid and sounded crazy."

"Mark, he was having nightmares for a week or so, bordering on night terrors from the way it sounded. Said there was a homeless man and his dog. Talked about transformations, not really a man, not really a dog. Mentioned huge fangs and some other weird things, but he said it was the homeless man behind it all. The man supposedly was telling his coworkers, said he would make sure they killed Harry. It was strange as hell, Mark … Mark, what's wrong?"

Mark's face was slack, head lowering as his brain checked out at the mention of the homeless man and his dog. He was at the scene that night, in the crowd afterwards, eating a burger or something and sharing it with his dog.

"Holy Shit! There's been this new homeless guy in town recently, and he has a dog. He was at the scene that night after the guy jumped. I also talked to him the other week outside a grocery mart. Management called complaining about him begging outside. He was a very strange cat. And then Chad Bigleby claimed the homeless guy's dog bit him. But it didn't look like a dog bite. Nurse Jenkins let me see it after he was knocked out. It looked more like a huge snake bite."

Amy sat slack jawed and silent, hand over mouth.

"Man ... this is freaky," Mark concluded.

"Wow ... you ain't kidding. I think I need to watch something happy now. That was terrible. I know it's getting late ..."

"What do I care?" Mark laughed briefly and smiled. "I don't work till tomorrow night."

"How bout we just watch 'How the Grinch Stole Christmas'?" Amy suggested.

"Sure."

They plugged in the short animation and forgot about all the weird drama for a while. Mark thanked Amy for the invite, and Amy thanked him for coming then they thanked each other for the gifts as they hugged. Mark kissed her on the forehead gently.

"All right, you sleep well. I'll see you later, and I'll let you know when I get a date set with the department counselor, Dr. Wilkins, like we talked about."

"Sounds good."

Mark went to turn for the door, but Amy held his hand, tugged a little and let her other hand slip behind his head. She slid towards him in one smooth, coordinated motion and kissed him lightly on the lips.

"I miss you. I miss us. Don't you go thinking you're free to play the field."

"Who me? I just beat the women away, with all their offers of no strings attached sex. It's not ethical, and, of course, it's just plain yucky. Eww." Mark smiled and made a disgusted face, but it didn't help. Amy bristled with jealousy all of a sudden.

"Hold on a minute, Don Juan! Who the hell is offering you 'no strings attached sex'?"

"Well … there's been a couple of girls while I was at work. One girl told me if it wasn't for my 'silly morals', quote, unquote, she could make us both real happy."

Anxious resentment and shock seized Amy all at once, her cheeks flushing with insecurity, immediately skeptical of the strength of his resistance to temptation.

"Hey, don't worry," Mark reassured her. "I've got my morals. It's tough sometimes, but I'm still standing. Besides, I'm counting on us having awesome makeup sex for a while when we get through this."

Mark grinned big, and Amy felt a little better.

"I love you," she whispered.

"I love you too," he replied, "and I miss you a whole bunch."

He leaned back into her and gave her a light kiss on the lips.

"All right. I better go. Come on Toby Bear. Tell momma goodbye."

Toby loved on Amy and she hugged him tight, then he and Mark trotted out the door, leaving Amy all alone with her mind a whirlwind of fears and doubts hiding behind the strong front she held out until the door shut. Then she cried herself to sleep that Christmas night, afraid of what lay ahead.

FRIDAY, DECEMBER 26

Adams jerked awake, immediately aware of the sweat beaded across his body and soaked into the sheets.

"Fuck." He glanced at the alarm clock. 3:00 a.m. glowed red and menacing.

He unclutched his fingers from the sheet and wiped the sweat from his brow and face. He closed his eyes for a moment then threw them wide an instant later, the last image from his dream too disturbing to relive again.

Amy lay beneath him, innocent eyes, but a forked tongue flickered out from full lips glistening with honey sweetness. He kissed those lips one last time, a Judas Kiss paid in kind for the many before. He gave up gladly then, and let the rage within consume him, his mind ablaze with hate, a colossal violence bearing down with locomotive inertia, every fiber of his flesh stretching, a vessel incapable of containing the torrential flood of hate.

Innocence fled Amy's eyes right then, pupils dilating with fear, drowning in the dark depths of panic, a creature found out, its camouflage suddenly useless, cornered, trapped beneath Adams' body straddling her chest, a psychopathic, bestial countenance looming above, lolling tongue dripping spit into the pools of oblivion gazing back at him.

Adams' left hand crawled up between her heaving breasts and found the soft indentation in the center of the clavicle with his thumb. His fingers stretched until he could clamp down on the back of her neck, a bear trap slamming shut. He pressed his thumb in and up against her trachea. A light choking cough reflexively escaped her lungs. Her wind was sealed, now; no air was coming in or going out.

Her beautiful breasts ceased to heave, the struggle for life all that was left. Hips bucked, legs kicked, spinal muscles exploded in movement, a twisting coiling snake pinned by the head. Arms flailed against him in primal simian fashion, all hopelessly ineffective.

As the burning built within Amy's chest, desperate for the air just beyond her lips, her hands seized his wrist and forearm, pulling, pushing, and clawing, unwilling to go quietly. Her tongue flickered in and out trying to plead her case but unable to form words.

LIES, LIES, LIES beat the native drums inside Adams' ears, all LIES, every word that witch's tongue ever spoke.

He leaned in and let her feel the weight of all his pain and brought his face close; his eyes locked on her eyes, waiting, waiting for the life to let go and limply slide out of sight.

When it finally came, a bud of joy burst forth within him, and he woke in disgust.

"Holy Fuck," escaped his mouth, an unconscious mumble as he stood, walked to the bathroom and grabbed a towel to wipe down with.

Sleep beckoned him after that, but he could not bear it.

Adams bypassed roll call with Hicks' permission and drove down to The Body Shop, hoping to find Jenny Pages. Walking up to the door, he recognized the heavyset bouncer from a distance. Adams greeted Huck with a handshake and man hug.

"How ya been, Adams? Ya look like you're stayin' n fightin' shape, eh?"

"You bet, Huck. Was just at the dojo earlier."

"Sweet! So what brings ya out here tonight?"

"Gotta talk to one of the girls. Got a missing person case, and Jenny Pages was supposed to be a good friend. Just covering all my bases and hoping maybe she's heard from her. To be honest though, I don't have a good feeling about it."

"Who's the missin' girl?"

"Annie O'Reilley."

"Hmm. Is that the red headed looker that comes up here every now and then?"

"Sounds like Annie. She's a redhead and hotter'n two hells. I'd wager she'd draw more attention than a lot of the girls working in here if she gave it a whirl."

"Yeah. That sounds like the one I'm thinking of. I haven't seen her here in a few weeks, but go on in and talk to Jenny; maybe she can tell ya something. I think she's on stage right now."

"Thanks, Huck." Adams shook hands and clapped his shoulder before turning to head through the door. "Catch ya on the flip side."

Music flooded out as the door opened, grinding rhythms to match the gyrating hips on display. Adams spotted Melissa, the bartender, and sauntered over to speak with her, eyeing the three women on stage briefly.

Melissa stood wiping out glasses behind the bar and called out over the music to Adams as he walked up.

"Well, if it isn't Officer Mark Adams, the man who selfishly broke my heart."

Adams reflexively spread his hands palms out. "Uh! Shots fired, girl! You still holdin' a grudge against me on that?"

"A woman's heart never forgets what could have been, especially when it looked and felt so good. Unh! You look better than the last time I saw you. No fair. You workin' out or somethin'?"

"Yup."

"What's your secret? Maybe I'll have you put the girls on a workout plan."

"Kettlebells, martial arts, and a lot of grueling effort."

"Shit! Not much chance of getting 'grueling effort' out of the ones that would need it. Oh well." She placed a dried glass on the shelf and picked up another to towel out.

"So ... rumor has it you might be in the market again. You come to check on my availability, huh?" Melissa let a wry smile tease at one corner of her mouth as the opposite eyebrow arched high, her eyes looking Adams over like a five- course meal.

Adams cleared his throat. "Well, I'm sorry to disappoint, but rumors of my availability and consumer status have been somewhat exaggerated."

"Back together already, huh?" She eyed the inside of the glass for spots. "Damn."

"Not quite yet, but seriously working on it. I'm commit-ted to the process."

"So, how long since you had sex, big boy? This place must be killing you right now."

"God, don't remind me. It's been over four months now."

"Wow ... well, sit back and enjoy the show from back here. That's Amber on the far left, Jackie in the Middle, and Jenny on the far right. They're all pretty good. The real show, though, will be Pebbles. She's on in about 10 minutes, so hang around."

"You said Jenny. Is that Jenny Pages?"

"Yeah." A confused look spread across Melissa's face. "How'd you know that?"

"Well, actually, I came here to talk to her about a missing person case I'm working. Girl was a friend of hers. You prob-ably saw her in here before. Annie O'Reilley. Real hot red-head. Ring a bell?"

"Yeah. I know her! She's missing? O my god! That's horrible!"

"You ever talk with her when she was hanging out here with Jenny?"

"Yeah, a few times. Last time I talked to her was around a month ago. She was flying high on Cloud Nine. Said she had hooked up with a smokin' hot lawyer guy at the firm she worked for. Said she had a good chance he was going to leave his wife for her. I warned her to never count on that till he signs the papers for a new place and moves his shit out. Until then it's just more bullshit to get in your pants."

"Well, that all sounds on target with what I've found out already. Anything else that might be of interest?"

"Nope, can't think of anything."

"Think you could call Jenny over for me? Shouldn't take but a couple of minutes or so."

"Sure." She picked up a microphone and spoke into it. "Jenny. Jenny. Exit stage and come to bar please."

Adams looked up and saw her bend over to pick up some bills off the runway. She was facing away, legs locked out straight, the progress down and back up deliberately very slow.

"Wow" he mumbled.

"Yeah, she knows how to play it up, and she's a solid eight or nine, depending on your taste. So … is she your taste, Mark?"

"Well … right now my tastes wouldn't be too picky, but, yeah, looks-wise she's definitely in my flavor category. But of course, she can't hold a candle to you, 'Lissa. I mean, if I were going to be in the market, I know where I'd go shopping first, if you know what I mean?"

"Ahh, Mark, you know just how to tease a girl. Don't break my heart again."

Jenny came walking up, counting a wad of bills. "What's up, boss?"

"Jenny, meet Officer Mark Adams; Mark, meet Jenny. Officer Adams needs to ask you a couple of questions. I'm afraid your friend, Annie O'Reilley, is missing. You heard anything from her?"

Jenny's hands flew to her mouth. "Oh my God! I knew it! I haven't heard from her in a month. I mean, she can just go off the grid every now and then, but this time was getting long for even her. She hadn't answered any of my phone calls either. This is crazy! I was just talking with Pebbles last night about maybe filing a report. Shit! I can't believe this." Tears slid from Jenny's eyes. She choked up and stopped talking. Adams let her work through it as he grabbed a napkin and handed it to her.

"It's just … Annie is such a sweet girl, good head on her shoulders, stays out of trouble, behaves, ya know? I mean, other than seeing that married lawyer boyfriend of hers, but he sounds like he really could be leaving his wife from the way Annie talked. God! I just can't believe this. Do you have any leads yet?"

"I'm sorry, nothing solid yet. Her ex-husband's alibi checks out, her mom doesn't know squat, and her lawyer boyfriend has an alibi."

Jenny shook her head. "Damn. 'Lissa, I need a couple shots of Tequila. Let me have it." She fanned herself with a menu and waved her fingers at Melissa to hurry up and bring it.

"Comin' up. Think I'll take one myself. This is way too close to home." She poured the drinks and downed hers in one gulp. Jenny composed herself, a shot glass in each hand, then tilted back twice and was done. She composed herself, then turned to Melissa.

"All right. Well, I'm finished for the night. I'm going to go change." She paused for a long moment then looked at Adams.

"You gonna be around, Officer Adams? I'll feel a whole lot safer if you are …" She smiled a coy, naturally seductive smile.

Melissa smacked Jenny's hand. "Back off, Bee-otch," she said in a joking manner. "Keep those grubby paws to yourself. If anyone's gonna get a piece of this rock here, it's me. He owes me from waaay back when. Ain't that right, Markie Mark?"

Mark smiled, dropped his head, and nodded. He peeked up at Jenny, "But I'm flattered, ma'am," he said, then, in his best Elvis impersonation, "Thank you, thank you very much." He tipped his head and gave a casual two finger salute in jest.

Jenny held up her hands, palms forward, acquiescing to her superior, and shook her head. "That's too bad, but no problem, boss. I know better than to mess with you." She turned on the chair and walked off to the dressing room.

Melissa looked over at the runway and stage. "Uh oh. I don't stand a chance now. Here comes Pebbles. You'll want to watch this. Hell, I'm not even bi and I get turned on sometimes watching her. Girl is bad ta da bone …"

Adams sat down on the bar stool. Pebbles was extremely fit, muscular thighs and butt, toned arms, but not un-feminine in appearance; abs that were firm and defined but still lithe and smooth. Her perfect tan complimented the naturally black hair that hung down in loose ringlets and flowing locks to the middle of her back. She moved like a cat stalking its prey, fixing each man with her sultry, hungry eyes. Her movements were intentionally slow, grinding and controlled one moment and the next convulsing as she burst into a series of ecstatic jerking motions. Adams ogled, mouth agape, as her hips careened up and down, squatting and popping back up, swinging back and forth and then slowing down again.

To say it was mesmerizing was an absolute understatement. Every man's eyes were locked on her and some women's too. The music began to build and her movements increased pace and intensity, until the pounding rhythms reached their crescendo, and Pebbles dropped to the hardwood floor on spread hands and knees. Arching her hips to the floor slowly—once, twice, then three times—before exploding downward; she slammed her pubic bone into the hardwood stage like a jackhammer, five times in rapid succession—WHAM! WHAM! WHAM! WHAM! WHAM! Then she immediately bounced back to her feet to continue swirling her hips, grinding up and down; gasps still hung in the air from the first impact with the stage, mouths were wide, tongues lolled, eyes ravenous with an insatiable appetite for her.

She finished by bending over to grab her ankles, then slowly uncurled her torso and reached to the sky with one hand, head thrown back, hair bouncing, while her other hand patted her pubic bone gently a couple of times, nice and slow. Just as the song ended on a crashing cymbal, she popped her hips forward and up violently and slapped her pubic bone and clitoris hard while giving a rock girl shout and throwing the devil horns hand sign. Her head and hair flipped forward and back all in one coordinated movement of seductive glory.

The crowd broke loose in hoots and hollers and even applause. Guys who had been too entranced to think about tossing bills did so now, and Pebbles did a little curtsy and picked up the money. Adams was speechless until Melissa smacked him upside the back of his head. "See? I told ya. Now you're ruint!"

"Wow …" was all Adams said at first. "Wow …" Adams shook his head and looked back at Melissa. "Ho-ly shit! I … I don't know what to say … I am so fucking turned on right now by that, I … My God … I didn't think a woman could do something like that … wow … I think I'm in love … or at least horny beyond measure …" Adams turned to Melissa with a slack faced, punch drunk, puppy-love look.

Melissa shook her head. "She's one of a kind for sure. Incredible …"

"Get your fucking hands off me, pig!" The scream cut through the music and bar noises. Adams spun around to look where it had come from. Some asshole was grabbing Pebbles by her arm and waist, pulling her down into his lap. She was yelling and struggling to get up, but he had her held fast.

Joe, the bouncer inside, took off across the floor. He peeled the guy's hand from her arm and lifted up Pebbles.

"Keep your hands to yourself, bro. No touch policy. Time to go."

Joe was a big boy, but so was the asshole. Looked like some Neo-Nazi skinhead type, covered in tattoos.

"Fuck you!" he shouted as he stood up and headbutted Joe in the nose, knocking him back. Melissa picked up a radio and screamed into it.

"Huck! Get in here! Now!"

Adams was already off and moving, covering the floor in long steady strides. The drunk asshole was moving forward now, away from Adams, a man on a mission. Adams saw everything play out in slow motion. The man grabbed a beer bottle, smashing it on the table as he took his first step. Joe hadn't recovered his vision yet. He was clueless as to what was coming. Adams was two steps away now from the skinhead's back.

"I'll fuckin' gut you like a fish!"

He saw the guy's meaty forearm flash out, slamming into Joe's chest, hand trying to grab the clothing at his shoulder and pull him in. Joe stumbled back, off balance, before the skinhead's grip was secure. It probably saved his life. It meant another step before the guy could begin the sewing machine process of stabbing him repeatedly. It meant Adams could reach him first.

Everything kicked back into full speed as Adams lunged forward, wrapping both hands around the front of the guy's face. A fraction of a second later, both arms snatched back with all his coordinated might, hips popping forward into the guy's hips, knocking his base out from underneath him as he ripped his head backwards and his body fully horizontal in the air. Adams hugged the guy's head to his own abdomen as he dropped to both knees and bowed forward. The tattooed giant hit the tiled floor, cracking it, at the same time his head folded violently under the weight of Adams' torso, chin slamming into chest.

"Ughhh!" The air blew out of the man's lungs, and his arms reflexively shot straight out like an electric current had gone through him, then he lay still, body in shock, grip on the bottle weak, barely holding on. Adams pinned the guy's head with his left hand, turning his face to look away as he put his right knee on the weapon forearm and peeled the bottle away.

"Joe! Hold this! It's evidence." No response, still holding his nose, trying to see the world again, probably.

"Here! I'll take it." Adams recognized Huck's voice behind him, turned, and handed off the broken bottle, then scanned 360 degrees before proceeding. The skinhead's body was still in shock. The takedown nearly broke his neck. He was going to feel this one for days. Hell, maybe even weeks or months, Adams thought and chuckled to himself silently. A few quick moves, and the guy was cuffed behind the back, ready to be searched for weapons.

He didn't have any weapons, but there were several packets of Meth in his pocket. Enough for a possession with intent to distribute charge.

"Hell yeah!" he said out loud and dropped the packets into his shirt pocket.

"Hey! 'Lissa! Kill the music for a second will ya?"

The sound ended a few moments later. Adams keyed his mic.

"113 to Dispatch."

"113 go ahead."

"Dispatch can you send a unit to The Body Shop along with EMS. While out here conducting follow up investigation a fight occurred. Subject is in custody but may be injured. Also, pursuant to search, there will be a PWID charge for Meth. Copy?"

"Copy 113. Units will be en route."

Huck knelt down next to Adams and whispered to him.

"Man, I thought you killed the guy the way his head folded up and his whole body went stiff like that. Did you do that on purpose, Mark?"

Mark felt alive, more alive than he could possibly ever remember. It was like the best high he could think of, high on life, high on the potential of death, high on sex and violence and the authority he held at this moment in time. He thought about Huck's question for a moment and gave an off the cuff, but honest answer.

"You know, I think I did. Didn't want this big son of a bitch making it through to turn that broken bottle on me."

"Wow. Dude, that's intense."

"Fuck him! He would've deserved it, lucky bastard."

A few minutes later, back up arrived along with EMS. They put a collar on the guy and strapped him to the stretcher. Adams asked one of the officers to go sit with the prisoner at the hospital while he got statements, secured evidence, and obtained warrants.

An hour later, Adams was saying goodbye to Melissa when Pebbles came walking up, dressed now, a timid, almost shy look on her beautiful face.

"Officer Adams, right?"

"Yeah. That's me."

"I … I just wanted to say thank you. Thank you for sticking up for me and for saving Joe." She ducked her head for a moment, pivoting back and forth as she worked herself up. "And … if you come back when you're off … umm" she paused and looked up and away for a moment, then looked him directly in the eyes, "I'll thank you … properly." Her head did a little roll and tilt to the side, an inviting, almost submissive, sensuality about it.

Adams blushed, tried to speak at first, and couldn't. "What is," he unconsciously cleared his throat, "'properly'?" Pebbles stepped close enough that her breasts brushed his shirt, and her breath was warm on his throat. She spoke slowly, each word purposefully formed, every facial expression and micro-movement calculated to seduce.

"Oh … well … first, I'll take you in that room" pointing slowly, leading his eyes to a place where heaven would meet earth, "and then I'll give you the best damn lap dance I'll ever give in my life. After that, we can go back to my place … or yours … if you want to, of course."

"Hooo-Eee," escaped uncontrollably from Adams lips as the air blew out sharply, cheeks puffing out slightly.

"Holy mother of God," was all he could say at first, a deer in the headlights of her bright, alluring eyes. "Pebbles, you just don't know how tempting that is, I mean, we're talking Greek goddess or succubus seductions, off the chart … but … I'm married."

It seemed to genuinely hurt him to say it at that moment, visibly painful.

"I mean, I'm separated but married, and trying to fix things right now. Otherwise, I don't think an army could keep me away. I'm absolutely tempted beyond … well … wow … I can't believe I'm even saying no right now as I listen to myself … I mean … you're so unbelievably hot in every way possible … geez … I … I just can't, not if I want my marriage to work out. I'm sorry. Really. I mean so, sooo very sorry. Believe me."

Adams was beet red, and flustered. Pebbles smiled big, full of life and sensuality, then stepped up even closer, her mouth almost touching his, reached up and scratched her fingernails over the nape of his neck.

"Well … if you happen to change your mind, I can be available any time … night or day. You got a good memory, right?"

"Umm." Adams gulped big, uncontrollably. "Yeah."

"Good. Here's my number. It's easy to remember. 567-PBLS, you know, like Pebbles."

"Yeah," he said breathlessly, "I can remember that. Honestly, I don't think I'll ever forget that."

"Good." She leaned forward, pulling his head down, and kissed him on the lips once, long and lingering. Adams was paralyzed, a fly in the web. "Thanks again, and I really, really hope you change your mind. Stay safe out there, Adams. I'm sure I'll see you in court for this guy, if nothing else. Ciao!"

She let her hand glide down his chest and her fingers brushed his groin and trailed around his hip as she moved past him, leaving Adams to turn and stare after her, weak and more than a bit enthralled.

Whack! Melissa's hand slapped the back of his head. "Pathetic. I swear. Get to work, and don't wait so long before you come back by to talk … and stay safe out there." She smiled, but it was a longing, depressing smile, fully aware she couldn't have what she wanted.

Adams smiled sheepishly, rubbed his head.

"Thanks, 'Lissa. It was good to see you too." He leaned forward and gave her a quick kiss on the cheek. "I'll catch you around. Later."

DECEMBER 27

It was 1:00 a.m., and Nurse Santos was on duty in the psych ward watching all the camera feeds from her desk. She was struggling to stay awake, the rain outside unconsciously affecting her, even though she couldn't hear it. She nodded off briefly then opened her eyes and looked around. Something odd flickered in her peripheral vision, a distortion of reality. Training and hours of observation time logged caused it to stick out immediately.

It was Chad's camera feed. She noted two distinct visual disturbances on the TV screen. One was medium sized and located in the upper right corner of the room on the floor. The other was larger and covering Chad's upper body. It looked almost like a smudge, but it didn't wipe away. She stared hard, not blinking, trying to focus on Chad's body, looking for anything unusual. She noticed his breathing was labored, his chest seemingly constricted. His head began to twitch; his lips pressed firmly together and flattened, cheeks sunken. She stared at the screen.

Suddenly, Chad's neck seized, and his head turned back to the left, his body acting as if it was trying to arch. It looked as if something was restraining him. She dismissed the thought immediately. Night terrors again, she thought, of course.

It was time for Chad's medication anyway, and his vitals were beginning to spike.

Nurse Santos grabbed a syringe full of Haldol and walked down the low-lit corridor, yawning and rubbing her eyes. Her mind was on autopilot, lost in the mundane details of her job until she neared Chad's room and realized the door was slightly ajar. It shouldn't have been. She closed it herself earlier. She was sure.

Suddenly feeling full of dread, she crept quietly toward the door, her bladder weak, goose bumps rising all along her flesh. She fought the irrational need to flee, stepped forward, pressed her hand gently against the door, and slowly began pushing. The room gradually came into view; a series of thin wedges were revealed as the door swept open. The top of Chad's head appeared first, and then a stabbing pain shot through her right temple. She squeezed her eyes shut in attempt to rid herself of the pain, but it refused to go away.

The door continued on its trajectory; Nurse Santos never told anyone, except her priest, what she saw next.

Another head came into view; only a partial profile was visible, the face hidden completely, pressed close to Chad's right ear. She stood like a deer in headlights—like someone seeing the vehicle bearing down on their door but unable to respond—overcome by events they felt impotent to alter.

A wiry hand firmly gripped Chad's lower jaw, twisting his head slightly in her direction, his muscles trembling as they instinctively resisted the iron vise holding him down, his eyes rolled back, the whites clearly visible. Her stomach dove for her bowels.

The skin was a blotchy olive complexion, leathery and sprouting hair that was visibly growing longer. The fingers were bony talons with taut tendons leading to muscles like knotted cord, coiled and bulging; The whole body was a lean mass of sinewy flesh and bone, black hair rippling over the deceptively powerful frame.

Nurse Santos heard it whispering to Chad, a scratchy, articulate voice with intermittent moments that bordered on growling.

"Tamen oculi scelestus vadum deficio quod suum refugium vadum abolesco quod suum spero vadum existo maero

meus pro ¹id est prodigium of scelestus vir ex Deus quod hereditas statutum tempus pro vir per Deus²."

She thought it might be Latin, but she was not sure, though she would hear it in her dreams for years to come, never quite able to remember the exact words.

The head slowly lifted into view, still hovering over Chad's face. Its skin appeared scorched, as if covered in a charred crust. The ears were long and pointed but flat, the skull broad and thick, a forked tongue winding circuitously down to Chad's cheek. Its lower jaw was unhinged, dropped down well below Chad's chin, huge fangs jutting out of fleshy sheaths in the upper palette, dripping some yellowish liquid in Chad's eyes.

Nurse Santos' hands went limp, and she dropped the syringe. Mr. Phailees turned, looked her in the eyes, and spoke in Latin again, his chin tilting upward on the last word. *"Si ego existo scelestus vae per mihi, quod si ego existo justus tamen mos ego non levo neus caput capitis³?"*

A gasp of breath escaped her lips, but her arms hung like broken branches at her side, unable to rise and cover her mouth. She had no idea what he was saying, but it was not necessary. His eyes alone communicated his contempt, his judgment, his hate, as well as a disturbingly unshakeable sense of righteous purpose. His eyes were seared into her brain, the shocking vividness of amber irises shot through with a multitude of dark hazel fault lines, while the pupils were vertical obsidian slits and fixed on her.

All her life, she would never purge those eyes from memory. No matter how many times she attended mass, no

---

[1] *"But the eyes of the wicked shall fail, and their refuge shall perish, and their hope shall be sorrow of mind." Job 11:20*

[2] *"For this is the portion of a wicked man from God, and the heritage appointed unto him by God." Job 20:29*

[3] *"If I be wicked, woe unto me; and if I be righteous, yet will I not lift up my head?" Job 10:15*

matter how many times she went to confession and served penance, she would never shake the fear of imminent judgment nor the keen awareness of all her hidden sins, both small and great. Those eyes saw through it all. She was convinced of it.

Lightning flashed as the creature began muttering some incantation. A strong breeze blew in suddenly through the open window, the rain gusting momentarily to a torrential downpour. As the creature finished speaking, thunder cracked, incredibly loud, startling Nurse Santos.

She found herself looking down at the syringe she dropped. Chad began to scream for the first time tonight. Startled, she looked up again. A doctor was standing over Chad, but his eyes looked at her, not Chad.

"Are you ok Nurse Santos? You look exhausted ... and pale. You see a ghost or something?" he chuckled.

She wasn't sure exactly what to say, her mind's processing speed trying to keep pace but falling behind. After a few seconds, she finally answered.

"Yes, I'm tired. I think that's all."

"Well, how 'bout giving Mr. Bigleby his dose of Haldol and Dr. Danner will try to figure this one out tomorrow. In the meantime, try to get some rest."

With that, he turned and walked past her, exiting the room and moving out of sight. Later, she would not remember his name, but more strangely, she could not explain the padding noise accompanying his footsteps as he left or the odor of wet dog that hit her after he walked by.

It was mid-afternoon when Chad finally woke, confused and bewildered after almost two weeks of drug induced sleep. Panic seized him, instinctively, first from the pain in his throat and his inability to speak beyond a raspy whisper, then from the unusual hospital room he found himself in, and lastly when he realized he was restrained. Even more disturbing, there was simply no recollection of his actions.

He tried to call out, but his throat was wretchedly sore. His breathing spiked as waves of anxiety swept over him, his desperate efforts at recollecting how he could have arrived here being futile. He remembered being bitten by the dog. He remembered the fever and aches, going to work and feeling exposed. He vaguely recalled disturbing bits of dreams his brain did not wish to dwell on at all. But that was it.

"I see we're awake at last. I bet you're parched. Here's some ice chips."

The nurse unbuckled his right hand and moved his fingers around the small Styrofoam cup, then guided it to his mouth. The chilling pieces felt like heaven, melting and sliding down his burning throat. Chad tipped the cup again, then tried to speak.

"Where am I?"

"You're in the Grace Memorial Psychiatric Ward. You've been here for almost two weeks."

Chad's mind was stunned.

"What the fuck?" he muttered. "What happened to me? What did I do to get here?"

"I think it best if the doctor explains it to you. He knows all the details. I'll go get him now. Just sit tight a minute."

Fifteen minutes later Dr. Danner finished giving him the rundown.

"So, doc, you're telling me I had a screaming fit, kicked the shit out of some medics, and kept screaming until I ruptured my vocal cords? And, it took 12 days of heavy sedation to bring me out of it?"

"In a nutshell, yes."

"Holy shit."

Chad lay silent, staring out the window, shocked and deeply unsettled by a helpless feeling of victimization, as if someone had abducted his mind and abused him on a level so terrifying his sanity had snapped. Not only was his psyche scarred, but his ego was crushed. He was not strong enough, resilient enough, man enough. Something had broken him inside, and that was gnawing at his marrow.

Chad looked back at Dr. Danner. He stood patiently, waiting for Chad to process the situation.

"And all this is a classic case of night terrors?"

"Classic, yes, but extraordinarily acute. In fact, I've never seen a case like yours before. Physical or emotional trauma can be a trigger in adults. I understand you were attacked recently by a dog?"

Dr. Danner pointed at Chad's left calf.

"Yeah. A black dog and some weird homeless man. But that was about a month ago, I think." Chad remembered the man in the white sports jacket in place of the homeless man but did not bring it up.

"That could definitely be a potential trigger, but I would expect something greater to be involved as well, to account for the radical nature of your experience. I'll let you rest now, but consider what else may have impacted you recently in a deep emotional way, and we'll talk later. Also, a police officer will probably be coming by some time in the next day or so to speak with you. Probably just a follow up for his report from the night you assaulted the medics."

"Wonderful …" Chad gulped, wondering if it might be about something different entirely.

Chad's phone rang again, slowly drawing Samantha out of her afternoon nap. She crawled to the edge of her bed, reached over into her purse, and grabbed it, thumbing the answer button as she lifted it to her ear. "Hello."

A bouncy, airhead blonde voice bubbled on the other end. "Well hi! Um, is Roger around?"

"I'm sorry," Samantha mumbled, still coming around. "There is no Roger here. You must have the wrong number."

"Yep! I'm sure I do!" The line clicked dead.

Samantha was tired, but her female Spidey-sense was tingling: two different women in a short time frame "accidentally" calling her husband's phone. Pure coincidence? What were the odds?

She lay back on the bed, took a long, deep breath and blew it out slowly, letting any thoughts of betrayal go. Her phone rang. It was the hospital.

"Hello?" Samantha's voice was cautious, fearful, like a man's feet when he knows he's treading on thin ice.

"Hello, Mrs. Bigleby?"

"Yes …"

"Hi, I'm Nurse Callahan at Grace Memorial Psychiatric Ward. I'm calling to let you know your husband, Chad, is awake. He seems to be doing ok; the doctor just got done checking him out and explaining things to him. He woke up a little while ago. I wanted to let you know."

Samantha's heart leapt, a seed of hope sprouting roots.

"Thank you. Thank you so much. I'll be there shortly."

Samantha walked through the door and Chad's eyelids fluttered open. He was propped up in bed, watching some sports channel in between nodding off. He smiled sheepishly, inwardly ashamed of his current state. Night terrors were about as unmanly as he could imagine. But with Samantha, he did not feel the need to prove anything. He was happy for the lack of pressure her presence brought.

"Hi, Sam," he croaked.

Sam squeaked out a return "Hi", her balled fist pressed to her lips, her eyes squinting, trying not to cry, deep breaths working her lungs like a bellows. The unexpected emotion of the moment gripped her. She could not shake it, and instead, gave up and rushed to Chad's side. She hugged him as if he might disappear, tears soaking into his gown.

"It's ok, honey" he whispered. "It's ok."

After a while, Samantha's chest stopped heaving, and her breathing returned to a normal rhythm.

"My God, Chad. You just don't know … how, how horrible it was … to see you like that, to hear you. God, the sounds you made, I've never heard anything so terrible in my life. It was absolutely awful!"

"I'm sorry, Sam. I'm sorry you had to see it. I don't know what to say. I haven't got a clue what caused it."

Samantha crawled up on the hospital bed with Chad and snuggled into his side, head still on his chest.

"I know, Chad. I don't blame you. Hell, the doctors don't even have a clue what triggered it all. I just wish I never had to see or hear you like that. I'll never be able to forget it."

They were quiet for a couple of minutes until Sam broke the silence.

"I love you," she whispered and squeezed him tighter.

Chad thought about it for a couple of seconds and decided despite all their differences, all her faults, somewhere inside his heart, he still loved her. Not as much as Emily and Robbie, but he still loved her.

"I love you too," he whispered back and squeezed her in return.

They drifted off to sleep for a while. Samantha woke first, while Chad still slept soundly. She slipped off the bed, crept over to her purse, withdrew Chad's phone, and slid it back into the hospital bag with all his clothes and personal effects, then slid back into bed and let herself fall asleep again.

Around ten o'clock she roused, gave Chad a kiss, and left for home.

DECEMBER 28

It was well past midnight and the clock ticked slowly, painfully slow, in fact. Amy couldn't believe just how agonizing this was. Sitting, reading, playing solitaire, surfing the internet, Facebook, Twitter, watching the video feeds, making your rounds, and sitting again. It would have been excruciating on day shift, but midnights? Her eyelids were like rain soaked quilts, sagging beneath their own weight.

Nurse Callahan glanced over at Amy, observing the unending struggle, while she sat filing her nails.

"First night's always the hardest, hon." The words had a white trash southern accent that could never be shaken no matter how far from home she moved. Amy's eyes jarred open, and her head bobbed erect.

"Huh?" Brief confusion and then her mind made the connection. "Oh, I'm sorry, Linda. It's kicking my butt. I could not fall asleep earlier tonight to help prepare for it."

Amy stood, rubbed her eyes, and grabbed her coffee cup.

"I'm gonna grab a refill from the break room. You need anything?"

"Nah, sweetie. I'm just peachy. Thanks though." Nurse Callahan continued filing her nails.

A few minutes later, Amy returned and sat back down. Coffee in hand and face freshly washed, she readied herself for round two and hoped to give a better showing. Perhaps talking would help her efforts, she decided.

"Linda, do you mind if I ask your advice on something personal?"

"Not a bit, girl. You got man problems?"

"That obvious, huh?"

"Not quite, but with most women, any problem they've got can usually find its roots with a man. I know mine did."

"Well, I've been married almost seven years now, but we separated about three months ago."

Linda continued filing away, but looked Amy in the eye. "What made ya want to do that, girl?"

"You know, the more I think about it, the more I'm of the mind it was a bad decision. I was angry and rash when I did it, and I've been too damn proud to back out of it. I want him to come home, but I want him to admit he was wrong. When we lost the baby a few years ago he wasn't there when I needed him. He spent too much time at work and training. I hated him for it, and every time he justified it I just got angrier. Eventually, he got angrier too."

"So, how did he manage the stress of losing the baby?"

"I don't know for sure. I guess working out did it for him."

"Did y'all ever talk about it much?"

"No. I didn't want to talk about it. I just couldn't. It was too much for me."

"Did he want to talk about it much?"

"Huh. Ya know, I'm not sure. I can't remember. I think he did at first, but … I'm just not sure."

"Did he talk with any friends, counselors, coworkers?"

"I think so. I think he talked to their critical incident counselor at work, but besides that, I couldn't say. He never said."

"So y'all didn't talk, he didn't spend enough time with you, you're not sure what he did to cope with his own grief, and you're still hurt and resentful over the fact that he wasn't around for you as much as you wanted him to be? That about right?"

Amy's face scrunched a little, a slight scent of possible hypocrisy wrinkling her senses for a moment before she let it go.

"Um … Yeah. I guess. I want him to admit he was wrong for not spending more time with me and helping me through it. I want him to say he's sorry, and I want him to spend more time with me than he used to."

"Well, I know exactly what you mean. I have walked a few miles in your shoes. Took me a while to learn the lesson." Linda trailed off, staring at her nails from various angles, blew sharply, and then polished them on her scrubs.

Amy waited patiently for several seconds. "Well ... what lesson would that be?"

"Oh, the lesson of priorities, honey. You have to figure out for yourself what's more important: being right all the time or being together the rest of your life. You can't have both. You each have to serve your time in the hall of shame. Ever thought about how you not wanting to talk with him about y'all's loss and not being concerned about how he was handling the grief made him feel? You might want to chew on that one when you're considering who was right and wrong?"

Linda picked up her nail polish before continuing.

"My point is ... consider the cost of insisting you're in the right all the time. It's more than just' denying what you did was wrong. It's denying him the validity of his own pain, the justice of knowing he was hurt, and the freedom of forgiving you when you clearly accept responsibility and apologize. Routine denial tells him his heartache and pain is insignificant and unimportant to you. He doesn't matter, and therefore, he is not loved. And if someone feels they are not loved, they cannot be happy. Run this cycle enough times and it will drive a wedge of dissension and resentment between you both that cannot be removed.

"And the other part of this lesson is to not think you're entitled to his attention just because you're married. If you want him to want to be around you, the way to get there isn't by demands and angry criticisms. It's simple; try to be the kind of person he wants to be around. I'm sorry to be the one to pop your bubble, honey, but if he don't want to be around you, it's probably not entirely his fault, if you know what I mean. There's always two sides, two lanes of travel, two to tango, and all that jazz. You need to decide just how important being right is, and then don't wait for him to make the first move. Consider what you could have done different then, how you could have helped support him in his grief, and also consider what you can do different now. Figure out what you need to take responsibility for and what you need to say to him, what you need to apologize for, and what you need to just forgive, let go, and move on from."

Amy's mouth had slowly gone slack, and her eyes were wide. She felt slightly offended, but at the same time she had this nagging warmth of conviction spreading through her chest and flushing across her face, and somewhere deep in her gut a sinking weight of guilt was pulling her stomach south.

"Wow, Linda. That was … rough. I've never had someone tell me something like that. But … but I think you might be right."

"No offense, honey, but I know I'm right. I lost my first husband for those very same reasons, always too critical and never able to admit my own wrongs. Took a lot of counseling to figure that stuff out, but I won't even send you a bill. Pro bono for you."

The telecom chimed just then. Linda pressed the answer button. "Linda, we've got a suicidal subject coming up to you shortly. He's also experiencing hallucinations. Just wanted to give you a heads up."

"Thanks, hon," she drawled over the speaker phone. "We'll leave the light on."

Amy sat in silence and stared at no particular screen in front of her, vision diffused, unfocused. Her mind's eye still tried to dodge the burden of blame she knew deep down she shared in this bloody civil war.

A moment later, something caught her eye. She thought she saw the door at the end of the hallway close shut, ever so slightly, as if she had completely missed the slow march towards stillness until the very last second. She looked around, an uneasy feeling washing over her they had been watched, and never had a clue.

She scanned the video feed. Everything looked normal, except one. The howler, Chad Bigleby. He was sitting up, hands clutched around his neck like two clamps, chest heaving, puffs of visibly cold air blowing out with each breath from his pale lips, despite the warm temperature inside. He suddenly breathed in deep and held it, eyes flying wide open just before he screamed.

Amy rushed into the room, while Nurse Callahan grabbed Chad's Valium prescription and followed. They both kept a safe distance.

"Chad … Mr. Bigleby … It's Nurse Adams … you're safe, you're in bed, here in the hospital. It's another bad dream, it's just a dream. It's ok." Amy kept talking in soothing tones, reassuring him everything was ok. Chad screamed once more, then seemed to come around to consciousness. Rapid, hyperventilating breaths panted in staccato rhythm, eventually slowing to a steady pace. Within a couple of minutes, he was breathing normal enough to speak in between gulps of air.

Amy maintained a tone both empathetic and conciliatory.

"Chad … Nurse Callahan is going to give you a pill. I want you to swallow it. Ok? It'll help calm you down."

Chad nodded, took the pill and glass of water, and quickly downed it. Amy continued talking.

"What did you dream this time, Chad? Do you remember? Can you tell me?"

Chad took another deep breath and tried to respond, sputtering words out in between still ragged breaths, his lungs still winded and taxed from adrenaline.

"I was here … in bed … the homeless man came in with his dog … he said something … then he grew long fangs … hair like a dog and eyes like a snake. He grabbed my arms and pinned them to my side ... sat on my chest. I struggled for every breath ... then he bit my neck ... or my spine, I think ... it hurt bad. I couldn't move ... I ... I heard slurping noises. God, I couldn't move, I couldn't stop him ... he moaned ... like he was enjoying it. It seemed to go on forever ... and then he stopped ... pulled out some metal flask and ... and stuck his fangs in it ... one at a time. It was like he was milking his fangs into the flask ... whatever he took from me ... he put it in there. Then he left ... and I screamed, and you came in."

Chad took another sip of water. Breathed deep again and tried to continue to compose himself.

"How do you feel now, sugah?" Nurse Callahan asked kindly.

"Dirty. Violated. But better than when I woke up."

"You don't want to hurt yourself or anything right now do ya?"

Chad shook his head. "No."

"Is there anything you want right now, hon?"

Chad nodded unconsciously and leaned back on his pillows, sweat beaded up on his brow.

"Yeah." He gulped hard. "I want to sleep and never dream again for the rest of my fucking life. You got a pill for that?"

Amy had just clocked out and was grabbing a coffee for the drive home when Dr. Danner came walking into the break room.

"Good morning, Amy!" He flashed his bright blue eyes and perfect teeth then ran his hand through stylish blonde hair as he stepped in close to whisper, "How's my favorite nurse?"

Amy seemed surprised, pleasantly, for a moment; her body even relaxed and leaned in closer. But then something pricked her conscious with a growing unease. She stepped back, trying to present a proper professional front.

"Why, Dr. Danner, I'm doing just fine, thank you, even better once I get home and crawl in bed. I just got done with my first night shift in a while. I'm dragging." She gave a half smile and sipped her coffee, keeping it in between them, chest level.

Dr. Danner looked around quickly then reached out, touched her upper arm, and rubbed it twice up and down as he spoke.

"Well, I wish I could join you, Amy. I've missed you the last few weeks. I was hoping we would see more of each other ..." His voice trailed off, but the strength of his concupiscence lingered, his eyes sweeping over her body in one long covetous scan. "I thought you would want to see more of me after last time. I'm not sure I've ever seen a real woman enjoy sex that much." He smiled a sly, devilish grin.

Amy felt drawn to him. Their first date had been heaven, real conversation with a man truly interested in her, who she was at heart, what she loved and liked and hated, and though she never thought she would have jumped in bed on a first date, between the alcohol and her deep longing for anything that felt remotely close to genuine emotional and physical intimacy, she had done just that. And it had been unbelievable. The passion was high and incredibly freeing. She hadn't screamed like that during sex in a long time. She hadn't felt that invigorated by the idea of sex in a long, long time. She was torn. Part of her shouted and pleaded its case before the judge, declared what she deserved, but the other Amy charged her with treachery, betrayal, adultery, and she knew she could not deny the reality of what she had done. She was human, and weak, but that didn't make it right. Adams was trying hard to make things right between them. She couldn't turn her back on him. She couldn't betray him again.

"Todd ..." her voice paused, pregnant with disappointment, a pin to pop the balloon. "I'm sorry ... but I'm really trying to sort things out with Mark. He's trying hard. I've got to give it a solid effort."

"Oh … I see." Both face and voice dropped with disappointment. "Well … are you back living together yet?"

"No, but we're working on the relationship. Who knows?"

"Well, I can't say I'm happy, but just remember, you were miserable for a long time before the two of you split. We talked off and on for months before the final straw broke your back. Tread carefully, and if you need anything let me know."

"I appreciate your concern, Todd. Thanks."

Dr. Danner looked around again then reached out, brushed her hair back, and tucked it behind her ear.

"You sure you don't want one more time to get you through? I can tell you want it. It's like electricity on your skin …" He let his voice trail off and watched Amy as her eyes closed, her coffee cup dropped to her side, her body swayed, and her head tilted, leaning towards his chest. Then she opened her eyes—sad eyes, guilty eyes, conflicted eyes—and looked at him. When her lips parted they were wet; when she spoke it was a breathy, defeated whisper.

"I'm sorry, Todd … I just … *can't* … I've gotta go. Bye"

And in an instant, she was gone and out the door, clutching her coffee to her chest, anything to warm the cold void she felt inside.

DECEMBER 31, NEW YEAR'S EVE

Adams was on his way in to the office for shift change, the streets already busy.

"Dispatch to 113."

"113 go ahead."

"Respond to 125 Lakeland Drive. Caller advises there is a naked white male outside screaming and brandishing a knife."

Adams responded, "113 en route."

"60 en route to assist."

"119 en route as well."

Hicks and Greer were backing him up. Adams' mind focused on preparing his body for the coming encounter, accepting the crazy description of reality awaiting him.

The world is just fucked up sometimes, he thought.

The house at 125 Lakeland Drive was at the very end of an overgrown cul-de-sac. Adams and Greer turned in at the same time. Hicks was seconds behind. Blue lights filled the night, strobes flickering, whirling shadows and wig wag lights alternately revealing and hiding houses as they sped for the dead end. When Greer and Adams pulled up, they saw a naked, large-framed, white male with a beer gut stalking back and forth in his front yard, turning and spinning as he went; talking to the night. A large, survival- style knife with serrations was clutched in a death grip, held out in front of him like a torch warding off a pack of wolves closing in.

They exited their vehicles, Adams rolling around the rear to take up a position of cover next to Greer inside the inverted "V" formed by their cars. They both drew their Glock 21 sidearms and held them down at their sides, out of view. Adams glanced over at Greer who nodded at him. Adams nodded his head up and down accepting the lead role, then looked out at the man and spoke, trying to key off his hunted body language.

"Sir! It's ok. We're the police. We're here to protect you. Put the knife down and come to us. We'll make sure you're safe."

The man's head snapped in their direction, as if he was totally unaware they were there before now. His voice dripped hopelessness, a convicted man on his way to the hangman's noose.

"Oh no. No, no, no, no, no ... you *cannot* help me. No one can."

"It can't hurt to let us try, sir. Just put down the knife and come to us. We'll do everything we can to keep you safe."

"No! There are some sins no one can forgive. Sins people *shouldn't* forgive. Sins that a man can only *attempt* to offer restitution for."

Adams decided to try and argue from within the man's worldview. Giving up the knife and letting them help would have to make sense to the man and be consistent with his own logic.

"All right ... I can understand sin, sir. I think we all can. You obviously believe in a moral order, right and wrong, sinners and saints ... but if God exists he can forgive your sins. It doesn't have to end here tonight."

"You're wrong! How can I *earn* forgiveness for the despicable things I've done? HOW?"

The man's naked frame trembled with desperate rage, a frightened shiver quivering forth from his spine until it spread along every inch of flabby flesh.

Adams opened his mouth to respond but was cut off by the man's continued outburst.

"All my efforts are nothing compared to my crimes against the innocent … just an impotent scream at Lady Justice and her sword. If God is just … there can be no mercy for me, no forgiveness."

"That's not true. Many who believe in God believe He is both just and merciful. There's hope for you if you give up the knife, and come with us. We'll help you figure it out. Just put down the knife, and start walking to us."

The man stared at the knife, a long sigh escaping his lips. The moment stretched out, almost offered Adams hope, right before the moment suddenly ended, strangled by guilt.

"I deserve the sword and I can fight it, or I can give myself up to it. Live by the sword, die by the sword. That's justice, but if I go willingly that may weigh in my favor. I know, now, there is a reckoning, a Hell for men like me, a judge to condemn and avengers of His wrath to see that I end up there. I deserve wrath, and I have felt their breath on my heels the last few weeks. It's now or never. Die on my own terms … or theirs."

Adams didn't like where the man's words were pointing. Part of him wanted to stop and ask who 'they' were, but he knew he needed to interrupt and redirect the man's train of thought.

"Look, sir. It's not hopeless. You say you've done wrong. We all have, but true redemption is in confession and assuming responsibility. Tell us what you did. Take responsibility. Let the burden go, and we'll help you. It doesn't have to end badly tonight. Let's write a better ending, ok? Put the knife down, and walk over here. We'll sort all this out. We'll help you do the right thing."

"Do the right thing? I'm sorry, but *your* idea of the right thing and mine are entirely different. I want to confess, yes."

He paused, looking around again, the knife still held out in front of him, fear gripping his mind, threatening to break it once and for all.

"But there are really only two choices for me. Run and be hunted down … by them."

He spun around again, head flinching sideways as if someone had spoken in his ear. His head turned rapidly back and forth, eyes squinting into the dark. After several seconds of fruitless searching, he looked back at Adams and picked up where he left off.

"Or I end it tonight. Confess and end this myself. I've done all I can to make things right for the ones I hurt. I'll confess to all of you, and I'll do what it takes. That's better than waiting for *them* to catch me."

He shuddered, his beer gut jiggling briefly, his face twitching, neck rigid, twisting beyond his control. A current of fear ran through his whole frame, a flood of hormones and chemicals cascading from his brain, uncontrollable and undeniable. He might as well have grabbed a live wire pulsing electric current. Adams tried to at least buy time and figure the guy out. It wasn't going well.

"Who are 'they'? Who's after you?"

The man looked all around again, scanning for his tormentors.

"A devil and his dog, Avengers of Wrath sent to punish me. They've shown me what they'll do, in my dreams, just a small idea of what's to come … the thought of what they'll do …" His face scrunched in terror, unchecked dread contorting his mouth, his eyes seeing the hideous possibilities. "I can't risk it. I just can't. I'm not strong enough. But I can do this. I can make myself pay."

He looked down at his groin, flaccid and shrunken with fear. He mumbled, barely audible to Adams.

"I'm sorry, Mindy. I was a monster, not a father. You and your friends were never safe, but now you are. I'm so sorry, honey. Daddy's gonna make it right."

Adams shook his head out of movie mode. He could feel himself being drawn into watching something inevitable. His gut knew this wasn't going to end well. There was nothing he could do to stop it at this point. The man was a runaway train, the bridge out just ahead. No hope of stopping it now. Still, he tried.

"Sir! Don't hurt yourself! We'll protect you. Come with us. Just put the knife down and come with us!"

But it was too late.

"You won't take me now, you hellhound bastards!"

In the blink of an eye, the man reached down with his free hand, grabbed his penis by the head, and pulled it firmly away from his body. The knife moved quickly. He laid it across the base of his member. With explosive might, he cut down violently, the flesh coming away easily in his hand. Blood sprayed out in pulsing rhythmic jets, matching time with his pounding heart. Greer nearly hurled. Adams just stared then calmly asked the question burning on his mind.

"Why?"

The man looked up at Adams, confession springing to his lips.

"Because I am a child molester. I have molested my daughter for years and many of her friends. I am a monster, and I deserve to die. This is the only way ... the best way. And now ...you're *going* to help me."

The man flipped the knife into an ice pick grip, blade facing towards Adams. He took a deep breath, blew out hard as he threw his near- bloodless cock across the street, bouncing it off of Greer's cruiser. His voice became shrill, his words injecting courage into his veins, setting his will for the final sprint.

"Because if you don't help me ... I swear to God, I'll kill you!"

The world slowed down for Adams as the man took off straight at him, unusually agile for someone his size, arms pumping as blood sprayed. Adams observed the man's face suddenly turn from fear to a beady, black-eyed, monstrous hunger. A piggish snout with wolfish teeth rotting in his drooling mouth of horrors grinned wide as a serpent's tongue slithered into view. Adams couldn't explain, but somehow, he just knew the man had scarred little girls for life in order to satisfy his own deviant appetites.

A series of images flashed across his mind's eye, a slideshow completed in .9 seconds of slow motion reality. Adams saw a little girl cringing beneath her bed, hiding, hoping her father wouldn't find her. He heard the child's pleas as hands drug her out, day after day, year after year. Then, finally, he saw the light in her eyes go out as the naked man strangled her. She was free from a life of torment at last, from her father's grotesque touch, but at the cost of death. *Her soul escaped but her life had been taken from her in so many other ways before she died*, Adam's thought.

Righteous fury rose up within him, and time cycled back to its careening, chaotic pace. Adams raised his gun, pulling the trigger without hesitation. Greer fired as well. Hicks watched in horror with no clean line of fire.

Round after round struck the man's hulking frame. Chest. Chest. Chest. With each one, his torso flinched away but stayed on course, his face focused on the kill, his mouth jerking into a fiendishly cruel smile: a happy smile with happy black eyes. Greer lowered his sights. Another bullet fled his barrel. Pelvic girdle broken, but still he came, stumbling back into a balanced, lumbering mad dash ten feet away. Remembering the failure to stop drill taught in training, Adams aimed just above the bridge of the nose and fired, hoping to shut down the brain. Miss.

The man's head snapped sideways as his right cheek exploded in a shower of bone fragments, blood, and enamel, the meat train continuing forward. Squaring off again, a jagged half-moon smile spread across the man's mutilated face, eyes locking onto Adams. One final surge of fury and he vaulted onto the car, legs crouching like a wolf. Quad muscles contracted violently, calves forcing his feet downward, buckling the hood as they extended in vicious effort. He leapt through the air, knife raised, and his enormous mass behind the blade as it devoured the space, a collision course with Adams' heart fractions of a second away.

Adams broke out of his shooting stance at last, stepped sideways as far as he could, hand slapping the blade offline to his right as he raised the barrel to touch beneath the double chin and pulled the trigger one last time. The .45 caliber hollow point passed through the larynx, tongue, and upper palate into the brain then out the top of the skull, carrying pieces of each part with it into the night sky.

The body fell, sudden stop, smacking the pavement with a sick, wet *thwack* a mere two feet away from Adams. Forcing himself to breathe, he trained his gun at low ready and stared at the smoke and steam rising from the large hole in the top of the man's head. It was over.

Later, inside, they found the child's corpse, her limbs limply askew on the bed where they came to rest once struggling ceased. They found the letter confessing to all he'd done and professing everything he carried out to make it right. He released Mindy from the hopelessly damaged life she would have had if he left her alive. He left the account number for the trust fund where he dumped all his liquefied assets and a list of names of every girl it should be divided between, and lastly, a PS to the hunters in his dreams that they would not feed on him. He would do the right thing. They would see. They would see. Next to the letter were several small boxes, his little treasure chests, full of Polaroids, hundreds of them depicting various young girls in pornographic scenes, some with each other, many with him.

It was exceedingly disgusting.

Adams walked outside and wretched forcefully. Other officers arrived to assist. The scene was taped off as Detective Andrews rolled up. Adams spit repeatedly to clear his taste buds. He didn't see Mr. Phailees standing in the yard next door with his dog till after he heard the voice and looked up.

"I told you, Officer Adams … you have a gift. You know who is just and who is wrong. You know he took the coward's path. You saw the truth, you saw the lie … *you* saw the wicked in him before he died."

"What the fuck is that supposed to even mean?" Adams blurted out. "And where the hell did you come from?'

"I walk the night, Officer Adams, and blue lights have a way of finding me nearby. I see the darkness hiding from those lights. And you … you know what I mean. You see monsters now. You can't go back, only forward into the night. Adieu."

Before Adams could gather himself, the man and his dog slipped into the shadows. Adams searched the whole area for them, but with no success. He returned to the scene and began the laborious task of processing it and taking notes, but first he stopped and looked at the fat man's dead body, dark, viscous blood and grey matter pooled about his once frightful frame.

"Fucking monster. Good riddance, you filthy, fat bastard. I only wish I could have put a bullet in your head years ago before you ruined all those innocent girls."

He almost spit on the corpse, but knew he couldn't corrupt the scene. He turned his head and spat away, the need to physically express his disgust too strong to deny.

It was a long night, and more than once he had to refocus on the work at hand, stopping his mind from telling him just how crazy all this mess was. How crazy he just might be. He needed to find that homeless guy, pin him down, and find out just who the hell he was, what he knew, and especially what he knew about what Adams saw before he shot that fat bastard. Maybe he could explain what the hell was going on with the world and with Adams' mind.

JANUARY 1, NEW YEAR'S DAY

Adams never really went to sleep, just stayed at the station waiting for the chief and deputy chief to come in so he could do a critical debrief. Megan came in for a minute when her relief arrived at 6:30 a.m. She tried to make him feel better, asked him if he wanted to talk. He thanked her but told her not right now, maybe later. He turned on music at his computer, made sure all his reports were done, and zoned until 8:00 a.m. when the brass arrived.

Greer, Hicks, and Adams each gave a rundown of what they saw firsthand. Detective Andrews then reviewed everything found while processing the scene. It was all rather grotesque and the photos were either grisly or just plain disturbing. Everyone praised Adams for his attempts at a nonviolent resolution then applauded his decisive action. The chief spoke up when they were all done.

"Take a couple of days off. We'll clear this one in no time. It doesn't get any more justified than this, suicide by cop or not. You did an outstanding job. Now, get some rest and make sure to go see Dr. Wilkins on Wednesday, or sooner if you need it. She'll need to clear you before you return to duty. Call if you need anything, Mark." The chief stood and extended a hand which Adams shook.

"Thank you, sir. I hear my bed calling now."

Adams walked out to his car, took a deep breath, closed his eyes for a few seconds, and then picked up his phone. A few seconds later Amy answered.

"Hi, Mark, what's up?" She sounded sleepy. He completely forgot she was working night shift, probably just got in bed. Dammit, he thought.

"I'm sorry, Amy, did I wake you?"

"Yeah, but that's all right. What do you need?"

Adams sighed heavily, a long pause, bordering on uncomfortable.

"I need to talk, Amy. Crazy shit went down last night. I had to shoot a guy."

"O my God, Mark! Are you ok? Are the guys ok?"

"Yeah. We're all good. None of us got hurt, but damn, it was close for me. I swear to God, I'd be a dead man right now if I hadn't been training all these years. It really saved my ass. No doubt."

"Oh, Mark, I'm so sorry you had to go through that! Come on over. You don't need to be alone. I'll make some coffee, and you can tell me all about it."

"You sure? I don't want to keep you from sleeping."

"Bullshit! Get your ass over here now, Mark. I'll be waiting with coffee and some breakfast."

"All right. Thanks, Amy ... I love you."

"Oh, Mark, I love you too. C'mon. Hurry it up. Bye."

When Mark arrived, Amy met him at the door and immediately embraced him and firmly held him to her body, the threat of loss birthing a fresh awakening of old love inside her. She didn't let go for a long time, eventually crying on his shoulder. Adams' eyes blurred with wetness, and he squeezed her tighter.

"Thanks, Amy. There's no place I'd rather be right now."

"There's no place I'd rather have you be right now. So, come on over to the table and tell me all about it. I got coffee, cheesy eggs, and some waffles."

She released the hug but held his hand and guided him through the living room to the kitchen table. They sat and ate and talked while sipping coffee for a couple of hours. Adams told her everything, except for the really crazy shit he saw. He even told her about the strange homeless guy and the things he said.

"Mark. A homeless guy and his dog? You talked with them?"

"Yeah. And it wasn't the first time recently. Why?"

"Oh my god. This is freaky. That screamer, Chad Bigleby, the night before last he woke up screaming. When I asked him what he dreamed he said a homeless man and his dog came in his room. The homeless man changed, his head like a wolf but with snake like fangs. He said the guy bit him in the neck and sucked something out. He was really freaked out. You think he's talking about the same guy?"

Amy's hands suddenly shot to her mouth, which lurched open in a big "O".

"What's wrong, Amy? What is it?"

"Mark! That other guy, the jumper we talked about, remember he mentioned a homeless guy and a dog that were following him too!"

"The homeless guy, Mr. Phailees, and his dog, they were at both scenes also, just watching, like they knew what was coming."

"Get the fuck out of here! Are you kidding me? What the hell is going on here?"

Adams paused and shook his head to gather his thoughts. "I don't know, Amy, but it's definitely not normal and the guy has a definite interest in me, has since the first time we met. I need to find him and have an in-depth discussion."

"What did you say his name was?" Amy asked.

"Mister Phailees. Was on his ID."

"Mister Phailees?" Amy paused, her brain searching for something in the recesses of her mind. Suddenly a strange dread filled her face. "Mark! Mister Phailees, that's awful damn close to Mephistopheles—the devil in Goethe's play, Faust. Who the hell is this guy?"

Something cracked in Adams' paradigm of reality, the weight finally too much.

"Holy shit," he mumbled. "I don't know any more, Amy. Shit has just gotten too weird … but if I'm going to figure out what the fuck is going on I need to find him and have a long talk."

"Mark, you need to be careful. This is too strange." Amy's concern was genuine.

"I will, baby. You know I will." Despite the fear stirring in his gut, his mental processing speed was waning, his body beginning to shut down, extraordinarily tired all of a sudden.

"Amy, I'm sorry, but it's finally catching up with me. I need to sleep something terrible. I need to go home."

"No. No you don't. Come to bed. You can sleep here today, as long as you need to. I'll get back up in a little while and go take care of Toby for you. Right now, I'm going to tuck you in and curl up for some more shuteye myself."

"You sure? You don't mind?"

"Mind? It's all I want to do right now, Mark. C'mon."

Once again, she held his hand and led him into the bedroom. Together they removed shoes, socks, shirts, and pants. He crawled under the covers with his underwear on, and Amy kept her PJs on, curling up to against his back and wrapping her arm over his chest to hold him close.

"Sleep tight, baby. I love you."

Adams was already drifting away in a sea of unconsciousness as his head snuggled into the pillow. He mumbled back to shore, "I love you too, Amy."

No strange dreams came, just ones of him and Amy on vacation, having fun and making love. It was the best sleep he'd had in years.

JANUARY 3

Adams sat in front of Dr. Wilkins. She had a very disarming demeanor, intellectually sharp but very non-threatening, empathetic, and non-judgmental.

"So, Mark, how are you feeling today? Have you been sleeping well?"

"I'm feeling pretty good actually. I slept like a baby when I finally crawled into bed that morning. Didn't wake up until around 9:00 p.m. that night. Went back to bed around 4:00 a.m. then slept in until noon. I don't think I've slept that good in a long time. Last night was restful as well."

"Always a good sign. Are you feeling any emotional angst over the shooting? Any wrestling over the morality of what you did?"

"Honestly, doc?"

"Of course," she said giving him a friendly sarcastic smile with raised eyebrow.

"I don't feel bad at all. I sorted out my moral issues a long time ago when it came to this job. When I was a more religious man I squared what I do with my religious and ethical beliefs. I've been in martial arts for years and have strong opinions on a person's right to self-defense. Whether he wanted me to kill him or not, the second he came at me with deadly intent, I had no qualms with taking his life. I'm justified. His blood is not on my hands."

"So it doesn't bother you at all that you took a human life?"

"I'm not one of those guys who hopes for the day he gets to drop the hammer on someone. I've never gone out of my way looking for that, and I don't really feel any kind of elation at having done it either. I regret that it had to be this way, but I don't regret what I did and no, it doesn't bother me."

"You said you don't 'really feel any kind of elation'. What do you mean by not really? Do you feel some elation or something else?"

"Doc, when I first shot that guy, I didn't feel anything good, but after I saw all the photos, saw his daughter's strangled corpse, I wished I could have put a bullet in him a long time ago before he ever ruined all those girls' lives. I wish I could have prevented all the destruction that fat bastard inflicted on those children. And at that moment of absolute disgust, after I vomited, I was happy I was able to end his life. Maybe that's wrong. I'm not entirely sure. Maybe it's not healthy. I don't know. But I feel fine. So, you tell me."

"Well, Mark … I appreciate your candidness, and I think what you're feeling towards the man because of the heinous nature of his crimes is natural. The fact that you were impacted by it, that it made you sick, shows you're in touch with the pain in the world. You haven't insulated yourself and disconnected. You still have a capacity for empathy. It seems to me that you're coping very well. If you need to talk at any point, give me a call, day or night. Here's my card."

"Thanks, Doc. I appreciate that."

Mark stood to leave but turned around when he reached the door.

"Hey, Doc, I gotta question for you."

"Sure, Mark. What's that?"

"Do you do marriage counseling?"

It took a few days before Chad began to feel a little better as the images grew vague, the sharp lines of terror blurring, fading. His voice was recovering with rest. Samantha spent long periods of time sitting with him, watching TV or reading.

They didn't talk much, but Samantha seemed unusually friendly to Chad, while at the same time uncommonly observant. He couldn't put his finger on it, but it was nice to have the company after what he had been through, though he wished it was Emily and Robbie instead.

Dr. Danner came in around 3:00 p.m. and released him with a prescription of Haldol and Valium to keep things in check until his follow up. Dr. Danner seemed to know there was more behind Chad's problems than marriage issues and a dog bite, but didn't press the issue.

"You can return to normal activities. Try to get plenty of sleep; do what helps you manage stress best, and try to sort out any emotional undercurrents that could be impacting you negatively. Counseling is helpful, both individual and marital. I recommend you check into it. Here's a card for a colleague of mine."

Samantha spoke up. "Thank you so much, Dr. Danner. I can't tell you how much I appreciate everything you've done for us."

She was sincere, tears welling at the corners of her eyes.

"Hmm." Adams stood in front of his DVD shelf, scanning.

"Ahh. This will do the trick."

He kicked back in the recliner, a beer in one hand, a bag of chips in his lap, and Toby lying by his side on the floor waiting for another BBQ treat. As the intro appeared on screen, Adams considered the recent string of square pegs that didn't fit round holes and how so much of it seemed tied to the homeless guy and his dog. There was no solid answer that made sense of these things, no matter how much he had tried to analyze them.

So here he sat, listening to Mulder lecture Scully.

"Whatever happened to playing a hunch, Scully? The element of surprise, random acts of unpredictability? If we fail to anticipate the unforeseen or expect the unexpected in a universe of infinite possibilities, we may find ourselves at the mercy of anyone or anything that cannot be programmed, categorized, or easily referenced[4]."

Hmm, he thought, that's the way my life is beginning to feel here lately–not able to "be programmed, categorized, or easily referenced."

He recalled Shakespeare's play Hamlet, and a scene where a ghost had just appeared to Hamlet and Horatio.

"Horatio: O day and night but this is wondrous strange!"

"Hamlet: And therefore, as a stranger give it welcome. There are more things in heaven and earth than are dreamt of in your philosophy."

"Yes ... the wisdom of not thinking too highly of ourselves and our opinions. There is more to this world than any of us can ever fully wrap our minds around. Maybe I just need to have a little faith in the inexplicable wonder of the universe?"

Adams' mind wandered around various philosophical and religious ideas, trying not to categorize everything. He reminded himself he needed to be flexible and open to things he did not necessarily know.

It didn't take long before both he and Toby were asleep.

---

[4] *X-Files: Fight the Future*, movie

JANUARY 4

Chad woke the next morning refreshed and invigorated, physically ready to work. He walked into the H. P. Arkham office building fifteen minutes early, grabbed some coffee, and headed up to the suite of Krumbacher, Sachs, and Bigleby. Judy greeted him kindly. No one else was in yet.

"Thanks, Judy, I'm ready to do some work and get my mind off of everything. Hold my calls this morning so I can sort out the backlog."

"Sure thing, Mr. Bigleby. Glad you're back."

"Glad to be back." Chad sipped his coffee and sat down to tackle the mountain of madness on his desk, currently leaning like the Tower of Pisa. But first, he picked the phone up and dialed Emily.

"Chad!" She was happy and a little perturbed all at the same time. "Where the hell have you been? I tried calling your phone twice from two different phones. I had to make up shit and try and sound different just so Sam wouldn't figure out it was me."

"Em, I'm really sorry I haven't called, but I have an impeccable excuse."

"Yeah, well it better be really damn good, 'cause Robbie has missed you bad."

"I've been in the hospital. Matter of fact, the first few days I was sedated."

"Get out of here!" she yelled in dismay. "What the hell happened? Are you ok? Holy crap! Are you sick? You sound terrible."

"I'm ok ... now, pretty much." Chad hesitated, shame welling up inside him again, ego challenged by the reality of his current weakness. "Em, I had these really bad night terrors. They said I was screaming and wouldn't stop. I freaked out and assaulted a paramedic. I don't remember any of it. I woke up in the psych ward. I just got released yesterday. It's been really freaky, Em." Chad's emotions bubbled to the surface, small sobs wracking his torso, voice constricting to a squeak the more he spoke. "Em … I … I don't know … what's wrong with me …" He paused, breathed deep. "I'm scared, Em. I'm real fuckin' scared."

"Oh, baby! It's ok. It'll be ok. Just come over tonight. Stay for a while. Hell, stay all night if you want. I'll take care of you, Chad. I love you."

Chad reigned in his sobs and whispered into the phone. "I love you too, Em. You and Robbie both. I'd do anything for y'all. Anything."

Chad breathed deep.

"Em. I wanted to let you know. I mailed you a letter with all the details you'll need to know about the account and how to access it. The money will show up as having been transferred from a business in California as a charitable donation for Robbie. I didn't want it to be traced to me at all. As far as you're concerned I had nothing to do with you acquiring this money. It's a miracle to you that someone heard about your son's problem through a website and donated all that money. Got it?"

"Of course, Chad. No problem."

"There should be enough money to cover all the expenses plus some extra to start a college fund."

"God, that's awesome!" There was a long pause then her voice softened. "Chad, please come over tonight. Please?"

"I'll do my best, Em. As long as nothing else pops up, I should be able to. Anyway, I gotta get to work. I'm way behind. I'll see you later, I hope. Love you."

"Love you too, Chad. Bye."

The rest of the day was a monotonous procession of pity. One person after another coming in to greet him, welcome him back, ask him how he was doing, cast long faced, condolent looks of feigned empathy. "Look at the screamingheebie-jeebies-chicken-shit-freak" he could hear their looks say. He had anticipated awkward questions with long pauses and sympathetic looks and responses. What Chad had not expected, though, was the whole emasculating effect it would have on him. The longer the day went the more his ego suffered, still more fragile than he cared to admit.

Adams returned to work that night, not wanting to take off any more time. He'd rather stay busy, plus, he needed to find Mr. Phailees and have a talk.

"Well, boys," said Sgt. Rose, "it's been fairly quiet. Not a lot of foot traffic this evening. People seem to be intent on going and coming, but not hanging out."

Sgt. Rose looked at Adams. "Hang in there, cowboy. Damn fine work you did the other night. Don't feel bad one lick."

Sgt. Rose didn't need an answer, as Adams was caught off guard. He flipped his clipboard closed, stood, and left without another word. Adams felt a rush of pride. Rose wasn't known for his compliments.

Hicks issued zone assignments, and Adams started his car to let it warm up. The cold had a bitter bite tonight. He popped into Dispatch long enough to check the warrant box.

"You be safe out there tonight, gorgeous. Drop in and talk if you get bored." Megan flashed a wink and a smile his way.

Adams blushed and walked out before the conversation went any further. As he patrolled his zone, he kept his eyes scanning for Mr. Phailees.

He spotted Glenda, aka "Dr. Harris", standing out in front of the Gas N Go station. She didn't usually hang out on the street, especially not in the high traffic drug areas. Glenda had gotten her act straight and secured a regular job a couple years ago after she was arrested for distribution.

Adams served the indictment on her himself. It was the first time they met.

"All right, Glenda, you're under arrest for two counts of distribution of cocaine. They have video and an informant who will testify you sold to him. You got anything to say?"

Glenda answered Adams with her distinctive southern accent, her voice and demeanor like a teacher talking to a child, carefully explaining her side.

"Well ... it's like this, Officer Adams. People got problems ... hard times in life they can't deal with too well. Sometimes they just need a little ... prescription." A playful, guilty grin crept across her face as she paused momentarily. "And that's what I do. I just write 'em a prescription to help get 'em through, you know, help 'em feel better. That's all."

"So, you're kinda like a doctor, huh?"

"Yeah!" she said, a sly look on her face as she turned her head slightly. "You got it."

"Dr. Harris!" Adams exclaimed and laughed. They both knew there was a real Dr. Harris in town.

And so, from that day on, to Adams, Glenda Harris was always "Dr. Harris." He pulled into the lot and rolled up alongside of her.

"Dr. Harris! Whatchu doin' out here on this chilly January night? I know you aren't back in the prescription writin' business." Adams smiled.

"Officer Adams. I was looking for you. I knew you were out here somewhere. I heard you on the scanner earlier. Figured you'd ride by here at some point. I need to talk to you, Officer Adams. It's real important."

Adams could see genuine concern in her face.

"Ok. Are we good to talk here, or should I swing by your place later?"

"Oh, here's just fine. It's not anything I'm worried about anyone getting pissed over. I'm worried about you, Officer Adams. There's some real bad juju goin' down. I've been readin' the cards. It's just not looking good. Somethin' powerfully dark is here in Pleasant Grove. Something that's hungry, seeking to devour. People are on edge lately. Lots o' folks comin' to me with bad feelings, bad dreams, feelin' guilty about things they do and have done that they hadn't ever been worried 'bout before. Why, Rashid Whitman came to me before he died. Said he felt like somethin' was following him, stalkin' him in the shadows. He couldn't put his finger on it, but when I read the cards for him, nothin' but the Fools, Swords, Justice, and Death showed up for him. I knew immediately he wasn't long for this world. It scared the hell outta of him. Two days later, I heard he'd been eatin' or somethin'. Now, listen and listen good. I keep gettin' this feelin' that whatever is goin' on, you are way involved. I did a readin' for you earlier tonight. Lots of things popped up. A Pope, a Chariot, Strength, the Moon, a Sword and Cup, Justice, and the Hanged Man. I'm not for sure what it's all going to mean, but you need to be careful. There are going to be intense struggles ahead, sufferin', and maybe worse. I don't know. You're going to be tested and tempted, power and women and what not. Relationships will change dependin' on what you do. Be ready for self-sacrifice to see this through, but most of all, don't abandon your beliefs and sense of justice. It's who you are. You're a good man, Officer Adams. Stay just. Stay true to yourself."

Adams was a little taken back. He didn't really believe in this stuff, but it was way too close to home.

"Glenda, I don't know what to make out of all that, but thank you. Thank you for thinking of me and taking your time to try and help me out the best way you know how. I appreciate it a lot. There is a bunch of weird shit going on around here, and you're right, I'm right in the middle of it … I think. Let me ask you a question, though, ok?"

"Sure. Shoot."

"Have you seen a homeless guy with a black dog wandering around town? He's only been here the last couple of months or so."

"You mean that creepy old guy with the long coat and that mangy black dog? He talks real nice with a bit of accent, but gives off vibes that would run off Mother Teresa? That the one?"

"Yeah. You know anything about him?"

"Not really. Talked to him outside Harris Teeter one day. Seemed nice enough but just gave me the willies. Couldn't explain it. Saw him awhile back too, right here behind the store one night. Scared the bejeezus out of me. Man felt like the devil hisself … awfully strange." A shiver ran down her spine and wiggled her heavy coat, ending in a visible quiver of her face as it cast off the fearful chill.

"When was that, Glenda? Do you remember?"

Glenda's eyes suddenly got big. "Oh my God, Officer Adams … it was the same night as the last time I saw Poo-Dick hanging around the store here."

"You're sure of that?"

"Absolutely," she said, head nodding vigorously.

"I'll be damned. I don't know what to think about that man, but it ain't good. Stranger all the time. Well, Glenda, if you can find out anything else about him that would be very helpful, but don't put yourself in any danger, you hear me?"

"For sure, Officer Adams. I'll see what I can do, and I'll stay safe doin' it." Glenda smiled shyly then reached in her pocket. "In the meantime, I put together something I want you to have. Here, take this. It's for good luck and protection from all this bad juju."

Glenda handed him a piece of tin foil about the size of a rabbit's foot. He pried back a piece to see what was inside. It looked like tobacco mixed with pieces of twigs, leather bits, and some other stuff he couldn't make out."

"Don't be openin' it up, Officer Adams. Keep it closed up, and keep it on you at all times. It's a little root magic, that's all. Made it and blessed it myself."

Adams let slip a little concern in his face.

"Nothing in here a drug dog's going to hit on is there?"

Glenda swatted her hand in the air. "You silly, Officer Adams. Nope. There's nuttin' illegal you gots to worry about. Remember. Keep it on you. You ain't got to believe. It'll do its job either way. I'll let you know if I find out somethin' useful about that weird homeless man. All right?"

"Sounds good."

"All right, then. I'm gonna head home. You stay safe, Officer Adams."

Glenda patted his arm and turned to walk away.

"Bye-bye, Glenda. I appreciate all this. God bless ya."

Glenda smiled over her shoulder, pulled her jacket collar up, and walked off.

Adams was frustrated he never spotted Mr. Phailees, but at least it didn't get crazy either.

THURSDAY, JANUARY 5

Adams swung by the church before he headed home after work and knocked on Pastor Dave's door.

"Well hello, Mark. Come on in."

"Hello, Pastor Dave."

Mark stepped in the office, shook Pastor Dave's hand, and slid into the leather chair across from his desk.

"So, what brings you out here today, Mark?"

Adams was unsure exactly how to approach the subject without sounding a little crazy, but if anyone would listen and give advice without thinking he was crazy it would have to be a pastor.

"Well, Pastor Dave, I've been seeing and experiencing some very unusual things here lately. You might even call them supernatural or spiritual. I'm not sure. It's complicated."

"Really? Exactly what are we talking about?"

"I guess you would call it visions and dreams, or some sort of ability to see things that are demonic and going on behind the scenes, maybe. I'm not sure. I've had weird dreams about real events before I even found out about them. I've worked two cases in the last two months, one suicide and one suicide by cop where, before the men died, I saw them for what they appeared to be inside—twisted, evil people, ugly and horrible looking, almost demonic. And then there's this homeless guy who has come to town, and he has been showing up at all this weird stuff. He told me I had a gift for justice. Said I could see the truth and see the lies, that I could see the wicked in men before they die. He told me I see monsters now. He knew what I was seeing before I ever told him. I don't know what the hell is going on with me, Pastor Dave."

Pastor Dave's face had grown progressively more concerned and marveled at Adams' testimony.

"Mark, that is incredible and terribly freaky all at the same time. I'm not sure what to say about it. I mean, I could make an educated guess. God has often used dreams to communicate something to His people. Dreams are not uncommon, but what you're experiencing is definitely of a supernatural character. They are revealing information you could not know. The visions of demonic proportions you have seen could be attributed to certain spiritual gifts, depending on how you interpret Scripture. A spiritual gift of discernment is often thought to be the ability to discern what type of evil spirits are at work in a given person's life or situation. However, I personally don't attribute most people's sins to demons themselves. I think they can tempt us, but they don't normally control us. Man's heart is deceitful and wicked, perfectly capable of committing gross sins all on its own. But you may be getting a peek into what kind of sins these persons are plagued by and what they are guilty of. As far as the homeless man, that's very hard to say. He knows more than he should, definitely, but beyond that, I can't say what may be going on with him. There's no way to tell with the amount of information you have at your disposal right now."

"Wow. So, you don't think I'm crazy or anything?"

"Crazy? No, not at all. I think God has a plan, and revealing these things to you will somehow fit into that plan. We just don't know what the puzzle looks like yet or even what all the pieces are. If anything else happens, feel free to come by and see me again, or call me. I'll help in any way I can."

"Thanks a lot, Pastor Dave; I really appreciate it. I don't feel so crazy now. I'll catch you around."

"Ok, Mark. I'll be praying for you."

9:30 a.m.

Adams' mind raced, struggling to deal with the Pandora's Box that had opened in his life.

He couldn't explain the things he'd seen in the last couple of months; especially that freak Phailees and his dog. "Seeing the truth and seeing the lie."

"What the fuck does this guy know?" he mumbled.

Adams didn't know what to think, for sure. His faith faltered a few years back, and his belief in things supernatural was mediocre at best. He was a doubting Thomas, let me touch it or see it kind of guy. But the odds of repeated coincidence were attaining astronomical proportions. And the things he had seen at the two suicides, along with that dream, either he was going crazy or there was a lot of shit going on behind the cosmic curtain. He wasn't sure which one was easier to believe in at this point.

A timely glance to his right spotted Mr. Phailees, sitting on a park bench positioned close to the street, either talking to himself or to the dirty black dog. All night he looked for Phailees and now, alakazam, there the son of a bitch sits, pretty as you please.

"Time for some goddamn answers," Adams said.

Adams was instinctively disturbed by Mr. Phailees. The man was no stereotypical oddity. You couldn't box or label him. The mask covered the man beneath, and even that seemed too complicated to simply name. Crazy? Maybe, but articulate and deliberate. He spoke with authority, not a scattered anxious belief. He knew things he should not. He spoke of things men should not understand. He had an inhuman eye for observation, callous and disconnected from his fellow man. The most daunting attribute though, he was without any kind of fear.

Despite the unnerving feelings wriggling inside his gut, Adams pulled up and made eye contact as he exited the car. Mr. Phailees held his gaze. Beneath the surface, Adams thought he saw a cold, calculating sadist, but anything more was hidden from him. It was particularly unsettling when the man smiled at him, as if he knew something Adams didn't, as if he knew Adams … almost intimately.

Adams spoke first.

"I've been looking for you since the other night. Nice little disappearing act you pulled off."

"The shadows are my home, Officer Adams, my own briar patch. You cannot find me there if I don't want to be found. But that's not what's really disturbing. No. It's what you see and what I say about what you see that has your mind in a knot. You want rationality, closure, and comfort in a world that has broken outside your paradigm. What you need, Officer Adams, is a new paradigm. What you need is a little faith that your great playwright Shakespeare knew a thing or two more than you moderns, when he penned 'there are more things in heaven and earth than are dreamt of in your philosophy'[5]."

Adams went pale. "I don't understand," he said while shaking his head, frustration building as he continued to speak. "How can you know what you know? How can you know what I see?"

Adams regained some semblance of authority. "But what I really need to know …" There was a long pause as Adams swallowed with difficulty, his mouth suddenly dry and feeling like cotton, before managing to finish the question burning up his brain. "Is it real, or am I crazy?"

Adams stood and stared down at Mister Phailees, a pleading espression set like flint, begging an answer.

"Officer Adams, you are not crazy. What you see is real, and you are one of a very few who have this … gift … to see the truth and the lie."

---

[5] *Hamlet* - Shakespeare

"Mother of God," he moaned and shook his head, then cupped his face and slowly wiped his hands away, as he leaned on his car, not sure whether that was really the answer he wanted to hear or not.

"Why? Why me?"

"That I cannot fully explain ... yet, but know this: By occupation you are an avenger of wrath. As your God's word says, "Therefore whoever resists the authorities resists what God has appointed ... for he is God's servant for your good. But if you do wrong, be afraid, for he does not bear the sword in vain. For he is a servant of God, an avenger who carries out God's wrath on the wrongdoer." It is your profession, your gift, your birthright. Embrace it, Officer Adams, in its fullness. Do not let the dreams disturb you. Focus on the task. Pursue justice. That is all I can tell you now ... You should leave. I need privacy for private thoughts."

Adams was unsettled, but, his authority challenged, his ego kicked in.

"Well, actually, there's a report of your dog here biting a man. Perhaps I need to call Animal Control? They probably want to talk to you and take your dog in for quarantine."

Phailees' face hardened, then he let a flat smile barely stretch the corners of his mouth.

"Well, Officer Adams, I've got a valid rabies tag for Phobos right here. No need for a quarantine. And I doubt Mr. Bigleby will have time to think about pressing charges right now. His world is out of joint and collapsing."

"You've got an answer for everything, don't you, old man?"

"Now, now, Officer Adams, I may be old but that just means I'm full of wisdom you have yet to gain. Envy is not becoming, nor are insults to try and make yourself feel better. You are distraught and confused, and I understand. It will all be made clear in due time. Patience. Revelation is at hand."

Phailees stood, and Phobos took up his position at the left heel.

"I'm afraid I must bid thee farewell. Till next time." Phailees tipped his head in respect and sauntered off.

Adams, feeling powerless, tried to compensate.

"Ok, but there's something not right about you; I just can't see it all yet, but I will. I'll figure out what's behind this whole façade you're maintaining." Adams held up his palm and circled it about to emphasize his last words.

Mister Phailees did a casual about face to listen to Adams then smiled coyly, a devilish charm playing on his countenance which, for a moment, did not look quite so old, or homeless. He turned back around to walk off, but called out over his left shoulder.

"You do that, Officer Adams. Be who you were designed to be. I expect nothing less."

Adams kicked a can lying in the gutter in frustration. More mystery to scratch at his sanity. He shook his head and got back in his patrol car, the universe spiraling, entropic forces deteriorating his grip on reality.

11:00 p.m.

It was dark and the night was cold indeed, but that wasn't what bothered Mr. Phailees and Phobos. The gnawing pain was setting in again—a twisting in their guts. It was an ache deep in the bones that could not be eased, a demoralizing misery capable of immobilizing one in an abyss of hopeless resignation.

Phailees sat in the alley, his skin clammy and pale in the moonlight as he shook the ornate metal flask, a thing of pure silver with beautiful etchings of angels falling from heaven then rising to hunt like hawks amongst the fields of men. There was the slightest sound inside, the noise as light as the transfer of weight within. He unscrewed the silver cap inlaid with red jasper, a dark, fiery red stone streaked with tiny obsidian veins. The color alone could make one think of hell and burning brimstone, of souls and demons and devils suffering for all eternity.

He placed the opening beneath his nose and inhaled deeply until his eyes rolled back, the odor alone sparking a cascade of fond memories, all happy and buoyant, full of blood and fear and death. His instinctive response to the pheromone essence was inbred and unavoidable. His jaws rippled; his throat convulsed in transformative growth. His tongue swelled, stretched, parted, then flattened into narrow forked prongs that began flicking rapidly in and out, shivering as it smelled the air. The aroma of fear lived in his nostrils, danced across his tongue, and filled his mind with glory and pleasure.

"Damn those two cowards," hissed Phailees. Phobos laid his head on the master's lap and whined lightly in agreement.

"If the greedy backstabber and the deviant pedophile had not committed suicide, we would have enough to fill the flask by now. As it is, we are at our supply's end, and can ration no longer. Our bodies and minds are in withdrawal. Our hearts fail for lack of joy. We must consume the last of it now and scrape up whatever else we can. In the meantime, we need the others to go the distance, to attain a full harvest, and see the fruition of our labor."

Phailees pulled a metal bowl from behind his leg and carefully poured a small amount of liquid from the flask into it.

"Here, Phobos. This should make you feel much better. The first time is bad, but alas my son, it only gets worse the longer you walk amongst the descendants of Adam."

Phobos lifted his head and stretched until he could reach the bowl and lick the pungent, yellow fluid. As he did, Phailees tipped the flask and held it up for a long time, allowing every possible drop to slip inside his feverish mouth, forked tongue licking deep inside. They both sighed when done, eyes closed, heads swaying to the cadence of relief, peaceful smiles on their faces for a time as their hearts found the closest thing to rest they could ever possibly know.

After several minutes, Phailees opened his eyes in the dark and looked out over the trash-strewn alleyway.

"This won't be enough to cross the threshold. We'll need to take a bit more, now, or the withdrawal will return quickly."

A shuffling noise came from the end of the alley just then. Phailees looked up and saw an older gentleman he recognized. A homeless veteran, a widower and father no more to a dead son. A good man with a fractured psyche and nothing left to remain sane for. Phailees had no choice, except how much to take. He swore to himself he would not kill the man. In truth, he could not. The consequences were worse than the symptoms it would relieve.

Phailees closed the distance without a sound, slipping into one shadow and out of another, his face morphing into something out of tales told to keep children from wandering off in the night. The man suddenly rebounded off a wall of flesh and nightmare. Startled hands shot up, face flinching away reflexively. Phailees hand caught him by the jaw, squeezing each side firmly so he could not look away. The horror too much to bear, fear overcame him, adrenaline, endorphins, and pheromones all releasing like a massive bomb exploding into his system. The blood drained from his face as the urine drained down his legs. He unconsciously whispered his first words in three years. "Dear Lord, save me."

Phailees cupped the back of the man's head and pulled it down sharply. The fangs entered just beneath the base of his skull through the foramen magnum, penetrating to tap the spinal column's precious fluid, awash with a chemical cocktail of raw, naked fear.

Phailees took just enough to finish crossing the threshold, then lifted the man's head back up, changing his appearance back to something normal.

"Thank you for your sacrifice. Go in peace, and do not return here."

The man stumbled off in the direction he came from, rounding the corner without hesitation and never looking back, overcome temporarily by the shock of what his mind was already wanting to deny ever happened.

Phailees returned to Phobos, spit into the bowl and told him to drink it. Phobos licked it up gladly.

Phailees was angry, licking his lips clean.

"This is beneath our kind, Phobos. We should be feasting at our leisure, not licking spit from bowls or suckling scraps from just men. Soon, soon Chad Bigleby and the others will be ready, and we will have more than enough to provide the promise of relief for a long time. Yes, indeed."

Phailees leaned against the brick wall, and Phobos curled up along his leg, neither really bothered by the cold night closing in.

The freezing wind cut right through Adams as he hurried inside the station for roll call. Everyone was kicked back in a chair as Sgt. Rose gave them the run down.

"Colder than a witch's tits on ice out there, boys. Snowin' too with lots more to come. With most folks stuck inside, there's been a few domestics tonight. Shaquita Jones had a fit when her boyfriend took her root magic, ripped it up, and flushed it down the toilet. He had his hands full then. She swore somethin' evil was about town, and that was her protection. We told her she'd be protected in jail and arrested her for assault. Been quiet since then. Hope it stays that way."

Rose pulled on his heavy coat, grabbed his furry hat no one else on the force but him would ever dare wear, and moseyed out the door.

Adams and his shift mates all sat around, nobody ready to brave the treacherous weather yet. Greer decided to break the silence.

"All right fellas, story time!" He grinned big, looking from one to the next for some ascent or approval. "So, topic for tonight: who's the dumbest person you've ever dealt with? I'm saving mine for last because I know it's the best."

Dexter piped up and took the first shot.

"All right, so I stopped this car with a couple of white kids in it leaving the projects at about 2:00 a.m., probable DUI and maybe some dope. His eyes were bloodshot, and I smelled beer. When I had him get out of the car I noticed his shirt. It said, in big creepy red letters, 'I see DUMB people.' I told him I liked his shirt 'cause I see dumb people all the time, then I asked him if he'd had anything to drink tonight. Of course, he said 'two beers.' So then I asked him if he'd smoked any marijuana tonight. All of a sudden, he's real sincere, 'oh no officer, honest, I don't do drugs.' 'Really?' I said, almost laughing. 'Yes, sir; my daddy taught me better than that.' I asked, 'So you don't have any drugs inside your vehicle or on your person then?' 'Oh no, officer; no, sir. You can check me.' At that point, I was about to bust a gut, so I went ahead and asked the kid, 'Hey man, what's that?' as I pointed at the huge marijuana blunt tucked over his right ear. He gets this confused 'huh?' look on his face, and then it hit him, and he just hung his head and muttered 'shit.' 'Yup,' I said, 'I see dumb people every day. Gonna have to get me one of those shirts.'"

Everybody laughed. "What a 'tard," Greer said. "That's funny, man. All right Adams, you're next."

"All right, so I had a call to the 7-Eleven for a shoplifter. A very tall, thin black male, who was a regular customer, reached behind the counter and took a carton of cigarettes. As I pulled up into the lot, I saw Clifton James walking away. You know how tall he is, and he lives just a few blocks away. Anyway, I got out of my car and called 'Hey, Cliff, let me talk to ya for a minute.' And what was his immediate response?" Adams grabbed his crotch with one hand and raised the other, moving' it to emphasize each word spoken in a low, stupid liar voice. 'Yo! I ain't stole no cigarettes from the 7-Eleven!'"

"Wow …" was Dexter's only response.

Greer just shook his head. "Man, they don't get much more stupid than that. Dexter's right. Wow. Ok, Sarge, your turn."

Hicks took a long sip on his coffee, kicked his feet up on the desk before starting his tale.

"Well, there was this one night when another unnamed officer was working on my shift, and we got out on two guys who were drinking beer next to a car on Wilson Street. We were going to just write them for open container, but one of them turned out to be Kyle Patton—well known drug user, possible dealer, and suspected armed robber of a burger joint once a couple of years before, though we never could get enough to solid ID him. Anyway, we start asking if they have any weapons on them—knives, guns, grenades, atomic bombs. They of course say no, and we asked if they would mind if we pat them down for our safety, and theirs, before we write the ticket for open container of alcoholic beverage.

"The first guy goes fine, nothing on him. Kyle, though, as soon as he turns around, starts acting hinky, like he's about to bolt. The other officer didn't spot it in time, and as I stepped forward to block his path, he bolted. The chase was on. We went a few blocks behind several houses before finally catching and cuffing him. We didn't find any drugs on him.

"Another officer met us and put him in their car, while we back tracked and looked to see if we could find any dope he might have ditched along the way. Still, no luck. So, we get back, and we're standing around the car with Kyle inside. The windows are up, and the heat is blowing. My unnamed partner cracks a joke and says, 'Hey, wouldn't it be funny if we told Kyle that we found some heroin, and he was going to get charged for it. I bet he'd shit himself.' We all laughed, and went back to our cars."

"I'm driving behind the car with Kyle in it, and we're almost to the PD when suddenly I see the rear door pop open and Kyle rolls out of the backseat, bounces down the road a few times at 45 mph, hops up, and takes off stumbling, trying to run. The officer driving was quick. He slammed on the brakes, jumped out in a jiffy, and ran down Kyle in just a few seconds. I pulled up as he put Kyle up against the car, leaning on the hood. That boy had some huge ass patches of road rash. One on his head about two inches across, one on his left shoulder that was almost a perfect four-inch circle, another good-sized one on his left forearm, and one on his left knee through torn jeans. He was wide-eyed, panicking, and maybe in a little in shock from the injuries. I walked up and asked him point blank, 'Kyle, what the fuck were you thinkin'?' He says, 'Man, I can't take no heroin charge. I got time hangin' over me. I can't go back to prison, I just can't!'

"I looked at my partner, like 'holy shit, how'd he hear that?' His jaw was already scraping pavement. We couldn't believe the guy heard us jokin' with the windows up and the heat blowing inside the car. It was nuts, but I was quick on my feet. 'Kyle, I don't know exactly what you think you heard, but we didn't find any heroin, and we aren't charging you with anything but open container and obstruction of justice. No felonies.' He looked relieved for a second, then he looked down at his shoulder, and arm and I thought the boy was gonna cry. So, I don't know who was more stupid, my partner for saying that shit or Kyle for jumping out of a car based on hearing a few words through the window. Either way, it's pretty damn funny."

Dexter was laughing his ass off; so were Greer and Adams. Greer finally got his voice. "Man, Sarge, that was some quick thinking. Guess that's why you got the stripes and get paid the big bucks!"

"And don't you forget it either, Greer," Hicks said as he sipped more coffee. "All right Greer, you're last. It better be good."

"Ok, so it was a really freaking cold night, like tonight's supposed to be, but even worse—low single digits. Around 6:00 a.m., I get a call to one of those shanty shack places at the end of Tower Road, you know, those nasty shitholes with no electric and plumbing. So, I get there and knock on the door. It opens and the stench of kerosene is so strong it takes my breath away. Old man Taylor greeted me through a mouth full of rotten teeth, says I need to check on this guy Harvey cause 'he not doin' so good.'" Greer made the bunny rabbit ears with both hands.

Greer's voice went really low and gravelly, broken and uneducated sounding every time he quoted Taylor. "He shows me out the back to their porch, and I see this guy sitting in a chair, his jacket pulled tight, his chin on his chest, still as a statue. Old man Taylor proceeds to tell me what happened. 'Ya see, Harvey was in here wit' me an' Coop an' James. We wuz all playin' poker round the keer-zine heater, but Harvey starts a'cussin' Coop uh cheatin'. Wants ta go ta blows. I tells 'im ta take 'is ass outside tills 'e can act right, else ahm gonna knock 'im one wit my bat. So's 'e listens, grabs 'is bottle uh Mad Dog, and goes out on the back poach. Guess'n 'e never wanted to come back in, cuz we didn' hear nuttin' else from 'im all nite. I's comes out here dis moanin' and find 'im sittin here. I says, 'Harvey! Wake the fuck up, an' come inside.' But you know, 'e didn' listen one lick. I toles 'im agin and 'e didn' even lift 'is head or speak. So's I shook 'im, shook 'im hard, but I couldn't make 'im move. 'E kinda stiff.'"

Dexter and Adams chuckled right then, but Greer didn't break stride.

"'I told Coop 'Harvey don't look so good, we better callz the law or somebody.' So Coop went down da street and called y'all and here you's are, and here Harvey is. I don't tink 'e looks too good, though. Prolly asleep reel deep. Can you's wakes 'im up?'"

Hicks let a "holy shit" slip and covered his mouth, trying not to laugh too hard.

"I laughed. Couldn't help it. The frost on Harvey's head and beard were clearly visible. The poor bastard was frozen. Had probably been that way for a few hours. It was cold enough I was shivering like a dog shittin' razor blades and the Mad Dog probably made it even easier to freeze him good. I looked at old man Taylor after I checked for a pulse, just to say I did.

"'Taylor! Harvey's dead.'

"'Wha?' he said. 'Nawl. Harvey don' looks good, but 'e ain'ts dead.'

"'Taylor! He's frozen harder than a stiff cock, man. He's dead.'

"'Frozen? Well, uh, how bouts we jus' bring 'im in here an' set 'im by da keer-zine heata? 'E'll thaw out fo sho an' be awright.'"

All the guys were about to cry by this point.

"The old man smiled a little, nodding his head as if trying to convince me of what he believed to be true. I stared dumbfounded then broke the news to him.

"'Taylor. I'm sorry, but once you're dead, you're dead. You can't thaw him out and him just be alive.'

"He just gives me this dumb look and says 'Oh …'

"So I call EMS and they come down and have to pry old Harvey out of that little aluminum folding chair. There were little pieces left behind. They heaved him up on that stretcher, strapped him down and then wheeled him off, lying on his back like a dog playing dead, arms and legs up." Greer simulated it, lying on the squad room desk, knees to his chest, legs bent and arms up, wrist bent forward. Then he rolled back down to his feet.

"Taylor just stood next to Coop saying, 'I knows 'e didn' look good' as I walked back to my car. And that, my friends, is the stupidest person I've ever seen."

Everyone nodded in agreement, wiping tears from their eyes.

Kaitlin cracked the door to Dispatch. "Hey, Adams, got a call in your zone."

"What is it, Kaitlin?" he asked.

"You need to meet a Roger Vasser at Fifth Avenue and Vine Street, reference a complaint of assault."

"Oh boy, good luck with him," said Greer, kicking back in his chair, feet on the desk. "I can never get that poor guy to talk."

Dexter spoke up.

"Yeah, poor guy's wife died in a vehicle accident four years ago, and then his son got killed in Iraq a few months later. His son was Army Special Forces, just like Roger was in Vietnam. Poor dude's been mute ever since. Lost his mind, lost his job, and lost his home. The shelter on Vine Street saves a spot for him every night."

"Well, let me see what I can do for the guy."

A short time later, Adams pulled up near The Least of These Homeless Shelter. He saw Roger standing on the corner, multiple layers of clothing insulating him, a long trench coat overtop of it all. Fairly new gloves kept his hands warm, along with a soviet style fur hat pulled down snugly to his eyebrows. A scarf wrapped tightly around his neck; a little too tightly, Adams thought. Roger appeared in his early sixties, albeit still fairly fit. There was a white male next to Roger. A shelter worker by the look of it.

Adams pulled up next to them, against the flow of traffic with flashers on, so he could just roll his window down and stay in the warmth of his vehicle.

"Mr. Vasser, I understand you need to report an assault." The man nodded and extended his gloved hand. Adams took it and shook.

"What happened to you, and are you hurt?"

Roger unwrapped the scarf, bent down and showed the back of his neck.

Adams jerked back in horror, sucking air into his lungs in a whistling rush. It might as well have been the plague.

There was some dried, caked up blood on Roger's neck, as well as fresh blood oozing from two holes at the base of his skull.

Adams' brain didn't want to admit it, but it looked exactly like the wound on Chad Bigleby. His heart raced, but he controlled his breathing and exited the car to get a closer look with his flashlight.

"What the hell bit you Roger? A dog maybe?"

Please say it was a dog, Adams pleaded mentally.

The old guy shook his head and looked at his companion.

"Hi, Officer Adams; I'm Jerry from the shelter. The best I can gather from talking with Roger is that another homeless man, a new one to our area, attacked Roger and went Goth on him, pretending to be a vampire or something."

"A homeless man made that bite?"

"That's what Roger swears happened."

Adams' mind raced. It had to be Phailees. No one else.

"Was there an argument that led up to this attack, or did it just come out of the blue?"

"Oh, it was a total ambush; one second Roger was walking down an alley, the next, the man surprised Roger and bit him."

"Does he know who the guy is?"

"No. Just that he's new. He's seen him around but doesn't know who he is."

"Do you know who he's talking about, Jerry?"

"Not sure, possibly. I think it's this new guy, really old and worn looking, pretty tall, fairly thin, and has unusually good posture."

"Does this guy have a black dog for a companion?"

"Why yes, he does."

"Roger? Does this homeless guy that attacked you usually have a black dog with him?"

Roger nodded in the affirmative.

"All right. I know who that guy is. Do you want to press charges, Roger?"

Roger shook his head back and forth in the negative. Jerry elaborated. "Roger doesn't want to press charges. He just wants the law to get on top of things with this guy so no one else gets hurt."

"All right then, umm, can I see the wound again?"

Roger nodded and bent down again. Adams inspected it closely and snapped a picture with his phone.

"Hey, Jerry, take a look at this." Jerry leaned in, looking at it again. "You see these holes, Jerry?" Jerry nodded, "uh huh." "Well, that sure doesn't look like normal teeth. Looks more like puncture marks, like a dog's incisors or maybe a snake. And look at the spread between the holes. Pretty wide, about 5 inches." Jerry's brow furrowed in confusion.

"Yeah, you're right, Officer Adams. What do you think?"

"Well," Adams paused, "Roger, do you think this guy was wearing some kind of fake teeth or freaky dentures or something?" Roger shrugged his shoulders, the universal 'I ain't got a clue.' Adams continued. "Well, I can't say for sure, but either way the human mouth is a hell of a lot nastier and germ infested than a dog or snake. Best you get it looked at and cleaned out. You may even need antibiotics. I'll call EMS and let them check you out, just to be on the safe side. Ok, Roger?" Roger nodded his head in agreement.

"Thanks for your help, Jerry. I'll wait with Roger." They shook hands and Jerry walked back to the shelter.

"All right, Roger, EMS will be here soon. One more question, though. Did he look normal, or was there anything strange about him?"

Roger acted uneasy, as if he didn't want anyone to think him more crazy than they already did.

"It's ok, Roger. I'm not gonna tell anybody else what you tell me. I know something's up with this guy, and the measurements on your bite don't match a human mouth. Anything else you can tell me?"

Roger motioned for paper and pencil to draw with. Adams produced his notepad and pen. Roger scribbled violently at first and then added in the fine details. After a few minutes, he turned it around to show Adams, who took a step back without thinking.

The head was completely inhuman, hairy and wolf-like but wide, flat, and scaly underneath the hair, with a forked tongue and very large snake-like fangs. Roger, apparently, was still a very good artist. The picture was highly disturbing. Adams took it from him and said thank you. Roger extended his hand and nodded his head in thanks as Adams shook hands. A few seconds later, EMS pulled up. Erin got out of the ambulance, smiling at Adams while he gave her the scoop. She asked how he was doing and offered to meet up for a drink, just to talk. Adams thanked her and hurried back into his car as she turned to attend to Roger, disappointment spreading across her face. He couldn't help but glance back at Erin as he drove away. She was glancing over her shoulder and made eye contact. A knowing smile teased at the corner of her mouth.

The next hour, Adams scoured the city for Phailees but had no luck. Roger's artistic depiction sat on the seat next to him and continually drew his eyes, his mind unable to stop thinking about it. The implications were dreadful … paradigm shattering, in fact. He decided to distract his brain and met Dexter.

It was cold, but addictions never rest, neither do the dealers who supply them. An abandoned house on Hobbs Street was a good candidate. Drug addicts used it all the time to smoke dope, shoot up, screw, and sleep in. Adams and Dexter bundled up, parked a block down from it, and began sneaking through some backyards.

As they got close, Dexter spotted someone walking down the sidewalk. He held his fist up and they both squatted down, fully immersed in the shadows, maybe 50 feet away. They could clearly see the scrawny girl, a local prostitute and crack addict. She was wearing a long coat with a mini skirt on underneath. She stopped, took off the coat, and laid it on the sidewalk. She took one step sideways into the grass, hiked her skirt, and squatted. In the moonlight, they could see her shit slide out and hit the ground. She stayed there for a few more seconds, stood, pulled her skirt down, stepped back on the sidewalk as she grabbed her coat, put it back on, and walked off.

Dexter couldn't hold back. He whispered to Adams. "That was fucking disgusting. Ughhhhh! And now the bitch will go flag some guy down, and he'll screw that dirty thing without a second thought. Geez, its worse than animals. At least they clean themselves, got some fucking sense of hygiene. Man, that's just gross. Fucking gross." Dexter's head shivered and twitched sideways involuntarily.

Adams nodded in agreement.

They waited a few minutes, then stood, and continued on toward the house, taking their time picking a path through the shadows of each yard. They knew better than to walk up to the back porch, you'd step in human shit for sure. No plumbing. They'd squat right over the edge of the porch and let it go. The biggest damn collards Adams had ever seen growing were beside that back porch. The memory gave him a shiver.

Slipping around to the side where a porch swing once hung, Adams noticed the door was closed. He moved forward and checked the handle. It was unlocked. He eased the door open; they tread forward quietly, flashlights ready but not on, guns in hand and by their sides. They crept along carefully, the moonlight providing a little illumination through the windows. There didn't appear to be anyone in the main living area. Adams gave a quick flash of light to scan as they approached.

There was a mattress in the middle of the floor, stains covering the center of it. Forty-ounce beer bottles lined the edge of the entire room, but they were full of urine, not beer. They heard a squeaking noise from upstairs. Adams pointed up, and they made their way to the stairs and ascended, the rhythmic squeaking noise helping to cover any sounds from the worn-out slats on each step. As they cleared the landing, they saw a flickering light from the end of the hallway, probably a candle. More sounds assailed their ears the closer they got—carnal, vulgar sounds. Slurping, smacking, animalistic moaning. Adams just knew it was going to be disgusting, but there was no turning back now. He cleared the door frame, still using it for partial cover, light on high illuminating the whole room, gun up.

It was disgusting.

There were two guys and one girl, all on a box spring and mattress lying on the floor. The guys had their pants unzipped, but she was on her hands and knees, naked and sucking one off while the other took her from behind. The body odor alone was stifling, but Adams thought he smelled shit as well. His stomach lurched even as he said, "Police, get on the ground!" They all startled at once, both guys pulling out, hands reflexively rising in the air, palms out. They just stayed that way for a couple of seconds, all three staring at the light like deer on a roadway, their eyes hollow and feral, pupils tiny, the female's face sunken from too much drugs and not enough food. The whole thing was inhuman.

Another roaring command, "I said get on the fucking ground right now!" and instantly they all dropped, face down. "Get your hands out at your sides where I can see them, palms up!"

Adams called for backup then turned and smiled at Dexter. "I'll cover them; you cuff 'em."

"Fuck me" was all Dexter said then moved forward. He cuffed the two males first, put his gloves on, and moved them away from the female one at a time to pat them down. The smaller of the two had a twisted-up baggie with probably ten crack rocks inside of it. "We've got our dealer here," Dexter said. He checked the second, bigger guy and found a metal crack pipe inside his pocket, cocaine residue plainly visible inside. "And here's the hired muscle. Gets paid by the rock, I'd wager." The men said nothing. Dexter moved on to the female.

Adams heard him almost puke. "Urrrhh, urrrhh, urrrhh." Dexter turned away sharply and waited for his stomach to stop trying to reject its contents. "Fuck, Mark! It's the chick we saw outside. She's still got shit on her ass. Fuck me! You gross bitch!"

"All right, Dex. Check her clothes, then make her stand up and get dressed." Dex did it, but protested the whole time. "Mark, I swear to God, you get the next one like this. Hell, you should be doing this one. It was your bright idea. I could be in a warm car right now." He picked up the clothes and crushed the pockets carefully with his hands, asking the girl "You don't have any needles in here do ya? Nothing that's going to stick me?" Her voice was quiet, but Dexter made it out, "No, I don't shoot drugs; I just smoke and snort. I don't like needles." Dexter finished checking her clothes, then told her to stand up and get dressed. Once clothed, he cuffed her and made her sit down near the guys. There was another metal crack pipe sitting on top of her purse.

He touched it. It was still warm through the gloves. "All right, so they paid her first with a crack rock, and she smoked

it so screwing these guys could be a little more tolerable."
The girl tried to protest. "That ain't mine." Dexter just took
it in stride, unconcerned. "Honey, first off, I saw you carrying
that purse outside, two, it was with your clothes, and three,
that pipe damn sure didn't just jump up there. It's yours; I
don't care what you say. Besides, I can send it to the lab and
match it with your DNA." The girl just sat quietly and hung
her head.

Greer and Hicks arrived on the scene and came upstairs,
each taking one of the males back to Greer's car. Greer
pinched his nose the whole way.

Adam's brought the girl down and stuck her in Hicks' car
and retrieved some evidence bags. Dexter packaged the dope,
and they walked back to their vehicles.

At the station, each prisoner was placed in a different
cell. As Dexter closed the girl's cell door he told her, "And
for the love of God, use the sink and paper towels to clean
your ass, will ya please? That shit's gross." She had come
down from the high already. She didn't really care about it.
She just wanted another hit.

Adams looked through the cell door window. Her body
was bony, skin loose from rapid weight loss, her face gaunt,
eyes dark and baggy, lips blistered and fingers burned from
the pipe. Her hair was matted and tangled. She probably
hadn't showered in a week or more. She was dead inside
though still breathing, and she knew it. The only time her
heart came alive was when she hit the pipe. Everything else
was just a depressing hell. She didn't care anymore.

Dexter was washing his hands for the third time already
when Adams walked into the restroom to wash his own. But
you can't wash that kind of shit out of your mind's eye, he
told himself, no matter what you do. Once you've seen it, it's
with you for life.

JANUARY 6

Adams could not move. His limbs would not obey. It was as if an avalanche of darkness covered him and consumed all the space around him, smothering him. He tried to push, pull, flex, anything; but it was useless. Fear gripped him. He began breathing shallow and rapid. It was then he noticed a particularly heavy weight upon his chest. He could feel two distinct points of contact, large and oblong. His brain searched for a reference. "Feet?" He felt it now. Could visualize it. The weight more on the heels, but the toes were curling into his collar bones, their curved talons pressing painfully against his flesh. He struggled frantically to open his eyes, the only thing that might obey him, but not without a contest first. A sharp pain burned across the back of his neck, followed by a wetness pooling on his pillow. An eternity of helplessness stretched out, nearly strangled Adams in an ever-tightening cycle of panic. When he couldn't bear it any longer, he heard a long sigh, felt it breathe upon his face.

"Aaaaaaaahhhhhhh … that explains so much. Your ancestors walked with the shadows long ago and received a gift. It's in your blood."

Adams thought the voice was familiar yet deeper, rougher. Fear fueled his efforts, and he finally forced his eyelids open. A creature that was part man, part monster and shrouded in shadows leered above him, its index finger elongated by the curving claw it held up to its flickering forked tongue. Blood dripped down the length of the preternaturally keen nail … Adams' blood. Large eyes stared out from the darkness, amber orbs enveloping vertical slits of oblivion.

"Soooon" it hissed, drawing closer to Adams' face, "you will seeee …" What else it might have said Adams did not know. It was gone, and the darkness with it.

The face was seared into his retina, though. It was
Roger's drawing. It was Mr. Phailees.

His pillow felt saturated with sweat and his neck stung.
Adams wiped at the back of his neck and sat up, his eyes
simultaneously seeing the blood on his hand and the red stain
spread across the white pillow casing. He lost it for a while—
pacing, cussing, kicking, and throwing things before he finally sat and forced himself to breathe slowly. He broke
down and prayed to God for answers, the first time in years,
hoping this time He would answer.

10:35 p.m.

Adams signed on for his shift over his police crusier's
radio, a man on a mission, determined to find Mister Phailees.

After an hour of riding around the usual hangouts for
most of the city's criminally questionable citizens, Adams
decided to try a different location off the beaten path. He
drove to the back corner of the park where a lot of homeless
and older street thugs liked to hang out around a bonfire, especially on frigid nights like this. It was the spot the first
strange murder happened on Halloween, and Adams was
ready to bet money Phailees was responsible for both suspicious deaths. He showed up right around Halloween, as far
as Adams could recall.

With lights off, Adams drove the car slowly over the
grass to the back corner of the park, the bonfire a beacon of
blazing light guiding him in. On foot, he could see there were
only two men left sitting around the flames. One was a crazy-
ass old fella, named Buddy. Didn't like the police one lick.
Always spouting off about crazy stuff and government conspiracies. He was facing Adams as he approached, seated on
the other side of the fire. The other man appeared to be Mr.
Phailees, his back to Adams. Lastly, Adams spotted Phobos

lying at his master's feet, curled up in front of the fire pit, eyes fixed on Adams, silently watching.

Adams stepped out of the shadows, but before he could open his mouth, Mister Phailees spoke.

"Nice of you to join us on this blustery night, Officer Adams."

Buddy jerked his head up, saw Adams, and immediately got to his feet; his eyes locked in on the uniform, the badge, and the gun, anxious at the surprise. He faltered between running and pissing himself, but all that happened was a stuttering rant.

"You, you, you can't … snee sneak up on a man … like dat. Why, why you comin' 'round here with dem clothes and dat, dat, dat gun!? This is our space! You, you belong out there!" He pointed towards the city lights and began to pace back and forth before the fire. "Dis, dis is su suuupposed to be a safe place!"

Adams tried to deescalate Buddy's increasing agitation before it got ugly.

"Buddy, I'm sorry, I didn't know you were here. If I had known, I wouldn't have even come. But I'm not here to see you. I came to see this man right here. He and I need to talk. Do you mind if I sit by the fire to stay warm and just talk with him for a little bit? I promise I'll leave right afterwards."

Adams made sure to project body language that said he was not in charge here—slightly hunched posture, head partially bowed, and hands folded one inside the other against his upper chest to appear sincere in conceding to Buddy's judgment, while also keeping his hands far away from his gun so as not to appear threatening. He was deferring to Buddy's territorial claim and authority to make a binding decision. Adams knew it was easier to give a person a choice first rather than imposing his authority from the start.

Buddy looked unsure but felt empowered. He looked around at Mr. Phailees, then Adams, then back at Phailees.

"Dat true, man? You got buh bizness with dis officer?"

"Why yes, I do," Mr. Phailees replied, picking up on Adams' approach. "I do indeed. Would you be so kind as to let him stay a little while so we can speak?" Phailees reached in his pocket and with a flourish produced an unopened pack of cigarettes and a nice flip-top metal lighter. "I'll make it worth your while, Buddy. What do you say?"

Buddy almost reached out without thinking, checked himself, and looked around some more. He mulled it over for a few seconds before giving in to his craving. He stepped forward and took the proffered gift.

"Well ... since you, you both asked so ni ... nice ... I su ... suppose. Just for a little while ..."

Buddy sat down, lit a cigarette, then pulled out a little iPod and plugged his earphones in. Leaning back, he closed his eyes and drew the smoke inside his lungs, held it, and slowly blew it back out into the night sky.

Mr. Phailees gestured to Adams. "Have a seat, good sir. No need to stand."

"Don't mind if I do," Adams said, taking a seat not quite directly across from Mr. Phailees. Adams propped his elbows on his knees, hands folded but tense. Phobos eyed him cautiously, but without fear.

"So, Officer Adams, what would you like to ask me? I'm sure you didn't come here to roast marshmallows." Phailees' face wrinkled into a slightly mocking smirk.

Adams felt his stomach tremble as he remembered his sleep paralysis earlier that evening. He turned it into anger.

"Damn straight I didn't. First off, what the fuck were you doing in my house earlier today?"

"Is this on or off the record? And aren't you going to read me my Miranda Rights if you're going to interrogate me like this?" Phailees grinned wickedly.

"Don't fuck with me," Adams commanded, leaning forward. "I've got a fuck load of questions, and there's way too many dots that need to be connected. I need some fucking answers, and you're the man to hand me the marker and point the way. So, stop jerking me around, and tell me what you know."

"I'm flattered, Officer Adams, that you would value my poor, humble input on such matters." He smiled wryly then picked something up from beside his seat. A bag of marshmallows. Adams stared in disbelief.

"Seriously?" Adams could think of nothing else to say.

"What? A delicious winter treat. I find them quite tasty, plus ... I like to watch them burn occasionally." Phailees stuck a couple on a small metal rod and held them out over the fire. "Don't let me distract you, Officer Adams. Go ahead, ask your questions, but save the first for last."

Adams sighed then took a deep breath, grabbing a stick to prod the ashes as he started to speak; idle hands were an impossibility in his agitated state.

"Did you bite an old homeless guy last night? Name's Roger."

Phailees glared at him for just a fraction of a second before he chuckled and popped a marshmallow in his mouth. He pressed it around with his tongue, enjoying the texture and taste before swallowing.

"Aaahh. Delightful. I must say, Officer Adams I can think of far better things to sink my teeth into than an old homeless man."

"You didn't answer my question."

"I assure you, my intentions are not to hurt innocent people."

"Then why the hell did you bite Roger on the back of the neck?"

"Seriously, Officer Adams, what do you take me for— some crazy cannibal homeless man? Perhaps you think I'm a vampire or something edgy and charming like that? I certainly hope not. It's so cliché."

Adams pulled a folded-up piece of notepad paper from his shirt pocket and held it up for Mr. Phailees to see in the crackling firelight. The monstrosity Roger drew for him was clearly visible.

"Well, this is what Roger said you looked like just before you bit him. The man may be mentally disturbed, but I don't take him as the sort to have B horror movie hallucinations."

Mr. Phailees bristled at the subtle insult.

"Hmmm. B horror movie hallucinations, eh? I rather think it looks better than that, and quite a bit scarier."

"I agree. Especially after seeing it myself this evening. But your diversionary humor is not working. You obviously recognize what's in this picture. I can see it in your face. What the hell is this thing? Is it you or your dog?"

"There are secrets in this world you do not understand, Officer Adams. Secrets your mind is not prepared to comprehend … yet. All I can tell you now is I meant Roger no real harm. I do not hurt innocent people. It's not what I'm here to do."

"And just what is it you are here to do? That's what I'm really trying to figure out, because I know you are connected to all this weird shit that keeps happening lately. I just can't prove it all. Right here, roughly three months ago, a man was murdered and gnawed upon, supposedly by some dogs or something. That was when you showed up in town. Somewhere else, not too long ago, a drug dealer was murdered in similar fashion. I dreamed about that the night it happened. Dreamed I was part of a pack of wolves that chased him down, killed him, and devoured him! Ain't that some coincidental shit? Afterwards, two suicides with men who had been considered, up until then, to be sane, and there you were at the scene of them both. Weird-ass bite marks. The one on Chad Bigleby perfectly matches Roger's bite. I don't believe any of this is mere coincidence. So, why? Why are these things happening? Why are they all landing close to me? Why the dreams? I want to know fucking why?"

Adams tone grew edgier as his volume slowly increased. He finally looked up and stared into Mr. Phailees' eyes, refusing to look away.

"Humph. I must say, Officer Adams, you are rather astute and dogged. I tell you what, how about a story?"

"A fucking story?" Adams sat up straight, flabbergasted. "Are you kidding me?"

"All of life is a story, my friend, a stage on which we each play our role. So, indulge me, and perhaps my story may answer your questions. Is that fair?"

"Fine. Just don't waste my time."

"Fair enough. Let us begin then. Once upon a time, my great-great-grandfather was a lawman on the frontier—Wild West and all that—before the legal system really got stabilized and legislated into its nice, cookie-cutter roles with its boundaries on what one could and couldn't do. He worked in a fairly large town that was a bit isolated, up in the Rocky Mountains. Took a week or more to get to the nearest community before the railroad made its way to them. People took care of their own problems, but they wanted to be civilized, so they had the lawman. Justice was swift and sure then. My grandfather had a knack, like you, for knowing when people were lying to him. He had a nose for gross sin, could smell it on a man. Had eyes that demanded the truth, cut a man's soul to the quick, and spilt his secrets."

Phailees popped another marshmallow in his mouth, mashed the brown crust against the roof, and felt the sweet center slide out en masse and slip right down his throat.

"There are certain people in this world, certain levels of wickedness that cannot be tolerated, cannot be forgiven, at least not before they are punished … severely. Mercy is fine, when it doesn't allow the sickness to incubate and multiply. That's the problem we have today. Everyone thinks people are entitled to mercy. They think that just because they try to be good in other areas, it excuses their chosen sins. They believe people deserve a free pass, so to say, but if you give them that pass their wickedness is allowed to fester, and they spread their disease to their offspring and to society at large. Well, in my grandfather's day, they didn't put up with that. The Lord might forgive your soul, but my grandfather made sure you never hurt anyone in the realm of the living again. Nobody has the stomach anymore, though, to do what is necessary. Nobody but those of my kind, and some of yours. We're our own breed.

"Takes a special kind of person to deliver justice. Someone who doesn't mind getting their hands dirty. Someone who can enjoy their work, most of the time, and sees the necessity of it. A certain type of moral conscience, convinced of the right in what they do even though they may be damned for what they do and who they are, always risking getting infected by what they see and touch. My granddaddy knew what had to be done to uphold justice, to enforce the plumb line in this fucked-up world. The hearts of men are deceptively wicked and hungry to glut their desires, even at the cost of abusing their fellow man. But whether a man be wicked or not, wrong is wrong, and it must be avenged. Men think, because they're weak, they can excuse their degeneracy. They prefer to minimize the evil of their actions, redefine the standards of immorality, and then hope their sins will fade with time ... but they don't, and Phobos and I ..." Phailees patted the dog's head as he spoke, "we're here to make them pay, just like you made that fat pedophile bastard pay."

"Not like me," Adams interrupted. "That was self-defense."

"Oh, Officer Adams, let's not quibble over professional idiosyncrasies, methods, manners, labels, and what have you." Phailees' hand fluttered past his head as if the whole concept was so ephemeral, it was already dissipating on the night air.

"Forgiveness isn't in our job descriptions. Unflinching justice in the face of viral corruption, that's our task. We know what men will do to one another to get what they want, and it is appalling. Granddaddy knew it was a filthy job watching man's atrocities, seeing their wretched, corpulent souls. He knew you had to be committed to the cause, willing to sacrifice your soul to do the hard things. And he did it, freely, not always gladly, not always proud of what he was, proud of the world he made, a world where men pay for what they do. He held his head high, and I do too."

"But there are limits to what is allowable," Adams butted in again. "I'm not judge, jury, and executioner! I can't just punish criminals all on my own. We have a justice system, not a bunch of sanctioned vigilantes!"

"Yes, I know, and how's that working out for you? Your people so like to maintain a sense of order, they're willing to sacrifice the rights of the victim, willing to let hardened criminals go free on minor technicalities even when they know the bastards are guilty. They are so desperate to maintain a clear conscience that they doggedly refuse to believe in the righteousness of vengeance!"

"It's called ethics," Adams blurted out, "checks and balances, preventing the abuse of authority!"

"It's called weakness, ignorance, naivety, and above all, willful abdication of responsibility!"

"Responsibility? Responsibility to what?" Adams blurted out in confused contention.

"Why, to heed the call of those who have suffered wrongly and avenge them and secure the safety of their fellow man; men and women who are too vulnerable to secure their own freedom from fear. That is your duty, and you know it!" An accusing bony finger jabbed in Adams' direction, its critical authority apparent to him even through the flames.

"But your 'system'," Phailees continued, a tone of disgust filling his mouth as he said the word, "it binds your hands with a multitude of rules and limitations and your conscience with myths of morality and guilt. These notions should not apply to those like us. We who are weighed down with the burden of trudging through the waste of man's daily depravities cannot allow these meaningless concepts to hold us back. We have a responsibility to secure justice for the victimized and bring punishment to the perpetrators of heinous violations committed against their fellow mankind."

He paused for a moment to see if Adams might jump in again, but he was silent. Phailees pushed on.

"Thankfully, some of your fellow men in blue recognize the truth I speak of and pursue justice as far as possible, without getting caught. They are committed to the cause of real justice."

"Yeah, but the only way they can sleep at night is to lie to themselves about the morality of what they do."

"The weakness of a human conscience," Phailees quipped, "but at least they have braved the path of upholding their oath to protect and serve and pursue justice."

"Or," Adams raised his voice, unconsciously trying to assert his own moral authority in the debate, "They're just arrogant enough to think they have the right to make their own rules. They think they are better and above everyone else!" Adams contempt for the latter category was obviously riddled with ambiguity, though he would deny it ardently if pressed.

"Ah! The confident sign of greatness—you must first believe before you can achieve." Phailees chuckled at his own little joke.

"You cannot second guess the righteousness of what you do, Officer Adams. I know from whence my authority comes. I know what I am allowed to do, despite what the laws of men may think. I am beyond regrets. I know my role, my position. I know what I am and what I'm designed to do. I know how to enjoy my job, and I know how to find relief when it all gets overwhelming at times."

"Hah," escaped Adams lips before he could seal the door.

Phailees cocked his head, lips pressed together tightly, and leaned forward slightly.

"What do you mean 'hah'?"

Adams could see the perceived offense clearly displayed. Something deep within his psyche, perhaps forgotten childhood fears, told him to tread lightly.

"I'm sorry, no disrespect intended, but if you are so confident in your identity and authority, then what could possibly overwhelm you?"

Phailees' features settled faintly as he spoke, but Adams still felt like a hunter caught unprepared by something more dangerous than what he was originally stalking.

"Why, Officer Adams, it's the taste of hubris, the stench of arrogance, the nails of entitlement constantly clawing at the blackboard of reality, the incessant madness, no, the absolutely indefatigable, narcissistic insanity driving mankind to always place himself at the center, to think so highly of himself when he is worth so, so very little. Sometimes it's more than I can bear."

Phailees feigned fainting, placing the back of his hand to his forehead and acting as if he might swoon. Adams smirked at the drama.

"And just what do you do when you're down? Hmm?"

"That's when I remind myself how far above the ants I sit. I remember my power and my position; that I am like unto the Assyrians and the Romans. I am a rod of affliction, sent forth to punish the people who are getting away with all their hidden sins. And then I go forth and do what I was made to do … and I take great joy in it." Phailees' eyes seemed to glow as he spoke the last phrase, but it could have just been a reflection of the fire.

Adams face was a question mark. "And just how do you punish people?"

"My but your modern blinders hide so much from your eyes. You will see when you are ready, but what you need to know right now is that your justice system is unaware and impotent, incapable of meaningful action and impact. But you, Officer Adams, in you there is something very special waking up deep inside, something which sees the concealed vices, the lies, the secret crimes men and women heinously commit against one another. You see the monsters that some men are, truly see, not just some abstract moral concept, but the essence and flesh, and it is deeply disturbing … as it should be to you."

Adams remained puzzled, but his heart felt the tug of temptation.

"How?" The simple but powerful question fled his heart first and then his dry lips.

"You can be free, Officer Adams, if you want it bad enough. I think you will have to make a choice … sooner rather than later, I believe. Will you be the hand of justice, at all costs, or not? Be ready to face the beast, the beast in you and the beast beneath your neighbors' skin, perpetuating their transgressions against one another. But don't worry yourself with Phobos and me. We are not your concern. We are beyond your justice system. There is nothing you can do to us, but maybe interfere in some ultimately insignificant way."

Phailees patted Phobos' head with one hand as he popped another marshmallow in his mouth with the other. Adams stared rather dumbly across the flames into Phailees' face, searching for something not normal, some indicator of 'otherness' to support his conclusions. It was there, visible but elusive, too sly to be isolated. It occurred to Adams right then perhaps he could not put his finger on it because Mr. Phailees was entirely "other" by nature, but the thought was fleeting, too radical to hold onto.

"That's some story," Adams commented after a long silence, trying not to sound as baffled as he felt. "Somehow, I don't think you were talking about your actual granddaddy. Even so, I'm not sure how to take it all."

"You are quite perceptive and suspicious, but I assure you, Officer Adams, the time for games is nearly over. I sense your uniqueness and would rather help you than hinder you in your professional and personal development."

"Well then, last question: is this you?" Adams held up the picture again.

Phailees grinned and slapped his knee. "I tell you Phobos, he's a dogged lawman, this one!" Phailees paused for a moment as he stared Adams in the eye.

"Yes, Officer Adams, that is one version of me, one way I present myself to the sons of men, when I wish to provoke extraordinary fear … and for when punishment is due. I'm sure that comes as a shock to you, but surely, you know by now that not all things are 'easily categorized or referenced', are they?"

Adams was caught off guard by Phailees unexplainable knowledge, but pressed on.

"What were you doing in my house earlier today then?"

"Simple. Getting answers. I had to taste your blood. The answers are always in the blood."

Adams opened his mouth to speak, but Phailees cut him off, holding up a hand.

"That's all I can say about that for right now."

Adams stared at him, dumbfounded but determined. He shifted gears and blurted out more interrogatives.

"Did you kill the man here a couple of months ago? Did you kill Rashid Whitman, the drug dealer, and Poo-Dick?"

"I'm afraid you said your last question was the 'last' question, Officer Adams. However, I will say this, the man who died here and Poo-Dick, both, were rapists many times over who never fully paid for all their crimes against the young and innocent ones who trusted them at some point, and Mr. Whitman, as you well know, was a blight upon this community and much deserving of what came his way. As to the manner in which they perished, well, you have the picture and you have your dreams. You figure it out."

Phailees' smile was broad and smug and high above the ethical judgments of men. Adams was at a loss. Phailees was right; he was above man's justice system. There was nothing

Adams could do to prosecute him, no way to prove anything, except maybe he was insane.

"Well, I guess that's all I can ask for given the circumstances, though I don't trust you anymore than I did before."

"I would expect nothing less," Phailees said cheerfully.

Adam's paused in thought for a moment before speaking again.

"And Chad Bigleby? What about him?"

"Oh, Officer Adams, Chad Bigleby is far from innocent."

"How do you know?"

Phailees chuckled lightly. "I see," he said, gesturing towards his two eyes with his index and middle finger. "Remember? And so do you. Trust your gut instincts. You've known it from the beginning. He's guilty."

"What are you going to do to him?" Adams inquired.

"Oh, he will suffer. We're making sure of that even now. But you, Officer Adams, you must catch him."

"I can't prove it, though," Adams blurted out in frustration.

"Patience. Soon. Soon the evidence will reveal itself. Keep searching."

Adams stood and stretched. "My brain is on overload. I suppose I should go and process all this." He shook his head and continued, his voice dejected and frustrated. "It's just too much for a normal man to comprehend and believe."

"But you are not normal and you are awakening to your potential. It will make sense … soon."

"I suppose you don't want to elaborate on that yet, do you?" His heart was incapable of struggling further … for anything.

Phailees smiled. "Not particularly. You must wait until you are ready. Worry not, you are almost there. Now, enough of that," Phailees dismissed Adams' dreadful feelings. "Come, good sir. Have a marshmallow before you leave. A sign of generosity amongst coworkers. Hmm?"

Adams looked at him for a few seconds then quietly extended his hand, slipped one off the wire rod, and popped it in his mouth, rolled it around, eyes closed, then swallowed it smoothly, the heat bleeding out into his torso, warming him from the inside.

"Man, it has been awhile since I had one of those. That was good. Thank you."

Adams turned and walked away, his mind a humming bird caught in a blizzard.

Phailees plucked another marshmallow off the hot metal and fed it to Phobos, his chops slapping twice before trying to swallow the sticky sweetness. The last marshmallow Phailees held over the fire, watching it turn brown then catch fire and burn slowly to a smoking black crisp.

JANUARY 7

The phone rang at Detective Andrews' desk around 11:00 a.m. He finished keying in something and picked it up.

"Detective Andrews."

It was Dispatch.

"Hey, Matt, I just got a call, in reference to the Annie O'Reilley case Officer Adams has been working. Another jurisdiction recovered her vehicle about an hour from here. Nobody in the car but they have a white male in custody. They want to know if we're going to send someone."

"Absolutely. Tell them I'm on my way."

Andrews grabbed his folder and camera and headed out.

By lunch, Chad was ready to get out of the office, so he walked down a few blocks to a little café called the Java Hut.

He ordered a sandwich and espresso. The young girl at the counter was a bit weathered and robotically nice. She took his order, his money, then offered a very precise and measured smile, but only for a moment, before turning to get his order.

Chad sat and sipped his coffee, looking over the crowded café, lost in people watching. A cop sat across from a gorgeous blonde-haired woman. A large, bald-headed black male with numerous tattoos sat alone staring at the cop while he ate his sandwich. Chad thought they looked like prison or gang tattoos. A dumpy, middle-aged white male with a laptop sat camped out, typing away, his wireless connection clearly visible.

It was then Chad's eyes fell upon an older gentleman, seated directly across from him. He wore a priest's collar and looked very familiar. Chad tried not to stare, but upon look-ing back, realized the man was looking at him with the same question in his eyes. They looked at each other for a few sec-onds without saying anything, their minds working to make the connection. The man spoke first.

"Chad, right? Chad Bigleby?"

"Yes," said Chad, frustrated he still couldn't place the man.

He stood and walked over to Chad's table.

"It's good to see you again. How's Samantha? It's been what, seven years since I married the two of you?"

The cold storage locks finally clicked open for Chad, most of the memories coming back.

"Mind if I have a seat?"

"No. Go right ahead, Father."

"Don't call me Father, Chad. The elders will snatch my collar. I'm Episcopalian, not some papist infidel." The man smiled jokingly and formally introduced himself, extending his hand to Chad.

"Pastor Joseph McConnell."

Chad laughed. "Sorry, my denominational discernment is a bit weak. Not much of a church going man."

"Sorry to hear that … of course. So, seven years, right?"

"Yeah … seven years. You're good."

"And how's Samantha doing?"

"Sam's all right," he said. "Struggles with depression a bit. Could be worse."

"How about the two of you? Relationship still good?"

Pastor McConnell was fairly direct, but managed to carry such a tone and posture that one felt disarmingly comfortable. He sat sipping his coffee, not saying anything, just letting si-lence fill the void.

"Actually, it's very rocky right now. Gotta say, I don't know how much longer it will last."

Damn, thought Chad, this must be some Jedi-super-pas-tor trick they teach in seminary to get people to talk. Chad found himself opening up and saying things he wouldn't normally have divulged.

"I'm sorry to hear that. How are you doing with everything? A lot of the time we get so wrapped up in the problem we fail to see how it's really impacting us."

"I was doing all right until recently. But I guess it's affecting me more than I thought. I've been frustrated and anxious, not to mention sick."

Chad was comfortable with Pastor McConnell, but the lawyer in him was still measuring how much detail he let go and just what level of truth he would mix with metaphor.

"Well, one thing I've learned in my time, Chad, and this I know to be true, in relationships it's almost never a one-way street. Both parties are wrong in some way, often one more than the other, but both bear a burden of injustice."

Chad nodded, not quite acknowledging agreement and definitely not indicating any sense of guilt. The proposal of guilt made him instantly guarded. Pastor McConnell studied Chad's face and body language.

"Look, Chad, I can see there is some apprehension as far as admitting wrong. That's natural. To admit wrong means we have to look inside and see the dark places. It also means we must assume responsibility for the state of affairs, and who wants to do that? Often, people don't want to admit fault, don't want to admit their own part in the tragic play they are stuck in, simply because it hurts too much to change. I would suggest you consider your part and not focus too much on Samantha's. There is always a place for redemption if one is willing to confess and turn and do what is right. The hardest part is squaring with who we are and facing the consequences when exposed."

Pastor McConnell sat silently sipping his coffee, the Jedi-pastor trick working hard on Chad, but Chad did not want to confess. He did not want to face any consequences, and in fact, he refused to even admit fault. He had a million arguments to rationalize who he was and the choices he had made.

Even if, deep inside, he knew he was guilty, his conscious would never know it. The lies were too big and the truth too dangerous.

"I think I've already made my choice, and she has too. It's just a matter of time. We're both miserable.

"Well, Chad, here's my card. If there's anything I can help you with or you just want to talk, I'm in the area and available. I hope you reconsider your covenant with Samantha. You really were a cute couple."

With that, he emptied his coffee and stood up to go.

"God Bless. I'll see you around." He nodded politely, turned, and walked out the door.

Chad watched Pastor McConnell go and the further he got, the darker the room seemed to get, until the door shut, and all the light in the world seemed to leave with him.

Reality shifted. In mere moments darkness crept in, filling space of every kind; shadows consumed walls, tables, people, the print of the newspaper left behind by Pastor McConnell. It was pervasive, permeating all Chad could see, its presence malicious and oppressive. Chad's stomach dropped out, a lump catching in his throat as the darkness crawled inside him with one breath. His torso constricted, an elephant seemingly sitting on his chest. His heart ran wildly, palpitating in broken rhythms, anxiety devouring rational thought, until at last his vision faded into black oblivion, the light finally digested by the night.

It seemed an eternity before the suffocating ended and he breathed again, his vision slowly returning but changed, as if he suddenly evolved, adapting to a previously unseen and infernal habitat. A curtain had been lifted. The backstage workings driving this play of the damned now exposed to him.

He looked out the window. All things were made new. The air was full of ashen currents, small wispy eddies moving where they willed. There was a slight ambient glow, like moonlight tainted by blood and sulfur, allowing visual distinction of one thing from another. The darkness was alive,

morphing, swelling, swirling—the shadows, portals to unknown places. He could see twisted forms contorting their
way through the darkness, as well as grisly, impish, creeping
things of every kind. Some were spindly-limbed with pug-
nosed faces, bulging eyes, and crooked razor teeth, while others were squat and blind with huge nostrils flaring as they
sniffed their way about, large claws dragging ape-like from
fat, disproportionately long arms. Some were cautious stalk-
ers, peeking out from the shadows, disappearing and reap-
pearing somewhere else, searching, stalking. For what,
Chad's imagination dared not guess. Other larger beings
simply trudged along, hunched and oblivious, obviously
higher on the food chain and unconcerned as they plodded
toward some unfathomable destination.

The world was worn and weathered; nothing seemed
new. Everything seemed to smolder in some slight way.
Worst of all was the sky. It appeared as if someone formed
huge cut stones from pitch and red clay and laid a firmament
to trap everyone beneath the heavens then lit it on fire. It bled
prophetic declarations of judgment with every ounce of light
emanating from the inferno, a labyrinth of black smoke
snaking between the flickering flames.

Chad sat in horrific awe, his mind temporarily loosed of
sanity, overcome and paralyzed by events. Then he looked
back inside the café, and it only got worse.

The people were more than he could take.

Chad's eyes fell first on the cop and the blonde-haired
woman. The man's face was apish and unrestrained, his body
bulky and powerful, his eyes calculating, his authority evident in his posture, his willingness to abuse it for personal
gain equally obvious in his eyes. They screamed greed and
lust. His left hand, the one with the gold band, slid under the
table, then slid further up the lady's inner thigh. She wore no
such band on her hand, and moaned lightly. She disgusted
Chad. Her flesh was bruised and marred, deteriorating. Boils
covered her arms and uncovered thighs, some gross sickness

festering within. Her face was haggard, her mouth perverse, and her eyes lewd and lecherous. She sweated promiscuousness from every pore, and Chad somehow knew she was a disease-ridden whore, addicted to increasingly deviant sexual acts, degrading and unspeakable amongst common folk … and the cop liked it, was willing to pay for it.

Chad looked away and noticed the bald, black male staring at the cop, his rage barely manageable. Everything in his bestial visage screamed deadly intentions toward the officer, sitting unaware. He seethed beneath the weight of injustice he suffered from this same cop the night before. He was trying to do right, but disrespect was the hardest offense for him to swallow. His daddy was uncaring and inhumane. His mother cussed at him like a dog. Neighborhood kids harassed him mercilessly, their words biting ridicule he could never forget. Then he joined the gangs, and all that changed. He had a gun and a short fuse, and he killed many a man for no more than a stray word that bore bare resemblance to insult. He served time for assaulting one police officer already, and he did not want to go back to prison. He restrained himself when this cop stopped him and put him down at gunpoint, cussing at him before finding out he was not the person they were looking for. Self-control was a bloody struggle. Only a matter of time before his idol of respect demanded vengeance, pride overwhelming self-preservation.

A large, white male walked in then, jeans and a white undershirt stretched tight over a swollen beer belly. His hair was long and oily, his face somehow smaller than his frame and weasel-like, and his skin pale and pungent with some cowardly sweat. He enjoyed beating his wife, a tiny woman of frail build and timid disposition, easily abused and intimidated into silent obedience. He was cocky but unsure, always looking over his shoulder, a skulking hyena scared to face a full-grown lion.

Chad's eyes caught a disturbing peripheral motion and were drawn to the dumpy, middle-aged man with his computer. His face was swollen and obese, his jowls sagging, a toothless gumline partially hidden by the enormous tongue snaking back and forth, in and out, parting and licking his lips. His eyes were inhumanly predatory, a voracious, cunning beast hidden within the weighty, seemingly unfit frame. He was hunting young girls and boys, chatting on the internet, his free hand beneath the table, the movements minimal but still discernible and disgusting in public.

Chad closed his eyes, and laid his head on the table. It was cool on his forehead, which now seemed incredibly feverish. He did not want to see such naked depths of depravity, the faces of evil peeking out from behind a neighbor's mask. It was too hideous to bear.

"Hey, mister. You okay?" The voice was professionally concerned, but had no personal investment one way or the other.

He opened his eyes and looked up. It was the cash register girl. Her eyes were sunken but jittery, cheeks gaunt, her frame emaciated, the skin sallow and barely hugging her bones; what little attraction she had before gone. She was a masochist, addicted to pain; numerous cuttings, cigarette burns, and extremely rough sex. Her life was so horribly out of her own hands and depressing it was the only way she felt the slightest thrill of living or slim control over her day-to-day fate.

Chad was repulsed. He stood quickly and ran outside without saying a word, but there was no escape. Everywhere he looked he saw the hideous truth of cannibal beasts driven by wicked, self-consumed hearts, some hopelessly lost, others defiant and denying their own sin, righteous in their own eyes. And amongst them walked darkling creatures: whispering, hunting, feeding, but always stalking some sort of prey, at times even each other. Chad ran as best he could, his calf throbbing now. He tried not to think about all the dreadful things he saw on his way back to the office, a five-block gauntlet designed to unhinge him. Homeless people, corporate execs, taxi drivers, hookers and their Johns, joggers, all hiding some secret identity: cheating housewives, adulterous men, pedophiles, abusers, liars, thieves, and murderers. So many normal looking people hiding evil behind a smile. It was indescribably unsettling. The world had shifted and suddenly the ground beneath his feet was a foreign land, a "Twilight Zone" where the laws of nature and matter were no longer the same.

Chad shook uncontrollably, trying to get his hand in his pocket and retrieve his keys. He jerked and trembled spasmodically, until at last his hand slid in and grabbed the jangling mass. He managed to secure the key fob in his hand and hit unlock, but only after first pushing the panic button and scrambling to turn off the wailing siren. He got in the car, caught a vague peripheral glimpse of something hideous in the mirror, and whirled to look in the back seat. Nothing was there. He could not recall exactly what it looked like, and he did not want to. He closed his eyes and, on feel alone, fumbled and turned down all his mirrors, his breathing shallow and fast, bordering on hyperventilation.

He did not want to see himself at all.

He turned the key and his Audi purred until he backed up and slapped it in drive and stomped the gas. The vehicle was a white blur as he popped a Haldol and Valium and headed out of the city. The world was still changed, but there were less people to look at. He found a parking spot in the edge of a field he used as a teenage boy when dating in high school, and there he sat, eyes closed, breathing intentionally slow until sleep overtook him.

Amy walked into the Java Hut café about two minutes after Adams sat down at a corner table across the room from the door, neatly positioned near the emergency exit on one side and the counter on the other. He stood and greeted her.

"You ready to order?"

"Sure."

They stood in line, placed orders, and sat back down to wait.

"Well," said Adams, taking the lead. "I have some wonderful news."

"Really? What's that?" She could tell there was a punch line coming by the devilish grin he was trying to hold back.

"Well, a couple weeks ago, while following up on a missing person case at The Body Shop,"

"The Body Shop?" Amy cut him off.

"Yes, The Body Shop."

"A couple of weeks ago? Before I let you sleep at my place?"

"Yes."

"And this is the first I'm hearing of it?"

"Yes. I mean, you know, I've had a lot going on."

"Ah-parent-ly." Amy rolled her head with each syllable.

"Come now, don't be rude." Adams flashed a coy smile. "Let me finish."

Amy threw her hands up, "Ok. Go ahead."

"So, I'm at The Body Shop following up on this case, and some big neo-Nazi thug grabs one of the dancers, the hottest dancer I've ever seen, mind you, and proceeds to pull her into his lap and not let go. The bouncer jumps up and tries to intervene but catches a headbutt for his trouble, right in the nose. So I'm moving fast to get over there, 'cause now it's my problem. The big guy breaks a beer bottle and lunges at the bouncer. I snatch him off his feet by his head, almost kill him on the takedown—the way he lands—cuff him, stuff him, and drag him out of there on a stretcher."

"And that's the good news?" She shook her head subtly, as if to say, 'that's it?'

Adams held his hand up, palm out. "That's not all, Rude-Amy. As a matter of fact, the Lap Dancer from the Gods, with mystical skills no mere mortal woman could ere possess was so smitten with my wicked demi-god combat skills and rugged looks she nearly threw herself at my feet and wrapped herself around my legs, like a Frank Frazetta Conan cover, all the while looking at me with her heavenly eyes and offering me, quote unquote 'the best lap dance she would ever give in her life' followed by a blazing night of glorious, unbidden wild sex that would likely consume us both in ecstasy multiple times before the sun dawned again and she had to return to the heavens."

Amy's face grew more and more shocked, a bit jealous, and frightened. "Oh my!" she said nervously. "And that's the good news, huh?"

"Well, if you were a guy, it sure would be good news to you, BUT!" He held up one finger. "But, I am no mere mortal man, and as such, my explanation can only be that God is real and loves me very much, both for the offer and for empowering me to say no ... because I want to make us work." He pointed to himself and then opened his hands palm up to include the two of them as he finished his story.

Amy's gut relaxed. "Wow. You are just ate up with pride, huh?"

"Damn right. Cause if I don't feel proud, I'm gonna cry. So, on that note, if we're not getting anywhere, just let me know so I can go and enjoy what any man would give his right testicle for."

Amy laughed. How could she not, knowing what she had done in worse times and what she had been tempted to do just days ago. Temptation was real, a real beast. It was like a pit bull that went for the throat and would not let go, and for Adams to have turned something like that down when he hadn't had sex in four months—probably hadn't had great sex in well over two years or more, that was an accomplishment. It said a lot about his conviction and commitment.

Amy leaned forward and kissed him on the cheek.

"I am impressed, I must say. And I think I'm turned on right now by your whole demi-god charm or something, because I'm not sure any other man could have told that with a fairly straight face to his woman and not got his head exploded by eyeball death rays or something. You're just gifted like that, I guess. Favored by God, eh?"

"You certainly can say that … all day long, if you like." Adams grinned big, like a dog showing his owner a new toy, waiting for more praise.

"Yes, you're a good boy." She ruffled his hair and patted his head, her voice kicking up to a high-pitched frenzy. "Yes, you are!"

Adams pushed her hand away and laughed as the clerk brought their food and drinks out and set it down. After a second, the girl looked at Adams and spoke.

"You're an officer, right?"

Adams stiffened, suddenly adopting a professional posture. "Yes. I am. What can I do for you?"

"Well, I just thought I'd tell you. The other officer left before I could say something. Anyway, just a few minutes before you came in, there was this really weird guy in here. I thought he was sick at first, he was sweating like crazy, like he had a fever or something, but I think he was seriously tweaked out, you know on Meth. He looked at me like I was a monster or something. I've seen people have some crazy hallucinations on that stuff, looked like he was on a super bad trip, ya know? Ran out of here in a hurry. I just thought I'd tell you."

"What'd the guy look like?"

"Oh, he's real handsome. I see him in here a lot. Fit, early thirties, well dressed, clean cut, slightly tan with dark hair. Works for one of the lawyer firms nearby."

"Really?" Adams' interest piqued, but Amy piped up.

"Did he fall asleep?"

"I'm not sure. He laid his head down, but I can't say whether he fell asleep or not. But he sure did wig out after the pastor guy he was talking to walked out."

"Well, thank you for the heads up. I think I might know who you're talking about. I'll text one of my buddies working today."

"Ok. Thanks." The girl was melancholy and matter of fact in everything she said and did, turning away to trudge back behind the counter.

"Well, that's interesting," Adams said.

"Yeah, sounds like that guy Chad you brought in with the night terrors. He just got released a couple of days ago. Wonder if he's starting to freak out again?"

"Don't know, but I don't trust that guy one lick. I think he killed that missing girl, Annie. I just can't prove it … yet."

"Wow. A killer huh? Great. Wish I'd known that when we were working around him the other night."

"Well, you know how the system is, 'innocent until proven guilty.' Civil rights and all that. I believe in rights and freedom, but sometimes it lets the guilty go. What then? Who punishes the guilty who have gone free?"

"God, I suppose," said Amy, sipping her coffee.

"I don't know if I can wait for God to do His thing. Besides, the way I see Romans 13:1-5, law enforcement was established by God to be avengers of wrath, commending those who do good and punishing those who do wrong. Maybe he wants us to take the initiative sometimes, to be the tool in His hand …"

Adams rattled on, blurting out his private thoughts far beyond what he suddenly felt was prudent. Amy was looking at him a little odd.

"Well, I think we all have thoughts about being judge, jury, and executioner at certain points in our lives. I guess I'm just invested in this case. We don't have a body yet; I just have that gut feeling telling me she's dead, and he's the one who did it, but there's not enough evidence to pursue it. It's just frustrating."

"I can understand that," Amy said. "But enough of it. Let's talk about us. I know we can't fix everything overnight, but we can start at the beginning. I've been thinking hard, and I know I've been in the wrong in a lot of ways that I hadn't even thought about before. I try to justify my actions all the time, and I need to own my part in our problems. So, I'm sorry for what I've done to hurt you and what I haven't done to ease your pain in the middle of all our struggles. I'm sorry I haven't been there for you; I haven't been the wife you needed … but … I want to be. I want us to love one another again, passionately, deeply, and intimately. And I want us to be best friends again. I love you, Mark."

Amy's eyes teared up as she finished speaking. Adams grabbed her hand and held it.

"I love you too, Amy. I've been a fool. I disconnected from you and resented you, and I wasn't there to support you and love you like I should. I'm sorry for not being the husband you needed. I'm sorry, and I hope I can change and be better to you. I hope we can heal and forgive and grow stronger and closer."

He sat still, just holding her hand and looking into her eyes. A thought shot through his mind and he tried not to smile, but Amy caught the fleeting mischief dancing behind his eyes—the windows of his soul.

"What's so funny?" she asked, a grin spreading across her face.

"Nothing …" Adams was embarrassed; he failed to hide the random thought.

"Oh no! No holding back. Out with it!"

"Ok. I just had a passing thought … that … uh … I hope you desperately want to have wild, passionate make-up sex with me sometime really, really soon." He finished speaking and immediately grabbed his coffee and sipped to cover his face. Amy laughed hard.

"Oh my! Yes, there are always priorities. I'll have to see when I can work that one in to our busy schedule. Of course, if you can't wait that long, I hear there's this phenomenal dancer at The Body Shop that would love to bear your children or something." Amy grinned big and sipped her coffee.

"Shots fired! Touché! God, you are so wrong sometimes. Just so freaking wrong."

They sat and talked for an hour, hammering out things and feeling more hopeful for their future. Amy hugged Adams long and hard and gave him a long, soft kiss on the lips before they parted ways, both of their steps light and buoyant.

Adams didn't see Amy bump into a tall man in a white suit with olive skin and perfect posture. Didn't notice the man touch her arm apologetically and mumble some foreign words ... then smile and walk away.

Chad woke around 4:00 p.m. Everything was normal again.

He quickly drove directly to the hospital and saw Dr. Danner.

Chad explained how the world changed after Pastor McConnell left, but withheld the nasty details on specific people beyond saying they looked sick or monstrous. Dr. Danner sat quietly, listening intently without judgment the entire time, and then he spoke.

"Darkness can represent many things. It could indicate a desire to hide one's own actions from the sight of others. It could be fear of the unknown, or fear of specific suspected threats that have, as yet, not fully shown themselves. Or it could be a combination of different possibilities. It's hard to say when the individual will not divulge all the pertinent details. As a doctor, I can't connect the dots if I don't know about the dots to begin with. I told you to consider the sources of stress and conflict that are contributing to your emotional and mental turmoil right now. I can only help you so much with so little information to go on."

Chad sat quietly, weighing just what he could say without telling the doctor exactly what he had done.

"All right, doc, here it goes. First, I've been cheating on my wife for a long time, recently with two different women. Our relationship sucks, and the sex is almost nonexistent most of the time. Second, I blackmailed a fellow employee recently to get his position. I don't really think I'm that bothered by this one, though; he's an underhanded asshole. Third, I had a girl that I was considering leaving Sam for, and it fell through after a huge argument on the day before I got bit by that weird dog. She just didn't have the same ideas for our future that I did."

Dr. Danner finished scribbling down the details and looked up.

"Thank you for sharing this with me Chad. It's important to identify areas like these; they help point us to underlying issues that the body is responding to through the night terrors you have experienced and now day terrors. Though, I must say, the duration and intensity of these waking nightmares you have described is incredible, rather unheard of, even. I'm not sure how to really categorize it."

"Gee. Great."

"One more thing before we discuss our options. I have to ask you, are you feeling suicidal? Do you want to hurt yourself in any way, whether out of anger, depression, or simple desperation to end the terrors?"

"No, doc. Not at all. I don't go down easy for nothing. You don't have to worry about me killing myself. It's just not an option in my philosophy right now."

"Ok. That's good. So, you can take the Haldol consistently throughout the day, as directed, instead of just at night, and the Valium can be taken when things get really bad. Just don't exceed the prescribed dosages. We'll schedule an additional MRI of the brain and a more in-depth blood panel. I also want you to go to a psychotherapist colleague of mine, Dr. Bon'Devant. He specializes in both 'brief' and 'systemic' methods of therapy. I think he might help you get to the heart of your situation and find a way to quickly deal with things and move on with a normal life."

"Sounds like a plan, doc. Thanks."

Chad got up, shook his hand, and left.

He got in his car and looked at the clock. It was 5:30 p.m.

"Fuck this," he said out loud. He put the vehicle in drive and headed for Emily's place, arriving in record time.

When the door opened, he embraced Emily and held her tight for a long time in the doorway before Robbie came out, and Chad scooped him up for a group hug.

After dinner, Chad played cards with Robbie for a while, relishing the time. As Robbie began to wind down, they put on a cartoon movie. Chad and Emily curled up on the couch and Robbie stretched out on the floor where he fell asleep in no time. It was only eight o'clock, but he got tired easily and often as of late.

Emily leaned into Chad and whispered in his ear. "Come on." She gave his arm a slight tug, and he followed. They held hands, and she led him through the bedroom door, closing and locking it behind them. Chad kicked his shoes off and laid back on the bed. Emily crawled up next to him, slid her hand around his head, lifted it, and laid it on her stomach, where she began to run her fingers through his hair in gentle, rhythmic strokes.

"Anything you want to talk about?" Her tone was full of warmth and genuine concern, full of love.

"I don't know, Em. I don't want you to think I'm crazy."

"I won't judge. Promise."

"Do you believe in anything supernatural? Angels … demons?"

"Yes. I do. I believe in God, the Devil, and their servants. I believe in ghosts too. I think I'm pretty open minded on this kind of stuff." Emily smiled slightly, proud of herself.

"Well, I've never put much stock in it till this last week. There's a lot of things happening that I can't explain. Either I'm going crazy, or I'm seeing demons or something like that."

"Wow." Emily was taken aback. "What happened? How did it start?"

"Well, you remember right after Thanksgiving when I got attacked by that dog, right?"

Emily nodded in the affirmative.

"It was some weird, old homeless guy and his dog, but then ... I could have sworn the homeless guy transformed into a suave middle-aged guy in a white suit."

Emily's head leaned back a couple of inches, instinctively disturbed by such an assertion coming from the mouth of a man she knew to be all too rational to say such a thing.

"Either way, homeless or well dressed, the dog didn't seem quite like a dog, even though it looked like one. The doctor said the bite looked just like a snake bite and it seemed to inflame like venom had been injected, but I know it was a dog. Anyway, days later I had the first night terror. It was a horrific dream. I mean fucking hideous. Then in the hospital, I remember the homeless man and his dog coming to me, holding me down. The man grew huge fangs like a snake, but his face became like something between a wolf and a snake. It bit me, drained something from me, and put it in a flask. He told me I was his now. I thought it was a dream, but the next morning I felt the bite marks under my hairline, near the base of my skull. I didn't tell anyone."

Emily was shocked by it all, but ensnared by the possibility at the same time. She reached her hand around and gently fingered the area. She jumped like electricity shocked her when her fingertip touched one of the holes left behind.

"Oh my God! Fuck! Hold on, honey. Roll over. I'm gonna grab the flashlight."

She skittered off the bed and retrieved the mini-flashlight, then scrambled back up on the bed.

Chad began spilling more information.

"And earlier today I started seeing terrible things while I was awake. Wicked people who looked like horror movie ghouls or something, repulsive and detestable. It was like, I knew exactly what their choice sins were, their addictions … all the evil things that defined them. It was too much. I saw the doctor again before I came to see you. I just couldn't go home."

"That sounds absolutely awful! I'd think I was going crazy too. Ok, honey, let me take a look."

Emily bent over his head, parted the hair, and shined the light on where she had felt the bite mark.

"Holy shit, Chad! You're not crazy! There's two big holes back here like a snake bite, but they're about as far apart as a large dog's canine teeth would be or further. God! Fuck! This is freaking me out!"

Emily shook her free hand as if she might fling whatever it was away from them.

"Oh! We should compare. Where's the other bite? Your left calf, right?"

Chad nodded his head. Emily pulled his pants leg up and surveyed the wound, which was still red and inflamed. She gasped and held one hand to her mouth. Her speech was slow, cryptic, and full of dread at first.

"Chad … they're the same. Exactly the same, only the one on your leg is all angry looking, and the one on your head is clean. But, I'll be damned. They're the same type, and I've never seen anything like it."

Emily suddenly flopped over to the nightstand and rolled back with her smartphone.

"We've got to take a picture of these. Hold still." She clicked off a couple of pictures of each bite from different angles, made sure they were clear, and saved them.

She pulled Chad upright and wrapped her arms and legs around him, cradling his back against her chest.

"It's ok, honey; you're not crazy. You're not crazy …"

Chad breathed in and out in time with Emily's rocking back and forth for a few minutes, both of them silent.

"Ok, so I'm not crazy … but you know what, Em?"

"What?"

"I think that scares me even more. There really are monsters; and I've got two of them hunting me, in my sleep and in the real world."

Emily was silent for a long time and then she began to kiss his head and face.

"I don't know what to do, Chad, but tonight I can make you forget about it for a while, and you can stay with me as long as you want."

Chad sat and turned around to face her. They kissed, embraced, undressed each other, and slid under the covers to lose themselves in the pleasures of the flesh they both so enjoyed.

And then they fell asleep.

Detective Andrews was waiting for Adams when he entered the squad room.

"Mark! Glad you're here. I can brief you and get the hell home."

Adams shot back, "Good to see you too there, Matt," a hint of playful sarcasm dripping off his tongue.

"You get my message earlier today? They found O'Reilley's car."

"Shit! Really?" He pulled out his phone and checked it quickly. "Damn. There it is. Well, what's the lowdown?"

"All right, it was about two and a half hours north of here in downtown Colonial Heights. Some crackhead thug was driving it. I drove up there, processed the car, and interviewed him. He said he found it parked behind a Dollar General at a strip mall, backed in, no front plate, like it belonged to one of the store owners, keys were in it. The locals collared him for vehicle theft. I verified the story on the car with the manager at the Dollar General. Lady said it had been sitting there since last week. She didn't use the space and didn't bother calling it in. Said it disappeared day before yesterday. Timeline is right with the guy's story. So, I processed the car. Nothin'. Not a damn thing to go on. No body. No blood. No damage of any kind. Nothing suspicious. But I did look around the area where the car was abandoned. Saw some old wooden pallets stacked up. Looked like they had been there awhile. Took a look behind them and found this."

Andrews reached under the table and retrieved a brown evidence bag, opened it, and pulled out a purse and wallet.

"These were behind the pallets. No identifiable prints." He opened the wallet and tossed it down in front of Adams, ID facing up. It was Annie O'Reilley. "No cash, either."

"Shit. Not good." Adams tone was defeated, the hope-balloon suddenly deflated.

"No. Not good at all. Made me think she's probably dead. So, we searched all the dumpsters in the area of the strip mall, and for a few blocks surrounding it. Nothing. Decided to bring in a cadaver dog and check the woods behind the strip mall. Nothing. Then we decided to run the cadaver dog on the trunk of the car. Got a hit."

"Fuck." Adams wiped his face and leaned back in the chair. "So now it's play 'find the body', eh?"

"Looks that way. But fuck me if I know where else to look. It could be anywhere, depending on how much thought the guy put in to it."

"Colonial Heights is about a half hour north of Westport. That's where Bigleby had his meeting that night. Why don't we check there?"

"Seriously, Mark? Bigleby? He had a solid alibi."

"Damn straight I am. His alibi isn't solid anymore. In fact, it's the most damning evidence on anyone we have. He was in the area where all this happened at the time it happened and has possible motive. Maybe Annie went up there to meet him and an argument broke out. It's plausible," Adams insisted, "and worth checking out. You got any better ideas?"

"Not really." Andrews sighed as he put the evidence back in the bag. "I don't know. We'll see what the lab results on the car come back with and go from there. Let's not tip our hand by talking to him again until we have more. I'll let you know what the test results are." He shook his head with frustration. "I'm going home. Stay safe out there tonight."

Chad woke to the ring of his phone, grabbed it, and hit the answer button just as he saw it was Samantha. It was 11:00 p.m.

"Hi, Sam, what time is it?"

"It's 11:00 p.m. I was getting worried when I didn't hear from you. Where you at?"

"Damn, Sam, I came back to the office this evening to try and catch up and fell asleep at my desk. You just woke me. I was beat after earlier."

"What happened earlier, Chad?"

"I … I had a day terror … I guess it was a hallucination, really freaked me out. I went back by Dr. Danner's office and got him to up my meds. Then I went back to the office."

"Oh God, Chad, are you all right?"

"I don't know, Sam, but I'm way better than earlier. Look, let me just finish filing some paperwork and I'll head home, probably stop for a coffee or something. Be home in an hour, ok?"

"Sure. Drive safe. Call me if you need anything, ok?"

"Will do. Bye."

Chad quickly showered and dressed, then tucked in Robbie. At the front door, he kissed Emily and hugged her tight.

"I can't thank you enough for believing me, for being here for me. I love you."

"I love you too. Drive safe and call me, whenever, and for whatever. I'm here for you, just like you've been here for Robbie and me. No matter what. Ok?"

"Ok." Chad smiled and headed for his car, glancing back over his shoulder, his mind taking a picture of Emily and all her beauty as she stood there in nothing but one of his button up shirts. Her eyes longed for him to stay. It was like leaving home. The home that actually mattered to him.

Chad made it to his house within the hour and even stopped for the coffee. Samantha was awake and concerned about his day terrors. He took his meds, explained as little as possible, and nodded off in the recliner.

THURSDAY, JANUARY 11

Amy had been struggling to stay awake all night. When her dinner break came at 2:00 a.m. she decided to just sleep for a half hour and nodded off instantly.

But it was not restful sleep at all.

She was riding around town in a patrol car with Adams. They pulled up at an intersection where five thugs were hanging out. One of them mouthed off.

"Fuck you, 5-0! We don't want you round here, ya cracker-ass muthafucka!"

Adams' head turned sharply, his tone and manner deathly cold.

"What did you say?"

"You heard me, muthafucka. Carry your cracker-ass out of our hood!" He turned and fist bumped with his buddies.

"Darien, right? Darien Pickett. Poonie. 834 Harris Street, Apartment C. Date of Birth 9-13-89.

The other boys busted out, "Daaaaayyyuuuuummmmn! Man, he knows you!" Laughter followed. For Darien, though, it was pure shame.

"Fuck you, pig! You ain't shit without your boys."

Adams put the car in park, and spoke as he opened the door and stepped out, collapsible baton already in hand and hidden by his side. "Darien. You've done fucked up now." The others instinctively took two steps back, sensing a predator in their midst.

Adams swung his hand in an arcing slice through the air, the metal baton opening en route to Darien's head. The tip caught just under the ear, unhinging his jaw at the socket and fracturing the bone. Darien hit the pavement, still conscious but screaming, covering up in the fetal position. Adams swung again, cracking his elbow joint. Again, and his fingers snapped. Then he laid into Darien's exposed thigh and calf, repeatedly hammering the soft tissue, the cries carrying for blocks. Adams' fury raged unchecked, his revenge insatiable, even when he finally stopped from fatigue. The others stood staring, aghast and afraid to intervene. Adams kicked Darien in the kidney with the point of his work boots as hard as he could and spat on him.

"*FUUUUUUCK YOUUUUU!!!!!*"

Adams' body folded at the waist in order to scream as loud as possible and look Darien in the eyes on the ground.

"You drug dealing piece of shit! You've skated so many times; a motherfuckin' cat with nine lives is what you've been. Well, tonight, I'm the motherfuckin' law, and you got no more lives left. Tonight, you fuckin' paid, didn't ya? Paid for all the lives you've ruined to make your dollars. You deserved every lick you fucking got, you parasitic, life sucking bastard, so don't go whining to anyone about it. Carry your punk ass home, and I swear to God, if I ever hear the word 'muthafucka' come out of your mouth again toward me or another cop it better be 'Sir, muthafucka, sir!' you hear me?! Do you fucking hear me?"

Darien managed a faint moan that resembled "yes, sir."

"Good. Fucking outstanding!" Adams looked around at the others. "What do you know; maybe rehabilitation isn't a totally hopeless cause after all. Now, boys, scoop up this shitbag you call a friend, carry him home, and don't make me have to ever do the same to you. Got it?"

They all nodded then picked up Darien, who cried out at every touch, bump, and movement.

Adams put his baton away and adjusted his uniform as he walked back to his car. He smiled big and proud at Amy, paused to wipe the blood and sweat from his brow, then got in and put it in drive, leaving his foot on the brake. Amy was speechless, terrified of his wrath, and horrified she ever married such a beast. Adams seemed to pick up on her fear and flashed a loving, tender smile.

"Don't worry, honey, it's still me; I'm still the good guy. Someone's just gotta do the hard things, the dark things. Someone's got to make all the sinners pay. And I'm just the man for the job, a rod of righteous affliction sent from the heavens, an avenger of wrath to punish those who do wrong. I was made for this. You'll see."

He held her head with his hand and caressed her face with his thumb, his eyes feigning softness, but deep in that black, inky center nothing lived but a sterile, ominous pit threatening to devour her soul if it found out what she had done.

Amy's mind screamed, terrified at the man she loved, at the grim devil she saw full of professional pride and zeal, no sense of contrition, no internal moral struggle or vacillation of any kind.

Doubts flooded her heart, but her mind told her it was just a dream as Nurse Callahan shook her and the world made sense again. "Just a dream," she said aloud.

Adams woke up in a sweat.

The night had been dead, and he had been unusually tired for no apparent reason, as far as he could figure out. So, while nothing was going on, he found a nice little hiding hole and closed his eyes. Just a few minutes, he told himself before he nodded off, barely able to stay awake a moment longer.

Twenty minutes later he startled awake, fists closed, muscles tensed, and forearms sore as if from great effort. He looked out into the pitch darkness then gradually rolled the interior light dial up until the dash glowed a dim green, illuminating his surroundings. He wiped his brow dry with a gym towel from his bag and looked at the time.

2:30 a.m.

The dream was still fresh in his mind. He felt invigorated, fearless, a deep sense of accomplishment undergirded by an unwavering conviction of righteousness. He was just in what he had done. He was beyond the petty judgment of others. Only God had the right to judge him now.

The details faded, but the impressions and emotions lingered on as he drove back out onto the streets to patrol his zone again.

FRIDAY, JANUARY 12

Thursday, Chad remained at home, in bed almost the whole day, not wanting to venture forth into a very uncertain and unpredictable world. By Friday he felt calmer and returned to work, wanting to reclaim some control over his own life. At the end of a day, with few breaks and all hard work, he'd finally chopped down the tower of files enough it no longer leaned dangerously to one side.

Content with his productivity, he headed out and got in his car, exiting the parking garage right at dusk. He looked right then left, and all was clear. Looking right again before turning left he found himself staring directly at an olive-complected man with perfect posture, a white sports jacket, and round sunglasses. The man was standing in the open, right where Chad just looked and had seen nothing. It was the homeless guy from the park. He was sure of it. The medium sized black dog that bit him sat at his master's heels, panting, eyes fixed on Chad. Chad slammed on the brakes, threw it in neutral and pulled the parking brake. He pressed the trunk release and exited the vehicle in a hurry, anger welling up inside him.

"You! I've been looking for you and your mangy mutt!"

Phobos yipped at the insult.

Chad scrambled to find his tire iron, clinched it in his right fist, and held it down by his side as he called 911. Mr. Phailees just stood, quietly smiling, watching Chad in his flustered agitation.

"Yes, ma'am, I am standing outside the H. P. Arkham office building on the north side where you exit the parking garage. I need Animal Control Officer Winslow to respond. I was the victim of a dog bite a few weeks ago. I have the animal and its owner here in sight. Yes. Thank you, ma'am. I'll be waiting right here."

Chad hung up the phone and looked squarely at Mr. Phailees.

"Your dog is the one that bit me!"

Mr. Phailees just stared and smiled.

"You think this is funny? You sorry son of a bitch, I'm gonna sue you! Don't you go anywhere!"

Mr. Phailees chuckled.

"I'm standing right here … Chad."

"How the hell do you know my name?"

"I know a lot of things about you, Chad. You're a busy, busy little bee! Having a bad time right now, though, aren't you, Chad?" Mr. Phailees voice rose to a mockingly sympathetic tone, before ending on a purely burlesque note, arms spread and a shit-eating grin spread across his tilted face. "Need a hug?"

Chad's temper flared at this apparent vaudevillian idiot. He clinched the tire iron and moved forward with a slight limp, his jaw set. Phobos took a step forward and growled.

"Heel, son!" Phobos sat obediently but kept his eyes on Chad, every muscle tensed and coiled.

"My, Chad! Such anger, such animosity, being a bit of a blowhard though, don't you think? I mean, what are you going to do, run after me on your bum leg?" Phailees let out a racous belly laugh. "Maybe if I walk real slow you can hobble after me and beat me to death with that tinker tool you got there?"

Chad's frustration at being the butt of Phailees' joke boiled over.

"Just who the fuck do you think you are, anyway? You let your dog bite me and then praised him for it, and I don't know how or why you did the whole homeless man get up, but I recognize you. I know you bit me in the hospital, you sick fuck! Who the hell are you?"

"What, Chad. 'What am I' is the appropriate question here."

"What the fuck do mean 'what'?" Chad exclaimed in frustration.

"Chad, I am a hound of the Ninth Circle, the father of all your horrors and someone whose attention you never wish to capture ... ever, but it is your guilty conscience that condemns you to this torment. You are a collaborator with me in this torturous play. You don't understand fully what I am, now, Chad, but I assure you ... you will before the curtain falls."

Mr. Phailees turned to go.

"Don't you go anywhere, you son of a bitch! I'm not done with you yet. Why are you following me? Why are you doing this to me? Why? Come here, you sorry bastard!"

Chad started forward, angry and indignant, raising the tire iron above his shoulder.

Mr. Phailees whirled about-face in a flash, his eyes blazing amber, the obsidian vertical slits swelling wide with anger.

"You dare lift your hand against me? You dare assault my kind? You insolent pup! I'll leave you a pitiful wretch. I'll take you for everything and leave you to the beasts of the field. You'll sink or swim in the hell you've made."

Chad recoiled in shock, his brain incapable of fathoming the meaning in those words.

"I have been planning all this since I arrived. You are a mark, a target, my prey."

Chad's mind balked at the incredibleness of Phailees' claim, but one thing was clear, nothing he had suffered was coincidence.

"Tell me, Chad, how is the leg anyway?"

At that, Chad's whole inner left leg seized up in a horrible cramp, the pain like a knife cutting up deep into his groin. Instinctively, he fell back and lay flat, straightening out the leg to try and find relief. The slightest attempt to raise his head caused the pain to double. He lay deathly still, afraid to flex a muscle at all. Phobos trotted over, sniffed his calf and then his crotch then trotted back to Mr. Phailees. Chad begged for pardon.

"Please. Don't do this to me. It's not right. I've done nothing to you. What do you want? I'll give you whatever I have, just give me my sanity back."

Mr. Phailees spoke, his tone coldly pleased.

"You can forsake your confidence right now, I tell you. The Just cannot be bribed, and he who knows he cannot lose will not extend peace to an enemy. I tell you, 'The wicked flee when no one pursues, but the righteous are bold as a lion [6]' I am a lion, Chad, and the beast himself would more likely release his prey once caught between the teeth than I am to let you go now. I know your wicked heart, Chad Bigleby, and I know your wicked ways. You cannot plead for what is right when you have done so much wrong."

Mr. Phailees approached Chad, straddled his torso and squatted on his chest, leaning over to get face to face.

"If I were your priest I would tell you to confess all your sins and repent before the end overtakes you in your path, but alas, I have no concern for repentance and no duty to be merciful. No Chad, my duty is to my soul, to soothe the ceaseless pain, to find a brief intermission from this purgative existence. You Chad, you and your kind are our inheritance, our portion, our relief in a world of anguish and misery, and we will have you, I swear, for the promise cannot be revoked."

Mr. Phailees stood. Phobos nudged the top of Chad's head jerkily, sniffing deeply the whole while.

"I hope you've enjoyed the bit of rest you've gotten, Chad. It's over now. Tonight, the world changes for good."

---

[6] Proverbs 28:1

Mr. Phailees turned and walked away, Phobos snorting in Chad's ear before trotting off.

"And by the way, Chad, don't bother going to the doctor again. No amount of therapy will help you through what's coming."

At that, Phailees walked away, humming that song Chad still could not place, Phobos trotting obediently at his heels.

Chad lay, his mind racing, trying to connect the dots, arrange the information in an orderly format so he could make sense of it, his leg screaming the whole time, his groin seized up, and upper body rigid. After a minute, it slowly began to fade, the pain lingering, but the muscles releasing. He stood cautiously, testing the leg at every transitional point. He was wiping his clothes off when Officer Winslow pulled up.

There was no way he was going to tell him what happened. The last thing he needed was the officers talking to that weirdo anyway. He obviously knew things Chad did not want the police to know. Plus, he'd look stark raving mad.

"Yeah, it was that homeless guy with the black dog. Looked the same, can't tell you any distinguishing characteristics. He wouldn't hang around, and I couldn't exactly catch him with my bad leg. They went around the corner. Left right after I got off the phone. I don't know which way they went from there."

Officer Winslow was obviously annoyed, but thanked Chad and left.

Chad picked up his tire iron, put it back in the trunk, carefully got into his car, and drove off.

Chad was still shaken and agitated when he arrived home. Samantha was in the kitchen cooking. He said hi and proceeded upstairs before she could ask him about his day, went straight to the bedroom, peeled off all his clothes, and climbed past the curtain for a long, hot shower.

Samantha took the opportunity to slip upstairs and check the call and text log on his cellphone. Her stomach knotted as she unlocked it, wanting the truth but hoping her suspicions were unfounded. The thought of it made her sick. She scanned over it quickly, finding nothing. She heard the shower cut off and was getting ready to slide it back in his jacket pocket when it began vibrating in her hand, startling her. She nearly dropped the damn thing on pure reflex, fumbled, but held on to it. Her stomach went south again, and she knew she had to hurry. She quickly opened the message. As she read it, nausea overtook her. It was a private number.

"Hey, sexy! I miss u. Last night was wonderful. I'm glad I could be there for you, body and soul. Can't wait till next time. Ur Baby momma BFWB ... Em."

At that moment, Chad walked out of the bathroom, toweling off then suddenly stopped, seeing Samantha staring down at his phone in her hand.

"What the hell are you doing?" he asked in a flat, challenging tone.

It was the tone that set Samantha off. She was suddenly filled with indignant rage.

"What am I doing? What am I doing?!?!? Are you shitting me? What are you doing, Chad? Who the hell is Em and what the FUCK does she mean Baby momma?" She held the phone up for emphasis, then threw it on the bed.

Chad stood silent.

"Well, Chad? Who the hell is Em? And who are the other two women that called your phone when you were in the hospital and suddenly hung up when I answered?"

Chad remained silent but looked down and shook his head side to side slightly.

"You cheating bastard! Don't stand there and try to deny it! Don't even try to pull some lawyer-speak crap on me, Chad. You've been cheating on me. How long, Chad? How many women? How many times? How many times have you played me for the fool? My God! How long have you had a fucking child with this Em girl, huh? I haven't even borne a child for you. You've denied me the joy of motherhood, but you let some cheap slut propagate your seed?"

Samantha turned away briefly, shaking her head, and grabbing her hair with both hands.

"GOD DAMMIT, Chad! I should have seen it. I should have known. Aaaarrrggghh! I've been such a fool!"

Samantha turned back on him in a fury. "Who else, Chad? Who else have you screwed?"

"Oh!" Samantha's hands went to her mouth as her hips sunk under the realization, and she turned in a full circle. "Oh, fuck me! That secretary that used to work for you, Annie, the really hot, busty one; I bet you did her, didn't you, Chad? Oh my God! How many times did she snicker when I called? How many times did she look down at me with contempt when I came to the office, knowing she was sleeping with my husband? How many times did she play the whore for you, Chad? Just how many times have you betrayed me? How long has all this been going on?"

There was a long pause as a light flickered on in Samantha's skull, and her mouth dropped to form a large "O". The sheer volume of her voice cut through the space between them, as if trying to skewer Chad with her increasingly violent screams.

"OH, FUCK ME!!! EM?!? Emily? My bridesmaid? You're FUCKING Em?!!!? Oh-My-God! And you have a kid with her? Are you FUCKING serious?"

She picked up his phone and slung it, striking him in the chest. Her voice reached its crescendo now.

"How long, Chad? How-FUCKING-long?!?!?"

Samantha was furious, her last words a screaming growl, her anger implacable. Chad stood statue-like, staring at her, face blank, mouth still. The moment stretched out, strangled by its own silence, until Samantha could take no more.

"You've got to be fucking kidding me! Say something, dammit! Don't you pull this 'I plead the fifth' shit, Chad!

Answer me. How many times have you cheated on me? How long has this been going on? How long have you been fucking Emily? How old is the kid? Answer me, dammit! For God's sake, answer me!"

Samantha stood, chest heaving, almost panting. Chad finally spoke—deadpan, calloused, cold.

"Samantha … shut the fuck up. I'm not telling you anything. You think I cheated on you? Prove it. In the meantime, I suggest you pack your shit and go to your sister's house, because I'm not going anywhere."

Chad stood like a rock, staring at her, watching her rage fizzle out, watching the tears begin to well, brim, crest, and roll in streams down her cheeks, multiple drops splattering on the hardwood floor. He'd be damned if he was going to be forced out of his house, and besides, if he left and went to Emily's now, he might as well admit to everything, and write the biggest alimony check she could think of. Fuck that, he thought as Samantha's composure began to show signs of pending collapse.

Samantha tried to hold it in, but she knew she could not and she did not want to give Chad the pleasure of seeing her suffer. She bolted and ran, grabbing her keys off the counter downstairs, still in full stride, refusing to stop until she got in the car, started it, and turned on the radio, dialing the volume way up to cover the sounds of weeping. Her chest began to heave uncontrollably, the sobs wracking her entire body in convulsive waves. At last, she finally knew for sure the dream was dead and she wept at its passing, even though they surely lost each other a long time ago. She wailed and moaned, head resting on the wheel, hands covering her face, her entire body violently jerking then resting, the intervals slowly lengthening until at last the spasmodic sobs stopped. She spent the bulk of her sorrow in those minutes, expelling years of depressed resolve and unconscious dread in that heart-wrenching, cathartic release.

She put the car in drive, pulled out of the driveway, and started towards her sister's house across town. She would not call, for she knew she would cry again. She would surprise Kristen and then talk and cry when her sister could hold her tightly and not let go.

Back in the house, Chad picked up the phone, ordered pizza and turned on football, trying to forget his encounter with the old man and his dog, trying to feel normal despite all that had happened and thinking about how he could protect his investments from Samantha during the pending divorce. A part of him was glad it was over at last.

When the doorbell rang he answered it, not remembering the words of warning, that tonight the world changes for good.

Amy ran for her life.

She had been standing on the loading dock at the back of the hospital, drinking coffee, and enjoying the night air during her break when it all went south. It was quiet then. The sound of the city was faintly audible, just enough background noise to calm a person while they thought. And she needed to calm down right then. Everyone at work knew she screwed Dr. Danner. Everyone knew she hooked up with that ER patient as well. Nurse Callahan had a big mouth; it was all common knowledge she was a cheater, an adulteress, a common whore. It was only a matter of time before Adams found out. She was panicking, hyperventilating, trying to figure out how she was going to manage to simply live around these people. The shame was too much. Her breath caught in her throat. She couldn't breathe in, couldn't breathe out.

Then she saw the pack of … dogs? Her first thought was they were rather large for dogs. Her second thought was there was something wrong about the shape of their heads. She counted three of them. They growled then, baring their teeth, and she had seen enormous fangs, like a huge python snake might have, but longer. Forked tongues flickered out and smelled the air, detecting her scent, pheromones suddenly released as a dreadful fear crawled out of her belly.

That's when Amy screamed, loud and long, releasing all the air trapped inside, releasing her diaphragm to breathe again. The beasts lunged forward. Amy spun around and ran for the swinging loading bay doors that led back inside the hospital. Stumbling forward, she careened through them and staggered into a full sprint as she regained her balance.

She ran for her life as three hellish hounds scrambled through the doors and closed on her heels, slavering the whole while. She tried to run faster, but the more effort she exerted, the heavier she felt, the weight of her guilt pulling her down, draining her vigor, and finally her will to fight. On she ran though, the pack seeming to allow her just a hairs breadth of distance, breathing on her back at every step. Down corridor after corridor she blundered on, careening off walls at every corner, her momentum uncontrolled.

She aimed for the stairs, yanked open the door, hoping it would shut in time, not daring to linger to ensure it did. The animals slipped through effortlessly, the hinges almost slowing for them as they passed. Amy's legs pumped hard, the blood flowing frantic through her limbs, less and less oxygen traveling to fuel the workers, more and more lactic acid building up. Each step began to feel like concrete boots were fitted about her ankles. Her quad muscles burned. Her hip flexors were growing exponentially weaker. She knew she could not escape. She wondered why she even tried. All her efforts were so futile, like the punch line to a joke she could not remember. "Don't run; you'll just die tired."

And Lord, was she tired.

Amy reached the next landing, pulled with all her might on the door. It opened just enough for her and she slid through. She heard a growl but didn't look back to see the first creature briefly caught before shrugging its whole frame, a wave moving through its body, snakelike, easily flicking the door wide open.

Adrenaline alone fueling her flight now, every step grueling, she rounded the corner and saw the elevator. Renewed hope strengthened her legs with a slight increase in speed. She crashed into the metal doors, one hand pushing the button rapidly, before flattening her back against the elevator, hoping her pursuers were not yet in range.

She gasped and moaned, her body desperately trying to push itself through the crack. The pack was standing still in a small semicircle staring at her, tongues flickering in and out, bright amber eyes alive with a light and life of their own, burning into her, looking through her. She begged them. Her voice dancing on the brink of full out sobs, the wind in her lungs fleeting and shallow, panting between words.

"Pleeease … pleeease … just stop … stay back … don't … don't do this to me … for the love of God … pleeeeeeeease!" The last word was a shrill, squealing plea echoing down the hallway as the elevator doors finally opened. Amy stumbled back into it, almost falling down. She reached forward for the only button available and hit 'B' repeatedly and begged.

"Pleeeeeease …"

The pack inched forward, growling and snarling.

"C'mon. Good boys. Good doggies. Stay?"

The leader stopped growling, twisted his head slightly sideways, as if deeply offended and just as the doors started to close, he leapt, both his companions instantly behind him. The doors closed and Amy screamed, over and over and over; the steel coffin descending as if to Hell, and Cerberus himself was present to carry her there … in pieces. She felt the fangs strike and rip and gouge, felt her body shaken violently enough to dislocate whatever limb they grabbed. The pain was searing hot, excruciatingly sharp and mind numbing, her eyes slamming shut temporarily.

Limbo enveloped her briefly, a psychic disconnect as her body twitched and jerked about to the rhythm of their tug of war, a will apart from her own, head bobbing every which way, neck nearly snapping more than once. There was a sudden pause, the inertia of their savagery coming to rest. A slight pulling on her left leg was all that remained. Amy chose that moment to plug back in and open her eyes … just in time to see the unhinged jaw and watch its huge fangs drive directly into her face.

That was when she woke in her bed, screaming, hands covering her face. Hyperventilation set in immediately, and it took a few minutes to get her breathing under some semblance of control. She looked at the clock. It was 9:30 p.m.

Time to get ready for work.

The doorbell rang at exactly 10:25 p.m. Chad paused the ball game on TV, grabbed the cash he set out for the pizza delivery guy, and limped to the door. The first clue should have been the door knob, so cold it stung his hand, but that wasn't all. The fluorescent aura around the door seemed weak and warped, as if something were draining its essence into the night, as if the dark itself was slowly infiltrating the lambent defenses provided by simple electricity.

Chad was oblivious as he opened the door.

The smell of ash and charnel struck his olfactory senses, his head rearing back reflexively from the threshold. His eyes spotted amorphous shadows stretching from the street to his front porch, marching to overtake the shrubbery, pressing against his windows and threatening to rush inside if not for the light at his back. Their unseen mass nudged the delivery boy forward, closer to Chad's face. The stench was of decay, a rotting body in a tomb. It infused the air that filled his lungs.

"Gotcher pizza right here, sir. That'll be twenty dollars even."

Chad drew back with an audible gasp, nearly yelped. The creature in front of him was obviously human ... at one time. Now, it was something corrupted, voluntarily transformed. It had conspired with a hidden nature to aid in its own descent into depravity.

The young "man" smiled, revealing pointy teeth filed sharp, a weasel nose and mouth, hungry, always hungry, perpetually searching for another high, another escape, or the means to pay for it. Chad observed the horrible skin, oily and full of acne and oozing sores. Even worse, the ulcerated gums, which Chad somehow knew could only have come from all the oral favors he performed on anyone willing to give a little money to pay for another crack rock. He was vile and disgusting. Chad's teeth were on edge just knowing this addict now knew where he lived. The man would surely steal his mother blind, much less a stranger.

"Here you go," Chad said as he held out the money and took the pizza. He immediately wished to God he had simply closed the door without looking past the part time gigolo/delivery boy.

The streets were beginning to glow that brimstone blackish-red, as if Hell were a bad moon rising to shine down on the world below, and as his eyes were hooked and reeled in to look upon the horrifying landscape, Chad wanted to vomit.

There were creatures everywhere, an incongruous medley of lumbering hulks, blood thirsty scavengers, bristly bipeds, and some emaciated weaklings. Two deformed goblins scampered along on all four, bodies canted, moving only along diagonal lines posturing to one another in passing.

Hungry faces roamed all about, hungry for wicked pleasures and forbidden food, seeking satisfaction at any cost and hunting whoever might feed them. Their eyes turned toward Chad and stared, hollow assessment, detached, no morality involved. One of them turned toward his house, an apish brute, ambling along with new-found purpose, gaze fixed ahead, tongue licking cracked, bleeding lips, pressing against jagged-eye teeth, nostrils flaring. Chad instinctively took a step back from the door as the delivery boy turned and walked back toward his car.

The boy was already dialing his phone, calling his dealer, oblivious to the monstrosity approaching him.

The attack was a blur, a raging animal pouncing on something significantly lower on the food chain, fragile and hopeless.

The brute's body slammed into the skinny frame, sending him flying through the air, only to rebound off the car door, a meaty hand catching him mid-air by the throat. His feet hovered above the ground momentarily before he was driven straight down, crushing head and body into the pavement. Primal fury rained down in repetitive blows. The ape-like fiend's fists rose and fell, flailing up and down, flesh hammers pounding imaginary nails through skull and torso. The young man's face was mangled in seconds and his consciousness snatched as if by a striking serpent.

The massive degenerate fumbled through the dirty pockets, found the keys, found the money, climbed in the vehicle, and quickly drove away.

Chad stared, a bewildering dread enveloping him, paralyzing him until he saw his neighbor's door open, and Bill Lashley stepped out to see what all the commotion was. Chad saw black, deadly eyes, a full mouth wet with drool and froth, spittle hanging from his chin. His body was drenched in sweat dressed only in boxers. A red face burned with lust as his whole chest heaved from exertion.

Behind him he saw a female face peek around, young but solemn in appearance, with vacant eyes … survivor eyes. She stepped forward, her tiny naked frame, fragile beneath the weight of darkness, signs of abuse visible from across the street. Bruised wrists, small nipples angry red and dark purple, teeth marks still imprinted in her soft flesh. She glanced around curiously then turned back in, disinterested, her buttocks bright red, hand prints clearly visible, outlined in welts.

Rough stuff, that's where she made her real money. Abuse and debasement always cost the client more.

Bill, unable to see because of a parked car, quickly dismissed the commotion and stepped back inside, his arousal already returning as he vanished from sight.

Chad slammed the door, but did not call 911, afraid of his name being attached to anything else crazy. What had he seen for sure, anyhow? Real? Hallucination? God, he hoped it was a hallucination. He threw the pizza away, too disgusted to consider eating it and no longer hungry anyway.

His phone rang right then, his whole body flinching away from the noise even as his head snapped to follow it. He breathed, cursed his jumpiness, and looked at the screen.

It was Emily.

Time stretched out between rings as his mind raced across increasingly hideous possibilities. His breathing was speeding up again, becoming ragged and staccato.

He ignored the call and threw the phone down on the couch.

All he could think about was what Emily might look like if she were outside his door, the images in his mind a ghastly dance of ghoulish figures on parade. His stomach couldn't bear the abominable burden any longer and decided to lighten the load.

SATURDAY, JANUARY 13

12:08 a.m., on patrol.

"What the fuck is wrong with people tonight?" Adams exclaimed out loud as he drove to a call. This would be the fifth disorderly subject call he responded to in more than an hour. Even for a Friday night, it was getting unhinged. First, they had a homicide right at shift change, and it seemed people were on edge everywhere, wanting to fight. Some of them were paranoid as well, convinced they were being followed and everyone else they saw was a candidate perp.

Adams pulled up at South and Washington Street, saw a familiar tall, black man wearing a white gown, the Koran held at his side. Easily six feet eight inches tall, a huge hand raised palm forward, fingers splayed as he spoke. His voice boomed for blocks.

"Brothers! I have seen Allah's servants of destruction come to punish the white man, seeking to devour. Prepare yourselves, lest they turn their eyes to you as well. Repent! Repent! The treacherous, the adulterous, the betrayers of their own kind, the friends of the white man, they all shall pay. Repent now and offer restitution, offer sacrifice for your souls. Take from the white man, and give to your own. Hurt them how you may. Heed the warnings of the great and merciful Allah and his prophet Muhammad."

Adams stepped out of his car as Dexter and Greer pulled up a block away to walk up behind the crazy street preacher quietly.

"Hanafi Khadafi!" Adams said loudly but in a jovial tone. "Haven't seen you in a while. You just get out of the hospital or what?"

Hanafi Khadafi pointed his long, thick, bony finger at Adams and began chanting loudly in a deep bass voice.

"The White Maaaan is the Devil. The White Maaaan is the Devil. Kill the White Devil! Kill the White Devil!" Each "kill" command was emphasized with a jabbing of his index finger in Adams' direction.

Several people were nearby. Most of them just moved on, intentionally distancing themselves from the street preacher. One man was standing beside him though, absorbed in the message and cheering Hanafi on with 'Amens' and other affirmations. Adams recognized him. Charlie Jay Justice—one of the many local crazies. Two peas in a pod, these guys were. De-escalation would be best, if possible, he thought.

"C'mon now, Hanafi, when have I ever treated you wrong? I respect you as a man, just like anyone else, and I respect your right to stand out here and preach to your brothers and sisters, but I can't have you out here trying to incite riots. We need to promote peace, not war, don't you agree?"

Hanafi spat on the ground and held his Koran up.

"Fuck you, you blue-eyed devil, you blue-eyed devil. Fuck you, you blue-eyed devil!" The words reverberated around them, Hanafi's voice thundering and deep.

Adams maintained a calm tone. He preferred not having to arrest a crazy man tonight, but the odds didn't seem in his favor. A different strategy then, he thought.

"Hanafi, you can't be talking to people like that. That's curse and abuse. Now I'm gonna have to write you a ticket.

Hanafi continued to chant his same insult. Some people stood at a distance watching, seeing just how much he would get away with. Adams walked back to his car and grabbed his clipboard, walked back to the front of his cruiser, sat down facing Hanafi, and began writing the summons.

Once done, he approached the street preacher again.

"All right, Hanafi, you're under arrest for curse and abuse. Just need you to sign this summons on the line, and you can walk away a free man right now."

Hanafi was crazy but not stupid. He puffed out his chest reflexively, breathing in deep for another round of chanting, then thought better of it and shut his mouth.

"Why you want to fuck with me, Adams? Why you want to fuck with me while I'm doing Allah's work?" Hanafi looked up at the people who had gathered across the street. "Don't you worry my brothers and sisters," he yelled, "the white devil can't silence Allah's servant."

Adams shot back quickly.

"Why you want to diss me while I'm doing the Lord's work of keepin' the peace? Huh, Hanafi? You know I can't let you cuss at me like that in front of everyone. Then they'll all think they can do it, and there won't be any order, just chaos. Now you tell me, is Allah a God of chaos or justice?"

Hanafi thought for a moment and shook his head, angry, but unable to contradict the basic argument. He grabbed the pen from Adams hand and reached for the clip board. Adams held it back briefly.

"All right, Hanafi, but there's one catch: you gotta sign your real name—Ricky King."

Hanafi blew up, shouting at the top of his lungs. "My name is Hanafi Khadafi! Don't call me by that infidel name! I am not Ricky King! I am Hanafi Khadafi, servant of Allah. Ricky King is dead!"

Adams explained to Hanafi if he refused to sign it by his real name he would have to arrest him and take Hanafi to jail.

Hanafi laid his Koran on the hood of the patrol car, stepped back, and thumped his chest with fist as he spoke.

"I'm ah black man, servant of Allah, and ain't no white devil gonna force me to become an infidel house nigga again." Then he began chanting and raised his hands in a boxing stance.

"Fight the power, fight the power, fight the power!" over and over, stuck on an unending loop. Charlie was getting into it, adding his voice to the dissident mantra.

Adams shook his head. "I am not in the mood for this shit tonight," he said with composed, but beleaguered, frustration. He drew his Taser and shot Hanafi center mass, barbed electrodes lodging in his hip and shoulder. His whole body seized, and like a board, fell flat and face down. His body remained rigid until the five seconds of current flowing through his tall frame stopped.

"That enough Hanafi or do I need to pull this trigger again? Don't matter to me one way or the other …"

Hanafi was quiet, trying to breathe.

"Weeellll…?" Adams persisted, a drawn-out tone full of disinterest.

"Fuck you, you blue-eyed devil, you blue Iiiiiiiiiiiiiiiii!"

Adams pulled the trigger again and listened to him scream for 5 seconds.

"Again?" he asked Hanafi. No response.

"You sure? I don't mind one more round?" A sarcastic edge crept into his voice, happy with himself, pretty as you please.

Still no response.

"Ok. I'll take that as a negative. Now put your hands behind your back and don't resist."

Adams knelt and pulled both arms behind Hanafi's back and cuffed them. He rolled the big man to each side and searched him while looking up at Charlie.

"All right, Charlie, unless you want some of this too, I suggest you move on down the street … now." The last word was emphatic but laced with a tired agitation.

Charlie never said a word, just turned and walked away.

1:30 a.m.

Adams just cleared from the arrest and headed downtown when he saw Mr. Phailees and his dog sitting at a bus stop. Adams pulled up next to them and rolled his window down.

"So, you know the next bus doesn't pick up till eight a.m., right?" Adams asked pointing to the sign bearing the schedule.

Mr. Phailees raised his hand to his mouth and exclaimed in a rich southern accent, "Oh, Lawdy have mercy! How could ah be so daft?" then slapped his leg and looked at Adams, a bit of sarcasm framing his face. His speech returned to normal. "Officer Adams, I am an old man, with old legs that walk almost everywhere I go. Sometimes these legs get tired, and I let the world come to me just like you have now."

Phailees smiled a large, deceptively pleasant smile that hid all but a faint edge of something unfathomable.

Adams stared at Phailees, then glanced at the dog for a moment before speaking. "So, just what has brought me to you this night; what lurid agenda is shaping my fate and guiding my steps?"

"Lurid, eh? Funny you should mention such things. Yes, it is shocking sometimes just how mysterious the ways of the universe can be, how providence, something so calculated, can be so surprising to us. But most disturbing of all is that the dark and gruesome things in this world have not been hidden from us. All things work together, Officer Adams ... yes indeed." Phailees chuckled to himself lightly.

"I wanted to speak to you again, Officer Adams. I think you know by now that Annie O'Reilley is dead, and you are sure that Chad Bigleby is guilty. I wish you luck in your endeavors to prove his guilt and punish him by the law of man, but I have first dibs on him. When I am done you can do whatever you wish with him. But until then, he lives. I just want that to be clear. I also wanted to encourage you to trust your instincts and gut feelings in the coming days. You are special, Officer Adams. Your gift also allows you to hear."

"Hear what?" Adams asked, puzzled.

"If you can learn to quiet your mind and listen you will hear the voices of victims pleading for justice. Listen carefully, and you will find Annie O'Reilley's body. I am sure of it. You have seen the monsters that men hide behind their masks. If you focus and observe the eyes of those you meet, you will see their lies and know the truth. You will see the wicked in a man … or woman. Pay careful attention to those you hold closest. Betrayal is the worst of sins, but is rarely possible by strangers."

Adams felt more puzzled than he looked, he was sure. Questions. Always more questions after talking to this guy. He shook his head and picked from the abundance of options.

"Hear the voices of the dead, huh? What do I look like, the fucking Ghost Whisperer? Quit with all the hoodoo-voodoo shit and cut to the chase. What makes me special? What makes me capable of these miraculous feats? Tell me that, will you?" Adams' frustration showed clearly.

"Mark, it's in your blood. You were born to judge, to hunt, to punish, an avenger of God's wrath who does not bear the sword in vain. But, the laws of man are holding you back. Your mortal attachments are dragging you down into the squalor of mediocrity. If you can embrace the depth of commitment necessary to inflict righteous vengeance upon sinful mankind, you can do wonderful and great works."

Adams was speechless, reality an opiate abyss spinning beneath his falling feet. Meaning an ephemeral mist he could not grasp.

"I don't understand …" was all he could manage to groan, his eyes staring, struggling to process, but looking only vacant.

"I know, Mark, I know, but soon I think you will. You will have a choice to make, a choice only you can make once your eyes are opened. Good night, Mark; I fancy a nap, now."

Mr. Phailees lay back on the bench and turned on his side, back to Adams, pulling the hoodie over his head. Phobos stretched out beneath him, alert to their surroundings. Adams nearly spluttered at the sudden end to their conversation but managed to hold his tongue. He sat for a few more moments, dumbfounded. A business alarm call came out for his zone.

He told himself, You gotta go a few times before his body finally, but reluctantly, obeyed. He released the brake and accelerated away.

Mr. Phailees heard Adams' voice as he drove off with his window down and hand striking the steering wheel.

"What *the fuck* is happening to me?!?"

SUNDAY, JANUARY 14

At 2:30 a.m. Adams walked into the hospital break room. Amy called earlier and asked him to meet her during her lunch break if he wasn't busy. She was already seated, dinner for two laid out.

"Have you eaten anything yet?" Amy's smile was controlled and timid, her face a canvas painted in big strokes of wary optimism, searching for his approval.

"As a matter of fact, I have not had the time until now. Been real busy tonight."

Amy's face beamed.

"Wonderful! I made extra today hoping you could eat with me." She patted the seat next to her. "C'mon. Sit down."

Adams eased into the chair, a hint of trepidation skipping like a stone across his subconscious, unsure as it processed her planning, anticipation, and particularly friendly attitude. His mind tried to calculate the meaning and whether there was anything more behind it than trying to work on their relationship.

As it was, they simply made small talk in between bites of food, leisurely passing the time. A half hour later, Amy finally breached the meat of the matter she wanted to discuss.

"Mark? I … I want to ask you something …"

"Ok. Sure. Shoot." He felt a slight hesitation, but nothing was setting off alarms.

"Tonight … or tomorrow night, however you want to look at it, I'm off. You're off too, right?" Her face radiated an anxious expectancy.

"Yeah. What's up?"

"I … I want you to come by the house …" her voice trailed off, the idea obviously not yet finished.

After a few moments, Adams interjected, "And …?"

"And I want you to spend the night." Amy blurted it all out very quickly, then paused for a moment. "There I said it." She sat back and looked at Adams, a bit proud of herself for going through with it.

"You want me to sleep over? You're sure about this? Don't think it might be rushing things?"

"Look. We don't have to have sex. I just ... I just want you ... there, with me, next to me, where I can hold you and curl up to you." Her anxiety was becoming more palpable.

"Amy, is something wrong? This doesn't seem like you? What's going on?"

Amy dropped her head and tried not to cry, tried to control her breathing. She raised her head and had to wipe her eyes, tears welling up. Adams squeezed her hand.

"C'mon baby. You can tell me. I won't judge."

Amy looked at him square and sighed, a short, puffing expulsion of air through the nose.

"I'm having nightmares," she confessed. "Horrible nightmares." Her face cracked, but she held back the sobs.

"Oh God, Amy. What about?" Somewhere, a monster with a fishing rod just lodged hook, line, and sinker in Adams' gut and began reeling it in, pulling it in unnatural directions, bad directions, nauseatingly disturbing directions he did not wish to travel.

"Different things ..." she sniffled. "Some are about you, you being in trouble or you working, but becoming like the bad guys—mean, cold, and scary beyond belief."

Adams was on the edge of a precipice not wanting to look down into a yawning chasm below.

"What else?" he said, mouth suddenly dry, a petrifying expectation filling his chest, immobilizing his limbs.

"I ... I've been chased by a pack of dogs ... except I don't think they were dogs. They had fangs like a snake and forked tongues and they were huge. They caught me and were tearing me apart when I woke up."

Adams sat, mouth agape, unable to say anything right away. In fact, the more he considered it, he did not know what to say. Mr. Phailees? was all he could think of as a possible explanation. "Why was Amy dreaming about him? seemed the only logical question. And what did it all mean? Was the same thing going to happen to her that's been happening to Chad Bigleby?

The questions fell into his mind like a meteor suddenly entering our atmosphere in flames, drawing all attention to itself. Why? That was the most crucial question. Why would Phailees target Amy? But his brain could not focus on that. It was inundated with "What if?" scenarios.

Unchecked in that long moment, Adams' mind was awash with questions that proffered potentially catastrophic answers—tragic, horrifying answers.

Finally, he managed a "wow" as he sat back in the chair, trying his best not to overreact and scare the hell out of Amy.

"Wow," he said again. "That … that's freaky, Amy."

"I know," she sobbed lightly, wiping her eyes again.

"I'll come over, Amy, of course. I'm not gonna leave you like this. We'll try to figure this out together, tonight. Promise." He squeezed her hand and touched her face. Gave her a light kiss on her forehead.

"I've got to get back on the street. I'll see you tonight. Around eight, ok?"

"Sure. Sounds great. Don't forget to bring your favorite pillow, k?" A loving smile slipped across her face without thought or effort as she stared into his eyes. "Thank you, Mark. I love you," she said without thinking and immediately worried if it was too soon.

"I love you too," Adams instantly replied. "Don't mention it. I'll see you later. Try to get some rest."

Adams left, and Amy desperately needed some fresh air, suddenly feeling very claustrophobic inside the hospital walls. She made for the loading docks, exited into the cool night air, and took a deep breath, once, twice, three times, forcing as much air in each time as she could, chest expanding fully.

Abruptly, Amy began to experience a feeling of déjà vu. A lump caught in her throat as she listened to the distant sounds of the city, then looked out beyond the loading docks and caught a glimpse of a homeless man and his dog standing beneath the fluorescent lamps. They stared at her. She blinked, her vision shimmered, and she realized they were walking toward her, but far closer than they should have been in those few moments.

A terrible dread spread throughout her bowels and sunk through her legs to the very soles of her feet. Fear seized her fully, and her only choice was flight. She tried to turn and run but her lower extremities were incredibly heavy, even numb and tingling, almost as if they had fallen asleep and were just waking up. She tripped, stumbled, and nearly fell, catching herself against the wall. She looked back again, and they were both on the landing striding towards her nonchalantly. She wanted to scream, but her vocal cords wouldn't work. She wanted to beg, but her tongue and lips couldn't coordinate.

Phailees closed to within about ten feet of her. He stood still and lit a hand rolled cigarette, puffing on it a couple of times before talking.

"Mrs. Amy Adams, such a pleasure to finally make your acquaintance. I've learned so much about you: wife, nurse, friend ... adulteress. I know this seems like a nightmare right now, but I assure you, it is not. You are quite awake, and I might add, hopelessly doomed."

Phailees took another deep drag and blew out six small smoke rings before smiling and speaking again, his tone taunting.

"Dreams are always so exaggerated and tend to give you a fighting chance. Reality is much more merciless. I'm afraid your hourglass is all out of sand little Dorothy. I could tell you 'run, rabbit, run', but it would grant you absolutely no benefit. I ran out of that good ole sporting spirit a long time ago. Nope. I'm afraid it's just time to pay for your sins … whore." He nearly spat the last word out, a growling accusation.

Phailees' face contorted into a wrinkled, snarling scowl. "Sick her, Phobos!"

She watched, paralyzed, as the dog's body contorted, bulged, flexed, and enlarged before her very eyes, muscles lengthening, thickening, skull expanding and flattening, fangs bursting forth from bloody gums, swinging into place, a forked tongue flickering in and out, just before the beast leaped forward.

Amy finally managed to scream as the huge fangs sunk into her side, the jaws working like a bellows, pumping terror into her system, a slow poison condemning her to a very personal hell. The pain was excruciating, and she blacked out; for how long, she did not know. But when she came around, the man and his dog were gone. Her scrub top had two holes along the front where her left oblique muscles started. The large puncture wounds leaked blood, slowly seeping through the material. It hurt horribly, but she managed to stand and walk inside. She made it to her locker, retrieved a spare top, then gathered some betadine, antibiotic ointment, bandages, and self-adhesive gauze wrap and proceeded to the bathroom where she cleaned and dressed the wounds as best she could.

She told no one. It was crazy. It was impossible. It was madness. But the man and dog were exactly like what that patient, Chad Bigleby, described. She feared for her sanity more than anything else, but as she touched the wound and felt the stabbing pain, she knew she wasn't crazy, just woefully ignorant of what secrets the dark corners of the universe hold hidden, just out of sight of the unsuspecting masses.

SECTION III

SUNDAY, JANUARY 14

Chad hadn't slept in three days, not since the night he witnessed the pizza delivery boy beaten to death. The world was changed, forever, it seemed. The darkness would not fade; the hellish sky would not relent. No rising of the sun, no rescue by the day. Everyone was a freak or worse, no longer hidden by their own skin. Chad hadn't dared look in a mirror and, God help him, he hadn't dared sleep. He set his watch alarm for every 10 minutes, just in case he drifted off. For two days, it hadn't even been a problem. Day three was becoming difficult, though. He found himself nodding at times; brief moments of chaotic, broken horrors rearing hideous heads before he snapped awake again, alarm blaring.

Micro naps had become micro hells.

He didn't dare go out of the house, and couldn't even bring himself to risk calling for take out again. Instead, he paid the sixteen-year-old boy across the street to make a grocery run for him. The kid had a wicked sex drive and lusted horribly after every pretty girl he saw, but what guy didn't half the time or more, he thought. Chad could empathize and the swollen, licentious lips and starving eyes living off porn didn't bother him so bad.

All the liquor in the house had been consumed in two short days. Murder was optional right now if it meant he could get a bottle of tequila. Merely existing was a living hell of its own, constantly struggling against a rising tide of unstoppable fear and loathing of cosmic proportions. The meaning of life had been redefined. Pain and suffering, punishment and judgment, vice and vile debauchery, corruption of every kind, they were all that existed to him anymore.

Emily had called dozens of times. He had only spoken to her once. Long enough to tell her that he was in hell, but she could not join him. He wouldn't allow it. "Don't come over," were his last words to her. "Whatever you do, do not come over!" She had listened thus far, but still persisted in calling. Chad couldn't bear to talk to her, terrified of what he might hear in her voice, what little clues he would find to point to her base iniquities; what gross ugliness he might find lurking beneath her skin.

Chad watched TV and ate his meal. At least people still looked normal on the screen. It hadn't completely gone to shit yet. The meat and potatoes sat heavy on his stomach as he watched women's downhill skiing on the sports channel.

His alarm brought his head back up as he began to nod off, fork tilting with the weight of a piece of steak as his hand relaxed. He reset the alarm for 10 minutes away and closed the phone, not noticing the settings had accidently rolled from p.m. to am. Within a few minutes, his head drooped again and sleep overcame him, this time defenseless without his guardian alarm.

Adams arrived at the house a little before eight and didn't even make it to the door before Amy threw it wide, pulled him inside and hugged him tight, the force of her grip seemingly borne of desperation. He hugged her back and she winced, but didn't want to let go. They stood and swayed in silence for what felt like a very long time, Toby ambling around their feet, patiently waiting his turn.

Finally, her hold on him relaxed and the silence was broken.

"Are you ok, Amy? What's wrong?"

She looked at him, at his kind eyes and caring face, the eyes that did not know who she had become after their separation. She tried to speak but could not at first. Head bowed, three deep breaths, and she managed to get it out, beating back the anxiety one second at a time.

"Mark, I … I told you I was having horrible dreams, and yesterday had been the worst. I … I felt like I was going crazy or something, feeling paranoid in general. At first it wasn't too bad, just a little anxious…" Amy turned away as she spoke and knelt to pet Toby, "but now, after last night … I'm freaking out, because, as absolutely insane as it all sounds, I know I'm not crazy, and that's scaring the shit out of me."

Toby was whining, licking her face and then began sniffing her left side and licking her shirt around her ribcage.

"What are you talking about, Amy? What do you mean?" Adams felt his blood pressure rising exponentially, his unconscious suspecting what his conscious did not want to entertain. Panic set in as he waited for her answer, an elephant sitting on his chest, constricting his breathing, his heart beating faster to try and deliver more oxygen.

"I mean … your homeless man and dog showed up last night at the hospital after you left … and … Chad Bigleby was right. They are not normal. That dog is not a dog. It's something wicked, something from hell. I watched it … transform."

Her voice cracked, spiking into a high-pitched whine with the last word, her closed hand coming up to cover her mouth with thumb and forefinger, head turtling between her shoulders.

The world tilted and swayed as Adams struggled to accept what Amy had just said. He told himself to just accept it, accept it and move forward. He forced his limbs to move, squatting down and reaching out to her.

"Oh my God, Amy! What did they do? Did they hurt you? Are you ok?"

He touched her shoulder, and she cringed away reflexively, looking down, not wanting to speak.

"Amy, you can tell me. You can tell me anything. I'm here for you." His voice was full of comfort, compassion, empathy.

She shook her head slowly, not looking up. "I can't …
you'll think I'm crazy."

Adams' tone was caring, but firm now. "Amy. Listen to
me. I've seen enough weird shit over the last several weeks,
particularly anything connected with that old guy and his
dog. I'm game for the X-Files confession. Tell me, baby. Just
tell me."

Amy sat back on her haunches, a defeated posture over-
taking her whole frame. She reached down and grabbed her
shirt, acted as if to pull it up but seemed to lack the strength
of conviction to lift it. Holding back the tears, she took a deep
breath and whispered, "It bit me Mark … the fucking thing
bit me." Her hand heaved at the shirt with all the courage she
could muster, lifting it to her armpit, revealing the large bandage. Adams just stared at it, not sure he was ready for what
he knew would be underneath.

"I need to redress it anyway," she said absently as she
used her other hand to peel it off.

Two angry puncture holes stood out on her pale, lower
ribcage about 5 inches apart, the surrounding area inflamed,
as if from some poison or venom. It looked just like Chad's
leg did that night at the hospital.

"Ho-ly shit." Adams reached out instinctively, a doubting Thomas needing to put his hand on the wound and make
it real. Amy gritted her teeth and winced, but let him do it.

"Amy, baby. I am so sorry. I am sooo sorry this happened
to you. I … I don't understand though. Why? Why you? Did
he say anything?"

"Whore," shot through her mind like an icy dagger, fear
welling up within her, but self-preservation ruled her
thoughts and will. She lied.

"No, Mark. Nothing. I don't understand any of this either."

And then she let the tears flow, she gave up on holding it
back and cried hard and long. Part of Adams wanted to rush
out into the city, track Phailees and his dog down and put a

bullet in them, but he knew Amy needed him here right now. Adams' muscular arms encircled her and pulled her gently into his lap as he sat down on the front porch. He slowly rocked her frightened frame back and forth, quietly praying to God, the first time in years he had really prayed, begging God to give him wisdom to figure it all out, courage to do what was right, strength to act, and above all, for mercy on Amy's body and soul.

They sat there until Adams' back began objecting to the position. He reached one arm under Amy's legs and hugged her to his chest, her head buried in his neck. He came up to one knee, stood and carried her in the house, closing the door behind them with his foot. He walked her to the couch and sat down with her still clinging to his torso.

And there they stayed, Adams holding her, nestled into his body, enveloping her like a blanket she never wanted to leave. She kissed his cheek once and nuzzled his neck, burying her face. Their breathing became slow and shallow and eventually synchronized, hearts beating calmly as they fell asleep in each other's arms.

MONDAY, JANUARY 15

It was just past midnight, and Chad drove like a bat out of hell. A gruesome panic seized his heart as he fled for his life. He sped along empty streets, shifting like a professional driver, revving the engine to the max along the straightaways and braking aggressively and snapping the wheel to sling the car through the corners. His only goal—escape.

The black Suburban with tinted windows was breathing down his back, sticking with him, toying with him. Chad tried to make a hard right and take a narrow cut-through. He pressed the brakes firmly, jerking the wheel left, kicking the rear end out slightly before snapping the wheel the other way and slinging the car back around. He punched the accelerator to shoot down the back alley. The Suburban did the same and stayed right on him, rubbing his bumper back and forth as it pushed him along.

Chad looked in the mirror. He already knew who it was. The driver, the olive complected man, was relaxed and methodical. His passenger, a medium built teenage boy, bordered on frenzy. Both were wearing police uniforms. Chad started braking early as he approached a T-intersection at the end of the alley. It was not helping much. The Suburban was still pushing him. He continued to brake as long as he could. As he exited the alley he released the brake and yanked up briefly on the hand brake, the rear end sliding out. He punched the gas again just in time to take off and avoid spinning out, the Suburban trying to push his rear end around as they drove through the corner.

Steadily accelerating, he flew down Main Street: 70, 80, 90, 100 mph and still climbing. The Suburban was about five car lengths back now. Up ahead, Chad spotted some homeless lady pushing a shopping cart full of possessions across the street. He downshifted, slowed slightly, shot around to her rear, the wind from his car whipping up the hem of her peasant skirt.

He looked in the mirror. The Suburban didn't flinch or brake. It sped up, slamming square into the old lady, her body flying into the air like some ragdoll tossed by a big brother tormenting his younger sister. Every detail became crystal clear to Chad. He saw the lady's body tumble limply back to the street, landing with a sick thud, her broken limbs lying terribly askew, like bony lots cast by angry hands. Chad did not have time to see what they might say.

Chad heard a howl and looked back at the Suburban closing fast. The teenage boy was practically bouncing up and down in the passenger seat, yipping and howling like a dog, and flailing his arms on the dash like some gorilla having a conniption. His face was transforming, looking more wolfish, elongating, thickening, getting hairier.

Chad forced himself to look forward again, but as he did he saw the intersection was full of cross traffic. He reflexively slammed on the brakes, bringing the vehicle to an abrupt stop.

The Suburban's driver never came off of the gas. The teenage boy held on to the "oh shit" handle while bracing on the center dash with his other hand, his frame now half man, half wolf, with a little serpentine flavor, the cop uniform still clinging to him. The Suburban's bull bar slammed into Chad's rear end at about 70 mph, driving him out into traffic and into a passing car. Front and rear ends crumpled from the double impact, causing all his airbags to deploy. The force threw his weight forward before rebounding to slam hard into the back of the seat. The car looked like somebody lit a fire inside with baby powder, smoke pouring out the shattered rear windshield.

Chad reeled from the impact, almost losing consciousness. Everything turned to black for a few seconds before slowly fading back in. His head was pounding, his neck hurt terribly, as well as his left knee, which had slammed into the lower dash. He looked in the side view mirrors and could see the two "policemen" get out of their Suburban, white smoke rolling out of their doors as well. Physically, though, they appeared uninjured and looked intent on ending the pursuit, but not too quickly.

Oh God, they're playing with me, he thought.

Another adrenaline cocktail dumped into Chad's system. He tried both doors quickly but found each one wedged shut. Chad hurried to crawl out the driver side window and hit the ground, already scrambling back to his feet. He cast a glance back to see the wolf boy creeping forward, waiting for him to rabbit away.

Chad ran for his life, ignoring all the pain in his left leg and neck. He hurled himself through the streets for several blocks, twisting and turning, hearing the beastly teenage officer behind him the whole way, toying with him. A bad decision led him down an alley with a fence, about fifteen feet tall. It was a dead end with nowhere to go but up and over. Chad never broke stride. He jumped and hit the fence climbing.

Suddenly, he didn't hear the wolf boy's footsteps.

Phobos' body slammed into the fence; claws gripped the interlaced metal next to each side of Chad's face. The beast's legs hooked inside of Chad's thighs; its groin drove into his back and its muzzle pressed against the terrified lawyer's head. A low guttural growl escaped the beast's lips before it hissed; a forked tongue flickered lightly in Chad's ear, and his whole upper body flinched away in fear and revulsion. A deep, throaty chuckle vibrated in his skull, and in the next instant, Phobos hooked his arms under Chad's armpits and threw himself backwards off the fence. Chad's tenuous grip ripped clear. They arced through the air, bodies flipping in unison, until they landed, Chad falling flat, face down, the beast landing perched upon his upper back. All the wind went out of Chad with a whoosh, sounding like a bellows violently compressed. Multiple ribs cracked, his whole chest lit on fire, and breathing was impossible.

"OOOOH! Epic fail! Helluva run for the goal line there, though, Chad! Missed it by that much," Mr. Phailees said in his best Maxwell Smart voice while holding up his left thumb and forefinger about an inch apart.

Phobos' weight was crushing Chad, asphyxiating him. He tried to scream, but he couldn't inhale. He tried to resist, but he had nothing left, no wind, no strength, and no will. He gave up, resigning himself to death, hoping it would come quickly.

"Good boy, Phobos! Well done. Well done, indeed. All right, get up off him now, before he croaks."

Phobos obeyed Mr. Phailees, climbed down off Chad's back, and stood over him, ready at a word to go back to work. Chad gasped, air rushing back into his lungs, burning but welcome. Mr. Phailees approached, adjusting his gun belt and tucking in his shirt, making sure the uniform was crisp and neat before drawing the police baton hanging from his side.

"Now it's time to pay up, Chad."

Mr. Phailees' tone was sedate yet buoyant, almost frolicsome. He obviously took great pleasure and pride in his job.

"You're not supposed to run, Chad. It's fun, don't get me wrong. But it's a bad thing to do. We always get our man, and if you run, we always make you pay."

Mr. Phailees smirked, a twinkle in his eye, a deviant look of pending enjoyment. A quick nod to Phobos, and he drew his baton as well. The two of them fell upon Chad in a vicious fury, a near simian rage. Arms flailing, the black polycarbonate batons whipped through the darkness, falling again and again from all angles as they hopped and bound and jumped around on hand and foot, every strike bringing another bit of malicious glee to their faces.

Chad instinctively curled into the fetal position, but soon lost faculties enough that all muscular tension fled. His head rested, face turned to one side on the trash strewn pavement, his limbs askew.

Chad's body limply rebounded from the force of each blow, sometimes like a fish flopping out of water, and at others like a puppet lying prone, his master pulling all the strings in random combination from varying oblique and perpendicular angles, creating obscenely queer jerking motions like a dying man's twitching dance before stillness reigns.

The whole time, Mr. Phailees and Phobos yipped, howled, and shrieked like a pack of chimps until they spent themselves in unfettered amusement, the grim misery of their existence temporarily expunged.

Chad would not die, and though his consciousness faded, it would not extinguish entirely. At last the brutal mauling ended. Mr. Phailees and Phobos backed away, leaving his body battered, bruised and broken, lying cockeyed and contorted, and his clothing disheveled and bloody. They stood silently, breathing heavily from the emotional exertion, but not physically fatigued.

They gave Chad a minute to come around before speaking.

"My! That was absolutely cathartic! And Phobos here, it was his first hunt. He'll never forget that rush. The first time is always special."

Phailees fumbled through Chad's pockets until he found his phone.

"Selfie time!" Phailees exclaimed, waiving Phobos over to pose with him and Chad, like big game hunters posing with their kill. Phailees grabbed a handful of hair and lifted Chad's head so his face was clearly in the picture.

"Try to smile now, good chap. It's a Kodak moment! All right guys, everyone say 'boobies'!"

Phailees took a few pictures, moving the camera around for slightly different angles, then put the phone back in Chad's pocket.

"Thanks for the memories, Chad," he said, slapping him on the shoulder.

Mr. Phailees smiled at Phobos and scrubbed his head.

"Come on lad, let's get him to the Suburban. You worked hard catching him, I'll take him back."

Phobos looked happy as he slowly changed back into a more human looking figure, his young boyish features returning. Mr. Phailees walked over, bent down, and grabbed Chad by the cuff of his pants leg, stood, and began dragging him, the weight seemingly effortless, his posture perfect the entire way back, whistling while he worked.

Through the mental fog, Chad could not help but try to figure out the tune and why it held significance to Phailees.

Adams raced through the city, his patrol car a couple of car lengths behind the black Suburban, right on the ass of the sports car they were chasing. Adams knew it was Chad Bigleby in the car, knew they had him pegged for the murder of Annie O'Reilley, and now he was running. The pursuit went on for several blocks, whipping around ninety degree turns, clearing intersections, avoiding pedestrians, until finally, Chad slammed on the brakes to avoid a collision with a vehicle in the intersection ahead. The black Suburban plowed into him, driving him forward into a T-bone collision with another car. A few moments later, Chad scrambled out of the window and took off on foot. Adams bailed out and sprinted full bore after him, passing Mr. Phailees in uniform and someone else as they exited the Suburban through a haze of airbag smoke, his vehicle still operational, but the bull bar pushed clean into the trunk of Bigleby's car. He heard Phailees speak as he went by.

"Get him, Adams! Get him boy!"

Chad was in good physical shape, but Adams could tell he was struggling to recover from the brutal shock of impact that was still reverberating throughout his whole body, unable to tell yet whether anything was seriously hurt or not. Chad's body would have to settle down first before he could pinpoint any potential injuries, an unlikely event right now as loads of adrenaline dumped into his system. Chad's legs pumped as he took every turn he thought might possibly put him out of sight of his attackers before they could round the corner and track him.

Adams was peaking: heart rate, muscles, motor skills, speed of thought, instincts, everything. He was locked in on Chad Bigleby and devouring the distance between them. He followed every twist and turn, silently moving in closer and closer, his light footsteps the only noise he made. Another anxious turn by Chad, and Adams saw a dead-end alley with a tall chain link fence. Chad jumped up on it and began climbing. He was nearly to the top when Adams jumped up onto a stack of pallets, cleared the gap to land on the top of a dumpster, cut back and leapt through the air, landing on top of Chad.

"Got you now, bitch," he growled in Chad's ear, before grabbing underneath both arms, clinching his hands together like a vise and throwing himself backwards into the air, arching his back to suplex Chad in grand wrestling fashion. They fell, interwined, like two tumbling meteors, bodies rotating in midair before crashing into the pavement. Chad landed face first. Adams landed straddling his back, knees bouncing off the pavement. It hurt like hell, but he quickly pulled Chad's arms behind his back and cuffed him.

"Now finish him, Mark." The voice was flat, commanding, matter of fact. It was Mr. Phailees.

"You know what to do, Mark. Be the Avenger of Wrath. Be the Sword of Justice … or," a light chuckle escaped his throat, "in this case, the Rod of Affliction."

Adams stood and looked at Phailees and his young uniformed companion, then looked back at Chad. He wanted to do it. He knew he needed to do it. Man's justice system was so weak, so unreliable—capricious judges, corrupt attorneys, manipulative media. It was all a hoax. Only one way to make sure.

"Mark!" The sharp voice called him out of his thoughts. "C'mon, partner." Phailees said the last word with a drawl that intoned sincerity laced with a wicked humor. "Just beat him to death, and let's go find another faithless, murdering traitor. Too many fish need frying to stand around and dawdle, to falter between two opinions. Duty calls, and the most committed wins, Mark. Always has, always will. Now get to it son!" Phailees clapped Adams on the shoulder, just the right amount of pressure to deliver that fatherly encouragement, the loving prodding of a mentor.

Adams drew his expandable metal baton and snapped it downward, fully extended and locked out.

"That's my boy! Showtime!" Phailees voice cackled with glee.

Adams screamed as he lunged forward and loosed a primal anger genetically passed down to him from so very long ago. A passion for justice and an indomitable desire for vengeance fueled the rage that beat down on Chad Bigleby. The first blow landed, the first stone cast; the dam broke and unleashed hell. Blow after blow rained down on Chad's body, crushing, breaking, bruising, bouncing his flesh up and down over the pavement, the force unyielding, irresistible, as the life fled his limp form. The last blows made the broken corpse dance around in a queer little jig. As he stopped Adams laughed, laughed long and hard, and then wiped the sweat off his brow, thankful for the fruit of his labor. Justice was served.

Phailees walked up and grabbed Chad's fractured leg by the cuff of his pants. "Well, ah B, B, B, B, B, B ... dat's all folks." And with that, in one fell motion he threw Chad's body through the air and into the nearest dumpster, clapped his hands, walked back to Adams, and embraced him.

Adams startled awake, Amy squeezing him tightly. He gasped for air, feeling out of breath. Amy opened her eyes and looked at him.

"There's my hero," she whispered softly to him and kissed his lips. Beneath her, his ribcage rose and fell quickly. Amy pressed her hand to his chest, felt his wildly beating heart, saw the sweat on his forehead. "You ok, Mark?"

He took a deep breath, slowed his breathing and answered. "Bad dream."

"I'm sorry, honey. You did wonders for me. I dreamed I was being chased, but you fought for me and saved me—my knight in shining armor." Amy pulled his head down gently and held him to her breasts, caressed his head, tussled his hair, drew her fingernails lightly across the back of his neck. His nerves danced, his hair tingled, goose bumps rearing wherever her fingers touched skin. His loins stirred, alive with excitement.

"Amy, please … don't tease me. I can't take it right now." Adams was consumed with sexual tension, a static electricity enveloping his whole body.

Amy whispered in his ear. "I'm not teasing, Mark," and then her hand grabbed his and guided it between her legs. She moaned, louder than she had intended. Her voice was breathy and desperate for him, her eyes seductive and lascivious, her mouth insatiably hungry. Mark's hand was wet, the heat of her warming his skin through the sweatpants.

"Mark, I want you now," she panted in his ear. "Take me now … pleeeeaaase …" She begged and moaned and began moving her hips, grinding against his hand, which was moving now all on its own, cupping and squeezing, rubbing, circling, pressing.

"I've missed you sooo bad, Mark," she groaned. "Pleeaase …"

Adams lifted his head and leaned toward her. Her mouth opened wide, lips moist and full joining with his, tongues intertwining like two snakes. She released his hand, confident it needed no further help and sought out the edge of his pants, unbuttoning and releasing the zipper before she plunged her hands within his boxers and wrapped her delicate fingers around him.

It was his turn to moan.

"Oh God, Mark … I have missed you! I want you now … now!" Her voice turned commanding, insistent, clamoring for an immediate response.

Adams scooped her up, stood, and headed for the bedroom, eyeing her as he smiled.

"You, little lady, are in deep trouble." He dropped her on the bed and pulled off her pants, socks and shirt, then gazed at her naked body, luscious curves, full breasts, gorgeous skin, and beautiful lips. Every part of her called to him, urgency apparent in the constant squirming of her body, desperate for his attention.

"Oh, I hope it's a lot of trouble!" Her face was beautiful, angelic, yet mischievous and full of passion and sensuality. She spread her legs slightly and motioned for him to come to her.

He grabbed her buttocks with both hands and in one sweeping motion pulled her to the edge and knelt to consume her like a fine wine. Amy groaned loudly, grinding her hips up and down as she panted, nearly hyperventilated, back arching, head thrown back. A shameless cry escaped her mouth as the orgasmic riptide dragged her out to a sea of all-consuming bliss. Floating along on rippling currents, tiny aftershocks from a cataclysmic force caressed her entire body. A small eternity later she sat up, kissing him deeply before she spoke, her voice quivering.

"Oh my God, Mark. That was glorious! But those clothes must come off, now!"

Amy yanked the shirt over his head, before snatching his pants down around his ankles and swallowing him whole in an instant. Sensation overload weakened his knees and he lay back on the bed. A minute later, his pants were ripped all the way off and Amy climbed on top, slipping him inside before swirling and grinding her hips, round the world, up and down, his own hips synchronizing their thrusting movements to match her own. In time they climaxed together, rested, then renewed their efforts, not yet content, their bodies still hungry for one another. With unrestrained passion, they enjoyed the fruit of their covenant bond, the two having physically become one flesh again, at last.

They both lay spent, Amy sprawled across his torso, knees hugging his ribs. Moments later, sleep embraced them both again.

Adams dreamed of the dead, of the victimized, the restless souls who have found no peace. He heard their cries for justice, their pleas for an advocate, one who would champion their cause among the living.

Annie O'Reilley sought Adams out in his dreams. He was the one, the Avenger of Wrath, whose name now drifted along the lips of the dead.

Adams listened intently until he could understand the words of her mournful song. Where she led he followed, into the city to see the place of her death and beyond to the abandoned warehouse. She brought him to the forgotten dumpster, a defenseless coffin for her rotting corpse, the maggots and rats feasting as they pleased. She whispered everything to him. Adams knew it all now—the scandalous blackmail, the money, and exactly how Chad Bigleby murdered her. Most importantly, he knew where Annie O'Reilley's body lay, anxiously waiting for justice.

Chad slowly regained consciousness, and with it, clarity, as the scraping of his chest and face on rough pavement brought him out of the fog. He rolled over to his back, instinctively protecting his face, realizing his right leg was lifted high, something tall dragging him along.

Mr. Phailees never broke stride, just spoke briefly.

"Get comfy, Chad; it's a long walk back to our vehicles."

It seemed to go on forever. Chad gritted his teeth at the pain in his back as small bits of glass embedded into his flesh, cutting tiny intersecting paths from one end to the other. Chad was glad when Mr. Phailees stopped, stood him up, and threw him in the cargo area of the Suburban. He lay still, almost thankful for the lack of any new injury or pain, content now to simply deal with what he had.

Mr. Phailees hopped in the driver's seat and cut out the deflated air bag as Phobos took up the shotgun position, antsy, his excitement showing. Phailees tossed the airbag in the backseat then drove off.

"What's next, sir? Are we gonna book this one?"

"Yes, Phobos. Yes, indeed. We'll book him, then stand back and watch the others do their worst."

"Cool." Phobos said it quietly as he looked ahead, anticipation filling him, a rookie's awe.

"What do you mean 'book him'?" Chad asked from the back. "Where are you taking me?" His voice was raspy and broken. It hurt to talk.

"A very, very bad place, Chad. I'm sure you'll feel right at home. Now just relax, and enjoy the music."

With that Phailees turned on the radio. Bob Marley's "Three Little Birds" was playing.

"My, my, Chad. I really don't think that man had a clue. You've got a lot to be worried about, Chad!" Phailees chuckled with some exhuberance. "Let's find something else, why don't we?"

Mr. Phailees hit the seek button and Mick Jagger's voice suddenly flooded the interior singing title phrase of the Rolling Stones' song "Time Is on My Side".

Chad recognized the tune Mr. Phailees had been whistling before.

"I'm afraid that one isn't for you either, Chad. That's our song, though Phobos! Yes, it is. Humph. Let's try again, shall we." Phailees smiled and hit the seek button once more.

"Mad World" by Tears for Fears came on just as the chorus was beginning.

"Yes, much more fitting, fairly accurate, though you may disagree with the 'best' part he mentions."

They drove for an indeterminate period of time, various songs organizing during the course of the trip to form some theme, it seemed. AC/DC's "Highway to Hell", Metallica's "For Whom the Bell Tolls", the Eagles' "Hotel California", Steppenwolf "Magic Carpet Ride", and Megadeth's "Devil's Island", as well as many others Chad could not recall for certain.

Eventually they arrived, but Chad could not see where "here" was. He heard what sounded like an enormous bay door roll up, clanging and banging as it went. They drove inside, and all the stars disappeared. Only shadow filled the world above as Chad looked up through the window.

"All right, Phobos, you get the honors," Mr. Phailees announced, his tone obviously proud.

Phobos lifted the back door, his body partially changing into half man and half bestial mix of both wolf and serpent. His skin grew leathery and sprouted dark hairs, as his brow widened and forehead thickened, amber eyes aglow, cut by vertical obsidian slits. He wore the uniform still, but now had the police hat fixed upon his head, tilted down, two fingers between his nose and the brim. He grabbed Chad by the cuff of his pants and hauled him out, letting him fall hard on the worn concrete. He began following Mr. Phailees, dragging Chad behind him, his posture perfect.

They were buzzed through a heavy metal door into a long corridor lined with glass on each side. Chad could not see through any of the windows, but he heard the screams, shrieks, bloodthirsty howls, gross grunting, sloppy gurgling, and finally, the quiet panting noises that some made once their initial excitement died down.

They continued on and were buzzed through another door, entering a large room with a desk on the left and a wall to the right. Phobos dragged Chad up to the counter and let him go. Mr. Phailees was already waving at someone Chad couldn't see. Lying up against the counter with an overhang above made it pretty much impossible, but something big moved in response to Mr. Phailees, the ground trembling slightly.

"Phobos, this is Charon and Mortis. Fellas, this is my new partner … and son, Phobos."

"Pleased to meet you, young fella," they both rumbled, the bass in their voices causing a vibration in the floor. Phobos returned the greeting and stood quiet, obviously proud.

"Chip off the ole block, eh Phailees?" Charon asked, smiling broadly.

"He's sharp looking," quipped Mortis, nodding at Phobos.

Charon chuckled then spoke. "So, he's got his first one for Level 9, huh Phailees?"

"Yes indeed! That's our man, a traitorous, greedy, lustful, murdering miscreant!"

"Sounds like fun," Mortis said. "I swear, you get all the good ones."

"Gentlemen, when you look this good and have mastered the job like I have, it's hard not to."

Phailees stood leaning one elbow on the counter, blowing the fingernails of his other hand and polishing them on his shirt then thumbed his hand in Phobos' direction.

"And my son is a dogged runner. No getting away from this one. Gonna be a regular serial killer right there. Traitors will be pissing themselves at just the smell of him."

Chad could hear two distinct laughs, dark and booming, reverberating within the spacious chamber.

"Ain't that right, Phobos?"

"You know it, sir!"

Mortis chimed in, still chuckling deeply.

"You're a hoot, Phailees! That's why we always love to see you. We know we'll get a good laugh."

"Thank you, thank you." Mr. Phailees bowed at the waist then knelt and grabbed Chad's face. Holding his jaw and cheeks in his left hand Phailees lifted Chad up, feet dangling well off the floor, then struck a pose, head tilted back, right arm bent up and to the side, his palm lifted in the air.

"But alas, poor Chadwick here must be dealt with. Ah, Mortis, I know him well, the cheeky conniving bastard! He will scream and wail and cower too, but there's a beast inside, he'll not remain quiet, he'll want his due."

Mortis and Charon laughed and smacked their thighs, tears welling in their huge eyes, Mr. Phailees' mock Shakespeare recital just what they needed. He bowed again, then dropped Chad to the floor and brushed his hands together.

"Purell, Phobos?" Mr. Phailees reached behind the counter and grabbed a small bottle of hand sanitizing gel, proceeded to apply it liberally, then handed it off to Phobos. The laughs continued behind the counter.

"Well, gents," Mr. Phailees nodded politely, and stood off to the side, out of the way, "we'll be letting ye be about ye business now. Don't mind us. You know we just like to watch." Phobos nodded and followed suit.

Charon came around to inspect Chad, while Mortis recorded all the pertinent personal data Mr. Phailees had to provide. Chad felt each step as the creature plodded forward, slowly and deliberately.

The first thing Chad saw were the huge cloven hooves, hairless tree trunk calves rippling beneath brown, earthy hide. Reverse jointed knees supported tremendous thighs, the muscles hidden by blue uniform pants. The creature's pelvic girdle was wide and thick, but the torso was enormous, swelling outward in a solid V shape, barrel-chested, the lat muscles freakishly broad and dense, easily apparent even through a short-sleeved uniform shirt.

It stood over Chad, silently studying him.

"Humph! You may be right Phailees. He's scared now, but give him some time to adapt, we may have a real monster on our hands."

Chad stared in awe. Charon's whole upper body was covered in coarse hair, matted and shaggy, varying shades of brown, black, and auburn. His neck was massive, the head broadening from nose to crown.

Charon bent over, bringing his head closer to Chad, in order to scrutinize him. Chad had to move his eyes side to side to take in the creature's whole face at this distance. Charon's forehead was the breadth of four normal men's put together and though his hair was most bountiful on top of the head, he also possessed an incredibly full goatee, hanging down past his collar bones.

Charon looked Chad in the eyes. His eyes were set wide apart, two large orbs blinking as they attempted to stare directly into Chad's soul.

Charon snorted through his nostrils, blowing air into Chad's face along with a slight trace of mucus. Chad winced, reflexively squinting his eyes shut and moving his head back a little, but otherwise he stayed still.

"So," Charon addressed Chad directly. "Do you think you're a monster in the making? Hmm?"

Chad opened his eyes back up and wiped his face cautiously with one hand. The last thing he wanted was for this behemoth to react to his movement and turn those bright ivory horns growing from the temple areas against him. They were thick and twisted and curved up sharply before running along the arc of Charon's skull.

"Well?" Charon inquired, standing up straight again.

Chad was sure he stood at least nine feet tall, and was undoubtedly male. Huge manacle-like polished brass bracelets adorned each wrist, and the arms were long and disproportionately muscular, ending in fists like huge mauls.

Chad's voice quivered, barely audible.

"I don't think so."

"Hmm. Interesting. Doubt of the darkness in your heart is a sure sign it has run amok."

Chad's eyes were suddenly drawn to Charon's belt. It was made of twisted hair, which looked peculiarly like human hair, fitted with a polished brass buckle. Chad's stomach twisted and grew ill.

"Very well, Phailees. Level 9 it is. We'll find the monster if he's in there." With a smile, Charon grabbed Chad by the cuff of his left pants leg and began dragging him with only his upper back touching the ground, his right leg hanging down awkwardly.

Chad could see a coiled whip hanging from Charon's right hip. It was huge, the thickness of a young boy's arm, tiny brass weights stitched to it in a spiral pattern that climbed from base to tip. Chad figured it had to be at least twenty feet long.

They exited through one door into another corridor. It was all stone, no windows, and only lit by an occasional torch, the darkness teeming with movement, just deep enough to stay hidden from common observation. Chad tried to keep his head up so it didn't constantly bounce off the worn stones.

After a short time, the path turned into a gradually increasing downward slope. Charon began humming, the same tune Chad heard Phailees whistling before. Oblivious to all else, the creature walked on.

In time, the declining path turned into a spiral cobblestone roadway, at least forty feet wide, bordering on what must have been a tremendous abyss. As they descended further, they came to what appeared to be a large terrace, open and flat, almost like a prison yard but incredibly large, stretching back farther than Chad could see.

There were people everywhere milling about lethargically: unmotivated, depressed, and downcast. Some were in groups talking. Chad could hear them. They were all debating how good they were, complaining about the injustice of their current situation. Others moaned and lamented out loud, but all alone. They were all restless and weary, each one unable to accept the reality they found themselves in, unable to square with what they truly were. Burdened and weighed down by denial, they struggled on in vain attempts to justify who they thought they had been in life, lying to themselves and each other. Never at rest, never knowing peace, they seemed obsessed with the unending toil of filling their mouths with arguments to prove they were worthy of more, attempting to convince their fellow fallen souls, but never truly convinced themselves.

Chad watched as he dropped below the terrace and out of eyeshot of the mob. The last thing he saw was a gaunt woman in dirty clothing who locked eyes with him and ran near the precipice to shout urgently.

"I don't belong here! I don't belong here! Do you hear me? Dammit! Listen to me. I don't belong here! I'm not guilty!"

Her plea turned to indignation, and she cursed Charon. Suddenly, something unseen grabbed her. In that instant, before she disappeared, her eyes flew wide and her face filled with a terrible recognition she had broken some law and would pay dearly for it.

Chad and Charon continued their descent, and soon another terraced courtyard came into sight. From slightly above, Chad saw the horde of people, their appearance quite inhuman. Uncontrolled appetites for one another had taken their toll, each cursed entity consumed by uninhibited passions. They engaged in hideous orgies, public spectacles of gross indulgence, ever escalating in excess, their degree of depravity boundless. Numb souls desperate to feel, they took no pleasure in the ordinary, tasted no joy within the limitations of the mundane. They would always toil in vain, forever seeking more, but satisfaction would never come. The object of their affections branded them slaves and demands absolute, obsessive commitment. They bear the burdensome yoke of futility, the curse of disabled hearts struggling to feel something.

Pain became like pleasure to them because feeling something was far better than the yawning nothingness that devoured their will to struggle on. Necessity of some relief drove them on to more deviant ingenuity. And so, they dehumanized and degraded one another, willingly accepting violations of the worst order, willingly possessing innumerable ways of abusing and being abused until their bodies could stand no more and disease and deterioration set in. They were dead, and dying daily, unable to resist their repulsive, yet gnawing cravings. Beauty fled their lives long ago when they rejected her pleasant calls. And now they are slowly consumed, the rotting worm within their flesh, never full.

Charon plodded ever downward, dragging Chad along. He stared aimlessly in shock, his face upturned and absolute horror filling his eyes as dread and hopelessness consumed his whole countenance. Each level was its own hell, something hiding in us all, something unavoidable.

In time, Chad saw a wasteland composed of brittle stone, boulders, stubble grass, withered bushes, dust bowls, and tumbleweeds. A wandering horde of sullen people staggered about beneath the weight of unmet expectations, shattered hopes, and perceived injustice; depression consumed their minds until, at last, frustration built to irritation and boiled over. Unable to take it anymore, they would fall upon one another to lash out in rage. None could find peace; nothing could ease their frustrations. An unwarranted fury flowed within their veins, their skin itself like thorns, full of venom,

and no one who came close could avoid injury or contamina-
tion.

Roaming amongst them were the bitter ones. Their faces
were like flint, smoldering eyes, hearts of cold stone—full of
fury. They were keenly cynical, sure of everyone's guilt and
never trusting anyone. They never felt anything but calculated hate for those who hurt them and were capable of little
but indifference towards the rest of mankind. They bite from
the shadows, their words caustic, dripping hostility. They
have completely rejected any offer of redemption. Resolved
to never forgive or forget, their resentment stank like a
bloated corpse. There was no place for them to find love,
peace, or community. In time, they destroyed everything
good.

Chad locked eyes with one woman and felt the icy poison
reach out for him. He covered his face and waited until he
was sure he and Charon were out of sight.

A battlefield of sorts came into view. From above, he
could see it stretch out of sight, hundreds of thousands of
souls engaged in conflict, a massive free-for-all with occasional allegiances of convenience and mutual benefit. Each
one lashed out in violent fury against his neighbor with motives unique to each one. Some lashed out in unrestrained anger, some in cold, calculated vengeance. Many shed blood
for mere personal gain, their greed unrestrained, their sense
of self entitlement demanding everyone else obey and supply
their needs, and if not, the consequences were swift and
harsh, often murderous. Tortures were plentiful in covert
places, ignored by the greater mass, the strong and demented
abusing the weaker vessels, violating them in every conceiv-
able way one could imagine until at last the weak grew strong
with bitter resolve and rose up to abuse their captors in turn
with zealous rage, gladly returning every brutish deed with
an escalating vengeance. For every last soul, the graphic
atrocities committed became the penalty received. Chad was

helpless to stop looking, some part of it all ringing true with him.

Deeper down, whole groups were consumed by artifice, misdirection, underhanded guile, and chicanery. Their sole defining drive and source of pleasure was weaving deceptive webs and refining their wiles on one another. They were fraudulent, maliciously strategic to a fault. They could never trust, always wary, paranoid of what they might lose if they believed a word. Each attempt at selling their own lies was another play at credibility. They were intent on stealing something of value, whether faith, emotional involvement, sexual favors, or material possessions. Everyone was victim and offender, continually stuck in a vicious cycle, using one another for their own gain.

At last, Chad and Charon reached the bottom. A vast plain stretched out as far as Chad could see, spotted by small rocky crags and large thatch-roofed huts. The only observable movement was some interspersed sightings of individuals being led from one hut to another by creatures that resembled Charon and Mortis.

Charon dragged him through the maze of huts. Chad's back was raw and ragged, his limbs aching and stiff, his wounds from the car crash and beatings having increased in pain during their descent. Chad heard horrible screams of both rage and anguish. He could only imagine what was happening behind the wooden walls, but he was sure he would not be curious for long.

Charon approached a hut from which Chad heard no noise of any kind. He opened the door, ripped Chad's clothes from his body, then tossed him inside, naked. The room was bare, except for a wooden stool and a few small shelves holding lightly flickering candles, shadows dancing on the walls. The floor was old wood, hard and full of splinters.

Charon spoke up, his voice deep and booming, but filled with dignity and sincerity.

"Welcome home, Mr. Bigleby. You have arrived at Level 9. Enjoy your stay."

With that, Charon turned and exited the hut, closing the door firmly behind him.

All was silent for a time. Chad lay on his side, facing the door, immobile, unable to command his body to do anything beyond slightly lifting his head and shifting his gaze. Sleep or unconsciousness finally overtook him.

He woke slowly as the door creaked open. Darkness filled the threshold until Charon stepped aside, allowing a lady to enter. Her naked body remained silhouetted against his shadowy form until the door was closed again. Candle light danced off her heavy, sagging breasts and stretch marks. Her moderate frame and full figure could have been attractive, but presently, a mixture of caked blood and dried mud were smeared across her torso and upper thighs like finger paint.

Chad caught her eyes just then in the low light. They were bordering on a lunatic fury, pupils dilated and whites jaundiced, her expression wild. Her chest was beginning to heave, shallow at first, but quickly deepening. The woman suddenly sucked in air violently and screamed, her whole body sinking, bending, projecting all her rage with arms at her side, fists clenched.

As the scream died down she scrambled forward frantically, launching herself onto Chad's helpless body in a brutal frenzy. Arms swung with a fury, fists slamming again and again before she leapt all around him, stomping and kicking from every angle. Then, at last, when that would not quench her thirst for wrath, she fell upon Chad and began clawing and biting his exposed flesh.

Chad felt every painful blow at first, but soon went numb, his mind unable to consciously handle what was happening to him. He found a happy place and went there in his mind. Clean beaches with crystal blue water, warm sand, a beach chair, beer, and a beautiful woman sitting next to him.

Chad did not hear the distinct thudding and thwacking noises emanating from his flesh, nor did he continue to feel the shock of impact. He was Zen. He was one with a distant dream.

Finally, exhausted of all emotional fervor, she ceased and stood erect, stomped the back of his head one last time as an afterthought, then slowly backed away until she tucked herself in the shadows beneath a candle.

Her right hand twitched violently as she tried to chew her fingernails. Periodically her eyes reflexively squinted, head seizing to the left simultaneoulsy, shaking and turning at an awkward angle. She squatted in the corner, buttocks touching her heels, whispering hoarsely to herself. A man had betrayed her. He led her along, made her think she was the one. Told her she was the best in bed he ever had, said "I do" and promised they would live happily ever after. But he was a traitor, an adulterer. He abandoned her for another woman, took all the money and left her penniless, his lawyer better than hers. There was agonizing pain, remorse, regret, guilt, shame, anger, bitterness, and plans of revenge, now finally fulfilled.

Chad was not that man, but it did not matter what was true, only what she saw.

"Why are you doing this to me?" Chad croaked weakly barely able to look up at her.

She screamed, left hand clutching a fistful of hair before yanking it out.

"Shut up! Don't you dare speak to me! Shut up!"

That was all it took to work herself back up, the emotional burden building to a punishing zeal again. She threw herself on Chad again with fervent drive, her cathartic passion demanding release once more.

Chad received the justice he was due, even if by a foreign hand. The woman finished. Charon entered and led her away. A short time later, he returned and let a man enter. He was naked, dirty, lacerated, bruised, bloody, and downcast. He took one look at Chad and fury flew up within him.

"You!?! It's you! I've been waiting years to pay you back. Do you know how long it took me to regain my position at the company after you stabbed me in the back? Do you know how hard it was to start all over and climb the ladder again? How overwhelming the financial burden was after my demotion? I had to be like you! I had to cut the legs out from under Harry Johnson, and Michael Candis, just to keep my head above water. For God's sake, I was their friend, but you left me no choice! It's all your fault, and now, finally, you're going to pay!"

The man strode forward, his actions fully measured, the rage articulate and intentional. He beat Chad methodically until his hands and feet hurt, and then he grabbed what lay near. Pieces of pottery smashed into Chad's head and knees. A candlestick was a fine club and the burning candle itself allowed him to melt his name in Chad's flesh. A cold malice fueled his vision of vengeance, unabated until another Minotaur creature came and led the man away.

More people arrived, bled their wrath on Chad, then left. Chad lost all sense of time, one beating blurring into another. Eternity became a sea current that he swam against, always trying to keep the beach in sight.

Then the door opened and a beautiful woman walked in, her face serene, pleasant, and kind. Her body was naked, firm, shapely, and clean; her skin tan and glistened with a slight sheen of sweat. Pity filled her eyes. She held a pitcher of water, a bowl of food, some form of liniment, and a thick cloth. She looked at Chad, clearly sympathetic, but when she took a step forward he still reflexively flinched away and covered his head.

She knelt, wet the cloth, and began wiping away the blood and wringing it out on the floor. She repeated the process until his whole body was clean, then rubbed the healing liniment into every cut and bruise. Slowly, over days it seemed, they healed, but his strength was sorely lacking. Chad's mouth opened mechanically to receive the food she spooned in, and his vigor gradually returned. The lady stood and retrieved a large blanket from a shadowy corner, laid it on the floor, and wrapped them inside together. Her lips found his, kissed him deeply as she slipped her leg over his hips and slid on top. She loved him, and all the gates of hell could not have threatened the joy of that moment.

That was Chad's life for an unknown time. Sleep, wake, love again, eat, and sleep some more, this woman nourishing him back to health. Time was immeasurable, but at last, Chad was able to stand, his thighs steady, his shoulders held back, head erect, arms calm, his center still.

The lovely lady stood as well, slipping away from the shadows, her feet gliding along the floor, her hips moved like silk flowing back and forth in a breeze. She approached, hands clasped coyly behind her back. They embraced, her right arm easing around his shoulders to grab his neck and pull him closer. She kissed him deeply, and even as her tongue slipped inside his mouth, the dagger in her left hand slipped deep inside his liver.

Chad felt an incapacitating pain. His knees buckled but held, his left arm tucking instinctively to his side. She pulled her head away and stared into his eyes. He stared back at her, uncomprehending. She held his neck still, smiled slightly, then ran his heart through as well. She kissed him lightly on the lips, pulled the dagger out sharply with a twist, and let Chad fall to the floor.

The door opened, but no one was there. Without a word, she turned and walked away, leaving him to die. Chad lay catatonic, awake or unconscious, one could not say. Time stretched beyond comprehension and coiled back on itself, almost as if he had stepped outside of it, but eventually his body did heal, two angry scars etched in his torso.

More people came and beat him, but Chad did not care. His happy place was one of retribution. He could hold out forever for a chance to avenge himself on the wench who betrayed him. He had visions of what he would do all day long, particularly vivid during each battery. It made him hard, resilient, and indomitable.

At last the people stopped coming, and Charon opened the door to find Chad sitting in a corner, eyes closed, whispering to himself. Charon motioned for Chad to follow. He stood and exited the hut, the sky above dark and red, but bright to him. Charon led him through the maze of huts, until they stopped in front of one. A glance back at Chad revealed a countenance of stone, a stiff neck, and cold eyes. He smirked and opened the door, gesturing for Chad to enter. Chad did so, his eyes quickly adjusting to the shadows and candlelight.

A naked woman lay on her side on the floor, beaten and dirty, but still beautiful, her eyes slowly opening, blinking tears away to roll down her cheek. Her face lifted slightly, trying to see who it was. Chad moved slowly towards her, curiosity peaked. His form cleared the shadows, emerging into the flickering candlelight, his face easily distinguishable.

"Oh God. Not you ..." The voice was terrified and weary, but Chad knew it.

It was her.

The two fresh scars over his liver and heart burned mildly. He touched them absently and smiled, a cruel anticipation spreading across his face.

Chad stalked across the room and kicked her hard in the stomach; the breath violently expelled from her lungs. His fury was torrid and unrestrained as he fell upon her in a primal rage, the bestial visions that kept him going throughout all the beatings now becoming reality. He leapt about, abusing her in every way he had imagined: beatings, biting her nipples, ripping her hair out and smothering her with his bare hands as he stared into her eyes, cursed her, and mocked her fear. But nothing satisfied his vengeance. Not enough. Not enough! was his constant internal dialogue. There was only one debasing abuse that could truly repay such betrayal.

He held her down, hands pinned by her head, and slid between her thighs, shoving his way inside then violating her with increasingly vicious thrusts where once she had willingly accepted him with feigned love. His rage boiled over, his hands engulfing her skull, thumbs seeking out her eyes, covering them, threatening destruction, her head immobilized against the floor as he continued his primal thrusting assault.

"Pay! Damn you! Pay for what YOU … DID … TO … ME!" he snarled in sync with the most violent and explosive thrusts he could manage, gasping for more air in between each one.

He wrapped his hands around her throat and squeezed, watching the life slip ever so slowly from her eyes. His breath blew heavily with every thrust, his arms locked out and rigid, spittle dripping on her face. Over and over again, she nearly passed out, but he relaxed his hold then began choking her again. At last, he was undone with rage, no amount of punishment able to satisfy his bitter obsession. Pinning her neck to the stone floor with one hand, he began slamming hammer-fist blows into her nose, pummeling her again and again, screaming like some rabid chimpanzee until at last her face was a swollen, bloody, crumpled mass.

Chad was sure she was dead, but it was not enough. Sitting in the corner breathing heavily, he whispered to himself of how she got her due, but it still wouldn't satisfy. His vengeful spirit wouldn't be content. His anger rose repeatedly like the tide, and each time he returned to defile her limp body, rolling her face down to penetrate her and pound her back. Then he'd drag her around by her hair or feet and throw her body into the walls repeatedly. Incapable of fully purging his animosity, his heart became a hate factory at full production with no moral restraint.

Mr. Phailees stood in the shadows the whole time, quietly chuckling and telling Phobos numerous times

"What'd I say? I told you so. You see? I was right. There's a monster in there."

Eventually Charon returned, placed a hood over Chad's head, and led him out of the hut. They walked for a short time, Mr. Phailees and Phobos trailing quietly behind, before a small rock outcropping appeared with a vertical face. Mortis stood next to a huge polished silver wall that resembled a mirror embedded in the face of the rock.

A large post was buried in the ground, a mere three feet from the silver wall. It bore a thick metal ring with a pair of shackles run through it. Charon secured Chad's hands with the shackles, removed the hood, and took a step back.

Chad looked at himself, not realizing it was him for a few seconds.

The image in the mirror was hideous. The head and face were near simian, apelike, an ancient frenzied hate clearly evident in his countenance. Large canine teeth were just beginning to peak beyond the edge of his lips. Blood spray spattered his body from head to toe, but his muzzle, teeth, and hands were drenched in it. His eyes were cold and full of a wicked fury, uncaring, unyielding, and purely narcissistic.

Mortis nodded at Charon.

The whip slammed into Chad's back, each tiny brass weight ripping through his flesh with tremendous force. It took his breath away and his knees went out, dropping him forward to the ground. He caught himself with his shackled hands. Another blow landed, splattering blood across the silver wall. Over and over, Charon let the scourge fly and snap and rend and return again to slither along the ground behind him, coiling for another assault.

Mr. Phailees spoke, plain and blunt.

"Your hubris is mythical and typical all at the same time, Chad. Perhaps Charon's chastening lashes may purge it from your soul, but I think not. Every beat of your heart carries it

to every cell. It's who you are. You refuse to change, to confess and accept responsibility, and that is why I will not relent. You are promised to me, Chad, and soon I will come to
take what is my due."

Mr. Phailees nodded at Mortis.

"Finish him. We're done here for tonight."

Mortis stepped up behind Chad, his right hand covered
in a huge brass gauntlet. Chad looked up as Mortis's left arm
slid around his neck as if to choke, but cupped over the top
of his shoulder instead. The gauntleted hand grabbed his chin
and twisted casually, removing all slack. Eyes swollen and
clouded by blood, Chad knew the end was inevitable. Mortis's arms exploded outwards, shoulder blades nearly crashing together on his back, Chad's head snapping sharply on its
axis, far beyond the natural range of motion. A tremendously
loud popping noise escaped from his vertebrae as they broke.
A flash of blinding light amidst all the darkness consumed
his vision, an explosive pulse spreading out from the center
of his mind's eye, filled only by shadow in its wake.

Adams woke early, the dream fresh in his mind, every
detail crystal clear. He slid out from under Amy's lithe frame,
tucked the covers around her shoulders, and feather kissed
her cheeks. She moaned slightly and nuzzled his face, but
never woke. For a short time, he got on Google maps and
surfed around trying to get the big picture, connect the dots.
First, he located the strip mall where they found the car and
pinpointed the building where Chad's business meeting was.
Then he scanned the surrounding areas, letting the dream
guide him. It didn't take long to find the abandoned warehouse about thirty minutes north of the office building. He
zoomed in.

"I'll be damned," he said out loud. "Looks just like my
dream."

Adams was motivated now; a hunter whose prey was finally in sight. He called Detective Andrews.

"Hullo?"

"Andrews. It's Adams. Wake your ass up, we got a body to go find."

Andrews glanced over at his alarm clock. "Fuck, Mark! Its only 6:00 a.m. and today's my day off. Seriously?"

"Andrews, I think I might know where the body is. I had an epiphany and checked a bunch of stuff on Google maps. Consider this, if you're an intelligent guy and don't want to get caught, are you going to dispose of the body near where you ditch the car?"

"No, I suppose not," Andrews mumbled, still groggy.

"And, if you want the victim to just appear to be missing you need to ditch the body somewhere no one's going to find it for a long time, right."

"Yeah ... and ..." Andrews was following the train of thought but felt impatient.

"So, add to those factors that you have limited time and resources, and you're in the middle of a very built up city, no woods, swamps, rocky cliffs, or anything else to help you out. You need somewhere no one goes, where no one is going to check. There's an abandoned warehouse about thirty minutes north of the office building Chad Bigleby had his meeting. Send the body north, plant the car south, and get all the police on a wild goose chase. She's there, Andrews. I'd bet my paycheck on it."

Andrews warmed to the proposition. "All right, I can see the logic in it, and I think it's worth checking out, but I got one question, Mark. What the hell made you think of this?"

Adams paused for several seconds before answering. "Matt, I'll tell you on two conditions."

Andrews wasn't sure whether he was going to like what he heard.

"One, you agree to go look now and don't change your mind."

"All right. Agreed."

"And two, you don't tell me I'm crazy or anything like that."

"Humph. We'll see on that one. Give it to me."

"I had a dream."

Andrews sputtered on the other end of the line.

"Shit, man! I'm serious!" Adams' genuine conviction came through in his voice. "Clear as day, every step of the way, like Annie herself was showing me how and why everything went down, where it happened, and where he dumped her body. It was surreal."

"Holy fuck, Mark! Have you been licking acid or something? Bad Ambien trip? One of your martial arts gurus slip you some mushrooms or mescaline? Seriously?!"

"Hell, no! Are you daft?"

"But if we find something, are you going to tell the judge a ghost told you in your fucking dreams?"

"No! I'll explain it just like I did to you at first. A logical approach that sounds reasonable."

"This is crazy …" he mumbled, "but all right. I'll meet you at the PD in forty-five minutes. We'll leave from there. Should take about an hour to get there, right?"

"Yup. I'll see you there. And, Matt … thanks, man … a lot."

"Yeah. You owe me, dude. This one's on nothing but blind faith. Out."

The line clicked dead, and Adams got ready. He wrote a letter for Amy, printed out directions to the warehouse, then rushed out to climb into his vehicle and sped off.

Chad sat up straight in the recliner, a brief scream escaping his lips as he grabbed his neck. He was feverish, sweating, heart beating in his ears.

The doorbell rang again.

He made his way to the door and peeked out the window between the curtains. A young man, sharply dressed, stood outside, slacks, and button-down shirt and tie. His hair was short, cropped and neatly groomed. He looked quite normal. In fact, outside looked normal as well.

"Thank God," Chad mouthed.

A quick glance at the clock told him it was 11:00 a.m. He looked back out the window and shrank back with a jolt. The man was standing in front of the window now, a badge held up to the glass. Chad saw the words Private Investigator stamped into the metal.

"Good morning, Mr. Bigleby," he called politely. "Could you open your door, please, so we can talk face to face?"

Chad was hesitant. The young man flashed a particularly charming smile with perfect white teeth.

"I assure you, Mr. Bigleby, it is of the utmost importance to you and to your future."

Chad reluctantly moved to the door and opened it, standing on the threshold.

"All right, then," Chad said, "who are you, and what's your business?"

The young man held his badge up again. "Allow me to introduce myself properly, then. I am Investigator Lupin, Private Investigator that is, and I am employed by the attorney representing Marcus O'Reilley during his questioning in the disappearance of Annie O'Reilley. Pleased to meet you, Mr. Bigleby."

Chad had no idea Marcus had an attorney for questioning. Investigator Lupin extended his hand. Chad reached out reflexively to shake it. Lupin's hand was lean but his grip was firm, a steel vise not quite fully cranked down.

Chad just nodded his head in response to the greeting. Lupin continued on.

"Well, Mr. Bigleby, can I come in and sit down, ask you a few questions or have you completely lost your upbringing?" His tone maintained a subtle balance between joking and contempt, while his eyes were completely emotionless.

Chad was taken aback by the brash behavior, the hidden insult. He was unconsciously determined to prove the man wrong.

"No, of course not. Come on in and have a seat. Would you like anything to drink?"

"No. No thank you. I'm fine."

Chad sat on the recliner and Lupin perched on the edge of the loveseat across from Chad, a coffee table in between.

"So, then … Investigator Lupin, what exactly would you like to know?"

"Straight to the point then, good. Well, Mr. Bigleby, or do you mind if I call you Chad?"

"No problem. Go right ahead," Chad replied.

"Ok, Chad, I've been looking into this Annie O'Reilley case, and a lot of things just aren't adding up to me. I'd like to try and find my way through the briar patch. You good with that?"

"Certainly. Shoot." Chad wasn't sure about this guy, but anything he could do to lead interest away from him was a good thing.

"Well, first, what can you tell me about Annie and Marcus's relationship?"

"Call it a train wreck. Never worth anything. Marcus was a verbally, emotionally, and physically abusive hothead, and poor Annie was trapped like a caged animal until she finally got the courage to leave his sorry ass. And he didn't like it when she did. The day Annie disappeared, our office had just served the divorce papers on Marcus, and I'm sure that surprise didn't sit well with him. Coincidence? I don't think so." Chad leaned back in the chair, fingers pressed together in a steeple, flexing slowly in and out.

"Well, I know that sounds all nice and gift-wrapped, but the reality is, Marcus has a very reliable alibi for the times in question, and I spoke to your partner, Sachs, and it turns out the divorce papers weren't a surprise. Annie and Marcus actually had a separation agreement drawn up two weeks before the papers were served. He knew it was coming. So, take away the angry ex's motive."

Chad sat silent, his eyes glancing up in surprise at Lupin before looking away. Annie had not mentioned that at all to him.

"How about you enlighten me on your and Annie O'Reilley's relationship. I understand you were romantically involved, correct?"

"Yes, we were, for about three months now. We were quite happy. I was very close to leaving my wife ... I've not handled her disappearance well at all. I was in the hospital for a couple of weeks and have been on medication ever since. Night terrors and stress-induced hallucinations, my doctor tells me. I miss her deeply." Chad worked his facial features to display the maximum emotional content and hopefully illicit the most sympathy from Lupin possible for all his suffering.

"My God, that's so sad, Chad. But ... I think you're leaving something out." Lupin's eyes fixed Chad with a piercing gaze that seemed to know much more than initially revealed. In fact, the longer Chad looked at Lupin, the more it felt like Lupin knew everything, no matter how implausible that might be. Chad began to squirm in his seat the more his brain became convinced Lupin knew what he had done to Annie.

"I spoke with Brad Buxton, Chad. Your old buddy, your chum. I must say, he absolutely hates your guts. I assured him the details of where the money came from would not come out, but he told me all about how the two of you blackmailed him, screwed him out of his job so you could advance, and then really raped him by nearly emptying his 'savings'." Lupin made little bunny ear quotation marks as he said savings.

"I have a hunch, Chad. A gut feeling, if you will, that Annie, being the smart girl she was, found something in the computer records that you tried to hide … like maybe all the money you blackmailed Brad for, and Annie didn't want to have anything to do with that. Busting a piece-of-crap like Brad and letting you, her beau, take his job, was perfectly acceptable to her, I'm sure, but I don't think that she would have been comfortable with becoming like Brad and using the money he had stolen from all those clients. I bet that didn't sit well with her … not one bit."

Chad sat quietly, his stomach a churning pit, his hands gripping the chair arms. He was desperately trying not to look alarmed or agitated and was failing miserably.

"You know, I spoke to your wife, just yesterday. She told me about y'all's break up, how you've been cheating on her with multiple women over the years. Mentioned some girl named Emily; boy, was she furious over that one, let me tell you. Furious enough, I might add, that she had no problems giving me access to all your phone records. We called up the company and got a list of all numbers called since Annie's disappearance until now."

Chad spit out "you bastard' through gritted teeth. Lupin ignored him.

"And you know what, Chad? I found something very, very … odd." Lupin's chin lifted up slightly, then dropped nearly to his chest for emphasis on the word 'odd,' his eyes staring out at Chad beneath squinted lids.

"You know what I found, Chad? Do you have any idea what was so odd?"

"Enlighten me," Chad said, anger beginning to put an edge in his voice.

"Well, I found all these calls between your cell phone and Annie O'Reilley's cell phone … right up until the day before she disappeared. From then until now you haven't tried calling her once … not once, Chad! That is so … unbelievably damning! If you cared so much, you would have tried to contact her the first day she disappeared. You would have called her probably dozens of times if you cared anything about her. So, the omission of such acts begs the question … what did you already know that everyone else did not, Chad?"

Chad continued to sit silent, breathing increasing, the fight or flight response beginning to build within him.

"Well, Chad, there's only one answer that makes sense, based on everything we know. You didn't call her because you killed her yourself. You knew where she was."

Lupin laughed and shook his head.

"Damn sloppy oversight there, Bigle-boy. You're caught. You did it, and I'll prove it."

Chad suddenly stood.

"Fuck you!" he said sharply, face contorting in a hateful rage. "Talk to my lawyer, and get the fuck out of my house … NOW!"

Lupin stood as well, calmly, unperturbed.

"Chad, I am going to go to the police with everything I know, and the spotlight will turn around and land on you again, but this time it won't go away. You've had your chance to repent, to confess. I'm going to nail you to a cross and watch you squirm."

Lupin spun on his heel smoothly, turning to go.

"Oh, and did I mention, Officer Adams just found Annie's body this morning? They're identifying her remains by dental records as we speak. They also have the murder weapon. A white gym towel. There's DNA all over it—hers and his, that is, yours. They've got everything they'll need to convict you, Chad."

Chad's mouth dropped at the mention of the towel. How? ran through his mind over and over. "That's impossible," he muttered to himself.

"No, Chad. Not only possible, it's a done deal. They have it, just like I'm going to get all that money that you got from

Brad. Maybe we'll see it put back into the proper hands …"
Lupin smiled wickedly.

Panic shot through Chad's brain at the mention of the
money. Robbie his mind screamed, and like a bear protecting
a cub, Chad instinctively reached for a weapon, something
heavy, his hand finding a large pewter statue. Without thinking, he lunged forward, swinging for the back of Lupin's
skull.

Lupin spun, and with uncanny speed and precision, de-
flected the attack, grabbed Chad by the nape of his neck, and
with one smooth motion, swept him off his feet. The vise-
like grip planted Chad's face into the hardwood floor first,
his body catching up a fraction of a second later. Lupin straddled Chad's back, prepared to smother any movement.

A hissing began in Chad's ear, and something wet tickled
it. He cut his eyes as far to the side as he could and wished
he hadn't. Lupin's face had transformed. Dark, thick hair fol-
licles springing out of dense skin, his skull wider, thicker,
with huge, jagged fangs swinging out as his jaw unhinged
and dropped down, forked tongue flickering in his ear. The
hissing came again.

"Pack your toothbrush and soap-on-a-rope, Chad. Oh,
and don't forget the lotion. You're gonna need it for those
lonely nights." Lupin growled low and long as he held Chad
down, hip to hip and hands to head. "I'm sure a pretty boy
like you will be a real popular bitch!" Lupin gave one quick
hip thrust to Chad's ass for emphasis on "bitch."

Lupin's tongue flickered, teasing the edges of Chad's
nostrils, then slithered slowly around his throat and ear until
it circled the puncture wounds on the back of his neck, toying
with them fondly. Chad's body jerked beneath him, muscles
seizing momentarily as if an electric current of fear shot
through him. Lupin chuckled quietly, then stood, face changing back to normal.

"See you soon, Bigle-boy." With that, he wiped his mouth and walked out the front door, not bothering to close it.

Chad scrambled to his feet to get another look at him.

No man was in sight. Trotting down the sidewalk, though, away from his house was a medium sized black dog that looked far too familiar to ever forget. Chad's calf throbbed at the mere sight of him.

By noon Adams and Andrews had finished processing the scene. Annie's body had already been removed to the coroner's office and dental records confirmed her identity. The cause of death appeared to be strangulation, though there was a pretty good bruise on her forehead as well. A white gym towel left with her body appeared to be the murder weapon.

Both men were ecstatic. There was a good chance of transfer of dead skin cells from the murderer in the process of strangling her. They would need to get a court order for a DNA sample from Chad Bigleby, but Adams was sure they had him. It was just a matter of time.

Andrews was packing up his crime scene kit and looked over at Adams.

"Man, I still can't believe it. This is some crazy shit. If I hadn't heard and seen it myself, I'd never believed it. How'd you do it, Mark?"

"Dude … I don't know. Best I can say, it's some kind of gift, maybe. I don't understand it any better than you."

"Hell of a gift, man. Freaky."

"Yeah, well, I'm still the same person, so don't go getting weird on me, K?"

"All right, all right. I'll try not to."

"Ok. Enough of that." Adams felt uncomfortable and wanted to get back to business. "We need to put a rush on the

DNA tests, get the DNA sample order for Chad Bigleby, and, most of all, find Chad Bigleby so we can grill him again."

"Well, Adams, you drive and I'll start making phone calls. Deal?"

"You betcha."

Chad packed an overnight bag with the basic necessities, a couple sets of clothes, passport, and as much cash as he had on him, and headed out the door, sunglasses and baseball cap covering his head. Once in the car, he turned the key in the ignition. The engine turned over but would not start. Again and again he tried, but without success. Fists hammered the steering wheel, lips cursed his luck. He popped the hood and looked underneath.

"MOTHERFUCKER!!!" Frustration reached a critical level. The spark plug wires were all cut, along with other stuff he didn't even recognize. "That fucking bastard!"

Chad slammed the hood closed. Time for Plan B. He turned up the street and began walking for the bus stop. The 12:30 p.m. bus rolled up right on time, and Chad caught a ride over to the park by the H.P. Arkham building. The subway was just a few blocks away, and his bank was en route.

Paranoia became overwhelming. Chad's eyes roamed constantly, searching for police cars, the homeless man, the dog. Safety was ephemeral, fleeting, and it could shatter at any moment. A sense of urgency seized him. He had to make it to the airport and get out of the country … now. "One step at a time," he told himself. "One step at a time."

At the bank, Chad withdrew as much money as he was allowed at one time and quickly hiked over to the subway. It was about 1:00 p.m. when he walked down the stairway and entered the underground.

He would take the subway as far north as possible, then grab a cab for the rest of the way to the airport. The crowd was light, with plenty of space between people and lots of empty seats. He climbed on board the last car and sat down. There was only one other person in the car with him. A red-headed lady wearing a hoodie sat three seats down from him, her face hidden by the loose-fitting material but with her spiral locks hanging out. She appeared to be listening to an iPod.

The cars began to move, and Chad settled back to consider his plans: airport, direct flight to Cambodia, fake ID, and stay off the grid. As he sat thinking he began blinking uncontrollably, his head suddenly swimming. The lights were sizzling, in and out, dim and dimmer. He rubbed his eyes and looked around. The lady had nodded off, chin resting on her chest.

Peripheral vision picked up movement.

Something black and leathery scuttled across the windows and was gone, disappearing into the shadows from where it came. Chad could hear nails scratch, joints pop, and wet flesh slither on the roof, a bumping, broken rhythm of movement echoing inside. What he heard next made his blood thicken and congeal in terror.

It was tremendously loud, a deafening screech within a trumpeting roar that rumbled throughout the tunnel, multiple tones blending into one maddening cry. It came from behind the subway car and reverberated all around him, through him, teeth rattling in his skull. Chad glanced out the side windows quickly, but all he saw was a current of inky darkness sweeping by as they sped ahead.

The primal bellowing noise came again, blasting forth like some clarion call of impending doom, some ancient titan bellow of the damned howling their liturgy of approaching wrath.

Chad's eyes were drawn inexorably, and against his will, to the rear window. Looking out in the tunnel through the small opening was a small death in itself. He saw the leviathan bearing down on him, moving through the shadowy eddies, its pale, pulpy tentacles grasping the tunnel walls, dragging the bulbous body forward.

The subway car shuddered, one tentacle encircling a frame rail along the roof. More tentacles whipped forward, wrapping around until the entire car was constricted by huge cords of flesh, suckers gripping at every contact point.

The car was battered and crumpled all about, creaking and straining; darkness oozed in slowly through fresh cracks in its weakened structure. Chad covered his face and shrieked at the darkness. The rear window shattered inward; a slick purple chasm covered the opening, its muscles contracting and swallowing, it seemed, the contents of the car. At its center, a massive, milky-white appendage coiled and twitched about, retracting back inside the gaping maw.

The orifice heaved and contracted, suddenly sucking in the air around him. A moment later, the trumpeting roar came again, a fog horn cry rising to a siren shriek. The glistening tentacle-like tongue quivered in its mouth; sickly white phlegm spewed out, sticking and jiggling wherever it landed. The noise debilitated Chad, his equilibrium gone, as he crumpled to the floor in the fetal position, hands covering his ears. The whole world shook violently.

There was a horrible belching noise that followed. His sinuses instantly burned, his stomach heaved. The smell of sulfur was unbearable. Chad opened his eyes, despite the stinging. A vaporous tentacle of red and black smoke reached out from the beast's mouth, like a ghostly arm stretching out on shifting angles, searching, seemingly hunting. As it moved overhead it slowed briefly, touched his hair, recoiled and shot forward, snaking its way toward the sleeping lady.

Chad stared in silence, afraid to speak. It wrapped about her neck once then suddenly slipped inside her mouth. She choked and coughed, but the sulfuric smoke continued to infiltrate her lungs, until at last her head snapped back, a wheezing noise escaping her lips before her head slowly settled, chin level, shoulders squared, and the lady stood and turned to look right at Chad.

"Chad Bigleby," the words were spoken in a deliberate manner and laced with contempt. "We need to talk ... and I want your absolute and undivided attention."

She took a step toward him, and the darkness seemed to swarm forward with her. Chad heard the scuttling sounds again: nails dragging, joints popping, a crunching melody accompanied by wet, sloppy, squishing noises. Out of the shadows came a dozen disgusting fiends, emaciated creatures moving on all fours. Limbs rotated about, popping in and out of joint as they crawled and leapt toward Chad. Covered in black, leathery hides, streaked with sweat and some pitch-like syrup, they twitched and jerked their way along in time with the lady's advance. When she screamed, "Get him!" they wailed in response, jaws stretching absurdly to the floor and eyes bulging. They channeled her wrath as if it were their own, as overrunning Chad in an instant. Hands like bony vices seized his limbs, pinning each to the compartment floor.

The creature holding his right ankle clamped down, clinching fingers to palm until his bones crunched audibly. Chad choked back a scream, head lifting reflexively to look at his foot, the pain agonizing. Long talon-like fingers grabbed his face, digging inside his nose, hooking the corners of his mouth, and pulling him back to the floor. Their pitch-like ooze creeped into his nose and mouth and smeared across his face. The redhead with the hoodie jumped deftly up onto him and squatted, feet planted in his abdomen, hands on his chest.

"Do you know who the fuck I am?" Her tone was obnoxious and brimming with rage.

Chad tried to speak, but only a mumble came out.

"Answer me!" A puff of sulfuric smoke escaped her mouth. "Shake your head … yes or no. Do you know who I am?"

Chad shook his head back and forth.

"Figures. Well, I know you. I know that nothing and no one matters to you but yourself. Greedy, lying fuck! That's what you are!"

Chad tried to say something else, but it was unintelligible. The redhead looked at the creatures. "Let him talk," she commanded, and they removed their fingers from his mouth. Chad spat multiple times, expelling the ooze, but not the overwhelmingly disgusting taste.

"Well, who the fuck are you?" he shot back, sarcasm dripping from his lips. Somewhere inside was a small part of him who was done with the suffering, who didn't give a damn any more, and who was tired of putting up with other people's shit. It was only a seed, not grown yet, but it had begun pressing through the soil of his heart.

"Who the fuck am I? You pompous, rat bastard! How dare you back talk me!?" She slapped him square in the face, a loud crack that made her feel a little better. "I'm Annie O'Reilley!" She coughed hard, a larger cloud of smoke swirling out of her throat.

"I'm the woman you betrayed, the one you killed for no other reason than your own goddamn greed! I'm the woman you sentenced to an unthinkable hell. I'm trapped in the gut of that thing, Chad!" She pointed to the broken rear window with the yawning gullet and albino tongue, both gesticulating slowly, patiently.

"My soul is tormented constantly. Fire and brimstone line its belly, maggots fill my body, fiery worms whose flames never flicker. I DIE ALL DAY LONG, Chad Bigleby!! Every day I burn inside and out! And you, you continue on with your life, as if snuffing mine out was of no consequence! And that's not justice! I don't deserve this! I mean,

I'm the fucking victim here. Me! You're the bad guy! I'm the good girl."

Chad laughed at Annie. "Ms. Goodie-Two-Shoes, eh? That what you fancy yourself? Geez! I'm sorry, Annie, but I throw the bullshit flag! You were a seductive, adulterous bitch who helped me blackmail a man out of his job. What the hell did you expect was waiting for you, the pearly gates?"

"Shut up! Shut up, you murdering asshole! I don't care what you think!" Annie clamped her hand around Chad's cheeks and squeezed, forcing him to look her in the eyes.

"I need revenge! Justice, dammit! This is my one chance, Chad, my one chance to grab one little fucking piece of comfort to last me for eternity. I need justice. I need to know that you suffer in life and in death. I need to know that you are exposed for the murdering piece of shit you are. I want to know that, if I'm damned, then you are too, four times over. Goddamn me, but that creature's bowels are disgusting, full of rot and slime, and worms slithering all over me, in and out of me. I vomit all the time, just this momentary reprieve is like heaven. Any hell would be better than this one you have left me in, Chad. I hate you. I despise you. Words alone cannot describe the level of sheer murderous rage I hold for you. You've corrupted me forever. You stole all hope away."

There was a long pause as she held back a cough and composed herself.

"Well now, it's my turn to steal from you. I'm going to expose you for what you are and make you regret every lie you told me, make you want to sell your soul to take back the day you killed me!"

Chad's arrogance shone full on his face.

"Don't bet on it, you fucking bitch! There's nothing you can do to me now. The important stuff is safe, and besides, this is all just a dream anyway. I went through worse than this the last time I fell asleep. This is gravy, girl. Go ahead, give it your best shot!"

"You stupid, ignorant asshole! Wait and see, mother-fucker, just you wait and see!"

Annie picked up a razor lying on the floor, crack cocaine residue clearly visible on it. She lifted Chad's shirt and began carving away at his chest, leaning in hard. Over and over again, she cut, twisted, and turned the blade, then cut again. Chad screamed once, then bit his tongue and held it in. He did not want to give her the pleasure. When she was done she sat back, admired her work and smiled, then pulled his shirt back down, the blood pooling on his chest and soaking through.

"Oh, and I'll be damned if you'll ever use those hands of yours again to kill anyone."

She motioned for the bony creatures to turn his hands palm up, exposing the wrists. She hacked deeply several times at his right wrist, making sure she sliced through the flexor tendons completely before moving on to the left. She coughed repeatedly at the effort, sulfur puffing out of her mouth as blood spurted in time to Chad's heartbeat. Annie stood up, threw the bloody razor away, watching it skip into the darkness.

"You think you have it bad now, Chad? Believe me, it gets a hell of a lot worse around here. I swear to God, I can't wait till you get yours, but this will make me feel a lot better for now. Enjoy your hell, Chad, and by the way, surprise! This is most definitely not a dream."

A scornful smile spread across her lips then parted in laughter, red and black smoke pouring out of her mouth. Chad felt the leviathan begin to inhale deeply and leaned his head back to watch Annie's essence get sucked back inside the hungry mouth. Darkness began to encroach on Chad's vision. He heard the bony creatures hiss, felt them release his limbs, and click and pop and squish their way into the distance, but he couldn't move. The world went black.

He hoped to God he was waking up.

A short time later, rescue squads responded to the subway for an attempted suicide call.

Medics and officers swarmed the scene. A redheaded lady in a hoodie was sitting next to a white male's body. Her backpack was open. There were tourniquets tied around both arms and gauze bandages wrapped around his wrists. Medics did a quick assessment, got the man on a stretcher, and made their way back to the rescue squad. An officer approached the redheaded lady for questioning. He noticed she was wearing scrubs underneath the hoodie.

"You a nurse, ma'am?" he asked.

"Yeah, now I am. I used to be a medic in the Marines. Good thing too, else that guy would be dead right now, I'm sure. He lost a lot of blood, but I always carry a med kit in my go-bag. I was able to tourniquet his arms and stop the bleeding. He should be ok."

"What exactly happened in there?" he asked, nodding at the subway car.

"I'm not entirely sure. I must have nodded off, but when I jerked awake I see this guy laid out on the floor, wrist bleeding everywhere, blood all over his shirt. I stopped the bleeding from his wrists first. Then, when the train stopped, I dragged him out and screamed for someone to call 911. I thought it was a suicide attempt, at first."

"What do you mean, at first? That's what it looked like just now." The officer looked confused.

"Well, it might be, but you need to go take a look under that guy's shirt. That's some creepy shit. You'd have to be pretty hardcore-motivated to do all that to yourself."

"What's under his shirt, ma'am?"

"Someone carved a message in his chest. Kind of hard to read without wiping all the blood away, but you should definitely check it out."

"Thanks ma'am. You work at the hospital?"

"Yeah. ER. Headed to work now."

"Can I get you to fill this statement form out, sign it, and I'll swing by a little later and pick it up?"

"Sure. No problem."

With that, the redheaded nurse left and the officer walked to the ambulance and knocked on the side door. Mack, the paramedic, opened up.

"What's up Rosco?"

"Hey, man, I need you to check something out on this guy. The nurse lady who saved his ass says someone carved a message in his chest. Can you clean it off, and tell me what it says?"

"Wow. That's nasty. Give me a sec."

Officer Rosco leaned in and watched Mack work quickly, clipboard and notepad in hand.

"Read it to me as you clean it up, ok?"

"Sure," hollered Mack.

"All right. Big capital letters across the top spell the word 'GUILTY.'" He paused a few moments to wipe the next area off, blood already seeping out to fill in the barren gashes. "Next is 'I killed.' Humph. Hold on a second … this part looks like a name … 'Annie O'Reilley.'"

"Annie, huh?"

"Yeah."

"What's this guy's name? You got some ID on him?"

"Yeah. Hold on. Let me finish cleaning off these last words. Ok. Last part of the message: 'Punish me.' Wait a second and I'll check that name." Mack leaned over, shuffled through some personal effects and pulled out the ID. "Here it is. Chad Bigleby. His name is Chad Bigleby.'"

"Son-of-a-bitch. We just got a BOLO for a Chad Bigleby. He's wanted for questioning in reference to a murder case, some girl whose body they just found. Girl's name was Annie, I think. I'll need to come with you to the hospital. This guy's going to have to be kept under guard."

"Well, look on the bright side; you can tell the detective we've got a written statement waiting for him at the hospital."

They both broke out laughing.

TUESDAY, JANUARY 16

Chad's nose itched. Without thinking, he tried to move his hand to scratch it but found he could not budge. He tried the other hand with identical results. Slowly, he forced both eyelids open, blinked a few times, and looked around the room. The clock said 12:05 a.m. Fuck, he thought. Not again. But then he looked down at his body. His arms were strapped down, large bandages covered his wrists. His fingers did not obey his commands to move, and his wrists hurt terribly when he tried. An IV was in his left upper forearm, and his mind was quickly waking up to the burning pain covering his chest. A dull throbbing began in his right ankle. A glance down told him there was an air cast on it.

"What the hell?" he mumbled under his breath.

Sitting just outside the open door, Adams heard the rustle of Chad's movements, stood, and walked to the door, magazine in hand.

"Well, if it ain't Sleeping Beauty, back from the dead. I'll call the nurse in here to check on you." Adams lingered at the door.

Chad stared at him blankly for a few seconds then it clicked, the cop who accused him of killing Annie. Great, he thought to himself. Last man he wanted to talk to right now, but he really wanted to know how he ended up hurt and in the hospital.

"What the hell happened to me this time?" he asked.

"Well," Adams began, "you pretty much fucked yourself up real good. Fractured ankle, carved a nice confession in your chest, and managed to slice both wrists to the bone, completely severing your flexor tendons and all blood vessels. If I may say so, though, I personally, really appreciate

the written confession you gave us. Out-fucking-standing."
Adams gave Chad two thumbs up.

Chad was indignant, incredulous even.

"Are you crazy? I didn't do this to myself. Some …" He
stopped mid-sentence and thought carefully about what he
should say. Do I really want to say some redheaded lady possessed by the spirit of my dead ex-girlfriend did this to me?
He pondered it over for a few seconds and decided, Better to
be thought of as crazy and guilty than just plain guilty.

"I'd love to hear what comes after 'some', but before you
start talking, you need to know that you are under arrest for
the murder of Annie O'Reilley. You have the right to remain
silent. Anything you say, can and will be used against you in
a court of law. You have the right to an attorney and to have
him present with you while you are being questioned. If you
cannot afford an attorney one will be appointed to represent
you before any questioning, if you wish. Do you understand
all of the above rights I have just explained to you?"

"Of course, I understand. I'm a fucking attorney. I try
cases every day."

"No foul intended. Just protocol, right? Only thing that
separates us from the anarchists. Ok. So, you were saying,
'some' … what?"

Chad frowned, but started back where he left off.

"Some redheaded lady was possessed by the spirit of Annie O'Reilley, picked up a razor off the floor, and carved me
up like this while her ghoulish playmates held me down."

Adams did his best contemplative look and waited a few
seconds before responding.

"Wow, no wonder they put you in the psych ward. That's
the best you can come up with? Seriously? Well, you've got
problems already. The redheaded lady didn't hurt you. In
fact, she's the one who saved you, put tourniquets on your
arms to stop the bleeding. She's a nurse, and you owe her
your life."

"Duh! I just said Annie's ghost possessed her and used her body. She didn't know what was happening."

"Well then, maybe we need to get the redhead in here and hold a séance or something, see if she can channel Annie again. Or maybe you just need a good whack upside the head to stir the memory? What do you think?"

"I think you're a sarcastic ass, and that's the only question I'm answering without my lawyer."

"Well, I knew your sorry ass was guilty the first time I spoke to you. And since you already confessed, you might as well just lay there all quiet-like and rest. You've got some healing up to do before we transport you to jail."

"What do you mean, I confessed?"

"Oh, I mean that nice statement you carved on your chest. 'GUILTY' in great big letters, followed by 'I killed Annie O'Reilley. Punish me.' Priceless." Adams smiled big.

"You're shitting me," Chad said in disbelief.

Adams pulled out his cell phone, thumbed a few buttons and turned it around for Chad to see.

"Right there it is, my man. Read it and weep. Or get the nurse to pull your bandages off and see for yourself."

Chad stared for several seconds. There was no denying what it said.

"I told you I didn't do this to myself. So, unless we're admitting messages from the dead into testimony, you don't have shit!"

Adams laughed out loud.

"You think the judge and jury are going to buy your bullshit story that someone else did that to you? Fat chance. But either way, you're fucking guilty. And we'll prove it."

Adams walked out and called the nurse.

"Hey! What about my phone call?" Chad yelled, intentionally being demanding. He was sick of this smartass cop.

Adam's looked back in. "What phone call?"

"The fucking phone call I'm entitled to. I want to call my lawyer!"

"Oh, I'm so sorry, but right now I'd have to hold that phone to your ear, and that would violate attorney-client confidentiality. Now, please, don't disturb me. I really want to read the 'Top 10 Things Men Don't Tell Women They're Thinking While Having Sex'." Adams rattled the magazine in front of him and slipped back out to sit down in his chair.

"This is bullshit!" Chad yelled. "When do I get to have my phone call?"

Adams leaned his head around the corner. "When you can hold a phone and dial it." His head disappeared again, but his laughing echoed down the hallway.

Amy was pleasantly surprised to see Adams when she came on shift and found him on suicide watch guarding Chad Bigleby. Now Bigleby was awake, and she needed to check on him. Knowing he had killed some poor young girl disgusted her, but she had a job to do and she would do it. As she walked past Adams she asked him, "How long has he been awake?"

"About 15 minutes. That's all. And, might I add, he is not a happy camper."

She nodded acknowledgement and entered the room.

"How are you feeling, Mr. Bigleby? Would you like some water?"

"Yes, please," Chad replied. Amy picked up a cup with ice water and a straw and lifted it to his mouth. Chad drank deeply.

"You're due for some pain meds. Amy reached over and pushed the clicker button to release another dose of Dilaudid into his IV. "The doctor will be in shortly to see you."

Chad thanked Amy as she left.

At 12:35 a.m., Dr. Danner walked in the room.

"Mr. Bigleby, how are you feeling?"

"Like shit, doc," Chad responded.

"Is your pain manageable?"

"Yeah, the nurse just gave me some more meds. It's starting to kick in."

"So, Mr. Bigleby, let's talk about how you're feeling emotionally. Do you want to hurt yourself right now?"

"Doc, I never hurt myself to begin with."

Dr. Danner looked up at him, an openly suspicious look on his face.

"Well, then, Chad, tell me how you got these very nasty wounds."

"Doc, I know this is going to sound crazy, and maybe I am, but I swear to you, it's the truth. There was some redhead chick on the subway. Annie's ghost possessed her somehow then took a razor off the floor and carved me up. It's the truth."

Chad was trying to maintain composure, but the more he talked about his experience, the more frightened and out of control he felt.

"You've got to protect me. I haven't felt safe to sleep in days, and now the real world isn't safe either. What the hell am I going to do, doc?

"Who are you afraid of now? Who's going to be back for you, Chad? Annie?"

"I don't know about Annie, but there are others, mainly the homeless man and teenage boy who are half man, half wolf or something, the ones who bit me. But sometimes, everyone I see looks like a monster. I've seen demons of all kinds slouching through the streets at night lately. The only place I've felt safe is at home, and I definitely don't feel safe here."

Chad jerked on the restraints to emphasize his point.

"Well, Chad, you've got an officer stationed outside your door 24-7. If you're not safe, I don't know who is. So, try not to worry about that. Now, first, we need to operate on your wrists, before they start to heal wrong. The surgeon will probably be in tomorrow morning to talk with you about it and line your surgery up. Second, your blood pressure is through the roof and your heart rate is staying elevated. We'll put you on some medication that should help bring both of those down. The less fearful you are the better your blood pressure will be. Relax as best you can. That's important right now. I'll check on you again before I leave in the morning."

"Thanks, doc."

Dr. Danner came out of Chad's room and walked right over to Amy where she stood at the nurse's station. He greeted her kindly, a little too friendly it seemed to Adams. His body language was far too familiar, too comfortable; his body was squared off, its proximity much closer than what normal coworkers would maintain. He touched Amy's arm a few times during a short conversation, eyes wandering over her as if recalling fond, lustful memories.

Amy's body language was conflicted. He could tell she was used to Dr. Danner being that close, but she seemed on edge about it right now. Amy glanced over at Adams a couple of times before turning her back to him, hiding her face, which he already saw. He noticed it had a certain softness towards the doctor, a softness she appeared to be trying to force into a professional stoic expression.

It wasn't working too well.

Amy took a step back, hugging a clipboard to her chest, creating a defensive barrier to redefine the boundaries between them. Dr. Danner finally took the hint, said goodbye, and walked away.

Adams knew right then, deep down in his gut … Amy cheated on him with that doctor. He felt furious, betrayed, an agonizing pain blossoming in his heart. His stomach flip-flopped, nausea weighing like a stone in his belly the longer he stared at Amy's back. Shame strangled him slowly until he looked away, unable to bear the sight of her any more.

The elevator door chimed, opened, and Greer stepped out, grinning.

"I'm here to relieve you, homey. Gravy job is mine now."

Adams forced a smile.

"Thanks man. I've had my fill of this place. I need some fresh air. Busy out there tonight?"

"Nah, not too bad."

"Good. I need a break right now."

With that, Adams walked down the hall and slipped into the elevator without Amy seeing him leave.

Inside his patrol car, Adams hammered the steering wheel and screamed at the night until his hands and throat ached. He wanted to cry from the pain, but he was too angry, too bitter. No tears would flow. His mind raced. How could she have done this? As hard as he was struggling to be faithful, the whole time she had already played the whore. It was a knife in the back for sure, but to make it worse, she kissed him and made love to him, knowing the truth would come out, and the wound would bleed eventually. He felt humiliated, horribly and publicly shamed, broken and utterly furious.

Surely that bastard doctor didn't know who he was. Adams was positive Dr. Danner was relatively new on the staff. But he knew she was married. She's worn her ring during the entire separation, at least every time he'd seen her, she had it on.

He looked down at his own wedding ring, pulled it off and stared at it, a warped circle, bent the first year of their marriage when he made a rookie mistake.

Guy cracked his window and held his ID just inside, out of reach. Adams slid his fingers through the gap when suddenly the window rolled up, pinching his wedding ring tight.

The car accelerated forward and he ran to keep up, drawing his expandable baton, still closed. In retrospect, he knew he should have drawn his gun, but as a wise man once said, "experience is something you get shortly after you need it. "

The car increased speed and he stumbled; his feet shot out from beneath him, dragging him down the road as he hammered at the window with the pommel, his lower body bouncing up and down against the pavement.

By the grace of God, it didn't last long. Hicks, responding to assist, ended up on a head-on path with the perp's vehicle, saw Adams dangling from the side of the car, and played chicken with the guy. Adams felt the vehicle move left, jerk back right, then slow. Hicks had moved to stay in front of the suspect's car. The guy slowed, looking for an out.

It was enough. Adams managed to land a solid blow in the bottom corner of the window. It exploded inward, his body falling away to roll repeatedly, momentum dissipating until he came to a stop. Relax was all he could think the whole time as he covered his head. Be like the drunk man.

He'd heard a crash then, looked up and saw the crumpled hoods, the white airbag smoke pouring out of the perp's broken window. Hicks got out of his vehicle, gun drawn, screaming at the guy to show him his hands.

Adams' body hurt all over, but he forced himself to stand and staggered forward. He got to the car, reached inside, and dragged the stunned driver right out of the window and slammed him on the pavement.

"Put your hands behind your back. Do it now!" he screamed. His limbs shook terribly, but he wrenched the suspect's arms behind his back, fumbled the handcuffs out, and secured him. Hicks came around the car and holstered.

"I've got it, Adams. Sit back and rest. Ambulance is on its way."

"You all right, Hicks? That was ballsy."

"I'll be a little sore tomorrow, but I'm fine."

He'd looked down at his hand then, his wedding ring was bent into an oval. He pulled out his multi-tool. It took a pair of pliers to mash it back into enough of a circle to get it off his hand before the swelling kicked in.

Months later he had it reshaped, but it would never be a perfect circle again. Much like his marriage. When they lost the baby, it put their relationship in a vice and slowly began to crush it. The circle became warped. But now, with what Amy had done, that misshapen circle had been mangled.

He thought of Pebbles, Melissa, and Megan. Why should he fight it anymore?

"I should fuck all three of them," he thought out loud. "One, it'd make me real happy for a while. Two, nothing like a revenge fuck to hurt her right back."

He put the car in gear, marked clear from the hospital, and headed toward The Body Shop, intent on lining up a hook up for after work. Hopefully Pebbles was working tonight.

Chad looked at the clock for probably the tenth time in the last hour. It was 2:00 a.m. The door was cracked, and he could see the cop outside his door appeared to be nodding off. It was a new guy. Chad checked the sturdiness of the bed with a few quiet and controlled jerks, looking for any possible means of escape. No luck. He sat frustrated, then reached for the male-end of the seat belt and found neither of his hands had the simple capacity or dexterity to perform any useful coordinated movement.

"I am so screwed," he thought aloud.

He became aware of a whispering voice, but couldn't pinpoint where it was coming from. It took a little time, but eventually the words became clear. It was a depressed young man's voice, groaning over the condition he could not escape: socially inept, unable to connect, adrift, worthless, and unloved. Life was emasculating, meaningless, death was all he wanted, oblivion.

Another voice started in. This time he could hear a middle-aged woman. She was in the hospital again: beaten, broken, and emotionally distraught. "My fault, my fault." She repeated the self-deprecating mantra over and over. Bearing the blame and questioning herself, what could she possibly do to not make her boyfriend angry again? What was wrong with her?

Voices began to swarm, a cacophony of misery, making it difficult to discern one from another. Some stood out, though, occasionally. Chad heard the hopeless, inevitability in the muffled cries of a cancer patient attempting to reconcile with impending death: alone, no loved ones, no comfort, terrified of what was to come. A Meth addict on detox after an OD. She nearly died, but still she longed for it like a lover, a savior, the only thing to fulfill her heart's desire even as it destroyed her body.

The horde of voices seemed to go on forever, louder and louder, overwhelming his senses. He was unable to shut out the cries. His mind loathed this monotony of unending afflictions. He had enough tragedy of his own to deal with. As he hardened himself to their torment, the noises began to fade, eventually only a murmur in the background. He sighed, happy for a reprieve.

It was then he heard the scuttling noises in the shadows, tiny feet scurrying across the tiled floor. He turned his head to look over the side just in time to catch a blur disappear under his bed. Beneath him, two little creatures, hardly two feet tall, wiggled against each other, their bulbous heads twittering back and forth, huge bulging eyes scanning all around.

Chad lay very still, terror cresting inside him until the panic was unbearable and he had to speak, had to find out if anything was really in the room with him.

"Who's there?" he whispered.

Chittering high-pitched snickers escaped from one of the little hobgoblins. The other slapped his hand over the loud one's mouth, finger to his own lips.

Chad's stomach lurched, back flipped; a sharp churning paralysis spread out from his gut.

O fuck, O fuck, O fuck, raced through his mind like a deck of cards flipping by. His anxiety levels leapt tall buildings with a single bound; the possibilities were enough to threaten sanity and send one into a conniption. His chest tightened with anxiety, the oppressive weight of helplessness crushing his resolve, panic becoming a runaway train inside his brain.

He turned his head back and forth, leaning as far out over the edge of the bed as possible. He looked towards the floor, straining at the straps holding him captive and vulnerable, a veritable sitting duck.

Dark green hands clambered out from beneath the head of the bed, clinging to the frame, frog skin bodies side by side, a pale moonlight beam glistening on their wet hides.

Chad heard a very faint slithering noise, but could see nothing. Behind his head, twin tongues snaked their way in between the railings, twisting, turning, and making their way to Chad's ears.

"Please, please, please go away …" Chad pleaded.

One of the hobgoblins snickered again. The other smacked him. Chad heard the noises, and was just about to scream when a third creature leapt onto his chest, pressing a hand over Chad's mouth and a single finger over its own large obsidian lips.

"Shhhhhhhhh …"

The creature's flesh smelled rotten with a hint of sulfur. But even worse was the wet, sticky, clammy cold skin practically smothering him. Chad tried to scream, but couldn't. The creature smiled, the corners of its mouth literally spanning from one side of its head to the other, small pointy teeth in multiple rows shining white. Chad tried to cry all the louder when he saw his own horror reflected in those bulging big eyes.

Both tongues found his ear canals and slithered deep inside, thin straw-like appendages on the end penetrating the flesh. They slurped and sucked, and moaned, smacking their lips. The one giggled again.

"Yum."

Chad squirmed and writhed like a snake in the throes of death, nerves firing all on their own, desperate to flee. The creature held his mouth more firmly, now with two hands, leaning in close to his face and keeping Chad's head pinned to the mattress.

"Be stiiillll, human," it hissed. "Don't make thisss rape a murder, ok?" It patted his cheek lightly with one hand, nodding its head vigorously, wide eyes bobbling around in its skull, its tone a disturbing attempt at assuring him it would only be bad for a little while.

Suddenly, out of the shadows there was a blur, and the hobgoblin sitting on Chad's chest flew across the room, slammed into the wall, and fell to the ground … still. The giggler was oblivious, but the other saw its companion's limp form and squalled, slapping its friend and skittering down back under the bed. The other looked surprised and didn't understand, but followed his partner. From beneath the bed they sniffed the air and shrieked before scrambling toward the shadows in a panic on all fours, sliding back into the darkness from which they had come.

Chad was about to breathe a sigh of relief, when he saw Mr. Phailees standing at the foot of his bed, olive skin, white suit, perfect posture, whistling his favorite tune. He heard a crunching noise and looked to his right. Phobos was in bestial form, wolfing down the hobgoblin whole, jaws dislocated like a snake, but still crunching down as muscles forced the body down his expanding gullet.

Chad pissed himself. He would have chewed his arms and legs off to get away right then, if only he could have reached them. A scream stood at the edge of his lips ready to leap, but Mr. Phailees was already there, hand over his mouth. He glanced hopefully at the officer for help, but the man was still asleep in the chair outside the door.

"Now, Chad," he whispered, "you don't think we're going to let some little bottom-feeding shit kickers come in and steal our meal, do you? Heaven forbids it, actually, the Hierarchy and all that. Doesn't stop those little urchins, though; gutless, dishonorable fiends. But now they know better. They won't come around here again. There are much easier pickings than you. No need to be scared of them. Us? A totally different story, I'm afraid."

Phailees smiled a large cat-that-ate-the-canary smile.

"Time is almost up, Chad. Tomorrow night is the end, one way or another. But first, one more withdrawal …"

Mr. Phailees' face shifted, jaws crackling as they spread out, head growing wide and thick, fangs ripping through the gums, hair knitting itself across a leathery, almost scaly, brow and cheeks. He turned Chad's head to the side. Phobos sat pretty and placed both paws over Chad's mouth while Phailees bit the base of his skull and began suctioning out the cerebrospinal fluid. When he was done, he milked his fangs into the silver flask, filling it with the unnaturally amber fluid.

"Now, Chad, one last dose to prepare you for the final harvest. Phobos, if you would do the honors, please." Phailees patted Phobos' side. "Give him all you've got this time, boy."

Phobos' jaw unhinged again, he leapt onto Chad's chest, facing him, and plunged his fangs into the soft tissue above the collar bone, penetrating into the subclavian artery. Venom pumped out in waves, muscles squeezing the poison sacs inside his skull over and over, until they were bled dry.

Chad's head was on fire, the chemicals going immediately to his brain. His adrenal glands began a critical response, dumping everything they could produce. Terror, unmatched by any prior experience to that point, gripped him mercilessly, overloading his cognitive functions. His body contorted, muscles heaving with unnatural might. The left belt snapped in two, his arm free, stretching for the ceiling, torso twisting until his face buried itself in his pillow.

Mr. Phailees smiled, capped his flask, and slipped it into the inside pocket of his suit jacket.

"Come now, Phobos. Time to go."

Phobos shifted back into his human appearance, a teenage boy first and then finally, Inspector Lupin. They walked out the door together. Phailees brushed his hand over the top of Greer's head as he passed. A few seconds later, Greer came around, thought he heard some kind of wheezing, whimpering noise from inside the room. He got up to check, rounded the corner, and stopped like he'd hit a brick wall face first.

"Holy shit," was about all he could think to say at the sight of Chad's contorted body, muscles seized up and frozen, a statue of flesh reaching for the heavens.

Adams sat outside of The Body Shop, tapping the wheel and trying to decide which voice he was going to listen to, Halo or Pitchfork.

Halo admonished him to recognize that Amy wanted him back now and to forgive her and move forward. Pitchfork told him he had a right to feel angry, to feel bitter, and above all, he was entitled to fuck at least one other woman, just to make it even. "And besides," Pitchfork said, "you want to fuck Pebbles something horrible …" which, of course, was true.

"God help me! What am I going to do?" he said out loud to no one in particular.

He pulled out his phone, stared at it for a minute, then dialed Hicks' cell phone. Two rings later, Hicks picked up.

"What's up, Mark?"

"You in the office, boss?"

"Yeah. Knocking out some paperwork."

"I need to ask your opinion on something personal. You got a minute?"

"Sure. What is it?"

"Let's just say, hypothetically, that you found out your wife had cheated on you while you were doing your damnest to stay faithful. Would you want to go out and screw some hottie just to get even and make yourself feel good for a little while, or would you just forgive her and move on?"

"Wow. Mark, you found out Amy is cheating on you?"

Mark lowered his head. "Yeah … and I am so pissed; I don't know what to do. I'm sitting outside of The Body Shop right now considering doing a business check and talking with some incredibly hot girl who told me just the other night that she wants to sleep with me. I'm torn, boss. What's your advice?"

"Well, Mark, as much as I can empathize with you on the feelings of anger, betrayal, and a desire to get even, and the desire to screw some smokin' hot dancer, you need to consider a bigger question first."

"What's that?" Adams asked, a depressed and somewhat confused tone dragging his voice down.

"What kind of person do you think you are, Mark? I've always known you to be a loyal, faithful, and honest guy whose integrity is beyond question. That's who you are, who you've been as long as I've known you. Never been a question in my mind about trusting you."

Adams nodded his head and looked up at the building in front of him.

"So, what exactly are you trying to say, boss?"

"Well, I don't think you'd be calling me right now struggling over this issue if you didn't already know, deep inside, that having a revenge fuck just isn't who you are. I'm not gonna debate the moral right and wrong of it, the justice of it or what have you. It comes down to this, Mark. What you do in life really isn't about what people do to you. It's about what kind of person you want to be. Period. So, ask yourself,

do you want to be known from here on out as a man who
cheated on his wife? If you can live with that and don't mind
being that man, then go ahead and have some fun. Lord
knows you only live once, plus Amy deserves it. But, if you
don't want to be that kind of man, if you don't want to have
to face that reality the rest of your life, then put that car in
gear and drive away. Oh, and don't come in here and talk to
Megan either the rest of the night. That one could tempt you,
too. Or do talk to her if you decide that route. That's the best,
unbiased advice I can give you, Mark. Any questions?"

"No, boss. That's pretty simple. I just need to decide.
Thanks for putting it in perspective."

"No problem, Mark. Anytime."

They both said bye and hung up.

Adams was tapping the wheel and looking at the door
when his phone rang. It was Greer.

"Hey, Greer. What's up? Bored?"

"Not anymore. You need to come back up here and talk
to that Doctor. Bigleby has had a new development, and
they're saying his vitals are through the roof. They're not
sure what's going to happen with him."

"All right, man. On my way."

Adams put the car in gear and headed back to the hospital.

"A sign from above perhaps?" he said out loud, mulling
over what it all might mean.

At the hospital, Adams spoke to Dr. Danner. It was hard
to look at him without showing animosity, but he managed.

"What's Bigleby's status, doc?"

"Not good. Not good at all. He is experiencing an acute
attack of catalepsy. His body has seized into one position,
muscles entirely rigid, and his brain is non-responsive to ex-
ternal stimuli. Look inside here, and see for yourself."

Adams did. It was a pretty freaky sight. Looking at Chad's contorted body frozen in place, one arm reaching for the heavens, as his face looked toward Hell below; it was as if he knew where he was destined to go, Adams thought.

"Wow. Strange," Adams said.

"Yes, Very, and very rare. On top of what you see right now, he's running a temperature of one hundred-four degrees and his heart rate and blood pressure are through the roof. We're giving him different medicines to try and bring them down, but are having only small successes."

"What's causing it? Do you know?"

"Viral fever possibly? Swelling on the brain? We're just not sure right now. I hate to admit it, but we really have no idea what exactly we're dealing with here. Bottom line though, officer, he can't last but so long like this."

"All right, Doc. Well keep us posted. Somebody will continue to remain outside his door round the clock."

"Will do, officer." At that, Dr. Danner walked off.

Adams went looking for Amy. He found her in the break room, alone.

As he walked in, she smiled.

"Hey sneaky. I never saw you leave earlier. You get a call or something?"

Adams stood there, silent. His body language screamed closed, distant, hurt, and angry. He went to speak but only opened his mouth, stopped, closed it, looked away, and stood there staring off into the unseen void, before he finally looked back at her. She knew immediately something was wrong. The smile fled. Her stomach dropped out. Everything in her wanted to run away, anything but have to face him right now. She knew by his eyes he was a wounded animal—pained, betrayed, his angst brimming over as tears welled up.

He knew.

In an instant she weighed her heart, her love for him, and knew, if there was a chance of still salvaging their marriage she had to confess everything now, first.

She started talking while he deliberated.

"Mark. I'm so, so sorry. I know I should have told you before now, before we made love. You saw me and Dr. Danner and you figured it out, didn't you?"

Mark stood stoic, stiff as a statue, shoulders sunken, head half down, but eyes still up on her. He nodded his head slowly, biting his bottom lip the whole time. He had thought he would scream and holler and cuss her like a dog, but in her presence, most of his anger evaporated and only pain reigned in his heart and mind. He struggled not to break down and cry right there.

"Mark, I've wanted to tell you, but I've been a coward. I've been so scared that it would sink the ship. I was stupid for doing it and stupid for not telling you before now. But I want to tell you the whole truth. I screwed up. I screwed up so bad. I know it. I can't say it enough. I betrayed you. Even though we were separated, you were being the honorable one and I was playing the harlot. I told myself I deserved something good when we first split up. God forgive me, but I cheated on you three times."

Adams cringed, stepping back slightly, arms coming up to fold in front, a shield for his heart. Amy noted his change in posture. She hurt for him inside. She cursed herself for her careless acts of faithless selfishness.

"The first time was half out of anger, half out of desire. Someone I met in passing and went out on a date with. The second and third times were with Dr. Danner. After a couple of weeks of talking with him at lunch each day, I was weak. He listened when I needed it. Once the dam was broken, it was just plain easier to do it again."

Amy's voice rose in pitch and broke periodically as she bordered on sobbing, tears streaming down her face. She hid her face in her hands and shook her head, then made herself make eye contact with him again. An unnatural darkness was all that stared back at her now. She found it difficult to speak.

"Mark, I … I was so … so wrong and … I'm so sorry that I hurt you like this … I never should have done it. I was selfish, greedy, and I didn't care about you or us when I did what I did. I … I …"

Amy stepped forward and Adams reflexively moved away from her, his back butting up to the closed door. She reached out to him.

"Don't you dare touch me right now," he spat out, hands reflexively coming up, palms forward, his voice deep and full of hostility.

"Oh, Mark! Please! Please forgive me! I've got no excuses. I was wrong. I was a horrible, selfish person! And I'm so, so sorry. I know I can't change what happened, but I love you, and I know I want to be with you, just you. Please Mark! Please forgive me …"

Amy was crying now, dropping to her knees as she begged for his forgiveness, begged for some sign of humanity behind his cold eyes. But she saw only distance in his posture, an impassable chasm of titanic proportions, and an impenetrable wall, terribly thick and incredibly tall. She knew right then he could not forgive her, not now. Slowly, she retracted her hand, a hand that, moments before, had been tentatively stretched out testing the air around him for any sign of mercy. There was none.

"Mark, say something … please, anything …"

Mark glared at her, a deep hatred filling his eyes, teeth gritted in righteous indignation. His voice was slow, methodical, and breathy as he restrained his tears.

"I … don't want … to talk to you right now. Right now, I hate you … right now you disgust me … right now I can't even bear to look at you. You have hurt me so bad I can't even begin to describe it. I've got to go."

In an instant, he shifted sideways, opened the door without looking at it, and backed out, closing the door behind him. Just like that he was gone, leaving Amy on the floor, stunned and hopeless. Despair washed over her, crushing her beneath its might and mass. For minutes, she struggled to breathe, and when her chest finally relaxed and breath came, it was in choking gasps.

Adams sat in his car while Amy knelt on the break room floor, both of them alone, both weeping bitter tears, one of pain, the other regret.

Chad Bigleby was in Hell.

The room was a tunnel of torrential winds and sulfurous ash, a pathway to darkness, drenched in shadows. But nothing was hidden from Chad now. He could see all the hideous beasts wandering about—fallen ones who had found their place, inflictors of pain, devourers of mankind, as well as damned souls still tied to this world, feeding on their own kind.

One after another they came for him.

Some were present for no other reason than to invoke fear and stare into his petrified eyes, a self-gratifying experience all on its own for them. Some licked his body, testing the time left to death so they could accompany his corpse, for they only fed on the dead, and the more rotten, the better. The bitter souls stood in an unending line as well, waiting to vent their rage on his heinous soul with numerous beatings, vicious pinching and twisting of flesh, violent shakings, and more. All day the whispers of the damned filled his ears, unable to shut it out. Rage, hate, self-pity, scorn, shame, pain, guilt, and constant despair poured from their ragged lips.

Bruises appeared and sometimes welts and small pinpricks of blood. Occasionally, his body convulsed but would return to catatonic paralysis, pointlessly reaching for the heavens. The doctors and nurses were baffled, looking at the officer on duty with increasing distrust.

But locked inside his mind, existing in both some neth-erworld as well as our own, Chad Bigleby suffered, his wick-edness finally having found him out and hung itself about his neck like some rotting albatross. He struggled to die as he drifted on a burning sea of darkness, unable to fully stay afloat, unable to sink and drown.

He begged for death, but it would not come. He pleaded for oblivion but justice said, "Too easy." His sanity was stretched to breaking, frayed ends ridiculously taut but refus-ing to snap. A babbling idiot would not appreciate the weight of his sins nor the equity of lawful punishment, the unim-peachable integrity of recompense extracted. No, you must be coherent to truly reap the consequences of your selfish deeds.

His hopes were crushed. He was bound and helpless, a weak child before all his abusers, a vessel for their insatiable wrath and wretched appetites for destruction. A scapegoat depository of shame to lay their hands upon in malice and bludgeon with their fists until they felt a momentary relief of rage. A small, brief bliss in an eternity of hopeless affliction.

Chad Bigleby could see no relief for himself in sight, no release from this Hell. His will to resist was spent. There was no rest for his wicked soul here. No rest at all.

All morning, Adams tossed and turned, catching only minutes of sleep here and there. He finally gave up and de-cided to go for a run, burn off some stress. Hopefully he would be able to sleep afterwards.

Ten laps later around the park, almost three miles, he spotted a middle-aged man in a white suit, olive skin, and dark sunglasses. The face was somehow familiar. A dog sat beneath the bench he was seated on. The man waved and called out.

"Officer Adams! Fancy seeing you here." Mr. Phailees smiled wide, shiny white teeth beaming in the noon day sun.

Adams stopped suddenly. I'll be damned, he thought, recognizing Mr. Phailees.

"How can you look so much younger? It's impossible."

"Like a snake sheds his skin, Officer Adams. I can put on the old …" and suddenly he was the homeless man, aged and wrinkled with dirty clothes, "or cast it aside." In a blink of the eye, he was back to the smoother olive skin and white suit.

Adams staggered back, right into the path of a lady walking by. They bumped into each other.

"Oh! I'm so sorry!" Adams sputtered. "Excuse me, miss."

"It's ok," she said, a little irritated, and resumed her stride.

Adams looked around to see if anyone else had seen what he had, but everyone passing by was apparently oblivious to any change. He looked back at Mr. Phailees.

"What the fuck are you?"

"Do you believe in God, Officer Adams?"

Adams faltered, hesitated. "I used to. I'm not entirely sure anymore."

"Well, I can tell you, on quite good authority, that I am not Him." He giggled at his own jibe. Adams just stood there, feeling the pointy end of his joke.

"Officer Adams, with everything that you have seen in your life, and especially in the last three months, all the strange wicked things you've been witness to, you must certainly believe in evil. Don't you?"

"I've always thought the heart of man was evil enough, all on its own."

"True. True. But why do you call one man's acts evil and another's good? On what basis? If there is absolute moral wrong or evil in the universe, then there must be a judge, a lawgiver, someone who is righteous above all else and makes

the rules. There must be an objective moral standard to measure men's wickedness by, to say this is right and that is wrong
and what some do is despicably evil. Otherwise, it's just the
subjective opinions of men, and the majority rules. 'Tyranny
of the fifty-one percent' as Thomas Jefferson said, I believe.
Or as Nietzsche put it, 'the will to power', might makes right,
the strongest make the rules and everyone else must just follow their lead. But, without anything beyond 'I think', without an authoritative 'you should', morality is always just a
man's opinion at the bottom of it. Just a man. And what
makes one man's opinion better than another? What makes
the chemical reaction in his head better than another's?"

Adams shrugged, waiting for the mystery answer.

"Not a damn thing!"

"So, what are you trying to say?" Adams felt frustrated.
"Just spit it out!"

"I'm saying that there is a God. There is a heaven and
hell, and a spiritual world behind the veil that most men do
not see, a place where devils and angels, lost souls and things
that languish somewhere in between, roam the shadows just
outside the sight of men but ever with them."

"And which are you?" Adams asked.

"I and my boy here," he said, indicating Phobos, "we languish somewhere in between. We can walk between the
raindrops, flitting from one side to the next. I myself am ancient. I have wandered the planes of existence for several mil-
lennia, since the time of the Tower of Babel when fallen
angels once again began to breed with the sons of men and
produce great men and women of renown. My mother was
the offspring of such a union, my father was worshiped as a
god in Mesopotamia. I am a prince amongst my kind, of pur-
est blood, so to say. I have laid waste to more men than I
could be bothered to remember. Traitors, betrayers of their
own kind, whether through murder, lust, greed, or lies, those
reserved for the lowest circle of hell, they are my promised
portion, my food, my reward, my merciful means of relief in

this agonizing existence as long as I punish them for their sins. I am an avenger of wrath sent to bring down the wicked betrayers of their own kind, but I am not limited by your government's laws. I am a devil on a chain, bound by covenants of authority that I cannot cross, but I have much, much more leeway than your pathetic badge allows. A shame actually, since you have the blood gift. You can see the lies men tell, you can discern the truth. Lady Justice is your true bride. Your breeding is that of a warrior, agile and born to combat. You could be so much more with the proper commitment."

"What do you mean 'blood gift'?" Adams inquired with more than a bit of trepidation. You didn't use that exact term before?"

"It's your heritage, stretching back hundreds, maybe even thousands of years. Somewhere, far back in your bloodline, there is a faint trace of my people's blood in you. I could call you cousin, but it would be extraordinarily distant." Phailees winked at Adams, knowing it would trouble him.

Adams felt revulsion at the idea, but stood, soaking this reality in, thinking for what seemed like a long time before he spoke.

"What the hell does that make me?"

"Oh, nothing too special just as you are. Potential is there, mind you, but you're still just a man, just a creature of flesh and bone and flexible moral fabric made in the image of your Maker."

The last word was said with a distinct dislike as if his tone was meant to carry a slur against the name itself. Adams decided to probe.

"What do you think of God?"

"Ah. An interesting question." Mr. Phailees' voice took on a theatrical tone. "He is glorious! Magnificent! Omniscient and omnipotent! Full of mercy and justice! For the chosen, His loving kindness renews every morning."

His voice dropped back down, bitterness dripping from his lips.

"And yet, do I curse Him! For I am a vessel of destruction, set forth to pour out His wrath at the end! And I hate Him for it! Yet it makes no difference. I was created for such as this. I am a Lion of Tartarus, a Rod of Affliction who will one day be cast into the fire when my work on earth is done. I am the Left Hand of God, if you will, touching what He will not, fulfilling His will of justice by doing what He will not personally do—a proximate cause punishing those who rebel."

"Martin Luther said, 'Even the devil is God's devil.'" Adams' brain had pulled that out of cold storage.

"Indeed, yes he did. Quite accurate I suppose. I was created, A Rod of Judgment in the Hand of God, to chastise wicked men. Spurned by grace, yes, but a very necessary evil to curb the hell that evil men impose on their fellow man. In the end, it is my fate, my design. It is my lot, my portion, and my heart enjoys the pain I bring. I hunger for their fear. I find myself reborn in their misery, comforted in their company of agony, healed by their wounds. What I take from them brings me blissful relief … for a short time."

Mr. Phailees paused, looking off in the distance as if trying hopelessly to remember a time when things were not so. "And you, Officer Adams, you have nothing to fear from me. You are a faithful man, a loyal man, a friend to your fellow man. You are not my portion." Suddenly a wry, smug smile spread across his face, a Cheshire cat smile indeed. "Your wife on the other hand … that little adulterous whore, she is mine, and when I am done with Chad Bigleby tonight, I will come for her too. Her suffering will begin in earnest very soon."

Adams bristled, something inside him instinctively stepping forward, husband, lover, protector. His voice was controlled, barely, a brewing violence lingering just beneath the surface.

"You stay away from my wife!" he commanded Mr. Phailees.

"Dear, dear. My, aren't we touchy? From whence cometh the guardian? You know what she did. I can see it. I can see your pain, your rage, your hatred. And yet you rush to her defense. Why, Officer Adams? Why? Don't you want justice? Revenge? Don't you want a clean break from her heinous deeds? I will be the sword severing the shameful ties, freeing you to move on. Stand with justice, don't defend the guilty!"

Adams hung his head then looked up at the sky, struggling with the same thought that had been gripping him all morning as he tried to not think and just sleep. He looked back at Mr. Phailees.

"It's my fault she cheated on me."

"What?!? How can you even say that? She did the deed! No one forced her hand!"

"I know she bears her own burden of responsibility. But the reality is I played a large part in pushing her there. When we lost the baby shortly after childbirth she needed me, and I wasn't there for her. I wanted to talk and she didn't. She wanted to return to some form of normalcy before she went mad, and I couldn't. I couldn't pretend when she needed to. Though I always blamed her for not being there for me, I was selfish in my own way. I could have found people to talk to and been there for her, providing continuity, support, security. I could have been the strong husband. But I was a coward. I couldn't look at her without feeling the pangs of death. I withdrew. I avoided her. I punished her by withholding my presence. I found another life to fill my void, excluded her, then condemned her for not loving me. Our collapse was inevitable, both of us holding onto our animosity, our rights, entitled to our own pain and rage, unwilling to forgive, unwilling to love as we should have, as we used to."

Adams grew quiet, eyes closed, swaying in the wind, oblivious to the cold. Phailees sat watching, index finger tapping his thigh in irritation.

"That still doesn't make her innocent!" he snapped.

Adams shot back. "No. It doesn't. But it does make me complicit! A collaborator in her demise! She does not stand alone. I'm a sinner as well. Just a different sort. We all are, in some shape, form, or fashion, I suppose. We all have our temptations, choice morsels that call to us to come and taste. I've been tempted the same as she was. I just managed not to give in."

"And why is that? What made you better than her?" Phailees pressed Adams, hoping he would embrace pride and damn his wife.

"I don't know. Deep down I didn't want to be that person. But even that doesn't seem powerful enough. Last night I was so damn very close to giving in after I found out. I'm still tempted."

"And what has stopped you then? What made the difference?"

"I don't know for sure. But I know a friend who made a difference. He made me feel something deep inside, something clawing to prevail, something not my own, perhaps the finger of God, scratching at my heart, a providential intervention. I just know I didn't do it on my own. That's my conclusion. As much as I have cursed God for the death of my child and the destruction of my marriage over the last three years, as much as I have rejected Him and raged against His will, and hated Him in my heart, He's still there. He's still faithful even when I'm not. It's like He's holding onto me and won't let go."

"Damn him," hissed Phailees. "Merciful God, everlasting … for men. Your kind makes me so grotesquely sick. He's always favored you above us. You pitiful, weak, human kind; too fragile to uphold His image. It's disgusting."

Phailees looked as if something nasty had flown in his mouth and reflexively spit it on the ground.

"I don't know why He has even bothered so long with your race. But you know what I do know?"

Adams stood waiting, a questioning look on his face.

"I know you can't forgive Amy for what she did. You may empathize, you may blame yourself to some degree, but still, when you look at her face, all you can think is 'traitor' and how you can never trust her again. You can't forgive God for what He did to you. You can't forgive her. Just accept it, and don't get in my way when I come for her."

At that, Phailees stood and turned to leave.

"But what if I can forgive her?" Adams called after Mr. Phailees.

Phailees spun around, glaring at Adams. "Don't you try to interfere in my affairs, Officer Adams. You're special, but not that special!"

Phailees walked away, Phobos trotting along, glancing back balefully at Adams before they were out of sight.

Amy woke in a sweat, clutching at her blankets, heart racing. Her head thumped with a horrible headache. She looked at the clock. She had only been asleep about 30 minutes. Every time she closed her eyes it was the same horrible dream. She couldn't sleep for more than 30 minutes at a shot, and she didn't want to sleep at all now; the dream was too much to bear.

Everyone at work shunned her. She had a scarlet letter upon her chest, a large 'W' covering her shirt. No one would speak to her, only about her as she passed. She heard the words whore, adulterer, betrayer, unworthy. She felt overcome by shame and fled, but they would not allow her peace. Everywhere she went, someone followed and told every stranger what she had done, how she played the harlot and cheated on her husband when he had been so faithful. Everyone's faces turned to horrified astonishment, and her shame grew by leaps and bounds.

She ran, but now the people were turning into wolves and giving chase, pursuing her relentlessly. She fled, all the way to her house, where she scrambled inside and locked the doors. Outside, they all sat and howled, baying like dogs with an animal caught up a tree. More and more arrived to join the huge pack. Then one stood on two legs and walked to the front door. He spoke with a growling shout, malevolent intent filling his voice.

"You better open the door little whore 'cause the Big Bad Wolf is coming, and your door will do you good no more! Your resistance will only make his rage vicious and sore."

He descended the steps on all fours and rejoined the legion of wolves dancing, running, and howling in her front yard with a bonfire barrel ablaze in the middle. For how long this went on, she was not sure, but at last the moon shone on a man striding across the lawn, a blue uniform on. He moved graceful and fast, bounding up the porch stairs in one motion to stand and scream. She could see his face. It was Adams.

"Little pig whore, let me in!" He hammered the door with his fist; pictures on the wall inside danced a jig.

Amy jerked away from the window, her back to the wall, thinking small. She was speechless, her throat constricted, palms sweaty.

"Little pig whore, let me in or I'm gonna huff and puff and kick the shit out of your door."

Amy could only stand quiet, fear overwhelming every fiber of her being.

Adams growled at her refusal to comply then roared like a lion as his foot shot out, striking the front door. The whole frame split from top to bottom, the deadbolt alone still holding on. He stepped back, roared again, his foot shooting out, and the door flew off the hinges. Splintered pieces exploded in all directions as he stepped across the threshold.

"Come here, you bitch!" The words were deliberate and menacing. Amy fell to the ground, paralyzed.

"Please, Mark," she begged, "don't hurt me! Please don't hurt me! I love you!"

Adams laughed then growled at her. "You think you love me? You don't know what love is. Just some stranger's cock between your legs. Apparently, that's all you know about love. But I've seen the truth, and I've seen your lies and now I see the wicked in you clearly. I can tell you exactly what I know you are … a fucking whore! And when I'm done with you everyone else will know it, and you'll never forget it! Now COME HERE!"

His command rattled the walls. Amy knew there was no escape. She submitted to his wrath, knowing her guilt.

Adams pounced on her then, dragging her around as he pulled her pants off, ripped her shirt in two, and snatched it from her limbs. He pushed her on her back then pinned her to the floor with one foot standing on her abdomen. Adams barked an order to someone outside and the wolf man brought him an iron rod with twisted metal at the end, glowing bright yellow-red in the night. Adams grabbed it and held it above Amy's breasts, perfect and pale in the moonlight coming through the window. He lowered the rod slowly, watched her upper chest grow red. Amy whimpered quietly, but when he slammed it down just below her collar bone and the flesh sizzled, she sang like a loon crying in the night. Adams held the brand to her longer than necessary, his glee apparent. When he finally pulled it away the smell of her own cooked flesh made Amy's stomach lurch. He tossed the rod out the door and walked over to the wall, pulled the mirror down, and came back to stand over her.

"Look in the mirror, Amy! See what you are? See what your mark is?"

Amy stared at the horribly painful burn marks, large letters spelling 'WHORE'. She wept, vicious, savage tears of contrition spilled in vain. Her husband did not care about anything but justice, and now it was due.

"Will you forgive me now?" she croaked, between sobs and tears and snot.

"It's too late for forgiveness," she heard the wolf man snarl.

"Run," Adams told her coldly, all emotional attachment vanished. "Just run."

She stared at him, helpless, hopeless … unbelieving.

"I said RUN, WHORE! Run and don't stop!"

Adams jerked her to her feet and shoved her naked frame out the door, kicking her in the ass, right off the porch. The wolves yipped and howled, leaping all about, working up into a frenzy. Amy looked back for just a moment and wished she never had. The wolf man stood beside Adams, his hand on Adams' head. He was already half changed, body shifting, growing, head taking on the wolfish features, his teeth already fangs, hair spreading over his whole body as his uniform shredded, unable to contain the building muscles rippling across his frame.

She ran, and ran for all she was worth, through streets and alleys, backyards and empty lots, jumping fences and crawling beneath wire, until she could not run any further and Adams caught her.

His claws were a swift fury, shredding her face and eyes, digging inside her mouth to tear her lying tongue out. He kept her alive as he attacked every part of her that had shamed him, had betrayed him.

As Adams ripped her apart she heard the wolf man's voice. "He'll never forgive you, whore. You cannot be saved."

Finally, mercifully, Adams spent his rage in one last flurry of slashes across her abdomen, slicing through to the spine, then buried his face in her neck, teeth severing all the major blood vessels. In seconds, Amy blacked out from the blood loss, death waiting with open arms.

That's when she woke up, every time; terrified of falling asleep again. She was deathly afraid of what was happening to her. The homeless man and his dog, the bite and the dreams, she realized what had been happening to Chad

Bigleby was happening to her in a similar way. That terrified her, threatened her sanity, made her want to flee and go hide in a hole somewhere. She felt doomed.

Her only desire now was for Adams to hold her, forgive her, and love her. She just wanted another chance to be the wife she committed to being before their lives went to hell. Just a second chance.

She pulled her knees to her stomach as she rubbed her upper chest. It almost burned for real. She bowed her head and prayed for the first time in a very long time. She pleaded for mercy, confessed her sins, and asked for forgiveness, asked for a miracle in Adams' heart. It was short, but humble and sincere. She didn't feel anything different, but she never had before. She sat and waited, her mind awash with dread, battling to believe in the seemingly impossible.

Could Adams forgive her? Could she be saved from the coming evil?

Adams needed advice. He'd gotten back in his car and driven to the church where he knocked at the office door. Pastor Dave looked up and brightened at the sight of him.

"You got a few minutes, sir?" Adams asked meekly.

"Of course, son. Of course. Come on in, and have a seat." Adams slipped on in and sat down.

"What can I do for you Mark?"

"I need your advice on something ... something concerning Amy and I."

"Ok. Are you two still separated?" His brow furrowed, wrinkles of deep concern showing clearly.

"Well, yes, but it's complicated. Long story short, we were almost reconciled completely, even made love night before last, but ... I found out last night that she cheated on me three times in the first couple months of our separation."

"Wow. I'm so sorry, Mark. I'm sure that's quite devastating." Pastor Dave's tone was low, somber, and consoling.

"Did she tell you up front, or did you find it out another way?"

"Well, I figured it out watching her interact with this doctor she works with at the hospital. Way too friendly. When I went to confront her, before I could get it all out she started confessing, told me about sleeping with the doc plus one other guy."

"All right. So that's the situation. What do you need advice on exactly?"

"I don't know if I should forgive her, and if I should, I don't think I can."

"Well, the first part of your question is easy. Yes. You should forgive her. Forgiveness is at the core of our Christian faith. Jesus tells us explicitly that we are to 'forgive others even as our sins are forgiven.' And 'if you do not forgive others your heavenly father will not forgive you.' If we are to be forgiven our sins we must be willing to forgive others of their sins, especially their sins against us."

"Does that mean I should seek reconciliation with her too?"

"Is she repentant? Has she apologized for her sin against you, shown sorrow over how she hurt you, and asked for your forgiveness?"

"Yeah. She did. I just didn't want to hear it at the time. It was too soon."

"Does she still want to be your wife? Does she want reconciliation?"

"She said she loves me and wants to be with me. Yes."

"All right. Then I would say, yes, you should at least try to reconcile with her. God commands you to forgive in this situation, but not to continue in the relationship. However, nothing images our faith more than a willingness to restore broken relationships, to resurrect that which was dead and give it new life."

Adams took a big breath and sighed. "Well, guess that answers that part. What about the how? I don't think I can do it."

"Mark, I don't think men can ever truly forgive others without the grace of God at work in their hearts. They may bury it, try to forget it, but somewhere it lingers, maybe festers, maybe rears its head years later. But to truly forgive someone, especially for such a hurtful, damaging sin as adultery, it takes a piece of you to die. You have to give up your rights to justice and leave it at the cross where true justice exacted payment in full. Christ died to pay for the sins that He forgives. Justice was served. When you forgive someone, you do it knowing that you have been extended a grace beyond measure. A debt you could never pay has been cleared on your behalf, and because of this mercy in the face of relentless justice, you can also freely offer forgiveness to someone else, knowing God has paid the price and covered it over by his sacrifice. God desires mercy more than sacrifice because He provided the true sacrifice. He wants us to be full of mercy because His mercy triumphed over the justice we were due. Love forgives and if the love of God abides within you, so must you. So, to answer your question, Mark, of how, it's not a matter of whether or not you can, it's a matter of whether or not the love of God is alive in you to enable you to do it."

"But Pastor Dave, I haven't loved God in three years, not since we lost Emily. I've hated and cursed Him, unable to accept why He would allow something like that to happen to my baby girl, how He would allow it to destroy my marriage."

"Mark, you have struggled with a burden I would not wish on anyone. I can't fully understand the level of grief you experienced, but I can try to empathize. Many people in the Bible were subject to God's harsh providence. Job lost ten children at one shot. When he found out he said, 'The Lord giveth and Lord taketh away. Blessed be the name of the

Lord.' And then he was struck with a terrible disease. He wrestled with the suffering, in very deep, dark, and personal ways before God healed him and gave him more children. We most often will not know why God does these things. The tapestry of billions of lives over thousands of years is far too complex in its interconnectedness for us to ever comprehend how deep the rabbit hole goes. And so, we are told what God is like. God is Love. God is a Just God. God is good and merciful, a God of glorious promises. His mercies renew every morning. He works all things out for the good of those that love Him. He will finish the work He began in us, to sanctify our souls. God is faithful and kind. He will never forsake us nor will He ever fail to keep His word. He is Truth. Faith is believing these things, believing that He is and that He is a rewarder of those who diligently seek Him. You have to believe that Father knows best. It takes faith to trust Him no matter what comes our way. You ever heard the old hymn 'It is Well with My Soul'?"

Adams nodded his head.

"Did you know the guy who wrote that did so on a ship after having just received word that his wife and four daughters had died in an accident?"

Adams mouth dropped. He was speechless.

"If he and Job can continue to love God and bless His name, I think we have good reason to hang on too and not abandon our faith. I encourage you to consider seeking God again, and ask Him to forgive you for your anger and unbelief and to help you believe again. Then ask Him to help you forgive your wife and mend both your hearts together again."

Adams nodded his head then looked Pastor Dave in the eye. "Will you pray with me?"

Pastor Dave smiled broadly, extending his hand, palm up, across the table. Adams took it.

The words were succinct, simple and genuine. Adams didn't have any crazy spiritual experience, but what he did start to feel was peace, a peace he hadn't felt since Emily's death. It wasn't complete but it was certainly unprecedented, a new beginning, new life in a withered soul. He left after Pastor Dave hugged him hard and long, feeling like a new man, a stronger man, more prepared to face the world of shit he lived in right now.

WEDNESDAY, JANUARY 17th 12:05 a.m.

Amy had arrived at work a little before 10:00 p.m., the air full of snowflakes falling steadily, a bitter cold biting through her clothes as the wind blew. Tired and emotionally drained but feeling better to be at work and not alone at home plagued by nightmares, she made her way to the elevator and up to the psych ward.

An hour later, her initial rounds done, she noticed Adams slip in to relieve the officer who was standing guard, informing another nurse he was covering the entire night shift tonight. Hopefully, Mark will want to talk at some point, she thought. However, after waiting an hour, Amy decided to take the initiative, ventured down the hall, and returned with a peace offering of coffee. It was just after midnight as she approached Adams cautiously, her movements tentative, fearful, her body ready to take flight in an instant.

"I come in peace," she said quietly. "I thought you might need this tonight, especially if you didn't sleep any better than I did today."

He accepted the coffee, gripped the cup, and immediately brought it to his lips to sip.

"Thank you, Amy. That's very ... sweet ... especially after the way I treated you last night."

Amy twiddled her thumbs and looked away, unsure of how she should react.

"I think I deserved it, Mark. You had every right. I don't blame you one bit. I wouldn't blame you if you never want to see me again. Though I hope that won't be the case. Anyway, I don't want to bother you. I'll let you get back to your reading."

Amy slowly backed away, watching him, hoping he would say something to stretch out the conversation. Nothing. Her body rotated incrementally, lingering as long as it could, wanting nothing more than to hear Adams' voice call her name again.

"Amy?" It was flat but not angry. Not cold, maybe even slightly warm. She twirled about, eyes wide and bright, unable to hide her excitement. Adams smiled at her, and all she could think was Yes! He smiled at me! He actually smiled!

"Yes?" was the only word that came out of her mouth.

"I've been thinking a lot and talking to some people today. I've done some soul searching, and I have some things I need to say to you." He sat the coffee down and stood as he spoke.

Only the worst seemed possible to Amy right then, like standing on a cliff waiting for that final nudge, just enough to shift your weight past the point of no return. Free fall.

"Go ahead, Mark. Say what you need to … I can take it." The last words were a sudden breath of courage that filled her sails.

"Remember what it was like between us after Emily died?"

Amy nodded, surprised at the direction Adams was taking the conversation.

"I wanted to talk, you didn't. I couldn't get past it. You needed to regain some sense of normalcy to maintain sanity."

Amy nodded again, this time in agreement. Her stomach was a tight knot, unsure where this would end.

"I couldn't let it go, and you couldn't help me. It was right then that everything changed between us. It was right then I started blaming you for not being there for me, and I withdrew. I didn't want to look at your face. I was angry, and it reminded me of losing Emily. I started my own life then, and I didn't include you. It's no wonder you were angry at me. Of course you wouldn't want to make love to someone who was emotionally, and often physically, not there any-more in a lot of ways. It became a vicious cycle, our resent-ment feeding on each other to breed a growing monster of animosity and bitterness. We both have our faults. We both bear responsibility for what we've done. But I, as your hus-band, as the head of the household, I sank the ship way back then. We were just bailing water up until three months ago …"

Adams grew quiet, thoughtful, stared right at Amy, through her, and she just stared back, speechless, but loving him more at that moment than she had in years, possibly ever.

"Amy, I'm sorry. I'm sorry for what I did to you back then. I'm sorry for checking out, for not being a man, for not being your rock, support, strength, a comforter in time of need. I'm sorry I failed you. And I'm sorry for all my anger and selfishness that followed. I was wrong, so wrong. I pushed you to the edge. I understand the temptations you felt, I felt the same. You were wrong for jumping … of course, you've already said that … anyway, I don't know if I can really forgive you for the betrayal … but I want to …"

Amy's hands had covered her mouth as the first 'I'm sorry' escaped his lips. Tears crept up, sneaking over the lids of her eyes one at a time, tiny streams escaping down her cheeks. Her heart swelled, a flood of emotions bursting through a dam erected and fortified over the last three years. She tried to manage the overwhelming flow, cognizant of where she was, but it was difficult.

Adams watched her as she broke, walls having long tow-ered between them seemed to come tumbling down in an in-stant. Part of him wanted to hold her, part of him wanted to run away, scared of being hurt again, still holding onto hate. His heart flexed as love gasped for air, a Titan wakened from torpor, and the stone encasement fractured ever so slightly. Amy's pain washed over him like water, and slowly he felt it wear within the crack, gradually eroding a path through years of hostility, offense, and layer upon layer of scars fused with malice, tortuous agony, and fierce indignation, all bound together into some malignant ore.

Love battered his defenses. Shaken, weakened but still standing, the siege went on.

Amy's body heaved slightly, great sobs held back. She barely formed the words.

"Hold me, Mark, please?" The words begged mercy. Her whole body pleaded for it.

She marched forward as if to death, but hoped for a pardon, their previous life together restored. Risking it all, she approached the cliff's edge, committed to falling, but still unsure if he'd catch her. She kept moving forward, one small step at a time. Adams did not retreat, he did not step forward. Inches remained. His body tensed, a voice inside screaming as if a hot brand were approaching a prisoner, shackled, unable to escape the coming torture. Final step, her body touched his, arms by her side waiting to be embraced and saved from the freefall. Seconds stretched out into infinity, eyes closed anticipating the impact, rejection, a death sentence.

But it did not come. His hands moved stiffly from his own sides, reluctantly at first, then with greater deliberateness. Unseen forces began to soften his limbs, his posture, and even his heart. Hands pressed against her back and hugged her to his chest firmly. He inhaled, as if drawing her inside him, and held his breath.

Amy felt her descent diminish, felt the hands about her drawing her back from the precipice. She cried softly into his neck, her own arms coming up to embrace him, tentatively at first, then moments later like a drowning man gripping a life preserver. Amy's longing embrace was a healing salve soaking through the expanding cracks in Adam's hardened heart and eventually reaching his wounded soul.

"Amy," he whispered, "I can't promise you anything right now. I love you, but I don't know if I can forgive you. It may take time."

"I know. I know. I just hope it's not too late for us …"
Amy tried to lose herself in the moment, but in the back of
her mind, somewhere a wolf man growled. "You're
miiiiiinnnne …"

They held each other for a long time, oblivious to their
surroundings.

Mr. Phailees and Phobos walked towards the hospital,
feet tracking through the snow as it continued to fall, huge
flakes obliterating the sky, near blizzard like intensity. Visibility was mere feet, the storm peaking as they approached
the corner of the building where Chad Bigleby's room was
located. Shadows covered the snow drift, piled up where the
two walls intersected, the 'U' designed structure catching all
the driving snow the wind could carry. Phobos walked upright behind Phailees, a young man in jeans and a heavy coat,
staying close in order to make out the outline of the white
sports jacket in front of him as they disappeared into the
shadows.

Phailees led the way, walking into the shadow realm,
traveling through dark shortcuts then stepping out inside
Chad's room. He saw Adams and Amy embracing and
growled to himself. He would see Chad Bigleby finished
first, then see to ensuring Amy's fate.

Phobos' fangs sank into the base of Chad's skull through
the soft indentation. He withdrew all the hormones and endorphins that had flooded Chad's system with fear. At last,
when done, he filled the metal flask and capped it, returning
to his human façade.

Phailees' hand touched Chad's forehead. They stood
above him in his dreams, all the wicked beings who had been
relentlessly assaulting him now stumbling back into the shadows, Phobos growling at them all.

"Chad? Can you hear me?"

Chad was still strapped down on the hospital bed. Relief flooded his body, the joy of a brief respite from such bountiful suffering. He opened his eyes and looked at Phailees, realizing at that moment he no longer felt any fear.

"Chad, you do not have long left in this world. Soon, my world, this world," he gestured all about them, "it shall be the only one you know."

Chad nodded casually, knowingly.

"But now, we have arrived at a juncture, one at which I am bound by duty to make certain offers to you. You, Chad, you stand at a fork in the road, and to quote an old proverb, 'you have a choice: be the hammer or be the nail.' Which one are you going to be, Chad? Hammer or nail? Your path is up to you from here. You must choose. It will not be long."

At that, Mr. Phailees slipped his hand down to the leg shackle and touched it. It clicked, the teeth slowly backing out one by one. Phobos unbuckled the arm and leg restraints and covered him back up with blanket and sheet.

"There's a beast inside that one, Phobos," he whispered. "You'll see."

Phobos nodded in apparent agreement as they moved to leave.

Mr. Phailees, dressed in his white sports jacket, sunglasses, and perfect posture, walked out the door. Phobos followed behind him, now dressed in similar fashion, his posture more confident than ever before.

As they passed Adams and Amy, still locked in an embrace, Phailees whispered to Phobos.

"We shall test his convictions, Phobos, very soon … if they live through the next few minutes, of course."

They both smiled and stepped back into the shadows.

Chad woke, his body relaxing from its contorted state. He felt his bonds were gone but did not want to move yet. He looked around, the bedside lamp providing a small amount of light. A man walked through the door right then, a priest making late night rounds, his eyes kind and sincere. Chad looked into those eyes, his own cold and careless.

"My son, I know you are close to death," the man said. "The Lord knows the things you have done. Every man must give an account of his actions. How well will you fare when your time comes before the judgment seat? Not well, I think, but there is hope. I, as an ambassador of Christ, offer you redemption. Confess, repent, accept the sacrifice, and bow your knee to the king. Like the thief on the cross, you too could be in paradise today. What say you then, murderer?"

The man was very old, but his eyes were sharp and bright, and he spoke with authority. Chad's heart was hardened, his neck stiff, his eyes full of rebellion.

"Father," he said with more than a hint of disgust, "I have nothing to confess. I did nothing wrong. I saved a life, the life of my son. Who is to say that woman's life was worth more than my son's? She did not have to get in my way. In fact, she was threatening his life, and I was defending him from the consequences of her actions. She brought it on herself. But I have seen to my son's well-being. He will live, and I will die. Better this way than for him to be slowly devoured by that disease when a cure was within reach. I don't care what your Bible says, priest. I don't care what the laws of men say. I reject your moral codes. I have made my own, and I am not ashamed. I would do it all again."

"Very well, son. You belong to the kingdom you have chosen."

With that, the priest hobbled out the door, disappearing into the light outside.

As soon as the priest was gone all the lights began to sizzle and dimmed to nothing. The darkening came again, this time worse than before. Shadows filled in everything, dulling lines, angles, and details. The walls became like gelatinous pitch. Then the whispers began, barely audible at first, but slowly building. Husky, bitter voices conjured up memories of goblins and trolls arguing over who would eat the hobbit. He wasn't sure whether the voices were coming through the ductwork or slipping through walls. They seemed to come from everywhere. The closet door opened, a black hole stretching to oblivion. Whispers turned to shrieks, echoing down that abyssal corridor. A thunderous rumble began to grow, louder and louder, shaking the floor. Chad imagined it sounded like horses, a horde of nightmarish steeds bearing down upon his room. In an instant, the room was a dark blur as creatures of all hideous kinds leapt from the closet and began crawling over him, hissing, licking, biting—eager to have their fill.

A mob of naked rotting corpses rushed his fetal form and unleashed their fury. Fear and despair threatened to smother him, but then Phailees' words came to his mind, a clarion call sounding in his head, echoing over and over again in his soul. "You gotta choice, the hammer or the nail … hammer or the nail … hammer or the nail …"

Something clicked inside Chad, a harmonic resonance with those words reached deep within him.

He was the hammer … not a nail.

The wretched multitude pressed him to the ground. They piled atop each other precariously, each one struggling to dig their way to the bottom. But at the bottom, beneath the burden of violence he carried, Chad began his metamorphosis.

It was then that he screamed, a primal wail.

Adams and Amy both flinched at the scream, reflexively pushing out and forcing themselves apart.

"Emergency in room 606! Page Dr. Danner!" she yelled, but one of the girls was already on it.

Rushing into the room, Adams saw Chad first. His whole body flailed about on the bed, all his limbs free. Chad writhed like a mad man, like a desperate man trying to breathe, as if fighting off invisible attackers crushing him with their weight.

"How the fuck did he get out of the restraints," Adams wondered out loud as he rushed to help secure Chad to the bed again.

Amy and two other nurses came in to help. They all began grabbing Chad, attempting to restrain his limbs, sinews like steel cord, unbending, unmoving.

Amy turned towards the door and shouted. "Dr. Danner, bring a sedative ..." She grunted at the effort of holding onto Chad. "He's loose! And he's fucking strong!"

In the dark netherworld all the ghouls, goblins, angry souls, and every hideous beast piled atop Chad's body failed to witness his transformation, but hidden beneath them, his body contorted and morphed, muscles palpitating as they shifted and grew. His spine bent, his head widened, his brow thickened. Arms elongated, crippled hands grew nails long and viciously sharp ... his head and frame swelled to apish proportions. His eyes turned blood red, his snout grew out slightly. Any aspect of humanity was removed.

Fear turned to fury, prideful defiance at their audacity to treat him like a nail. Chad breathed deep, filling his lungs with all the hate he could muster for the inferior beings assaulting him. Contempt then turned to something else. Rage. Violence erupted within him, a juggernaut of wrath that would not stop, fueled by unquenchable hostility.

Dr. Danner came running in the door, syringe in hand.

"Don't let go of him," he called, maneuvering into position to deliver the injection.

He slammed the needle into Chad's neck, depressing it on contact. Chad's eyes flew open, pupils dilated, blood vessels ruptured and bled, turning the whites of his eyes red.

Chad was a hammer and everybody looked like a nail.

His whole body coiled inward, tensing incredibly beneath the weight of his assailants. Dr. Danner and the nurses all looked on in horror, Chad's features grotesquely contorting with a demented indignation.

The pack of wicked creatures biting and clawing for his death felt the now powerful frame tremble beneath them. Something was not right. They paused, trying to feel what it was.

Chad opened his mouth, a roaring howl ripping from his guts, every muscle in his frame unnaturally tense.

His body exploded up, dislodging the masses holding him down, Bodies flew off at all angles, striking walls, tables, equipment, each other. Chad landed on his feet and immediately launched into action, sprinting and spinning about the room in a colossal frenzy, his rage fully simian. He flailed his arms back and forth as his body careened madly amongst the feeble crowd, displacing them entirely wherever he moved. They were like tiny bumper cars before him, bodies bouncing away as if struck by a much larger vehicle, the blows jarring and irresistible.

They could not hold his fury down any longer, and he made them pay: claws ripping, shredding, disproportionate arms pounding those who fell, grinding them into the floors. A whirling dervish of unrestrained rage, he slammed into each one again and again, falling upon those who crumpled beneath the brutal onslaught.

Adams was still trying to regain his balance after being knocked off his feet for the third time. Amy was in a corner rubbing her head and shaking off the cobwebs, but otherwise all right. The rest looked like they were in a pinball machine along with Adams, Chad hurtling all of them about the room, sending them stumbling away. A solid back hand blow struck Dr. Danner full in the chest, knocking the wind out of him as he crashed into the wall and bounced off to land at Chad's feet. Chad stood above him. Adams clambered to his feet trying to reach Chad before he tried to kill Dr. Danner. The doctor may have screwed his wife, but Adams wasn't going to let the man die like this. Not on his watch. Seconds seemed to stretch out. He was too slow.

A weasel-faced goblin lay splayed at Chad's feet then attempted to skitter off, but he fell upon it, pressed it down with crippled hands, clawing to find some purchase to temporarily restrain the wretched creature as it scrambled to escape. He knocked it flat with a crushing blow to the torso, secured it at last while its senses were staggered. The apish mouth opened wide and plunged huge canines into the soft throat of the creature. It shrieked, but Chad would not let go, bowed over on all fours, hugging it tightly, greedily.

Dr. Danner was overwhelmed; chest burning, struggling for air. It was all happening so fast and before he had fully regained his senses, the searing pain hit square in the side of his neck. The force of impact slammed Dr. Danner's head sideways to the ground and pinning it beneath Chad's growling body. Adams bent to grab Chad's shoulders and pull him off the doctor. A backhand palm strike sent him flying again, fingernails somehow cutting deep slashes into his Kevlar vest and ripping a shallow trail through the exposed flesh along the side of his ribcage.

Chad shook his head viciously, the body beneath him jerking about like a dead rabbit in his mouth. Arterial spray jetted between his teeth.

He was elated.

Adams got back to his feet, side burning. In three steps he reached Chad, who was snatching back and forth on every possible angle, shaking Dr. Danner like a dog killing a rabbit. Blood cast off in all directions from his bleeding throat, spraying the walls along with every person in the room. Adams braced both his hands on Chad's back and kneed him in the left kidney multiple times as hard as he could. It had no effect.

Adams switched legs and drew back for a knee to Chad's head. This time, his feet shot out from beneath him, as he slipped on Dr. Danner's blood that now coated the linoleum floor around them. Adams gripped Chad's body for balance, and, once anchored to his back, shot his forearm across Chad's upper lip, crushing the nose as best he could while his other hand reached over the top of Chad's head and found purchase in the bony orbits, fingers digging into the eyes. He stood and jerked back in one whole-body coordinated explosion, forcing Chad's mouth open and yanking him off Dr. Danner and into the air, his body floating horizontally for a moment. Adams continued with the motion and slammed

Chad onto his back, his head cracking the tiled floor on impact. Adams stomped Chad's face once for added measure, and was going to do it again, but it was no longer there.

Chad was not phased. Already turning and spinning to his knees, he stood and came at Adams. A stiff arm lifted Adams off his feet, and sent him soaring into the wall with supernatural strength.

Chad turned back towards Dr. Danner, intent on his death. Amy had immediately scrambled over to the doctor and was applying direct pressure to his wounds.

Adams screamed.

"Amy! Get away from him! Now!"

Without question, she heeded his voice and bolted around the edge of the room fast, sliding in behind Adams, feet almost shooting out from underneath her. She was gasping for breath. Terror gripped her heart.

Chad's eyes locked on Adams then on Amy. A wicked smile spread across his face just before his foot rose sharply and slammed down on Dr. Danner's face, the nose and cheekbones collapsing inward. Chad grunted, blowing air out his nose as he lifted his head slightly, a primal challenging gesture just before his body tensed to rush forward as his eyes still looked past Adams.

A popping noise could be heard as the electrodes launched through the air and lodged in Chad's body. Adams stood like a statue, gripping the Taser in an outstretched hand, trigger still pulled. Enough electricity surged through Chad's frame beneath the bloodied white hospital gown to drop a bull.

He didn't go down.

The first thought through Adams' brain was Oh shit! as Chad not only remained standing but yanked the barbed metal electrodes right out of his skin and threw them aside. To his credit, Adam's did not hesitate with any thoughts of "this can't be happening." Years of training found their moment of truth that night. His mind simply accepted what he saw. It is what it is, he thought, then commanded himself, "now do something."

Chad rushed forward, a locomotive with teeth, mouth stretching inhumanly wide. Amy screamed behind Adams.

His left hand shot forward as the right hand travelled down to grab his sidearm. He stiff armed Chad's face, force feeding his hand as far back in between those gaping jaws as he could possibly get it, a gagging noise escaping even as those jaws tried to find enough leverage to crunch down. The sacrifice bought him the split second he needed. His gun cleared the holster and leveled off at heart level. His finger squeezed quickly, then again, and two .45 hollow point slugs drove into Chad Bigleby's heart. Adams pushed him away, and he staggered back. Red eyes with large dark pupils looked at him, surprised, almost confused, then looked down at his chest. Two streams of blood were pouring down his body.

Adams stood at high-ready, finger off the trigger, prepared to shoot again in an instant.

Chad stared at Adams with blood gushing from his mouth, then lifted his gaze and stared at the ceiling, through it even, as if he were seeing heaven itself for a moment. Then his head tilted further back and, like a tower falling over all at once, his body crashed flat to the floor. Horrible gurgling noises, just barely distinguishable from Dr. Danner's own death sounds, issued from the back of his throat. Blood bubbled up and flowed from the holes in his chest, a babbling brook spilling onto the floor.

Adams reassessed the threat, his training running the show. Eyes scanned 360 degrees, checking for any other potential threats. He noted Amy's safe condition as well as the two nurses hopelessly trying to save Dr. Danner's life. He looked back at Chad's body, relaxed a little as he stared at the crimson flow. The arms slowly lowered, head twitching, contorted to one side. Within a few more seconds, Chad's legs ceased their restless struggle and he heard one last rasping exhale.

Chad Bigleby was definitely dead. Adams holstered his Glock.

He was covered in blood, some his own, but mostly Dr. Danner's. It was a horrible sight but one that attested to Adams victory. Nurses were applying direct pressure, yelling for assistance, and notifying surgery. An orderly rushed in, shocked by the scene, but listened to the nurse's screams for help. They put Dr. Danner on Chad's bed, Nurse Callahan riding on top trying to intubate him while the other nurse staunched the bleeding, and the orderly pushed the bed out the door, rushing for the O.R.

Relaxation crept through his body as he continued staring at the crimson flow, confident the threat was neutralized. His head bowed from fatigue and shock. He thanked God he had survived this crazy shit, then spoke out loud.

"What a hell of a day," he muttered. Amy hugged him from behind, holding on with all her might.

He glanced back at the body. The bleeding had stopped, but in its place a black tarry substance oozed from the two holes neatly placed side by side over Chad Bigleby's no longer beating heart. Adams shook his head. A trick of the light, he thought and wiped sweat from his eyes.

It was then, with head still bowed, he heard the window shatter. His head snapped up, eyes wide open, just in time to see a bloodied, white gowned form drop from the window, out of sight. He looked back at the floor where Chad Bigleby's dead body should have been, but only a pool of blood delineating a partial body outline remained. Heart racing, he ran for the window and looked down, a full six stories to ground level. The snowstorm had slowed, big flakes still drifting here and there.

He saw Chad Bigleby, exactly where he landed, squatting on all fours. He stared up at Adams for a moment, eyes feral and black as coal set in a Neanderthal skull, his frame seemingly too big for the bloodied hospital gown fluttering in the moonlight breeze. His knuckles dragged on the ground, wrists curled like gnarled stumps. He had a look of prideful rebellion upon his face, and four incisors curled well up over his lips. He had assumed the posture of a male gorilla, bold and challenging, snorted once, dark smoke blowing from his nose, then turned and loped away on all fours, straight into a patch of shadow draped along the corner.

In an instant, he disappeared.

Adams leaned out, looking for any glimpse of the man. Amy was by his side staring in awe. He found his radio, called it in, gave a description. Officers rushed toward the scene.

"I need to go downstairs and look for him, Amy."

He squeezed her shoulders as he told her, but she gripped his arms, not letting go, her face an expression of pure panic.

"Don't leave me, Mark! Please! Please don't leave me now. Not now!"

"Amy! What's wrong? The bad guy is gone. Six floors down. It's ok. Let me find him."

"It's not him I'm worried about, Mark. That man and his dog, I can feel them."

Adams jerked his head all around, scanning.

"I don't see anything, Amy."

"I don't care! He told me he would come for me tonight, after he finished with Chad! I feel him!" Her voice turned from emphatic to pleading. "He's here, Mark. Please believe me. Don't leave me alone."

"All right. All right. How about you come with me? I'll keep you by my side. Is that good?"

Amy nodded her head in agreement.

"All right. Let's get out of this room. Detectives will want to do the whole crime scene thing." Amy nodded again, and they turned to exit.

Phailees stood at the threshold of the door, Phobos lurking behind him.

Adams immediately held his arm out, pushing Amy behind him. Protective instincts kicking in.

"Officer Adams, I told you not to interfere with what was mine. The consequences here can be quite … deadly."

Phailees' mouth began to quiver, his head shook, neck twisting. His snout pushing forward; his teeth grew and his jaws unhinged, revealing huge, jagged fangs. His head swelled wide and thickened top to bottom, mandible joints flaring out. His whole body morphed before Adams' eyes. Muscles pulsed in waves, the fibers multiplying beneath the surface, every limb lengthening and gaining bulk as the tissues and bones were augmented by dark forces he now released unchecked into his own veins. Skin grew leathery, almost scaly, as black hairs sprouted and covered his entire form. Half wolf, half snake, he towered above a mere mortal man.

He growled at Adams and spoke, his voice deep and gravelly with a guttural, otherworldly tone unlike anything Adams had ever heard before.

"I would hate to hurt a distant relative, Officer Adams, but I assure you, you really mean nothing to me. Get out of my way, and give me the whore! She's mine."

"No!" he shouted. Authority in his own voice. A Covenant authority. "She's my wife! She's mine, and you can't have her!"

"Very well," Phailees hissed. "Over your dead body it is, then." Phailees chuckled darkly.

He stepped forward, smiling at his own joke. Bullets peppered his torso as Adams attempted to unload the magazine. Phailees waded through the hail of lead, swatting Adams' hand and knocking the gun across the room. His steely fingers shot out, grabbing for the throat that was no longer there, Adams' body slipping on the angle, avoiding the razor talons while trapping Phailees' arm. Adams secured it across his chest, one hand over top gripping the wrist, the other hand sliding under, shooting out explosively across Phailees' body to break the elbow across Adams' chest.

Phailees wailed briefly, surprised.

"No mortal man has hurt me in centuries," he growled, grasping the elbow with his other hand, wrenching it one way then another, a loud series of popping noises emitting from the joint. It swung back and forth along the natural hinged path once more. "See? Good as new."

He smiled and moved in a blur, palming Adams' face with a monstrous paw, driving him back while slashing claws through the lower abdomen of his prey. The uniform was tattered above the waistline, the gun belt deeply gashed, taking the brunt of the force, but his stomach was still ripped apart on the surface. Adams reached up to push the hand off his face. Phailees grabbed his arm and bit into his bicep, jagged fangs slicing deep, severing the artery and filling his mouth with Adams' blood.

"Yup. Tastes like family." He tossed Adams across the room at Amy's feet. His arm was spraying blood out of the mangled wound. As Amy knelt, his blood covered her scrub top.

Adams was in shock, weak, unbelieving of the strength of his enemy, the speed, the ferocity.

"Amy," he groaned, still struggling on, "tie my arm off … quick. I won't last any time if you don't."

"I know, Mark. I know. I'm on it." She reached over and grabbed a handful of thick rubber bands used for drawing blood and began tying them on. Four bands later, the blood flow seemed to have completely stopped.

Adams looked up at Amy and gazed into her eyes. "I love you. I want you to know that. And I forgive you, for everything. I won't ever leave you on your own again. Not today. Not for the rest of my life." Amy cradled his head and wept.

"Oh God, Mark. Thank you, thank you so much. I forgive you too. I love you. I just want to be with you. Just you."

Phailees stood by and looked on, allowing them all their futile efforts and meaningless words, and he just laughed.

"Your whole kind is so pathetic. You might as well all be trying to plug a breaking dam with your fingers. Your demise is inevitable ... it's just a matter of what poison you want to pick. You can't be good. Each man has his vice. Each man has his price. It's just a matter of how low you are willing to go to get what you want in life. And Amy, you went low enough to get me. Which means ... you're mine!"

Adams struggled to his feet to stand between Phailees and Amy, but it was useless. Phailees backhanded his face and sent him sprawling well out of the way, a path cleared to Amy. He walked slowly ahead enjoying the fear he saw on her face, the anguish at watching her man crumple to the ground, unconscious.

"It's just you and me now, whore. Time to pay the piper, and tonight, he's in the mood for a pound of flesh. I think I'll just do take out ... carry you off with me for a fast food meal."

He reached out to grab her, and she shrunk back, no-where to go. His hand passed in front of her. Again, he reached, and again his hand passed her by.

"What is this?" he sneered, stepping forward with his whole body, both hands grasping for her shoulders. He re-bounded, as if an invisible wall were there.

"What trickery is this?" he muttered, consternation spreading across his furrowed brow.

He snarled and hurled his monstrous body at Amy again and again, her tiny frame, seated against the wall, legs pulled up tight to her chest, arms covering her head. A loud banging noise like a hammer on anvil sounded every time Phailees rebounded. He cursed at the heavens, a baleful, guttural rage evident in his face.

"WHO IS HERE?" he snarled. "Show yourself ... Son of Light!" He spat the last word out bitterly.

A radiant shield began to glow between Phailees and Amy, growing brighter and larger until, suddenly, the priest who had come to give last rites to Chad emerged from behind the light.

"I thought I smelled your stench when I got here. You have no right to interfere. She is my portion. I claim her. She has the mark upon her. You can smell it yourself. By right of law, she is mine. Now leave, and leave what is mine for my disposal."

The old priest smiled kindly, gently, like a man who knows something crucial another does not.

"Actually, Mr. Phailees, or should I call you by an older name? Mephistopheles perhaps? Son of Moloch? Son of Baal? Anyway, I actually don't smell the mark on her. Why don't you sniff her again, brute?"

Phailees' lips curled back momentarily in anger and disgust, then he leaned in as close to Amy as he could get, nostrils flaring wide as he sniffed, forked tongue flickering in and out smelling. Suddenly, his head drew back in shock, brow furrowed deep.

"What is this?" he barked, eyes wide and bewildered. "How can it be?"

"It's the blood, Phailees." The priest gestured at Amy's scrub top, covered in blood, then Phailees' eyes followed the old man's finger as it came to rest on Adams' crumpled body. "His blood. He forgave her, and he shed his blood in her defense. He purchased her back. She belongs to him again, not you. You should know that portion of the law as well, or has it been so long you forget."

Phailees growled, but slowly returned to his human form as he did so. A malignant gaze fell upon Adams' unconscious form sprawled on the floor, sinister eyes, full of scorn, longing to devour him out of sheer spite.

"Very well, Michael. You are right. I have no authority here. I will depart." Phailees bowed his head slightly as he backed up.

"Go in peace, nephew. I rejoice not at your coming judgment."

"Bah! I'm sure you don't," he sneered, sarcasm dripping from his tongue. "Come, Phobos. We must depart."

With that, they climbed onto the window ledge and stood for a second. Phailees looked back at Michael.

"You know he has the blood gift, right?"

"Weak, yes, but there nonetheless," Michael replied. "Yes. I know."

"Very well, then. Adieu." And with that, they both stepped off the ledge and disappeared into the snowy night.

The light dimmed and extinguished, but the priest remained, his form that of a simple, elderly man who walked with a limp. He bent down with much effort, touched Adams' body, bowed his head momentarily, then looked up at Amy, waving her over. She stepped hesitantly, drawing close and knelt before him.

"He will be fine. He will recover. Get him medical attention." He reached out and touched her side gently, a warmth spreading over the tender tissue where she was bitten. "As for you, my child … go, and sin no more."

Amy nodded her head, tears welling up again. With that, the priest struggled to his feet, hobbled out of the room, and down the hallway.

EPILOGUE I

"Come my darling, it is never too late to begin our love again."
ATTICUS

"My soul was a burden, bruised and bleeding. It was tired of the man who carried it, but I found no place to set it down to rest. Neither the charm of the countryside nor the sweet scents of a garden could soothe it. It found no peace in song or laughter, none in the company of friends at table or in the pleasures of love, none even in books or poetry...Where could my heart find refuge from itself? Where could I go, yet leave myself behind?"

WALLY LAMB, THE HOUR I FIRST BELIEVED

Hicks, Greer, and Dexter all arrived on the scene. Detective Andrews was called out, as well as others, to help in the manhunt. K-9 units were brought in to search for Chad Bigleby. And all their efforts only resulted in corroborating Officer Adams' own eye witness account.

His eyes had it right, though his brain did not know how. It was incredible. Unbelievable, if he hadn't seen it himself. They located a large spray pattern of blood, where several drops were cast off as if from some sort of severe impact, trajectory indicating Chad Bigleby had indeed jumped from the sixth floor and landed. Some kind of black tar was spattered about as well. The snow and ground where he landed were deeply impacted with two large foot prints and two clawed hand prints, as if his knuckles struck the ground. The same prints made a beeline for the corner of the west side of the building where two wings met and a large snow drift lay beneath a blanket of shadow.

And that was where the trail ended. No more footprints, no more blood, no more black ooze, and no more scent. It all ended right there. K-9s turning in silly circles, barking, unable to find another path. They excavated the snow drift. Nothing. No doors. No holes. Nowhere to go, but vanished nonetheless.

Chad Bigleby was gone and there was no reasonable explanation for it or for anything else that had happened in that room.

Adams recovered from his wounds, in remarkable time the doctors said, Amy by his side every day. Two weeks had flown by since he got out of the hospital, and they were living together again, love and trust coming more easily with each day. The glory of a new beginning, when all had seemed lost, was bright and fresh.

It was a Sunday morning, and they were in church together for the first time in almost three years. As they stood in line awaiting communion, they bowed their heads and confessed their sins to God, asking forgiveness in Christ's name. The work of the cross had never been more real to them than in the last couple of weeks. It weighted heavy on Adams' heart and mind as he swallowed the bread and drank the wine.

'Repentance, forgiveness, reconciliation, and redemption. How did I ever abandon these things?" Adams asked himself, a feeling of regret washing over him before it was quickly lifted. "How did I abandon the King, who by His blood and by His broken body purchased Amy and I back from the Hell everlasting, as well as the one we made for ourselves?'

As Adams and Amy finished taking communion they both knew, by faith, that their lives would be different from here on out. They intertwined hands and walked back to their seats, a gleam in their eyes exchanged as they met briefly, part hope, the rest love.

EPILOGUE II

*"There are things known and there are things unknown,
and in between are the doors of perception."*
ALDOUS HUXLEY

*"All is not lost, the unconquerable will, and study of
revenge, immortal hate, and the courage never
to submit or yield."*
JOHN MILTON, PARADISE LOST

*"I am the punishment of God. If you had not committed
great sins, God would not have sent a punishment
like me upon you."*
GENGHIS KHAN

A nearby city, a short time later.

Phailees and Phobos sat together on a park bench, watching people pass by as they each sipped from small metal flasks. Phobos broke the silence.

"Father, are we really 'just' in what we do?"

Phailees looked at him as if a crazy man were standing in front of him with a unicorn horn growing from his forehead.

"Do not doubt the righteousness of our cause, son. We serve an important function in this world. Evil angels were sent amongst the Egyptians to punish them before the Exodus. The Assyrians and their gods acted as a rod of affliction sent to punish the other nations. Some of our kind were even sent to buffet the Apostle Paul so he did not get too proud. They enjoyed it, though the overall outcome hasn't been too good for our team. You just have to focus on what you know and what you do. We are the Left Hand of Justice, Avengers of Wrath, a Rod of Judgment to smite the wicked … and you know what, Phobos?"

"What," he asked, a hopeful tone building in his voice.

"I love my job, son! Who else can see the wicked humans suffer like we do? No one, I tell you. No one. Our cause is just, Phobos. Do not worry. And if it helps, in a very narrow sense of the definition, we are the good guys, though I know a host of relatives who would disagree with that entirely. But never mind them."

He held up his flask for a toast.

"To the good guys!" he cheered.

"To the good guys!" Phobos returned, in cheery form himself.

They clinked flasks and sipped together, returning their eyes to the throng of people passing by. Phailees broke the silence this time.

"Hmm. I smell liars, abusers, drug addicts and dealers both, violent men, murderers … aahhh. There Phobos, the man in the business suit. He runs a lucrative kiddie porn ring, cyber and hands-on. Sick bastard. Gotten away with it for so long he's absolutely cocksure and proud of himself. Oh, we're going to have fun with him."

Phailees capped his flask and slid it back inside his jacket pocket.

"Time to get to work, Phobos."

Phailees stood and walked off, following a ways behind the man, singing his favorite tune while they worked—'Time is On My Side' by the Rolling Stones.

Phailees did a little fast foot shuffle, followed by a single pirouette, leading to a tip of his hat to Phobos. Placing the hat back on his head, he pinched the brim in his forefinger and thumb and smoothed the fabric in a quick semi-circular swipe, smiling as he did so. Phailees slipped his arm around Phobos' shoulders and pulled him in tight, affectionately.

"Come on boy. Let's have some quality father-son time."

ABOUT THE AUTHOR

Mike Duke was a cop for 12 years, and has spent the last 10 years teaching the military, law enforcement and bodyguards how to drive fast, do bad ass tactical driving maneuvers and hand to hand combat. He enjoys martial arts and has been a practicing since 1989 in various styles.

69778161R00239

Made in the USA
Columbia, SC
17 August 2019